MERRY CHRISTMAS YOU filthy ANIMAL

New York Times, #1 Amazon and *USA Today* bestselling author, wife, adoptive mother and peanut butter lover. Author of romantic comedies and contemporary romance, Meghan Quinn brings readers the perfect combination of heart, humour and heat in every book.

www.authormeghanquinn.com

f : meghanquinnauthor

: @meghanquinnbooks

ALSO BY MEGHAN QUINN

BRIDESMAID FOR HIRE SERIES
Bridesmaid for Hire
Bridesmaid Undercover
Bridesmaid by Chance

STANDALONES
How My Neighbour Stole Christmas
Till Summer Do Us Part

MERRY CHRISTMAS, YOU *filthy* ANIMAL

MEGHAN QUINN

HODDER &
STOUGHTON

First published in Great Britain in 2025 by Hodder & Stoughton Limited
An Hachette UK company

This paperback edition published in 2025

The authorised representative in the EEA is Hachette Ireland,
8 Castlecourt Centre, Dublin 15, D15 XTP3, Ireland (email: info@hbgi.ie)

3

A CIP catalogue record for this title is available from the British Library

Paperback ISBN 978 1 399 74852 0
ebook ISBN 978 1 399 74853 7

Typeset in Arno Pro

Printed and bound in Great Britain by Clays Ltd, Elcograf S.p.A.

Hodder & Stoughton policy is to use papers that are natural, renewable
and recyclable products and made from wood grown in sustainable forests.
The logging and manufacturing processes are expected to conform
to the environmental regulations of the country of origin.

Hodder & Stoughton Limited
Carmelite House
50 Victoria Embankment
London EC4Y 0DZ

www.hodder.co.uk

PROLOGUE
MAX

NARRATOR: *NESTLED IN THE TREES, off to the left of the reindeer barn and yards away from the commotion of holiday lovers in the year-round Christmas town of Kringle, is the quaint yet grandiose log cabin that belongs to Otto and Ida Maxheimer.*

With their family of five, Otto and Ida live on the pine-covered land of Evergreen Farm with their three boys, Felix, Ansel, and Atlas.

Let me introduce them to you.

Felix Joseph Maxheimer, the oldest of the three, an avid weather observer known for his vast knowledge of lagers, loves being right about everything and enjoys watching men in black rain boots sans shirts, preferably wielding a snow shovel and dancing to the tune of "Run Rudolph Run." In town, he's part owner of Toboggan Tours, a touring company that takes visitors out on electric snowmobiles to Candy John Hill for sledding and through the mountains just past the town of Kringle.

Then there's Ansel Daniel Maxheimer, the middle child, known for insti- gating trouble with everything and everyone who gets in his way. He is a fan of jam, wingless angels, and chaotic pizza reviews on the internet, prefera- bly cheese ones. Occasionally classified as immature, he's the other owner of Toboggan Tours. Being the talent of the operation, he brings the entertainment to every patron on a snowmobile.

And finally the youngest of the brood is Atlas Peter Maxheimer, known around town as simply Max. He has an enigmatic charm about him and the

presence of a six-foot-four lumberjack with a knack for making people smile.
The complete opposite of his grumpy best friend, Cole Black, over on Whistler
Lane is full of life, slightly dramatic in the best way, and a bit overripe ... some
around town might say.

Which makes him the perfect character to frame an entire story around.

Let me set the scene for you.

Clears throat

It's a crisp Thanksgiving Day. A semidry turkey slathered in gravy has
been consumed by the bushel of men in the house, the famous Maxheimer
sour cream apple pie has been devoured, no crumbs left behind, and Grandpa
M is asleep in front of the fire, resting his geriatric body on the braided rug that
was constructed of clothes from Grandma and Grandpa M's early marriage.

Ida and Otto are engaging in an intense game of rummy at the dining
room table, where spiral-tapered green candles in gold angel candleholders
light the room.

Felix and Ansel are perched on the couch, beers in hand, watching football
while talking about the party of fifteen from Illinois they're hosting the next day.

The house is calm, quiet, and peaceful, and everything seems to be right
in the world until ...

"Mom! Dad!" I fling the door open to the house, panic constricting my
chest as I try to catch my breath. "Invaders." I press my hands to my knees,
gasping for air. "In ... vaders."

The house falls silent, only the faint sound of a football game playing
in the background as my brothers both turn in my direction.

"Jesus, Atlas," Ansel says from the couch, staring at me with a *what*
the fuck is wrong with you expression. "You startled Grandpa M." Ansel
gestures to Grandpa M, who's still sleeping on the braided rug in front
of the fireplace.

Grandpa M grumbles and then latches on to one of those realistic cat pillows that my mom insists is a charming decoration. Though the consensus among the men is that the cat comes alive at night and scratches on the bedroom doors.

Felix has sworn he's heard it.

Ansel has sworn he's seen it.

"What is going on in here?" Dad asks, walking into the living room in his white cable-knit sweater, hands on his hips.

I lift up and lean against the front door, still out of breath from the all-out sprint I just made through the backwoods of our family property, barely avoiding a cracked skull from tripping over a broken log. "Invaders on our land. There're invaders."

"Invaders?" Mom asks, joining us in her plaid dress, which she wears every Thanksgiving in preparation for the start of Christmas. "What on earth are you talking about?"

Keeping his eyes on the TV in front of him, my oldest brother, Felix, says, "Apparently there are invaders on the property. Alert the town crier." He lifts his bottle of beer and takes a drink.

Apparently football is more important to him than the possible chance of his family farm being taken over.

"There *are* invaders," I say, my breath more even now. "On the property. I heard them when I was on my after-turkey-consumption walk. They were talking, and I heard them—"

"Talking, ooo, scary," Ansel says as he picks up my mom's coffee table book of Christmas markets around the world and flips to the chapter on France. "*People talking* calls for battening down the hatches and calling in the National Guard. Felix, grab the blowtorch. If the talkers come close, we'll roast their heads off."

"Roasting heads off? Seems like a pretty harsh punishment for just talking," Felix adds.

Ansel lifts his fist to the air. "The talkers must pay."

And this is my family. Not a single one of them takes me seriously.

Expression flat—and somewhat annoyed—I say, "This is not a joking matter. They were talking about the property behind ours. You know the empty lot."

Grandpa M coughs, his whole body convulsing until he rolls to his back and snores into the air.

Dad rubs his forehead. "Atlas, you can't come charging into the house like that, startling us all just to say there are people talking on the other end of the property."

"Really, dear," Mom says. "We love you, but ever since you won the Christmas Kringle competition last year, it seems like your dramatic ways have kicked up a notch."

I beg your pardon, Mother?

Standing taller, I ask, "What's that supposed to mean?"

Gently, Mom places her hand on my shoulder. "You seem to have a flair for . . . embellishing. And this started when you entered the competition last year, addressing everyone in town as *sir* and *madam*, wearing a top hat and tipping it to every passerby . . . strutting up on stage as a dog again, panting in shorts far too short for you." Whispering, she says, "Sherry and Tanya are still talking about your jiggly bits."

Narrator: Just to step in for a moment, our matriarch of the story is talking about the town's Christmas competition to see who is the most Christmassy of all. It's an annual competition between six competitors who are put through several mini-contests to earn points. The year before last, Cole, the best friend, battled it out against his now wife, Storee. Last year, Max took on the treasured contest and won. His ego has yet to deflate since winning, especially since Cole didn't take the crown when he entered.

"There is nothing jiggly on my body," I say, insulted.

"I have video that proves otherwise," Ansel says while examining a page in the book, using his finger to trace the edges of the Eiffel Tower.

Letting out a frustrated breath, I say, "Listen, I'm not embellishing, and I'm not being dramatic. There were people talking out in the woods, discussing the development of the land. Development," I enunciate. "Don't you care?"

Stepping up, Dad says, "Atlas, I appreciate the concern, but there's no reason for you to be barging into our peaceful home like you did to let us know that people are talking about the land next to ours. You have no idea if they're just chatting or if they're really interested, nor will it have any effect on us."

"Uh, I think barging is necessary when they could possibly try to copy our idea. You know the acreage on that land? Thirty, Dad. There are thirty acres of prime space ready to just take over what we have created."

"Jesus, Atlas," Felix says, his eyes fixated on the TV in front of him. "First of all, that land has been vacant for years. No one even knows who owns it. Second of all, there are strict regulations within Kringle that prevent businesses from replicating another business in town, so even if the people who are supposedly talking on the other side of the property are thinking about purchasing the land, they have no ability or right to replicate Evergreen Farm."

"He's right," Ansel adds. "Which in return makes you wrong, Atlas." He clears his throat and then turns the book toward me. "Atlas, you're what the French call *les imbéciles.*"

What a douche. *Just say imbecile, you nimrod.*

Ignoring my brothers, I raise my voice. "I'm not fucking around. I heard them say *farm.* They're starting a farm."

"Atlas—"

"Dad, I'm serious, okay? They're going to take over Evergreen Farm!"

Grandpa M startles awake and nearly chokes on his own saliva as he sits up and sputters out a cough.

Ansel is quick to the ground, patting on Grandpa M's back, coddling the old man. "Hand me my beer," Ansel says to Felix, who hands him the beer. Helping Grandpa M take a sip, Ansel looks over his shoulder at me. "Look what you did, you jerk. Grandpa M is now awake from his slumber."

I rub my fingers on my temple, feeling like I've walked into an alternate universe where what I say has no validity. *Uh, hello, it's me, Atlas.* Doesn't anyone care? Isn't anyone worried? Evergreen Farm has been passed down from Grandpa M to my parents, soon to be passed down to me. The last thing I want to do is be the one who fucks up the family business by not exposing any potential enemies coming our way.

"Atlas," Dad says softly. "I think you should go upstairs and just . . . cool off. It's been a long day, and the busy holiday season starts tomorrow. Perhaps you should get some rest."

"Dad," I say in a pleading tone. "I'm not lying. There were people."

"I know." He pats my shoulder passively. "I know. But best you get some sleep."

"But I'm supposed to take Grandpa M home."

"The boys will take care of that. You just . . . you just go upstairs."

When I glance around at my family, noticing all eyes on me, a mixture of annoyed and humored, I take that as a sign that maybe I really should just disappear . . . for the night.

Head held high, I move toward the stairs. "Mark my words, when someone starts developing that land and starts their very own tree farm, I'll sit back and say, *You should have listened to me.*"

With that, I head up to the attic, where I'm temporarily living while I save enough money to build my very own log cabin on the family property.

They'll feel like such fools when this ends. Just watch. I'll sourly laugh in their faces and point.

Taking my phone out, I text Cole, because if anyone will believe me, it's my best friend.

He placates me.

He supports me.

He is the sounding board I need right now.

Max: There were invaders on the land today! Fucking scallywags thinking they can take over Evergreen Farm. Can you believe that? Not very Thanksgiving-y if you ask me.

I stretch out on my four-poster bed and let the rich red comforter suck me into its warmth as I stare up at the attic ceiling. They will regret not listening to me.

Regret it!

My phone dings with a response.

Smiling, I open up the text, ready to be welcomed with sympathy and understanding.

Cole: You're such a fucking disease, man.

Nostrils flared, I set my phone down and shut my eyes.

Jerks. All of them.

CHAPTER ONE
MAX

NARRATOR: THE HOUSE IS QUIET.

Not a soul in sight while Max lies half hanging off the bed, still in his shoes from his walk the night before. The sun is peeking in through the porthole window off to the right.

His mouth feels like cotton.

His muscles have been stretched in the most uncomfortable way.

And he's not nearly close to being ready for the Christmas tree season to begin. Because despite being told he was crazy, he could not stop thinking about the invaders from the night before, leading to night terrors and thoughts of Evergreen Farm going out of business.

Remember when I said he leans toward the dramatic? Well, here we go.

———————

"Do you really think that?"

Narrator: Um, you're not supposed to be interacting with me.

"I respect that, but just out of curiosity, will you be here the entire time?"

Narrator: Yes.

"Good to know. Then if that's the case, can I ask one thing?"

Narrator: Sure.

"The whole invader situation, did that really happen, or are you siding with my family on the he's crazy thing?"

Narrator: It happened.

"I fucking knew it!"

Narrator: Now, please, on with the story.

I rub my eyes as the sun nearly blinds me through the porthole window as I slowly sit up in bed.

"Motherfucker," I say as I grip my lower back. "Jesus. Why did I sleep like that?"

I lower my feet to the ground, realizing I wore my boots and coat to bed. Did my family somehow shoot me with a tranquilizer, and I didn't notice?

I shed my coat and boots, and head to the makeshift bathroom my dad and I built when I moved back into my childhood home.

At the age of thirty, the last thing you want to do is start a new chapter by shacking up with your parents again, but when my dad presented me with the idea of taking over the farm at some point and building my own home on the property, I knew I had one option: move back in so I could save the money to build my own place.

So here I am.

Living in my parents' attic because my childhood room is now my mom's craft room, and I prefer the privacy of the third-floor attic with low ceilings, even if I'm a six-four man and fear there's a spider in my bed every night. Not to mention the makeshift shower that consists of just a tub with a showerhead and a curtain circling around it. It all screams *I'm moving up in life*—definitely not nearing rock bottom in the slightest.

Also, fun fact: I use the shower as a sink and a place to bathe. Really high-end over here.

Don't worry, there's a toilet too. I refused to use the bucket Ansel jokingly gave me when he heard I was moving into the attic.

I turn on the shower and start taking care of business, making sure to do an extra special clean of the teeth, flossing and using two rounds of mouthwash. Once dried off, I slip on a pair of boxer briefs and a green robe. My morning routine usually consists of sitting at the kitchen island in my robe with a protein drink while watching what Grandpa M refers to as rubbish on my phone.

I stick my feet into my slippers and then head down the creaky wood stairs to the second floor where I catch my parents' bedroom door wide-open. Odd. Mom is usually getting ready at this time.

Maybe she had an early start.

Heading back down the stairs to the main level, I pause at the entry-way where the newspaper has been sent through the mail slot in the door but not picked up by my father.

That's strange.

I pick up the paper, tuck it under my arm, and head to the kitchen, where not a single soul is present. Not a dish out of place, not a warmed toaster in sight.

I scratch the side of my head and do a tight 360, taking in the entire kitchen.

"Uh, Dad?" I call out as I set the paper on the counter. I peek around the corner to the den, looking for any signs of him at his desk, possibly looking through the books for the farm. But nothing.

Straightening up, I move toward the dining room table, calling out, "Mom?"

Nothing but the hum of the furnace fills the house.

Scratching my cheek, I cinch my robe tighter and walk out to the back porch, where my parents sometimes drink their coffee in the morning, taking in the expanse of our tree lot.

When I open the door, the cold mountain air makes my entire body break out into goose bumps, causing everything to . . . shrink.

Yeah, shrink. Okay, I'm not scared to say it. I'm living in a town that's over nine thousand feet in elevation in the middle of the Colorado Rockies, and the only thing protecting my nether regions from windburn is a pair of cotton boxer briefs and a ten-year-old bathrobe.

I peek around the corner and call out, "Mom? Dad? You out here?"

When I'm only met with the sound of the wind blowing through the tall spruce trees, I quickly check the garage, where both cars are parked, and then tiptoe back into the house as the cold continues to seep into my body.

"Well, fuck. Where the hell are they?"

Needing my phone, I walk back up to my room and sit on the bed, where I shoot them a text.

Max: Hey, where are you guys?

I watch the text go through, waiting for the receipt that says *delivered*, but after a couple of seconds of it not appearing, the hairs on the back of my neck start to stand.

Okay, that's weird.

The text message should say *delivered*.

"Let's not overreact," I say to myself. "Because this is exactly what they'd expect, for me to fly off the deep end and start assuming the worst, especially after what we talked about last night. Stay calm."

I let out a deep breath and then head back down to the first floor.

I pull up my text thread with my brothers.

Max: Hey, do you happen to know where Mom and Dad went this morning? Woke up and couldn't find them.

I set my phone down and head to the fridge, where I grab a gallon of milk and then reach for my protein powder and shaker bottle.

Pausing for a moment, I pick up my phone, but once again, my text has gone undelivered to my brothers.

What the fuck?

I decide to send a text to someone else to see if maybe it's my phone.

Max: Can you read this?

I pop open my shaker bottle and start to pour the gallon of milk just as there's a knock at the front door, startling the fuck out of me. I drop the milk and spill it all over the kitchen counter.

"Fuck." I right the milk jug and start for the door.

I open it and take a step back when Cole moves forward, holding up his phone to me. "Why did you text this?"

I study his screen and then make eye contact with my less-than-charming best friend. Nearly a mirror image of me with his messy brown hair and brown scruff lining his jaw. The difference is I'm taller, far more attractive, with impeccable bone structure, and much more liked because of my stunning smile and cheery disposition.

"I wanted to make sure my phone was working."

"Why wouldn't it be working?" He scans me up and down. "And why are you in your robe? Dude, it's almost ten."

"Wait? Really?"

"Yeah. What the fuck have you been doing all morning?"

"Uh, freaking out," I say as Cole enters the house. "Now, I don't want you to think I'm acting crazy, because I'm not, but dude, I think—" God, he'll think I'm such a fucking idiot, but I swallow my pride and say, "I think my family disappeared."

"Jesus . . . Christ," he mutters as he grips the bridge of his nose. "Actually, I think I'll just head to the reindeer barn and start on my chores for the day. I can't deal with this."

He turns toward the door, but I grab him by the shoulder and turn him back toward me. "Dude, I'm not fucking around. They're nowhere—"

"Probably because they're out on the farm, helping everyone open up for one of the busiest days of the season while you traipse around the house in your robe." He plucks at it. "This thing is disgusting. You need a new one. It's pelting."

"It's fine," I say, pulling away from him. "It does what it needs to do."

"Really, because your left nut is hanging out."

"What?" I glance down only for Cole to chuckle to himself. When I look back up, I can feel the fire in my eyes. "Not fucking funny. And no, they're not on the farm, because if they were, then my text messages would have been delivered to them, and they weren't."

"What are you talking about?"

I take my friend by the arm and lead him through the family room and to the kitchen, where milk is now dripping down the face of the cabinets.

"What the hell are you doing in here?" Cole looks me in the eyes. "Your mom will kill you if she sees this mess."

I grab a bunch of red napkins that are left over from yesterday and toss them at him. "Help me."

Begrudgingly, he starts soaking up the milk, or at least attempts to. "These napkins are trash. Hand me paper towels."

While grabbing the multipurpose cleaner, I also snag paper towels and toss them to him.

We both set out on cleaning up the milk while Cole says, "Now tell me what the hell you're freaking out about."

"My parents aren't here," I say, knowing in my brain that it sounds crazy, but seriously, why wouldn't they have at least left a note or something? "Do you think . . . do you think they were kidnapped?"

Cole lets out a deep breath and then tears a few more squares of paper towel off the roll to start helping me again. "Maybe they're busy and they can't respond."

"The messages are going undelivered, man. That means they're not even getting them. And they always have their phones on. And I tried texting my brothers, but they haven't responded, and the text says *undelivered* too. I really think something happened."

Cole picks up the half-soaked newspaper that was on the counter and sets it to the side, only to pick up an envelope and say, "What's this?"

I glance at it with a shrug. "I don't know."

"It has your name on it."

"Really?" I snag the envelope. "It's in my dad's handwriting."

"Hmm, maybe it's a clue to the mystery you're trying to solve," Cole says with an eye roll.

"Maybe it is," I reply, head held high. I will not let his sour attitude tear me down. I open up the envelope while Cole finishes cleaning the counter. I read it out loud. "*Atlas, as you read this, we're currently on an airplane headed for Europe.*" I look up from the letter and say, "Europe? Why are they headed to Europe?"

"I don't know. Why don't you keep reading and find out?"

Clearing my throat, I continue. "*I surprised your mom with a trip to Europe to check out all the Christmas markets.*" I pause. "Ah, she's always wanted to do that. What a nice thing for my dad to do."

"Yeah, imagine that. They didn't disappear, just took a trip." Cole shakes his head.

"You know, I can do without the sarcasm."

"I could do without the idiocy, and yet here we are."

Ignoring him, I continue. "*I didn't tell you because even though I trust you with the farm, I don't trust you with keeping a secret.*"

"Isn't that the truth?" Cole mutters.

I side-eye my best friend. "*We will be gone until Christmas.*" I look up. "Christmas?!" I shout. "What the fuck? They're gone until Christmas?"

Annoyed, Cole snatches the note from me and continues reading. "*Everyone has been briefed about their responsibilities this season. Mitch will be watching over the day-to-day, while Kate will be taking over Mom's respon-sibilities with the vendors. They're in training and will be looking to you for any questions they might have. This is your chance to prove to us that you can really take over the farm. I'm trusting you to do a good job ... I know you will. We'll be in touch. Love you. Dad."* Cole tosses the letter to the side and takes a seat at the island. "There you go, the chance you've been waiting for. The farm is yours to watch over."

I pull on my hair. "Yeah, but ... I mean, a little warning would have been nice. Everyone was briefed but me? He didn't think I could keep a secret."

"I wasn't briefed, so maybe he didn't think either of us could keep a secret. But with me, it's because your mom always knows when I'm lying. You just can't keep your mouth shut."

I hate that he's right about that.

"I just ... I feel so unprepared."

"Unprepared? You've been working on the farm nearly your whole life. If Mr. Maxheimer gave me the role, I'd be able to do it in my sleep just from watching you."

"I can't tell if that's a compliment or an insult."

"Who cares?" Cole says. "Just take this opportunity and run with it. You've been wanting your dad to retire for a while, so now is the time to show him that he can leave the farm with you and he *can* finally retire."

I nod. "You know, I think you might be right." I puff my chest, letting the lapels of my robe fall slightly more open to show off my pecs. "I think I'm going to take charge, make this farm mine."

"Great," Cole deadpans. "But can you do it with some clothes on? Because"—he gestures toward me—"woof, man."

CHAPTER TWO
BETTY

NARRATOR: WHILE MAX GOES TO work—*after putting on some clothes*—*there's something else brewing around town.*

Something that could definitely threaten Max this holiday season.

Remember those invaders? Well, they weren't a figment of Max's imagination. No, they were very real. And we're about to find out exactly who they are. And what they want.

"Morning." Uncle Dwight lifts his cup of coffee in greeting as I walk into the kitchen, fully dressed for the day.

After going for a run this morning where the cold mountain air nearly froze my lungs and the ice on the sidewalks almost caused me to break a leg, I decided I might need to get a membership at the local gym. Well, if that's what you want to call it. It's a room in the back of the Polar Freeze with three treadmills, one weight-lifting bench, and several dumbbells in a variety of sizes that don't match up.

"Morning," I say as I pull a coffee cup from the mug tree next to his coffee maker and pour myself some much-needed caffeine.

"How was your run?" Uncle Dwight is at the kitchen table with a take-out container of eggs, bacon, and toast in front of him. Apparently he takes a walk into town every morning and picks up breakfast. It's his way of "exercising" despite it being a two-minute walk. But I can't knock a person's routine.

"It was good," I say, leaning against the counter.

He's only five years older than me. We're a part of one of "those" families where the uncle is nearly the same age as the niece. And oddly, I grew up calling him Uncle Dwight because my family thought it was funny, and it just stuck. I'd feel weird calling him anything else at this point.

"I will say maybe not the smartest decision. Nearly died running around the corner right in front of Baubles and Wrappings. I slid across some ice and knocked over a metal statue of Santa Claus. It fell over with a clunk."

"I know exactly what statue you're talking about. They always have it there."

"Why? Seems like a hazard if you ask me."

"The Dankworths, who own Baubles and Wrappings, are fined every year for having it out on the corner because it's been such a hazard. Bob Krampus has asked them several times to get rid of it and they won't. So now they just get fined."

"And Bob Krampus is . . ."

"Sometimes I forget you're not completely familiar with the town. He's Santa and the unofficial mayor of Kringle."

"Right," I say with a nod. "Still learning all this. So the Dankworths are okay with paying the fine?"

"Yup. Bob Krampus takes the money from the fine and invests in salt for the corner, which his son, Bob Krampus Junior, puts out every morning."

"Well, he missed it this morning," I say.

"You were out running before everything was opened."

"True." I think about it for a second. "But the statue was out. Do they not take it in every night? And if it's such a hazard, why don't people just steal it?"

"Great question. They have cameras on it at all times. No one dares to touch it. The Dankworths are one of the wealthier families in town, and you don't want to mess with them."

"Sounds like a real *Godfather* situation."

"You could say that." He takes a sip of his coffee. "So what do you think about the proposal I gave you yesterday?"

I take a seat at the kitchen table and cross one leg over the other. "When you say it like that, it sounds like you're referring to a marriage proposal."

He rolls his eyes. "You know what I mean, Betty."

"I know. I'm just procrastinating on answering you."

He sets his cup of coffee down and wipes his fingers on his napkin before sitting back in his chair. "I'll be frank with you, Betty, because it seems like no one else in your life is laying down the truth."

He's right about that.

"You're currently unemployed. You're single. And you're living with your parents in their basement, crocheting because you have nothing else to do with your life besides visit the senior living center on Thursday nights, where you puzzle with people whose names are Murgatroyd, Harold, and Henrietta."

"Murgatroyd, Harold, and Harriet," I correct him.

"My mistake."

"It's forgiven."

"Seriously, Betty. What are you doing with your life that could possibly prevent you from accepting my proposal?"

Nothing.

There is absolutely nothing holding me back other than fear. Fear of the unknown. Fear of moving. But most importantly, fear of failing.

After closing down my year-round Christmas shop—my baby—in Fort Collins after a year of being open, I just don't think I can stomach another project with the possibility of failing once again.

Not to mention I wasn't mentally prepared for such a proposal. When my family came to Kringletown for Thanksgiving, I assumed it would be a nice family get-together where we played some games, ate some pie, and fell asleep watching football, but then Uncle Dwight asked if I wanted to go for a walk, and since I had four slices of pie, I thought it would be a good decision to walk some of it off. I had no idea he'd take me to a piece of land that he purchased ten years ago, when he was a fresh twenty-year-old, looking to invest the money his mom's father left him.

And it is quite the piece of land.

Tall, full pines, a picturesque view of the mountains where the trees part, and a ton of acreage where you can do pretty much anything.

But Uncle Dwight has a plan. He wants to build a Christmas farm.

As he pitched it, a place where people can come and celebrate the season. Where they can enjoy hot chocolate they purchased at the hot chocolate bar and sit around the fireplace while live music plays in the background. A place where visitors can see the inner workings of Santa's workshop, a glimpse into the North Pole, with shops and rides. It . . . it actually sounds like a great idea. And the crazy thing, he wants me to head it up.

He nudges me with his foot under the table. "Come on. Say yes."

I shake my head. "I . . .I don't know. This is all such a surprise. I have a life in Fort Collins. I—"

"Tell me about your life again." He lifts a questioning brow.

"My family is in Fort Collins."

"Which is drivable," he counters. "It's not like you're moving to Alaska."

"Yes, but . . .Buzz is in Fort Collins."

"And who is Buzz?" Uncle Dwight asks.

"My tarantula," I answer. "And he cannot live without me. I bet he's barely surviving now, being all alone."

"Is Buzz in a cage cemented to the ground?"

"No," I answer.

"Then Buzz can move with you."

Yes, I saw that coming, but I thought I'd give it a shot.

"What, uh . . .what about my clothes? I have clothes in Fort Collins." It's a very weak argument. Even I know that. But I'm grasping at straws over here.

Uncle Dwight levels his gaze at me. "Betty, you need this. I know what losing the store did to you. I've seen how it's decimated your spirit. And yes, we have all given you time to run through the emotions of losing something so special to you, but now it's time to pick yourself up and do something new. Try your hand at creating and building again."

God, why am I feeling emotional?

I don't want to feel emotions, not in front of Uncle Dwight.

I look away and take a deep breath before saying, "I don't . . .I don't think I'm the right person for the job. I couldn't keep my little shop open, so how on earth do you think I can make your plans become a reality? This is so much bigger, so much more work, so many more moving parts."

"That's not something you need to worry about. I have the resources you need, and you're building a business in a year-round Christmas town, where people come to experience the holiday season. There have only been two businesses that have shut down in this town." He holds up his fingers. "The first one was an accounting business, and that storefront closed because they pulled their business in-house. The second one was a chain restaurant attempting to needle their way into our charming town. As a whole, no one went there on pure principle, so it went out of business. Every other proprietor that has opened a business in Kringle has succeeded. Trust me, the chances of success here are high."

I mull that over for a moment, because he is right. Every time I've come to visit, it's always the same restaurants, the same businesses year after year.

"And I could really use your help. You're so savvy with creating a charming aesthetic, with social media, with building a business in the digital age."

"Yeah, and then plowing it right into the ground," I huff.

"Hey," he snaps. When our eyes meet, he says, "The reason your business failed is not because of you but because of the location. If you started that shop here in town, you would be thriving. It wasn't the idea. If it was the idea, you wouldn't have over fifty thousand followers on Instagram."

I refuse to acknowledge that point because I'm still living in my feels of being a failure. Though I do still have all those followers, and I continue to feed them with content even though I don't have a store anymore. Would those followers increase if I opened my operation here in Kringle? Would they bring business? Would they still believe in my dreams and me?

"I don't know—"

"Tell me one reason why you can't do it. One solid reason."

I twist my lips to the side, thinking it over. I know whatever I say, he won't consider it a valid reason, so I decide to go with what I'm really feeling. "I'm scared."

He nods. "Now that's a valid reason but one we can overcome. This time, you won't have to do it alone, as I will be your sounding board as well as head up operations when it comes time to build. You will be the think tank, and I have the capital for you to do just that. The idea is there. We just need to execute, and I can't think of anyone better suited for the job than you."

I tug on the corner of my lip.

"Come on. Just say yes. I promise you won't regret it."

Blowing out a heavy breath, I close my eyes and say, "Fine, I'm in."

CHAPTER THREE
MAX

NARRATOR: *WITH A NEW GIRL—AND a new idea—in town, Max has no clue what's about to hit him. And I surprisingly feel bad for him. Because this is not going to be a walk in the park for him, and I think we all know how he gets when he's stressed.*

Though what would a story be without some tension and intrigue?

And a stressed Max?

Max: Do you want anything from Warm Your Spirits?

I wait for Cole to text back as I head down the sidewalk, avoiding ice patches as I make my way toward the coffee shop, the wind whipping around off the mountains and blowing snow up off the ground and into the faces of those walking the streets.

Jesus, it's nippy this morning.

My phone buzzes in my hand with a text.

Cole: Why aren't you at work?

Max: Had to make a deposit at the bank. Don't worry, dear. I'll be back soon. Is that a no on the coffee?

Cole: Just get back here, you fuck.

"I'm going to take that as a no." I pocket my phone and turn the corner just as someone runs directly into my chest. "Oof, watch the niblets," I say, their limbs almost getting me in the goods.

"Oh my goodness, I'm so sorry," the woman says in a muffled tone; the ski mask she's wearing is accompanied with a hat, only giving me a bit of her blue eyes. Smart to wear a ski mask with the way the wind is moving this morning. "Are you okay?"

"I believe everything is still intact. Are you okay?"

She pats her body and then says, "Everything checks. Unless . . ." She eyes me playfully. "Did you bump into me on purpose to steal something, maybe a pickpocket situation?"

I can see the smile in her eyes, so I play along. "Ma'am, you bumped into me, and how dare you accuse me of such an egregious act?"

"No, you bumped into me. It is known that when taking a curve, you stick to your side of the 'road,'" she says, using air quotes, and then looks down. "According to our positioning, you're crossing lanes."

I glance down as well and, *huh, would you look at that.*

"Well, you got me there." I raise my palm. "Guilty as charged."

She chuckles. "So hand it over." She holds her glove-covered hand out.

"Hand what over?"

"Oh, you know, what you took."

Pretty blue eyes.

Excellent repartee.

Consider me intrigued.

Hanging my head, I reach into my pocket and pull out nothing. "Fine, but I don't see why you are in need of a harpoon. It's Christmastime after all."

Why a harpoon? First thing that came to mind, so let's see where she goes with it.

She pretends to snag said harpoon and then, to my surprise, acts like she's polishing it. "My harpoon is none of your business."

Fuck, that's cute.

I eye her suspiciously. "You must be visiting then, because they out-lawed harpoons in Kringle about ten years ago."

"Not visiting. New to town." She sticks the fake harpoon in her belt loop. "And I got permission to wield one for purposes that cannot be spoken of. So best you keep to your own business, sir."

"New to town, huh?" I ask, liking this woman already. "Care to share a name?"

Slowly, she looks me up and down, and then that smile reappears. If only she didn't have that ridiculous ski mask on, then I could really see it. "Share my name with someone who tried to steal my harpoon?" She shakes her head. "Absolutely not." She starts to walk by me, but I stop her at the shoulder and then reach into my back pocket.

I hold my hand out to her and say, "Don't forget your harmonica either."

Her eyes widen playfully, and she snatches air from my hand. She points at me and says, "I'm watching you, sir."

Chuckling, I say, "Yeah, hopefully you don't bump into me again."

"Hopefully. I might have to put in a report to the police."

"Nah, they like me too much to arrest me."

"Ah, corruption in a small town. Looks like I'll have to use my harpoon after all."

I laugh. "A vigilante. Now that's something I can get into." I lean close. "Need a sidekick?"

"Perhaps." She eyes me again. "What qualifications do you offer as a sidekick, because I'm only looking for the best? Can't have you slowing me down."

"Qualifications." I tap my chin, trying to think of something good that I could bring to the table. Something unique. "Well, for one, I'm tall." Not unique, but I'm still getting warmed up here.

"How is your height going to aid me in any way? If anything, it will hinder us because you will stand out."

"You didn't let me finish. I'm tall, but I have the ability to shrink."

"Shrink where? In cold water?"

I snort so hard that I have to cover my nose. "How did you know?"

Her eyes peruse me, giving me a slow once-over before saying, "Solid guess. But I have to say, I have no use for any . . . shrinking, so unless you have anything else to offer, I think I should be on my way."

Just to be playful, I stick my hands in my pockets and smirk at her. "I think that's about it. Shrinkage."

From the twinkle in her eyes, I can tell she's smiling too. "Well, this has been educational, but I must be on my way."

"So that's a no on the sharing of the harpoon then?"

"How about this? If I bump into you again, then I'll call it fate and consider your use of the harpoon."

"What about the harmonica?"

Those makeup-free eyes smile up at me again. "Clearly the harmonica will be yours."

I nod in approval. "Then I look forward to bumping into you again."

"Only if you're lucky." And with that, she takes off.

Wow . . . I liked her . . . a lot.

Hopefully I bump into her again, catch her name . . . possibly her number.

Wouldn't mind seeing what's hiding behind that mask.

"There you go, ready for a new home." I pat the top of the black van that I just strapped a tree to.

"Are you sure we don't need netting?" the father of the family asks. "Every tree I've purchased at other farms was put in netting."

Keeping a smile on my face, I say, "The netting is just a gimmick. Trust me, the way I strapped this tree down, it's not going anywhere, and not a branch will be out of place. Not to mention netting doesn't give the tree room to breathe and more than likely flattens the branches, tugging on the needles." Also, the netting usually ends up in a landfill or in the ocean and rots away. I refuse to be the reason why a sea turtle loses a flapper.

Flapper?

Is that the right word?

Narrator: *The correct term would be flipper, referring to the fore and hind limbs.*

"God, you're useful. Thank you."

Narrator: Anytime. Now back to the story.

"Well, I'm holding you to that," the father says, pointing at me.

Hands on my hips, I say, "Please do." Then I pat the nimrod on the shoulder and head toward the tree shack to take a breather.

Kate is working the register, a job my mom usually works, so I take a seat behind her and grab my water bottle.

There's a lull in customers, so I ask, "How's it going?"

"Pretty good," she says as she turns toward me and leans against the counter. Kate is a pretty girl, short hair where it's buzzed on the sides but full up top. She curls her hair in just the right way where it falls over her forehead, sweeping to the side. I'll be honest, I had quite the crush on her a few years back . . . until Cole informed me that she has a girlfriend. I was gutted and jealous all at the same time. "Been nonstop in here, but I've been able to handle it. There was only that one question I didn't have an answer to, so I'm glad you had your walkie-talkie on so I could ask."

I nod and set my water bottle down. "Yes, you can find any vendor information in the drawer."

"I know that now," she says.

"Who was looking for vendor information?" I ask. "Did they want to sell here?"

"They wanted a list of vendors. She said she could just spend her time walking around, writing down the names of the vendors, as she planned to explore anyway."

"What did she want to do with the names?" I ask, the hairs on the back of my neck starting to stand.

Kate shrugs. "Not sure."

"What did she look like?"

Kate gives me a weird look before she chuckles. "Afraid you might have competition?"

I know to her, that's a funny joke, because Evergreen Farm is very well established and one of the centerpieces in Kringle, an iconic institution that maintains the idea that Christmas is the season of perpetual hope. But to me . . .my nether regions start to shake all over again.

Because—and don't fucking judge me for saying this; I swear I'm sane—but . . .the invaders.

"No, just curious," I say casually, trying not to bring any focus on the anxiety rolling around inside me.

"She had bright blond hair, almost white, and really rich blue eyes framed by black eyelashes coated in mascara. Not ashamed to say that they slightly captured me. She was on the shorter side and wearing a red sweater."

"Shorter than you?" I ask Kate, who is just about five foot.

She chuckles. "No, I'd say maybe an inch taller than me."

I nod, tucking that information away. "Good to know. Well, if you see her again and she has questions, just ping me on the walkie-talkie, and I'll meet up with her."

"Sounds good," Kate says while I stand from my chair.

"Well, headed out again. Let me know if you need anything."

"I will."

With a smile, I wave to her and then exit the tree shack. The moment the light whip of the wind hits me, panic overtakes me, driving me toward the reindeer barn.

Evergreen Farm is one of those places where customers can visit for at least half a day. Not only do we have a tree farm where we cut and plant trees, but we're home to Santa's reindeer, gingerbread-making classes, snowmobile rides, ice-skating among the tall pines, and a whole section of vendors where you can find a vast array of unique Christmas gifts. We embody the Christmas spirit, and we have for years, so someone snooping around the day after I heard invaders on the property? Uh yeah, not on my watch.

I hurry to the reindeer barn, bypassing a family tugging their sleds to the small kiddie hill we keep open for those who might want to participate in some sledding. The farm is busy, and I'm glad we have a plethora of workers helping out, especially with bundling trees, because I have some important business to tend to.

I push open the barn door and then quickly shut it behind me. My best friend's sweeping some spare hay that's fallen to the ground, clearly in his element, not ready for my tornado of neurotic behavior.

Thirteen years ago, if you'd told me my best friend would be working at my family farm as the reindeer handler, I'd have told you you might want to check your crystal ball again, because Cole was supposed to go to college and get a degree in something that didn't involve scooping up reindeer shit. I don't think his intentions were to stay in Kringle, but when he lost his parents on Christmas Eve, everything changed. He became a recluse and stopped celebrating Christmas, and that's when my dad stepped in and offered him a job. I know it was to keep Cole busy and to give him something to do, but I also think it was because my dad wanted to keep a close eye on him. My parents were friends with Cole's parents, and I know losing them was just as much of a hit to them.

Twelve-ish years later, and Cole is still working the reindeer barn, but now it's a little different because he brings his daughter, Florence, in to help.

"Cole, we need to talk."

On an exasperated exhale, he looks up from where he's sweeping. "Dude, if this is about the invaders, I'm not fucking doing this today. I'm tired, and I want to get home so I can just hang out with my wife and daughters."

"You know, it hurts that I'm no longer the person you strive to hang out with anymore."

"Yeah, because you're going on tangents about your parents disappearing and strangers trying to take over your farm."

"I'm glad you brought that up," I say as I walk up to him. "I was just talking to Kate over at the shack, and get this: there's a woman lurking around, asking about vendors."

He clutches his chest dramatically. "Oh no, not a woman. What ever shall we do?"

My expression falls. "You act just like my brothers, who by the way were not answering me on purpose just to be asses. But back to you. You don't have to be so sarcastic all the time."

"And like I said before, you don't have to act like an idiot all the time."

"I'm not acting like an idiot. I'm telling you, something's going on. Something is—" I gasp. "Fuck, do you think my parents are setting this whole thing up, wanting to test me? See how I can handle the pressure of competition while they're gone?"

"No, I don't."

"Why not?"

"Because they'd never do that to me." He points to his chest. "They know damn well the way you'd react to such a thing, which would in turn affect me, like it's affecting me right now. So no, I don't think they'd do that. They'd want you focused on taking care of the farm, not solving some obscure, irrelevant mystery about people you heard talking in the woods."

He has a point.

So we'll scratch that off the list.

"Okay, so then who is the lady walking around asking about vendors? Hmm?"

"I don't know. Probably someone visiting the farm, looking to buy some presents for people she knows. Having a list of vendors is helpful because you can have a general layout of what people are selling before going in and searching aimlessly."

I scratch the side of my head. "Yeah, I guess I never thought about it that way."

"Exactly, because your mind immediately jumps to the ridiculous. Seriously, Max, just chill, okay? Take care of the farm the way you know how, and when your parents get back, you can show them that you were able to handle everything on your own."

"You're right." I blow out a heavy breath, even though in the back of my mind, I still have this niggling feeling like something is awry. "I'll just focus on the farm."

"Thank you. Now, get that dustpan and help me out."

"As long as I can tell you about the woman I ran into in town this morning. I stole her harpoon and harmonica."

Cole tilts his head to the side, irritation written all over his face. "What the fuck are you talking about?"

Hunkering down, I say, "Listen to this . . ."

BETTY

Sitting on a bench in the middle of Evergreen Farm, I take out my phone and snap a picture of the vendor setup, one of the pictures Uncle Dwight wanted me to take while here. I think that's everything on the list other than the exit, which is the same as the entrance.

After we talked at the table this morning, Uncle Dwight went right into planning mode. He said the first thing I needed to do was to take a look at Evergreen Farm. I've never been, which is weird since I've visited Kringletown many times. It's just never been on the list. When I asked him if he was coming with me, he told me he had work to do, so I happily took his car and made the short trip over. I was surprised to see how full the parking lot was when I pulled in.

Then when I entered, I realized why. It felt like I was stepping into a German market with gingerbread hanging from booths, the smell of freshly chopped-down trees permeating the air, and happy families skirting from one activity to the next while Christmas music gently played in the background.

Uncle Dwight wanted me to take my time, to take pictures of everything, and to take notes because he said he wants to make sure I have an idea of what he's looking for in a business.

My only question is, why would we put up a business just like Evergreen Farm right next door? I mean, surely it's not good business practice to open a competing Christmas farm next to such a successful one, right? I mean, yeah, there are some things that they could add here and there to make it more of that one-stop shop Uncle Dwight is looking for, but the businesses would still be very similar.

Something to ask him when I get back.

I stand and stuff my phone in my pocket. I'm chilled and ready to sit in front of the fire and start planning my move. Uncle Dwight said he has the perfect idea for my living arrangements, which he's taking care of today, and he also said he would have movers bring all my stuff and my car so I wouldn't have to worry about going back to Fort Collins and I can just focus on the new project. It almost sounds too good to be true.

I head toward the exit, a warm fire on my mind, just as I see a woman walk in my direction, holding a cute girl in her arms who just happens to drop her stuffed reindeer on the ground.

"Oop, you dropped this," I say, picking up the reindeer and handing it over to the girl.

"Oh my gosh, thank you so much," the woman says as her eyes meet mine. "It would not have been good if we lost that. Not sure who would be more upset, my daughter or my husband."

I chuckle. "My money is on your daughter, but I don't know your husband, so I don't think I could make much of a judgment."

"Ah, which means you aren't from here."

"I have family who lives here, but yeah, not quite a townie . . .yet."

"Yet?" she asks. "Do you have plans to become one?"

"Well," I say, about to divulge my life to a complete stranger. "I actually just accepted a job, and my stuff is being moved here as we speak."

"Really?" the woman says and then switches the little girl to her other hip. "Let me be one of the first to welcome you. I'm Storee, and this is my daughter Florence. My other daughter, Evelyn, is with my aunt at home."

"It's very nice to meet you," I say. "I'm Betty."

"Betty, I love that name."

"Thank you."

"My husband is Cole Black. He takes care of the reindeer here on the farm. We live over on Whistler Lane, right across from the Dankworths."

"The Dankworths. Aren't they the ones who own Baubles and Wrappings?" I ask.

"Yup, that's them."

"Ah, on my run this morning, I knocked over that statue they have in front of the store."

Storee cutely clutches her chest. "Dear God, and you're still alive?"

"Apparently," I say on a laugh.

"Shocking. They're very protective of that statue."

"So I've heard."

"There you are," a deep male voice calls out just as a tall dark figure steps in next to Storee. I watch in fascination as a very attractive man with the carved shoulders of a Greek god slides his arm around both Storee and Florence, and lightly presses kisses to their heads. "Get me out of here."

Storee chuckles. "Atlas driving you nuts today?"

"You have no idea." He takes Florence from Storee and then spots me. "Is Evelyn with your sister?"

"With Aunt Cindy." Then Storee turns to me and says, "Look at me being rude. Cole, this is Betty. She's new to town, just got a job here."

"Hopefully not at Evergreen Farm," he says.

"Stop that." Storee elbows him. "You'll scare her away."

"Babe, you have no idea the kind of day I had. If she accepted a job here, she should run."

I laugh and shake my head. "No, not a job here."

"Glad to hear it." He nods toward the parking lot. "I'll load her up."

"Okay, be right there," Storee says, and then when he's out of earshot, she continues. "Sorry about that. He's a bit of a grump."

"That's okay. No need to apologize."

"He does have a kind heart."

"I believe it. From the way he looked at you and your daughter, I could see it."

That makes Storee smile. "Thank you." She looks toward the parking lot. "Well, I should get going, but hopefully I will see you around town. Florence, Evelyn, and I are always out and about. I take them to Ornament Park almost every day if it's not too chilly, just to let Florence run around as much as she wants. Evelyn is only a few months old, so she enjoys the fresh air."

"Great. Maybe I'll catch you out there."

"Yes, and if you ever need a friend, you know where to find me. My sister lives here too, so feel free to search us out."

"Thank you, that means a lot."

"You're welcome. And good luck with the new job."

"I appreciate it." I offer her a wave before she takes off.

Boy, she's nice.

Everyone seems to be nice in this town.

That guy I ran into this morning, joking around as if we were long-lost best friends, and now Storee.

Maybe this whole situation will turn out better than I expected.

CHAPTER FOUR
BETTY

NARRATOR: WERE YOU EXPECTING THEM *to have their meet-cute already? Well, a meet-cute where they actually saw each other's faces and introduced themselves? Maybe he'd search her out on the farm, looking for the girl in the red sweater? Well, I thought about it but then decided what I have planned might be more fun, because it's Max after all. Stumbling into her on the farm is too easy.*

Their first true encounter needs to be more exciting.

More unexpected.

More . . . Max.

But don't worry. I'll have some fun with them in the meantime.

———————

"Okay, should I be nervous?" I ask as Uncle Dwight drives out of the main part of town and toward the land.

It's been two days since I accepted his offer, and the only thing that I've accomplished since saying yes is to take a few pictures of a farm and draw Christmas tree after Christmas tree in my notebook.

"Why should you be nervous?" Uncle Dwight asks.

"Uh, because you said you'd show me my new home, and yet you're driving me out into the woods. Is there a tent in the trunk I don't know about? I'm not opposed to outdoor living, but I'm not accustomed to surviving in such harsh outdoor elements."

"Do you really think I'd stick you in a tent and leave?"

"I mean, I want to say no . . ."

"No, Betty." He laughs. "When I spoke to my dad about this idea, his initial response was to tell me to take care of Betty at all costs, and I'm sticking to that."

"I appreciate that, but why are we—"

My words are cut short when Uncle Dwight turns into the driveway of the property he showed me, and then a small cottage with a green roof comes into view.

All the lights inside are lit, giving me a view into the house through the windows. It seems like something you'd find in a storybook, with its Bavarian-style siding, red moldings, and a flower box full of evergreens.

"Is that . . .is that the place?" I ask, feeling slightly in awe.

"Yup," Uncle Dwight says, bursting with pride.

"But it wasn't there three days ago when you showed me the land."

"I know. I would have brought you over here yesterday, but they were still hooking up the water and septic. I wanted it to be ready for you."

"Wait, doesn't that take a while to set up?"

"Not when it's already on the property. Trust me, I've been planning this for a while. I just needed the yes from you to hook everything up."

"And the house, where did that come from?" I ask as he pulls in front of it. God, it's really adorable.

"It's one of those prefabricated houses. There's a company just over the mountain that sells them. I thought it would be the perfect place for you to settle in while we plan out this project. I also thought you would like to be on the property so you can be close and keep an eye on the construction."

"I mean . . . yeah, but this is all so . . . Wait, is that my car?" I ask, pointing to my Honda CR-V around the corner.

"Yup. And all your clothes are in the house as well. Your mom helped the movers pack everything you might need. They didn't unpack though. That's on you."

"I . . . I can't believe this," I say, looking through the windshield at the quaint cottage. "This all seems too good to be true." I turn toward my uncle in the car and ask, "Why are you doing all this?"

"What do you mean?" he asks, looking genuinely confused. "You're family. And we help family out."

"But this is helping out a lot. You're giving me a job, a salary, a place to live . . . This is more than just helping out."

"You're not the only one getting something out of this," Uncle Dwight says. "Remember, you're making a dream into a reality by helping me. I've been holding on to this land for a long time, waiting to do something with it, and now is the time. So consider it helping each other out."

"Well, it seems like I'm getting the better end of the bargain, but I guess I won't fight about it and just take it."

I step out of the vehicle and walk up to the small wooden porch, where I run my hand over the evergreen bushes in the flower box.

The door is painted a deep red, something I didn't notice until I got closer, and there is a wreath hanging from the door, welcoming me in.

Uncle Dwight holds the keys to the house in front of me. "Go ahead. Let yourself in."

Feeling giddy, I unlock the door and open it up. Immediately, I'm hit with warmth. The entire cottage is covered in wood, from the floors to the walls to the kitchen cabinets, but it's broken up by greens and reds scattered all throughout the space with rugs, furniture, and curtains.

I run my fingers over the back of a green velvet wingback chair.

"I hope it's okay that I went with the Christmas cottage. I thought it was appropriate."

"I love it," I say as I move into the small open-concept kitchen, which consists of a fridge, an oven, dishwasher, and an island that looks out over the living space. Behind the kitchen is a bathroom with a vanity, a shower, and surprisingly a combo washer and dryer. That's a really nice touch.

Back in the living room, there's a stove in the corner, which is generating the heat, and stairs off to the right, which seem to lead to a loft bedroom.

"This is . . . this is amazing," I say, taking it all in.

"The kitchen is fully stocked with everything you might need to cook. The bathroom has the essentials. And the bed upstairs is a double, because that's what could fit up there given the height of the ceilings."

"That is perfect," I say, taking one more spin around. "Oh my God, you brought Buzz too." I rush over to my tarantula's aquarium, which is bordered in a crocheted scarf, a little present I made for him before I left.

"Yes, miraculously his enclosure was movable."

I hug the aquarium, feeling all sorts of joy. "Thank you, Uncle Dwight. This is . . . this is wow."

He smiles. "I'm glad you like it. Just a heads up, Oh-Kay Plumbing will be by tomorrow to do the last installation in the shower. They were missing a part, so don't use the shower until they stop by, or else you might flood the house."

"Oof, don't want that. Might stop by your place then to shower."

"By all means. I also added a desk under the stairs over there so you can work on all the plans for the property. I wanted to give you your own space as quickly as I could because I know that my house isn't necessarily the ideal place to find creativity."

You could say that again. It's like living in a home that Delia Deetz from *Beetlejuice* would design. A touch cold and very unimaginative, which is why I'm so surprised by this house. It's warm, inviting, charming, and so much better than my parents' basement, where the furnace has a life of its own. And this might sound crazy, but I will swear on my left breast that one night, the furnace whispered my name.

"I love it," I say. "Thank you so much."

"You're welcome. I hope you're able to start a whole new chapter of your life here."

I nod, looking around again. "I think I will."

MAX

I finish tying my boots and then wrap my scarf around my head, covering my exposed facial skin; if anything, I've got to keep the moneymaker protected. Then I strap on my favorite knitted winter hat, with red reindeer, making sure my ears are covered by the wool-lined flaps. Just like any typical Colorado day, the weather changed on a dime. And instead of the simple flannel I wore earlier, I'm bundled up from head to toe, ready to make the trek.

Word around the farm is there was some noise heard out on the property behind ours. Construction-type noise. And once again, the hairs on the back of my neck were raised, so I waited until the farm closed, ate a hearty meal of Thanksgiving leftovers, and then made a plan.

My brothers might think I'm crazy.

My best friend might be questioning my sanity.

But I know something is up. I can feel it in my bones, and I'll be damned if I will stand by and let some vagabonds try to push my family out of business.

Standing tall, ready to go, I hold my flashlight at my chest like a BB gun and say, "This is my farm, and I have to defend it."

With my intentions set, manifesting my protective instincts into the universe, I take off out the back door and into the dark night, the sound of the wind whistling through the pines and my feet crunching against the five-day-old snow the soundtrack to my mission.

I'd prefer John Williams to set the scene for me, but wind and crunching snow will have to do.

With my flashlight turned on, I light up my path toward the property line, making sure to roam the flashlight back and forth, scanning all areas.

I do not want to be caught off guard or surprised.

Just to make sure, I pat the crowbar in my back pocket to make sure it's still there and didn't fall out. It was the only thing I could find in my dad's toolbox that I thought could be used as a sufficient weapon. It was either a crowbar or a blowtorch, and I am not about to light up the forest in case I come across a murderer or even worse . . .a murderous bear. Living in Colorado, you have to be aware of such things. So I went with the crowbar, an honorable but smart choice if you ask me.

Making my way, I stick my hand that's not holding the flashlight into my pocket to keep it warm while I crunch along the snow, not being quiet at all. To be honest, this isn't a secret operative mission where I'm attempting to sneak up on someone. No, I want it to be known that I will protect and defend my property.

When I reach the tree line that separates the two parcels, I pause and look in both directions, as if crossing a road and not wanting to be run over by a rusted utility van. When the coast is clear, I take a deep breath and cross over into enemy lines. When my flashlight illuminates a building, I pause.

On a low gasp, I quickly hide behind a tree, flashlight shining up my nostrils.

A building.

The rumors were right.

Slowly, I look around the tree, this time keeping my flashlight to myself as I spot a light off in the distance that I didn't see before because of all the large pines blocking a straight view.

"A house," I whisper.

Pulling out my phone, I hide behind the tree and text Cole.

Max: Alert. Alert. There is a residence on the neighboring property. I repeat, there is a residence on the neighboring property.

I clutch my phone and look past the tree again to get a better view, but with all the trees, I can barely make out what kind of residence I'm dealing with.

And how did this structure just magically appear without my knowledge?

My phone buzzes in my hand with a text.

Cole: What the fuck are you doing?

Max: Investigating.

Cole: Dude, not a good idea.

Max: Don't worry. I have a crowbar.

Cole: A crowbar? Why?

Max: To protect myself from murderers and murderous bears.

Cole: I really can't deal with this right now. You have put me through it today.

Max: You've been put through it? I woke up thinking my parents disappeared. Now there is a residence that popped up out of nowhere on the neighboring property that has been vacant for years, and this just after I heard voices talking in the woods. I told you something was up. And I'm going to find out exactly what's happening.

Cole: Please, for the love of God, don't.

Max: I can't just sit by while my family is being robbed!

Cole: Robbed? How the fuck is your family being robbed?

Max: Robbed of our privacy, of our farm, of . . . of my sanity.

Cole: The only correct statement you've made in the last twenty-four hours is your sanity being robbed, but it's not by anyone else; it's by you.

Max: You need to learn to be more supportive, compassionate. Especially in a time of crisis.

Cole: I am. This is a time of crisis. You are losing it, and I'm attempting to tell you to stop. Pack up the crowbar, for the love of God, and go back home. Investigating will only get you in trouble.

Max: It won't. I know what I'm doing.

Cole: You don't. Go back home.

Max: Never!

I stuff my phone in my pocket, ready to take charge. Flashlight in hand, I move closer to the house, bouncing behind tree after tree to avoid getting caught. And as I get closer, the building becomes more visible until I'm two trees away, taking in a small cottage-type house that looks like an oversize child's playhouse.

I remove my phone from my pocket and snap a picture for reference. Cole might not want to talk about it now, but tomorrow, when he's in the barn, I can tell him *I told you so.*

Now the question is who is living here? And how the fuck was it built so quickly?

Knowing this is risky, I skirt up to the tree that's right in front of the cottage and lean over, taking a peek inside the house, but the curtains are shut, blocking my view.

Damn it.

I assess my next move and notice that the window near the door isn't covered by a curtain. That's my only option to get to the bottom of this. There isn't a tree to shield me from view, but there is a flower box. I can be stealthy and go undetected behind that shrubbery.

Narrator: Spoiler alert: Max will not go undetected. In fact, this plan is about to very much blow up in his face...

Keeping my flashlight low, I duckwalk toward the cottage, keeping my six-foot-four body out of sight and off the snow until I reach the porch. I fall to my knees and then shuffle on them all the way up to the flower box. Smiling to myself about how I was able to channel my inner Tom

Cruise, I reach for my crowbar, pull back the branches of the shrub in the flower box with the curved end, and slowly start to raise my head to garner a peek.

I hold my breath, raising . . . raising . . .

Almost there . . .

Enemy, be prepared to be found out.

And just as my eyes peek over the shrubs, the front door opens, startling the ever-living shit out of me.

"Ahhh!" I scream out of pure reaction just as a feral warrior cry sounds through the silent night air as five words are screamed into existence by a female voice.

"Take that, you filthy animal!"

And then like a rocket being blasted through a cannon, a two-liter bottle of Pepsi flies right at my head, knocking me out cold.

CHAPTER FIVE
MAX

NARRATOR: POOR MAX. WHAT HE thought was a mission accomplished turned into a night of disaster, because our dear friend Betty is smarter than he expected. For she saw his flashlight moving through the woods. She heard the crunching of the snow, and she was prepared for when the intruder snuck up on her cottage.

She was aware of his approach, and when the moment was right, she busted out of her front door and nailed him dead between the eyes with the only weapon she could find.

And the hardheaded Max—pun intended—broke the bottle open, causing Pepsi to be sprayed all over. And as he lay there on the ground, dripping in the fizzy drink, knocked out, she called the cops, who cuffed him—looks like they would arrest him after all—and drove him to the small community jail, where he had one call . . . and one call only.

———

"I hate you," Cole says as he stares at me through the cell bars.

I grip my forehead, the massive headache throbbing, making it unbearable to deal with anything at the moment.

"Please," I beg of him. "I can't take it right now. It feels like I was hit in the head with an iron."

"More like a two-liter bottle of Pepsi," Officer Marv says as he undoes the lock to the cell.

I stand and slowly make my way toward the exit of the cell. "Am I bleeding?" I flash my forehead at Cole.

"No. The bleeding has stopped."

"Wait, was I bleeding?"

"You have a cut above your eyebrow," Cole says. "And a cut on the top of your hand where your crowbar impaled you as you fell."

Surprised, I lift up my hand, and sure enough, it's bandaged with white gauze. "What the hell happened?"

Marv clears his throat. "You were acting like a Peeping Tom, trespassing, and you were caught. Out of self-defense from your victim, you were hit in the head with a bottle of Pepsi where you fell to the ground and were impaled by your crowbar. You were then carted off in the back of my police car, where you dizzily rambled on about intruders. You were charged with third-degree trespassing. You will have a court hearing in the near future."

"A court hearing?" I yelp. "Am I going to jail?"

"It would serve you right," Cole mutters while Marv shakes his head.

"No, you'll probably need to pay a fine. Possibly community service. Given this is your first offense and you're in good standing with the town, the judge will go very easy on you."

I let out a pent-up breath, because *fuck, jail*? I wouldn't survive. There's no way. And my brothers and Cole would never let me live it down. I might look intimidating wielding an axe at the farm, but I'm not ashamed to say I'm a cinnamon roll.

"My suggestion to you: leave your new neighbor alone." Marv then takes off, leaving me with Cole, who is shaking his head.

"I told you to leave. I told you to go home. But noooo, you just couldn't listen. Jesus, Max."

I nod, feeling the shame of being caught pulse through me. There's only one thing to really say. "You were right, dear. You were right."

BETTY

I grew up in Colorado, and yet the weather in the mountains is so different.

Colder.

Windier.

More unpredictable.

The mornings are deathly chilling, especially if the wind is whipping around, which is why I find that I wear my ski mask in the mornings to avoid getting chapped skin during my runs.

I head down the street, passing the coffee shop, and look up just in time before I bump into the brick shithouse I bumped into yesterday.

But this time, he's wearing a winter hat over his head and a pair of sunglasses, his hands stuffed in his pockets with his head tilted down, like he's trying to avoid all humans.

Smiling, I bump into his shoulder, causing him to look up and say, "Oh shit, sorry—" He pauses, and then recognition falls over him, the smallest of smiles tugging on his lips as he leans in. "Vigilante?"

I can't hold back my chuckle. "Harpoon stealer? I almost didn't recognize you. Are you incognito?"

He slowly nods and then glances over his shoulder. "There has been a breach in the town cheeriness, and I've been forced to go undercover. Beware. If seen with me, you might go down as well."

Hate to admit it, but I was kind of hoping I would run into him again. This nameless man, who gave me such a strange but exhilarating interaction the other day. I kept thinking about him and how easy it was to just ... pretend.

Leaning forward conspiratorially, I ask, "And who is at the helm of this breach?"

He glances around, checking over his shoulders a few times before he leans in as well and whispers, "The Easter Bunny."

I snort all over my ski mask as he continues.

"Fed up with this year-round Christmas town, he's ready to take everyone down, me being the number one target."

I clasp at my chest in shock. "You?"

He points to his chest with a firm nod. "Me."

"Wow." I cross my arms. "What do I not know about you that would cause such close quarters to death by carrot?"

He smirks and says, "I spread too much Christmas cheer. I jingle, I jangle, I sneeze tinsel. It's too much, and that white fluff of a tail wants me out."

"Not the jingle, jangle, tinsel sneezing."

He slowly nods. "The very one. And I have to warn you, you must not be seen with me. Not if you have any chance of taking out Cottontail."

"You think I do?"

He places his hand on my shoulder and leans closer, his cedar-like cologne wafting toward me. "As the vigilante with the harpoon and harmonica, there is no doubt in my mind."

"Very well. I'll be on the lookout for jelly beans and eggs, a telltale sign of him being near."

"Don't forget the trail of carrot crumbs he leaves behind."

"How could I ever forget?"

"Silly me." He smiles. "Best of luck to you."

"You too." I start to walk away but then stop. "One more thing." Pretending to pull something out of my pocket, I open my hand to him.

He gasps and takes a step back, horror written all over his face, which makes me chuckle.

Because where is he going to go with this?

"It's . . . it's . . . you. You're Cottontail." He shakes his head in disgust, and it takes everything in me not to laugh. "No, get those jelly beans away from me." He playfully swats my hand away. "I will not surrender." He sidesteps me and moves away, only to turn around and walk backward with that smirk of his stretching across his lips. Goodness, he's handsome. "Later . . . vigilante."

I point my finger at him. "That's Cottontail to you."

He laughs and then takes off.

I should have gotten his name.

Maybe his number.

Then again, do I really have time for something like that?

Probably not.

———————————

"How was your first night in the cottage?" Uncle Dwight asks as he takes a seat across from me at the Caroling Café, where he grabs breakfast every morning.

The fifties-inspired diner is decked out in Christmas decorations, baubles and trinkets hanging from the ceiling, as well as garland. Every booth has Mr. and Mrs. Claus salt and pepper shakers, while up front, a stage is prepped and garnished in trees and fake presents, ready for someone to take the stage and start singing.

It's . . . cute.

And I feel like I'd appreciate it more if I wasn't so shaken.

"Um, it could have been better."

Uncle Dwight's brows crease. "What do you mean?"

"Well, I was getting ready for bed when I kept seeing a flash of light in the woods. I didn't think anyone should be on the property—"

"You're right. No one should be on the property but you."

"Well, I dimmed the lights, closed the curtain to the bathroom, and then waited. I perched myself in a position where I could see what was going on. And as I waited, I grabbed the one thing I knew that I could easily chuck at someone and do damage . . . a bottle of Pepsi."

Uncle Dwight leans in, concern etched on his expression.

"And as I heard the footsteps approach closer and closer, I moved toward the door."

"Wait, was there really a person out there?"

"Yup," I say with a nod. "And he had a crowbar. He was trying to get in my window, but before he could, I jumped out of the house with a swing of the door and chucked the bottle at his head, nailing him and knocking him out cold."

"Seriously?" Uncle Dwight says in disbelief.

"Yup. I then called the cops, and he was handcuffed and taken away." I dust off my hands. "Took care of the creep, but it left me a little shaken. I was thinking this morning about how I need to have better protection. I don't really want a gun, because they scare me, but maybe a BB gun or something like that would do me some good."

Uncle Dwight scratches the top of his head. "I'm sorry, I'm still trying to process the fact that someone was trying to get into your window with a crowbar. Did they say who it was?"

"Uh . . . Heimer or something," I say. "I was too shaken to really remember."

Uncle Dwight sits taller. "Do you mean . . . Maxheimer?"

"Yes." I yell. "That was the name. They kept calling him Maxheimer. Do you know who that is?"

Uncle Dwight's nostrils flare as he stares off at a space behind me. "Yes, I know exactly who that is."

"Is he dangerous?"

He wets his lips and mutters, "Very."

MAX

"What the hell happened to you?" Felix asks as he examines the cut above my eyebrow along with the bruising.

"Ran into a pole," I say as I sharpen my axe, trying to avoid all conversation about what happened last night. Most likely the real story will start circulating the town, because no one can keep their mouth shut, but I have no problem lying until it does.

I'll be honest; in the moment, I felt like a crusader, solving crimes for the innocent. But now, the day after, as I nurse my wounds and attempt to use my left hand to wield my axe, I just feel . . . foolish.

And yes, it takes a lot to set my pride to the side and admit that, but it's true. Who did I really think I was last night, traipsing around with a crowbar, sniffing out new territory? I might have felt like Tom Cruise at the time, but man, oh man, I was more like a wet bandit looking for trouble. And I know this because Cole gave me a lecture last night about it as he drove me back home. And he lectured me this morning as well when I was complaining about my hand hurting.

So, yes, embarrassment and humiliation have set in.

"Ran into a pole?" Felix asks, not believing it. "Then how did you hurt your hand?"

"Nail," I answer. "Nail in the pole."

"Uh-huh, and what pole was this?"

"One by the tree shack," I say as I put down my sharpening tool and examine the axe blade. The sharper the blade, the less whacks I'll need to take, therefore saving my hand.

"And what made you run into the pole?" Felix continues.

"Spider," I answer. "Huge one. On my leg. I let out a scream only dogs could hear, ran without looking, and then *smack*. Pole."

I thought about this.

I thought about it long and hard this morning while drinking my protein shake at the kitchen island. There would be questions about my wounds. And I wasn't about to tell them the truth. Therefore, I came up with a different story, one that is just self-deprecating enough that it's believable but far away enough from the truth that nothing could be linked.

"Were you knocked unconscious?"

"Yup," I say and then rest my axe against my shoulder. "Now, if you'll excuse me, I have some—"

"You were in jail last night?" Ansel announces, walking into the barn, sporting a shit-eating grin. "Dude, why didn't you call us to bail you out?"

And this is what sucks about living in a small town. Nothing is kept a secret. Absolutely nothing. News traveled quicker than I expected.

"Wait, you were in jail?" Felix asks, turning toward me with that big-brother look of disapproval pinching his brows.

"Yeah, for trespassing," Ansel says. "Cole was telling me all about it."

Cole?

Cole told him?

That motherfucker.

When has he ever engaged in gossip?

The betrayal! Almost hurts worse than my hand and eye put together.

"Where the hell were you trespassing?" Felix asks me. "And is that how you actually hurt your eye and hand?"

"Yup," Ansel answers for me. "The owner of the house he was trespassing nailed him in the head with a two-liter bottle of Pepsi. Knocked him out. And the hand was from the crowbar he was carrying around."

"Why the hell did you have a crowbar?" Felix asks.

Head held high, I say, "In case I crossed paths with a murderer."

"Little help that did for you, since you were taken out by a Pepsi," Felix says.

The heaviest Pepsi known to man. I can still feel the way it crashed into my head.

"My question is, was it regular Pepsi or diet?" Ansel asks.

"Great question." God, I hate them. Although if I were to guess by the heft, it was regular.

Both my brothers fold their arms at their chests, waiting for me to answer.

But I refuse to delight in their obvious ribbing. I have things to do. Trees to chop. People to avoid—ahem, Cole.

"Also, was it an unopened bottle?" Ansel continues.

"From the look of the cut, I'd say so," Felix answers.

"Confirmation would be great though." They both look to me for answers again, but like I said, I have things to do, so I head toward the barn door.

"As much fun as this is for the both of you, your tour should be done soon with their shopping. I suggest you get back to them while I get back to my job."

"Your actual job? Or your new job of trespassing? Also care to explain why you were trespassing?" Ansel asks.

"Fuck off," I call out, flipping them my middle finger and then heading over to the tree shack. As if I would tell them. It's best to keep them in the dark if for no other reason than the interrogation I was just put through.

The farm is buzzing today with even more visitors since all the vendors are having their beginning-of-the-season sales. The demand for real trees and artificial—yes, we sell those as well, in the tree shack of course—is booming, and the joy of the season is just starting.

When I reach the shack, which is more of a general store for everything related to Christmas trees, including ornaments, garland, and tree toppers, I spot Kate behind the register wearing an elf hat. When she sees me, she winces in an uncomfortable way.

Yup, word has gotten around.

"Do you know?" I ask her as I walk past an older couple checking out the personalized ornament section.

"I think everyone does."

"Great," I huff out as I take a seat on the chair behind the register and lean my head against the wall. "For the record, I wasn't trespassing in a creepy way. Just, you know, trying to gather information."

"Didn't think you were being creepy." She tries to hold back her smile, but I can see right through her. "For what it's worth, it looks like you went through hell to trespass."

"Yes, that's exactly what I want people thinking, that I went through hell to trespass." I groan. "Please, tell me something other than what happened to me last night. Anything good? Anything of interest?"

"Uh . . ." She leans against the counter. "The fake flocked trees from Larry Balzak and Company that you said would be a bestseller this season, well, we sold three already today. You were right."

"I'm usually right about trees," I say, attempting to pat myself on the back. I need the ego boost after last night's disaster.

"Oh, and the string popcorn kits you thought were a good idea, I sold a few of those as well."

"That's good news."

"I thought so. Oh, and that girl I was telling you about yesterday, the one with the blue eyes and bright blond hair . . ."

"Vendor girl?" I ask.

Kate nods. "Yup, well, she was back today, but she was asking about something else."

"She was?" I ask, perking up. "What was she looking for?"

"Asking about our suppliers and who we use."

"Seriously?" I ask, sitting even taller.

"Yes. She seemed genuinely interested, especially when it came to our decor suppliers. And I remembered her, because . . . those eyes of hers, seriously, so blue."

"Did you give her the information?" I ask.

"I mean . . . yeah." Kate winces.

"What? Why? Kate, she could be a mole."

"I don't know. She asked nicely, and I'm sorry, she's just . . . she's hot, and I thought why not?"

"Kate," I groan, sliding my hand over my face with my wrapped hand. "You can't be giving away information like that. Don't you see what she's doing? She's trying to steal all our information. First it was the vendors, now our suppliers. What's next? Our year-end statements?"

"Well, if she did ask for them, I wouldn't know where to find them, so at least you're safe with that."

I stand from the chair. "Is she still here?"

"I think so. I saw her walk off toward the gingerbread house."

"What is she wearing?"

"Uh . . . a long camel-colored wool jacket."

"Got it," I say as I move toward the door.

"Wait, Max, what are you going to do?"

I look over my shoulder and answer, "Protect my farm," then head out the door.

BETTY

It smells delicious in here.

Like actual heaven.

And it's cute, like being in an actual gingerbread house. Brown walls, brown flooring, brown furniture, all outlined with thick loopy white paint. Seriously, it's one of the cutest shops I've ever seen.

And from the smell of it, the gingerbread is not imported but baked fresh daily.

There's a sign outside stating this, but then again, I've seen my fair share of liars in business. Not the Evergreen Farm owners. They seem to be running a very upstanding establishment.

I walk over to the shop portion of the gingerbread house and examine the gingerbread house kits, the extra fixings and candy for decoration, as well as frosting. It would be cute if they did a make-your-own kit. Like a candy shop with bags and scoops for candy, but instead of buying candy for yourself, you're buying it to decorate your house. A pay-by-the-pound situation. People can pick out their structure, icing, and then candy.

Loving the idea, I write it down in my notes app, just as I feel someone step up right behind me.

"Can I help you?" a deep voice says, startling me.

I turn around, my eyes slowly scanning upward until a very tall and handsome man comes into view. Dark hair that curls at the ends, dark eyes, square jaw peppered in scruff, and a bandage above his eye . . .

Wait . . .

I know him. "Harpoon stealer?"

He leans back in surprise. "Vigilante?" His eyes scan me for recognition. When his gaze meets mine, I see the moment he connects the dots. "You're . . . you're the girl with the eyes?"

"What?" I ask as I back up, my attention focusing on the cut above his eye. Was that cut there before?

And why does he look familiar in a way that doesn't register happy, joking memories on the sidewalk?

Why does he . . . ?

His height, his width, the deepness of his voice.

Oh.

My.

God.

"You . . . you're him . . . You're . . . you're following me."

"What?" the man asks.

I clutch at my jacket and back up. "Stay . . . stay away." I reach for the closest thing to me and pick up a tube of icing. "I'm warning you, I'm not afraid to hit you in the head again."

"Hit me in the head again . . ." He pauses, and then his eyes narrow. "Are you the lady who pummeled me in the head with a Pepsi bottle last night?"

"Yeah, and I have no problem blacking out your other eye." I take another step back. "So s-stay away before I get a restraining order."

"Listen." He takes a step forward. "I'm not here to cause—"

"Back up." I wiggle the tube at him. "I'm not kidding. Not another step closer."

Hands up, he looks around the shop and then leans in closer, too close for me.

Before he can whisper whatever is on the tip of his tongue, I scream, "Restraining order," then chuck the icing tube at his head, nailing him right between the eyes before I bolt past him and out the door as I hear him groan behind me.

Outside, I make my way down the stairs, only for him to bust out the door as well, looking around while holding his head. When he spots me, he charges in my direction.

"Stay away," I call out and start to jog just as I look over my shoulder and spot him stumbling down the three stairs on his back.

A loud groan fills the cheery farm, and he grips his back as he looks in my direction. Determination sets in his features as he stands and starts limping forward.

Yelping, I hurry toward the parking lot, making sure to be careful, because even though they do a good job of clearing all the snow and ice, there are still some spots that are slightly slippery.

I reach the Evergreen Farm arch, and I'm about to turn right, toward my property, when my arm is grabbed, and I'm pulled up against a pole.

"Help! Help!" I call out just as the man's bandaged hand is placed over my mouth. There's a mark on his forehead from the sharp corner of the icing tube and visible pain in his features as he breathes heavily.

"I'm not . . . going to . . . hurt you," he says, labor in his breath. "Fuck."

He winces and leans forward, dropping his hand from my mouth and gripping his back again. "Shit, my back."

"Let me go."

"I'm not, ouch, fuck." He grips his back again, arching ever so slightly.

I attempt to slide away, but he keeps his hand on my arm, pinning me in place.

"Just give me a second. I need to . . . oh motherfucker. It's seizing. I'm seizing." And then before my eyes, he falls to the ground, rolls to his back, and stares up at the sky, a husky, painful groan falling past his lips. "Get . . . Cole."

"Huh?" I ask, staring down at the giant of a man. Honestly, I think his quad is the size of my head.

"Cole. I need Cole."

"Coal," I ask, confused. "Like coal from Santa?"

"No, Cole my best friend." He groans and winces. "He's in the reindeer barn. Please . . . get him."

Sheesh, he really looks like he's in pain.

Set on a mission, I'm about to head back to the farm when I pause, because if I've learned anything in my twenty-five years of life, it's that I need to be aware of stranger-danger situations. And this very well might be one of them.

Because this guy who tried to pry open my window last night is telling me to go find a man named Cole in the reindeer barn? A barn . . .

Barns are the perfect place for corruption and murder.

Uh, not falling for that trick. It's probably where they snatch innocent ladies like me and take them to their murderous dwelling, where they string them up and dance naked in front of them just for jollies.

Well, I will not partake.

I won't be tricked.

So instead of helping him and going to find this *coal*, I step over his twitching body and say, "Get your own coal."

Then I take off, head held high and safe from what I can only imagine would have been an abduction.

Nice try . . . Maxheimer—harpoon stealer.

Nice try.

CHAPTER SIX
BETTY

NARRATOR: HE SHOULD HAVE SEEN it coming, chasing after the girl he stalked last night. That was never going to end well, but if there's one thing we know about Max at this point, it's that he's determined. If he feels there's a threat to his farm, he'll take care of it. If only his imagination wouldn't run so wild, then maybe he wouldn't be in such a situation.

Then again, what kind of story would this be if Max didn't let his imagination take control of his actions? A pretty boring one if you ask me.

———————

"You doing okay?" Uncle Dwight asks as he takes a seat next to me on the bench, handing me a cup of hot cocoa, which he retrieved from the log cabin near Santa's house in Ornament Park.

I learned today that it's called Ornament Park because from overhead, it looks like an ornament, with Santa's house—a.k.a. the home of Bob Krampus—at the head. And it's quite the festive setup, with wreathes and garland strung from every lamppost, a stage near Santa's house, which is decked out in five-foot green and red metal presents, at least—from what I can see—five Christmas trees, and signs with arrows pointing visitors in the direction of where to find businesses and activities.

If you're looking to get into the Christmas spirit, Kringletown is the place to be, with its Bavarian-style buildings, brightly colored garlands, and perfectly manicured evergreens. Not to mention the vendor village behind the Myrrh-cantile is like a mini–German Christmas market, just adorable.

I take a sip of my hot cocoa, loving the hint of raspberry flavoring. "Yeah, a little shook but doing okay." I turn toward Uncle Dwight and ask, "Why didn't you tell me that Evergreen Farm belonged to the Maxheimers?"

"Guess I didn't think to talk about ownership."

"I know, but last night, when you were saying the Maxheimer guy was dangerous, you could have said it then."

"Perhaps," he says, staring off toward the stage where a family of nine have lined up from smallest to tallest, all wearing gold choir robes with white triangular collars.

"So why didn't you?"

He lets out a sigh and then looks down at his cup. "Atlas, that's his name. Atlas *Maxheimer* and I have a long history. You could say we've been enemies since high school, and I was trying not to bring that animosity into our project. I didn't want to thrust my opinions and judgment on you, as I wanted you to form your own opinions while living here. I guess he took his anger to the next level, making it hard to keep the two things separate now."

"Oh, I didn't know. What did he do?"

Uncle Dwight shakes his head. "Nothing that you need to know."

"I mean, I kind of want to know if his business is something you want to challenge. I think it will help me feel, I don't know, maybe less guilty."

"He attacked you, and you feel guilty?"

I sigh. "You know what I mean. If I had a little bit of fodder, maybe I would feel more inclined to seek revenge for you."

He slowly nods his head. "Without getting into details, he sort of messed around with my relationship with Jessica."

My brow knits together. "Like, he made a move on her?"

"Not really, but let's just say it wasn't great what he did. Really, uh, really made me lose hope."

I press my hand to his shoulder. "I'm so sorry. I know how much Jessica meant to you."

"She meant the world," he says softly, thinking about his girlfriend from high school. His girlfriend he lost to cancer.

"So there's animosity there," I continue, not wanting to dwell on something that makes him so sad. "Does he feel the same way about you? Like is the enemy status reciprocated?"

"Oh yes," Uncle Dwight says with a nod. "Very much so. And now that he tried to break into your cottage, I feel more animosity toward him than before."

"Well, you don't need to worry about me. I can handle my own." Though his comment about them being enemies since high school is a little suspicious. *Surely he's not using me to perpetuate this rivalry, is he?* "I need to ask you a question."

"Anything," he says as the choir finishes singing "O Holy Night."

"This project, this farm you want to create, is it your form of revenge?"

He sips his hot cocoa and then asks, "Would that be a problem?"

Okay, not going to deny it.

I lean back on the bench, thinking about it. I'm not someone who tends to fall in line with the angry side of the world. I'm not the grump; I'm the sunshine. I always have been. I've walked through life pretty oblivious to a lot of things, so joining in on someone else's vendetta doesn't exactly feel right to me.

But . . .

In a short amount of time, Uncle Dwight has done a lot for me. He's reinstated some of the confidence I've lost, just by believing in me. He's offered me a paycheck, a home, and a new chapter. Sure, it's now clear that it's because he's seeking revenge on someone who has hurt him in the past, but it's still a lot more than anyone has ever done for me.

And I can . . . skirt around the revenge a little. I wouldn't want the same business plan as Evergreen Farm, which is why I've asked about their vendors and their suppliers. I'd want to provide something different. So maybe I can get away with doing this while helping Uncle Dwight at the same time.

I turn to him. "No, that won't be a problem."

A large smile passes over his lips. "That's really good to hear. Really good." He stares off toward the choir. "Now we have to come up with a name."

A girl with bright red hair steps forward, performing a solo in "Carol of the Bells," her mouth moving a mile a minute as she sings the soprano part. Her angelic voice pulls me in as I listen to the lyrics.

"What about . . . *With Joyful Ring* Farm?" I turn to Uncle Dwight. "It can be themed around 'Carol of the Bells.' The shops and food trucks can be called things like . . . Bringing Good Cheer and Meek and the Bold. We can have a section with bells, where people try to ring them to the tune of the song—could be a kids section; that's something Evergreen Farm is lacking. It could be like . . . a pumpkin farm but for Christmas. And instead of cutting down all the trees and replanting them like Evergreen Farm, we can offer fake Christmas trees, although I know of a better supplier than they're using. We can have a choir who goes around, caroling to groups, all dressed in the old-timey garb. There can be a playground and a zip line through the trees, maybe a ropes course as well, and you go through, ringing the bells at each station you complete. We can have vendors as well, but we'll pull from real Christkindlmarkets. We can lean into reds and greens, with gold only being in the bells that are found throughout the farm. We can have scalloped edges and rickrack trim decorations and Christmas quilts. Genuine crafting stations. None of these quick kid crafts. True sewing crafts. It can be a place where people stay for an entire day, never getting bored, because they're going from one activity to the next. And instead of gingerbread, we can make Schneeballen."

Uncle Dwight blinks a few times. "Um, wow, that was a lot to take in all at once."

"Sorry," I answer bashfully. "When I'm struck with inspiration, my brain kind of moves fast."

"I can see that. Well"—he lets out a deep breath—"I actually love it all. Love it. I think it's unique and different but will bring in a new crowd, and I think . . . that's something people will appreciate. I only have one question."

"Yes?" I ask.

"What the hell is Schneeballen?"

I laugh. "They're a German deep-fried pastry that's extremely popular during the Christmas season. It would be the perfect thing to set us apart, because there are so many varieties of the dessert, you can play on some of the more popular flavor combinations with a general base of fried pastry."

"Well then . . . I think we have the start of a business plan."

"I think we do." I smile. "Now . . . to do a little more recon . . ."

CHAPTER SEVEN
MAX

NARRATOR: *WORD HAS SPREAD THROUGHOUT town, and now Max is known as a class A predator.*

Not really, but you know how gossip goes. You hear one thing, and then it's passed on from ear to ear, changing ever so slightly so that the truth becomes a mere memory of what's being told. Which means, guess who's on damage control? Our dear friend Max.

And it all starts at Kringletown's coffee shop, Warm Your Spirits.

———————

Cole: Be there shortly.

I pocket my phone, irritated that Cole is not on time. I know he has a kid, but I can't go into the coffee shop without executing my plan, so I lean against the side of the building, waiting it out just as a familiar masked Pepsi thrower rounds the corner.

When she spots me, she gasps and takes a step back, as if I'm the villain in this story.

Check the mirror, ma'am, because I'm not the one throwing deadly pantry items at heads.

"Are you stalking me?"

I roll my eyes. "Please, I have better things to do with my life." I grip my side and say, "My back is fine by the way. Thanks for asking."

"Then why are you just standing there...lurking? Are you practicing your Peeping Tom routine? Luring in innocent victims with your witty banter, only to try to break into their house and do know God knows what to them?"

My nostrils flare as I whisper, "I'm not lurking. I'm waiting for a friend—"

"I'm sure you are." She takes another step back as if I'm about to strike any second. "But you know what? I'm not falling for it, so just . . . just leave me alone."

"Gladly," I say, tossing my arms in the air. "Gladly. Just move on."

"You move on."

"No, you move on," I counter.

"Why? So you can attack me as I move by you?"

Grinding my molars, I say, "If anyone attacked anyone, it was you attacking me. So I should be the one calling for help."

"Don't you dare."

"Oh, I will." I lift my chin. "Help," I screech. "Help, the serial soda killer is attacking me."

"Stop that."

She glances around to make sure I didn't attract any concern, which I didn't. Real great, I live here all my life, and no one is here to save me. I'll take that into consideration next time someone is looking for help.

"Do not turn this on me. Typical man." She snorts derisively and then backs up, keeping her eyes on mine.

"What is that supposed to mean?"

"It means you can't take accountability for your actions."

"Says the woman who concussed me," I shout.

"Because you were trying to break into my cottage and harass me."

"I was not harassing you," I say, exasperated.

"Just . . . just stay away, Maxheimer. You hear me? Stay . . . away." And then just like that, she sprints across the street, walking on the other side to avoid me.

I have half a mind to lunge at her, make her think I'm about to attack, only to tie my boot instead, but knowing her, she will twist the move into something of a murderous attack. So instead, I lean against the building again and wait for my friend. I need to right my reputation, and it starts with him.

"Let me hold the baby," I say to Cole.

"Why?" he asks, clutching Florence, who's wrapped up in a snowsuit, to his chest.

"Because holding a child will make me seem more likable. Remember, we're trying to restore my image again."

"You're not using my daughter as a pawn in your scheme of making yourself look good."

"Then why did you come with me if you weren't going to help?"

"I didn't come with you. We ran into each other on the sidewalk after you chased me down, yelling my name. I came to have a muffin with my daughter, not attempt to make you look better."

I press my fingers into my forehead. "I wasn't going to bring this up, because I thought that maybe you'd help out of the kindness of your heart, but since I see that the old Cole heart is still black, looks like I'll have to resort to blackmail." Looking my best friend in the eyes, I say, "You owe me."

"I owe you?" he asks, brows raised. "How on earth do I owe you?"

"Three words: *holly jolly sidekick.*"

His jaw clenches as he stares back at me, knowing that I've got him.

Two years ago, when Cole was in his dark place where he couldn't celebrate Christmas, he pulled a 180 on everyone and entered the town Christmas Kringle competition. The reason? To beat Storee, who entered as well. At the time, they hated each other, but in their case, there was a very thin line between love and hate, and they crossed it without looking back. But during the time when they were hating each other, he volunteered me as his holly jolly sidekick for the competition, which basically meant I had to compete in the challenges with him.

And let me tell you ... there were some things that I did that I'd never do again.

Leaning in, he whispers, "You liked doing that."

"I enjoyed bringing the Christmas spirit out of you. But would I have really strutted on stage in front of the entire town in dog ears and booty shorts? No."

"Hey, you picked those outfits."

"To help you win." I roll my eyes. "Dear God, we had to use our bodies, and the best way to do that was to put you in lederhosen and me in booty shorts. And I was right. So you're welcome. Not that you ever thanked me at any point during that entire journey. But you know, if you want to continue to be ungrateful, you can hog your daughter to yourself and let me flail—"

"For the love of God," he mutters as he hands me Florence.

I knew it would work.

I grip her tightly and boop her nose with my finger. "Aw, you love your uncle Maxy Poo, don't you?"

"Don't call yourself that," Cole says as he opens the door to Warm Your Spirits and leads the way.

Putting on a smile and channeling my inner Kringle, I walk in behind him with my head held high. I did nothing wrong. I wasn't trying to break into her house. I wasn't trying to attack her. I was simply searching for the truth.

And that's what I'll lead with.

Let the *fix my reputation* commence.

"Good morning," Tanya, the owner, says. "Interesting seeing you in here, Max."

I smile at her. "Just wanted to take my niece out, share a muffin with her." I can practically feel Cole's eye roll from here.

Tanya leans against the counter. "Uh-huh, looking for some sympathy after the shocking news that's been spreading around about you? So you'll use a child to clean up your image?"

"Told you it wouldn't work," Cole says, reclaiming his daughter and ordering a blueberry muffin and some water.

Cutting the bullshit, I say, "Tanya, do you really believe that stuff about me? Come on, you've known me for a long time. Do you really think I'm a pervert predator, attacking a woman on my own farm?"

"No," she says, ringing Cole up. "But it's been fun to talk about, that's for sure."

"Tanya," I groan. "You know I don't like to be the subject of gossip."

"Which is why I'm glad you came in today, because I'd like to hear the truth."

"Trust me, you don't," Cole says.

"Ignore him," I say. "He's resurfaced his grumpy disposition." Shooing Cole away, I add, "Take your baby over there, and share a muffin while I lay down the facts."

"Let me text Sherry first," Tanya says. "You know she'll be the biggest asset to fixing your image. She has the biggest mouth out of all of us, and the picture of you dressed as a dog in those booty shorts is still the wallpaper on her phone. You know she's your advocate."

I tap the counter. "Yes, do that. Ring your friend. The truth will prevail."

I order a peppermint mocha and then take a seat at the counter, where I can talk to Tanya while she works and hopefully most of the shop can listen in. She drops off my drink just as Sherry arrives.

Rubbing her hands together, she says, "Oh, it's a chilly one today."

"I took the liberty of making you a coffee," Tanya says, setting her cup down next to mine.

"Such a good friend. Thank you." Sherry then turns to me and takes a seat. "Tell me everything."

This was the goal when entering this establishment—to clear the air and let people know what really happened.

So I start from the very beginning, telling them about the invaders I heard in the woods, then my parents disappearing—which Cole of course interjected in order to tell them how much of an idiot I was—then my search for the truth and protecting my farm. They patted me on the shoulder, told me that I was brave for going out there alone, and Cole rolled his eyes heavily. And then when I got to the cottage part, I admitted that I took it too far, that maybe I shouldn't have tried to peek in through the windows. If anything, my parents raised a truth teller. I told them I was justly arrested but made sure they knew I was not breaking in—I made that very clear. The crowbar was for protection, not for prying open windows and busting into an unknown residence.

They nodded, agreeing with my wrongs, and then I brought up the farm.

I told them some lady has been snooping around, asking about our vendors and our suppliers, so when Kate saw that she was there again, I wanted to introduce myself, ask questions, but that was when it all fell apart, because lo and behold, it was the same woman who nailed me in the head with a two-liter bottle of Pepsi.

"Wow," Tanya says with a shake of her head. "That's some story."

"I know, but it's the truth. I wasn't trying to attack her. I was just trying to find out what her angle was, you know?"

"That makes sense," Tanya says, and when I turn to look at Sherry for confirmation, that she believes my story, she's staring off into the distance.

"Uh, everything okay over there?" I ask.

She shakes her head. "No." She presses her hand to her forehead. "This girl, bright blond hair? More petite?"

"Yeah," I say. "Really blue eyes."

Like ... the bluest I think I've ever seen on a person, not that I noticed or anything.

Okay, maybe I noticed a little.

"I know who you're talking about. She's with Dwight."

"Dwight?" I ask. "As in Dwight Yokel?"

Sherry nods again. "They were talking on the bench yesterday in Ornament Park. Then I saw them walk off together."

She's with Dwight?

No fucking way.

Like I said, not that I noticed, but she is far too attractive to be with a guy like Dwight. He's a fucking disease. And she ... well, she's not—and I'll leave it at that.

"Were they holding hands?" I ask.

"No, but they were sitting close, talking, almost secretively."

Gross.

Woof.

Can't even imagine sitting close to Dwight, let alone talking to him. Makes me judge this girl.

"So you think they're up to something?" I ask.

"I think so. Wait, she's in the new cottage on the property next to yours?"

I nod. "She is. Why?"

Sherry worries her lip. "Hold on." She pulls up her phone and presses a few buttons before she says, "Hey, where are you? Great. Come to Warm Your Spirits. Now." She hangs up and then sips her coffee.

"Who was that?" I ask.

"BKJ."

I feel myself still. "You called BKJ?"

"Yup. I did."

BKJ, also known as Bob Krampus Junior, the son of Bob Krampus and currently in training to be the next Santa Claus of Kringletown, is a silent man. One who doesn't tend to ride the gossip train. Very aloof, you never know what he's thinking, and frankly, he terrifies me. An intimidating fellow with a beard that's already gray, galoshes that stomp through the streets, and a shovel always in his hand.

"Why, uh, why does he have information?"

"I heard him talking to his father about something this morning. I couldn't quite put the details together. All I heard was *sign*, a mention of the property next to yours, and *new girl*."

"A sign?" I say, feeling my heart start to pound a little harder.

I knew it.

I knew something was up.

Turning in my seat, I call out, "Cole, get over here."

Done with his muffin, he throws away his trash and then brings Florence over to the counter, where Tanya takes her and starts bouncing her up and down.

"What?" he asks.

"Remember when I said I thought there was something strange going on?"

"Yes," he groans.

"Well, I was fucking right. Turns out the girl who nailed me in the head with the two-liter is dating Dwight, my nemesis."

"Christ." Cole runs his hand over his jaw.

"And apparently there's some sort of sign out on her property now. I told you something fishy was going on. I fucking told you."

Before Cole can respond, the door flies open, and all eyes land on BKJ, standing tall, proud, and stoutly in a brown leather coat with sheep wool lining the collar and a Santa hat on his head.

In his giant black galoshes, he stomps into the coffee shop, shaking off the snow that must have started, and heads in our direction.

Intimidating is all I can say. And I'm four inches taller than him. But there's something about him being the son of the most powerful man in Kringle that has my nuts turning in on themselves.

"Merry Christmas," he says in a bellow.

"M-merry Christmas," I answer. "Uh, snowing out there?"

"Just a little sprinkle." He pats Cole on the shoulder. "Good to see you."

"How you doing, man?" Cole asks, dropping the pinch in his brow and smiling like a damn fool.

"Good. Good. Taking a break from the market for a moment to grab some coffee." He looks around, holding on to the belt of his jacket. God, he really has the mannerisms down, already puffing his chest, ready to shout out a *ho-ho-ho* that could shake the very timbers of this establishment.

"Let me grab that for you," Tanya says, passing Florence back to Cole.

While Tanya is pouring him a cup of coffee, adding his signature peppermint stick in the cup, BKJ says, "So I've heard you've had a rough go of it lately. Seems like you're on the naughty list, Atlas."

I feel myself cower, but before I can answer, Sherry says, "I'll walk you back to the Christmas market and fill you in, because I have something important to ask you."

Tanya drops off his drink and says it's on the house. BKJ offers her a wink and then takes a sip without even blowing on the liquid. Wow, incredible. What a metal mouth.

"Is this a private conversation?" BKJ asks.

"No, it's a conversation that I must have in front of everyone." Clearing her throat, she says, "I heard you speaking to your dad this morning about a new girl in town and a sign. Could you possibly inform us of what you were talking about? Because I think it has to do with the girl who Max had an interaction with."

"Betty?" BKJ asks.

Betty.

Huh, I kind of like that name.

"Yes, the girl living on the property next to Max, dating Dwight."

"Dating Dwight?" BKJ lets out a wallop of a laugh, so much that he starts coughing. "They're not dating. She's his niece."

"Niece?" I ask, surprised. "No, we can't be talking about the same person. She is not that much younger than Dwight."

"Her dad is Dwight's brother. Her grandfather had two marriages. One of those situations."

"Oh," I say. Well, that makes more sense, because there is no way Dwight could pull a girl like her. Not with how he eats his food, like a fucking chipmunk hovering over a nut.

"But, yes, that's Betty. New to town. Just moved onto the vacant lot that Dwight has owned for a long time."

I sit taller, dread starting to fill me. "He owns that land?"

BKJ nods. "Yup. I drove by this morning on my way out of town for some supplies, and I saw a sign out on the property, a *Coming Soon* sign."

I dramatically grip Cole's arm. "What did it say?"

BKJ pauses for affect and then says, "*Coming Soon. With Joyful Ring Farm.*"

Sherry gasps.

Tanya clutches her chest.

And I slowly mutter, "That motherfucker."

I knew it.

I knew something was happening. I knew someone was trying to put me out of business. I just didn't know the extent of it. Well, I hope everyone who didn't believe me eats their words, because who is the fool now?

Not me, that's for damn sure.

After we all let the news settle in, Cole asks, "But how is that possible? There's a rule in Kringle. Businesses can't overlap."

"Correct," BKJ says. "But that piece of property is just outside the town ordinance. Technically, it's not a part of Kringletown but rather part of the county instead."

And just like that, my stomach drops, everything becoming clear. The voices I heard. The plotting. The questions she was asking. The snooping. The ability to nail someone square in the head with a soda with zero emotion at all.

She's here to take over.

She's here to destroy me.

Slowly, I turn to Cole, and I don't have to say anything, because I can see it written all over his face. He nods. "You were right, dear. You were right."

"Can we just go over this one more time?" Cole asks as he hands me a tin of chocolate-covered pretzels and popcorn in a white paper gift bag. "You're going over there, knocking on her door, not peering in, and you'll offer her the pretzels as a peace offering. You won't accuse her. You won't start a fight. And you most certainly will not go on a tirade about how she can't start a farm next to yours."

I take a deep breath and fix my winter hat on my head. "I'm aware."

"There will be no mention of the farm. There will be no mention of her trying to destroy you. You are calm, cool, and collected."

"I know." I grip the straps of the bag tighter. "Trust me, I'm good at this shit."

"I don't trust you one bit," he says. "Not even a little. I fear that you'll get there and kick her door down, demanding answers."

I scoff. "Unlike you, I know how to control my temper. I'm a smooth talker, okay? I can do this." I flash my teeth at him. "Anything in my teeth?"

"You're good."

"What about my breath?" I blow at him.

He winces. "Eh, minty."

"Good, I just downed ten Junior Mints. Forgot how good those little fuckers are. I still have some on the kitchen counter if you want a snack."

"I'm good."

"You sure?"

"Yeah, I'm sure."

"Your loss." I tug on my mittens hanging from my jacket and slip them on.

"Dude, mittens?"

I pause. "My mom made them for me. I have to use them at least once a year."

"They're attached to your coat. What are you, eight?"

"No, I'm a smart asshole who doesn't want to lose the precious mittens his mother made for him and talks about constantly because by the time she was done knitting, her hands were bleeding. Jesus, insensitive much?"

"Sorry," Cole says, looking slightly guilty.

"Apology accepted. Now, will you be here when I get back?"

"No, I have a life, and it doesn't consist of holding your hand through whatever bullshit this is. I'm grabbing pizza and heading home."

"How many pizzas? Maybe I could come over for some dinner?"

"One," he deadpanned.

"Maybe grab ten?" I ask. "Then I could come over, and we could have a little strategy session. Invite Guy and Taran, because she's conniving and could help. Aunt Cindy would be a good one. Oh, and my brothers if we're desperate."

"No."

"Okay, then maybe just me. I have no problem grabbing a salad for all of us to share."

"No."

I blow out a heavy breath. "When a man is in crisis, you'd really drop him like that?"

"Can we just reconvene tomorrow? Text me to let me know how it goes, and then we can plan from there, okay? I want to spend a night with my wife."

"Fine." We head out the door, and I set the bag down so I can lock up.

"Don't set it down on the wet mat," Cole says, pulling the bag up. "You don't want the paper to break."

"Please, these gift bags are all weatherproof." I take the bag from him and then go in for a hug, but he palms my face instead.

"No," he says. "Just no."

"Fuck, you're no fun."

CHAPTER EIGHT
BETTY

NARRATOR: AND THROUGH THE WOODS, without a hug, Max trudges over broken tree trunks, under snow-laden branches, subtly tripping here and there but with one mission on his mind: to find out who this Betty, the niece of Dwight Yokel, really is and what her intentions are.

Because in his eyes, right now, she's seeming like a real wench.

———————

I slip my slippers onto my feet and then look at myself one more time in the mirror to make sure I rubbed in all my lotion. I turn off the bathroom light and start to settle in for the night when I see a flash of light in the window again. Startled, I pause where I'm at in the kitchen and reach into the fridge, pulling out another two-liter of soda, this time Coca-Cola, and I bring it up to my chest just as there's a knock at the door.

Ready to attack, I shuffle toward the door, two-liter in position to take out a human, and I call out, "Who is it?"

"Atlas Maxheimer, without a crowbar."

What is he doing here?

Didn't he get the hint the other day at the farm that I want nothing to do with him?

Or this morning when I sprinted across the street to avoid walking past him?

"I promise, I come in goodwill. I'm not here to hurt you."

Says the serial killer about to attack.

"How do I know that?" I ask.

"Because I'm not that kind of guy."

"You were trying to break into my window with a crowbar. You are very much that kind of guy."

"That was a misunderstanding," he says through the door. "And if you'd give me a chance to apologize and explain, I'd greatly appreciate it."

"How do I know you're not just trying to get me to open the door so you can bash my head in with your crowbar?"

"Because once again, that's not something I'd want to do. As much as it might seem that way from the two negative interactions you've had with me, I don't like to spend time in jail."

I think about it for a second. I mean, if I'm murdered, there will only be one person who gets called out for it, and it will be him. Given the freshly fallen snow and his footprints, all tracks will lead to him, so . . . I could possibly be protected.

Not to mention I'm curious about what he has to say and how he'll spin his little breaking and entering story. And sure, curiosity killed the cat and all, but I seem to want to test my fate tonight.

So I say, "I want your hands up where I can see them, and you will do what I say, or else I'll make sure the cops take your no-good keister off my property, understood?"

"No-good keister? What are you? An old-timey mobster?"

"Just answer the question. Understood?"

I hear him chuckle on the other side of the door, but then he says, "Understood."

"Hands are in the air?"

"Hands are in the air," he calls out.

I unlock the door and then fling it open fast, startling Atlas so much that he jolts backward.

"Jesus," he says as I hold the Coca-Cola over my head, ready to throw it. When he sees what I'm holding, panic seeps into his face. "Hey now, easy there. Put the soda down."

"What's that in your hand?" I nod toward the bag.

"A peace offering."

"What kind of peace offering?"

"Can I move my arms and show you?"

"Slowly," I say, watching his every move.

He starts to lower his arms, bringing the bag forward, and when he begins to reach inside, I cock back, ready to throw . . .

And then, like a bat out of hell, the bottom of the bag falls out, and a loud clang sounds throughout the still night, while a pop of brown and white shoots up into the air like firecrackers, startling the shit out of me.

Screaming bloody murder, I chuck the bottle over my head and right into his chest before I slam the door shut and scream out, "I'm calling the police."

I rush to my phone, pull up the SOS option, and I'm about to call for help when I hear groaning on the other side of the door, followed by, "Noooo . . . pretzels and popcorn."

I pause . . . slowly turning in his direction.

Did he just say *pretzels and popcorn*?

Finger ready to dial, I shuffle toward the door again, but this time, I squat down low to the doggy door that was included in the cottage. I unlock the latch that keeps it sealed off from the outer elements and then slowly lift it, focusing my attention on the ground, where I see an open Christmas can with chocolate-covered pretzels and popcorn scattered all over my welcome mat.

"Fuck, I think you cracked a rib," he grumbles.

"What, uh . . . what's that on the ground?" I ask. I don't care about the pain he might be experiencing. I just care about the contraband on the ground.

"Fucking popcorn and pretzels," he groans as I see him roll to the side. "A peace offering . . . like I fucking . . . said." He groans more, and I feel myself wince.

Crap, I think I might have really hurt him.

Feeling slightly guilty, I stand back up, set my phone to the side, and open the door, slowly of course, in case he's faking it. When I see him gripping his chest and writhing in pain, the Coca-Cola rolling off to the side, I feel that I'm safe . . . for the moment.

Stepping over the pretzels and spilled popcorn, I toe his leg and say, "Are you in need of medical attention?"

"I'm in need of National Guard protection from *you*," he groans. He rolls to his side again but this time he carefully sits up, rubbing his chest. "Fuck."

His eyes meet mine, and it's the first time I've actually had a chance to study him. For a burglar-predator, he's actually quite handsome. But that's how they get you. They charm you with their deep-timbre voice and their carved jaws, which are lightly peppered in facial hair, and when you relax, that's when they snatch you up. Well, not me. I'm prepared.

"I think you might have broken my sternum."

"I'd say that's being a bit dramatic." I cross my arms over my robe-covered body. "If you were a wafer of a man, I'd say that's a great possibility, but you're not that."

His brow raises as he looks up at me from where he's sitting on my porch, looking incredibly pathetic in a jacket with a winter hat and . . . Are those mittens? A grown-ass man wearing mittens? Maybe I shouldn't be as afraid as I thought I should be. "Are you saying that I'm a tall drink of water?"

"No. I'm saying that you have meat on your bones that would help absorb some of the impact from the soda."

"So . . . you're saying I'm muscular."

I roll my eyes. "Do you have friends?"

"Huh?" he asks. "That's a strange change of topic."

"No, it's very much on topic, because from the few sentences you've spoken to me, you're coming off quite annoying—"

"Uh, are you forgetting about the harpoon stealer? You didn't seem to find me annoying then."

"Those are two different men: charming man on the sidewalk and creepy pervert trying to break into my cottage. Which brings me back to the thought . . . I wonder if you have any friends. Or maybe the reason you're skulking around innocent ladies' cottages is because you don't have any friends and therefore are looking to eat the brains of the people you prey on because you're mad at the human race."

"Jesus," he says, scooting back on the porch. "You're not quite in the holly jolly mood, are you?"

"I'm just calling it like I see it."

"Well, you're seeing it all wrong."

"And how should I see it?"

He carefully stands from the ground, still holding his chest. When he straightens up, he says, "Maybe you could invite me in, and we could talk about it."

"Ha!" I scoff. "As if I'd let you in my cottage. I'm not naive. If you want to explain something to me, you can explain it to me right there, where you're standing on my porch. But hold on a second." I shut the door on him and grab a jug of Arizona Green Tea from the kitchen. When I open the door again, he's back on the ground, but instead of wallowing in pain, he's picking up the pretzels and popcorn.

When he looks up and sees that I'm holding a gallon of liquid, I see true fear cross his features.

Slowly, he backs away, holding his hands up and leaving the destroyed treats on the ground.

"Listen, I know what you can do with that liquid, okay? I'm not . . . I'm not going to hurt you. If anything, I should be the one on guard."

"Best you know not to mess with me." I gesture to him. "Now, go on and tell me why you're here so I can get on with my night. I have a fresh ball of yarn waiting to be crocheted."

He scratches the side of his head. "Well, I brought you some treats as a kind gesture, to show you that I'm not the animal that you think I am. But those, uh, those suffered a bit through a slight misfortune. And I was hoping to clarify what I was doing during both of our unfortunate interactions."

I prop the tea on my hip like I'm holding a baby and say, "Proceed."

"Well, the other night, I promise, I wasn't trying to break into your cottage. I was actually trying to figure out who lived here."

"With a crowbar?" I deadpan.

He grips the back of his neck. "Yeah, I know how that looks, but it was more for protection from murderous bears."

"Murderous bears. Really?" I ask sarcastically.

He shrugs. "I have an active imagination. Anyway, I wasn't intending to pry into your house. It was just a stupid thing I thought would protect me. And when I was looking into your window, I was just trying to see who lived here."

"And why didn't you just knock on the door and introduce yourself like a normal human being? Say, *Hey, I'm your next-door neighbor*? Instead, you chose to part my bush with your crowbar."

He smirks a stupid smirk. "Part your bush with my crowbar, huh?"

My expression falls. I point at him and say, "Pervert. I knew it. I knew you were a pervert."

He rolls his eyes. "Come on. That was so obvious. As if I could just let that go."

"It's called being an adult."

"Yes, and as an adult, I can laugh at the fact that it was a funny slip of the tongue. I'm not a pervert. You can ask anyone in this town. I'm an upstanding guy. So maybe you should . . . I don't know . . . unclench a little."

"Excuse me?" I ask, shifting the gallon of tea, causing him to take another step back.

He holds up his hands in surrender. "Listen, all I'm saying is that maybe if you just lightened up a bit, you'd see how this all has just been one big disaster from the beginning."

"Yeah, for you."

"Not intentionally."

"Uh-huh. So then why were you chasing me around at your farm?"

His jaw grows tight. "I was not chasing you around. I was just trying to have a conversation. You're the one who freaked out."

"Well, pardon me for not wanting to be confronted by my attacker."

He pinches his brow. "I was not attacking you. Yes, I should have knocked and introduced myself rather than peeking in your window. I get that. But for the love of God, I wasn't trying to harm you. Now I have a cut on my arm, a cut above my eye, and a bruised sternum that proves you're the dangerous one."

"It's called self-defense. Apparently I need it living out here in the woods."

"Trust me, nothing will bother you out here."

"Other than large farm owners looking to dominate."

His expression falls. "The only time I ever dominate is in the bedroom." He quirks his brow as if thinking about that. "Well, and other things, like competition, but that's beside the point. I won't intimidate you. That's not who I am, and maybe we can, you know, try to get to know each other better."

"Absolutely not," I say. "I know enough about you to know that we won't have any pleasant interactions, so it's best you just move on."

"That's not being fair. You barely know me."

"I know that you peek in windows and lurk around coffee shops. That's all I need to know. Now, if you'll excuse me, I have to crochet."

With that, I shut the door on him and set my iced tea down on the counter, only for him to knock on the door one more time.

Sighing, I open the door and say, "What?"

He holds up the broken bag and the can of pretzels and popcorn. "Is it fair to assume you're uninterested in my peace offering?"

"Very fair," I answer and then shut the door, a shiver pulsing through my spine.

Sheesh, the nerve of that man.

I reach for my phone and send a quick text to Uncle Dwight.

Betty: Atlas Maxheimer just stopped by. Tried to give me treats as a peace offering.

I stick the iced tea back in the fridge and then head up to the small loft in my cottage just as my phone dings with a response.

Uncle Dwight: Did you take it?

Betty: I'm no fool. Of course I didn't.

Uncle Dwight: I raised you right.

Betty: You're five years older than me. You did no such thing.

Uncle Dwight: Just let me have this moment. I love relishing in Maxheimer's rejection.

Betty: Fine. You raised me right.

Uncle Dwight: Thank you.

MAX

"Do I even want to hear it?" Cole asks as I walk up to him with two cups of coffee I grabbed from the employee lounge. I wasn't in the mood to head into town and see Tanya. Not after last night's failure.

"No, you don't." I hand him a cup and take a seat on a wooden stool to watch my friend prepare the reindeers' breakfast.

I tried helping him once, and he said that I was not helping, I was causing him irritation, and if he wanted help, he would ask for it.

Talk about ungrateful.

So now, I just sit and watch, sometimes loving the moment where he struggles, knowing my help would make life a little bit easier on him.

He leans against a barn pole and sips his coffee.

"Isn't that the pole you tied Storee up against?" I ask.

"Yup," he answers, leaving it at that.

"You know, I might take a picture of that pole, put it in a frame, and give it to you for Christmas along with a pineapple-flavored candy cane."

"It would be the best present you've ever given me," he answers with a smirk.

Did you see it? Did you see that little moment of levity? He drops the Grinch act only for mentions of the girls in his life. For me? Not so much.

"Consider it done." I sip my coffee and lean my head against the barn wall. "Things are not—"

"Atlas?" Kate's voice sounds off in the barn as she peeks her head past the door.

"Hey, Kate, what's up?"

Glancing behind her, she says, "She's here again, but this time with a notebook."

I spring from my chair. "No, the fuck she's not," I grind out in outrage.

"She is."

I turn to Cole and point at him. "She's trying to ruin my life." Then I take off toward the barn entrance. "Where is she?"

"The tree shack. Mitch is watching the register for me so I could come tell you."

"Thank you. I'm about to catch this mole and exterminate her."

"Dude, lame," Cole says.

"I thought it was clever."

"Nah, that was embarrassing."

I turn to Kate to look for her opinion, and she slightly winces. "It had a bit of a cheese factor to it."

"Can't catch a goddamn break," I mutter as I move past Kate out of the barn and toward the tree shack, where I burst through the door and see her over by the tree catalogs, just browsing.

One hand holding my coffee, the other in my pocket, wanting to show her I'm not a threat, I walk up to her and say, "Can I help you?"

She startles and looks over her shoulder. She's a jumpy one, that's for sure.

And is that . . . is that lavender perfume I smell?

Fucking delightful.

"Why are you sniffing?" she asks, breaking my thoughts.

"What? I'm not sniffing."

"Yes, you are. I know what sniffing looks like, and you're clearly trying to sniff me."

Narrator: She's got you there, man.

Thankfully, I'm a quick motherfucker.

"Why the hell would I want to sniff you? I got a good whiff last night, and I was unimpressed. Smelled like a moldy pirate's belt if you ask me." Her face contorts in confusion. Yeah, not sure where that description came from either. "If you want to know, I have a touch of the sniffles and didn't want to present myself with snot."

She eyes me suspiciously and then turns back around, continuing to flip through the pages of the catalog.

Growing very irritated with this woman, I say, "Like I asked before, is there anything I can possibly help you with?"

"You? No."

Do not lose it on her, Atlas.

Keep it together.

Remember, you're in your place of business.

Taking a calming breath, I ask, "Well, it seems like you might need help, given how many times you've been here. Maybe I can help you find what you're looking for, so I don't have to see you here again."

She turns and crosses her arms over her chest. That camel-colored jacket's tight around her waist but slightly large over her shoulders, making it seem like she's wearing shoulder pads. "Do you treat all your customers like this?"

"Do you treat all your competition like this?" I ask, unable to hold back any longer.

A smile creeps over her face. "You see me as competition?"

"I see you as encroaching on someone's space, which is not allowed in this town."

"So I've heard, but since the property isn't in town limits, those rules don't apply to me." She turns around and takes a picture of the catalog with her phone's camera.

"Hey," I say, slapping my hand on the page. "Don't do that."

"Do you not allow pictures in your establishment?"

"I don't allow people trying to copy my family's business to take pictures. Seriously, what the hell do you think you're doing?"

"Trying to improve the business you created by not making the same mistakes."

"Mistakes," I nearly roar but then lower my voice as I lean in. "I can't imagine how a business that's been running for over thirty years has been making mistakes. Maybe show a little respect to the establishments that have created this town where you want to do business."

For the briefest of moments, I see a flash of regret register on her features. It's brief, but it's there. Just enough for me to realize that she is in fact not the devil incarnate. Pretty close, but not quite all the way committed to playing the role.

Head held high, she says, "I think I have everything I need anyway."

"Wonderful. I'll see you out."

"Not necessary," she says as she walks by me.

"Oh, it's completely necessary." I follow close behind her.

I see her waver, wanting to go farther into the farm where families are posing in front of one of the many tree murals painted on our buildings. But then she pauses.

I point in the opposite direction. "Exit is that way."

"Are you kicking me out?"

"I'm asking you never to return."

She folds her arms and juts out her hip. "Are you really that scared that I might take business from you?"

Yes.

Terrified.

I don't do well with competition and confrontation put together when it comes to business. Goofy contests, no problem, but when it involves my family's livelihood, not so much. I've had a stomachache since the moment I heard about her. And last night, I could only have one gingerbread cookie instead of two. That's saying something.

"No," I answer, trying to play it cool. "But I think it's awfully rude of you to think that you can replicate an already established business. You might be getting away with it with your coordinates and such, but I will tell you this. There's something in this town you don't have, and it's loyalty. It's also something your weird uncle doesn't have either. The minute you start your plans, this town will rally behind us. It will be like the Shop around the Corner meets Fox Books all over again, but in the end, we will prevail."

"What are you talking about?" she asks, looking confused.

"Uh, from *You've Got Mail.*"

"Never seen it."

"What?" I shout, feeling my eyes pop out. "You've never seen *You've Got Mail*? Well, Jesus." I scratch the top of my head. "That explains a lot about you. Did you know that it was inspired by *The Shop Around the Corner*, a classic Christmas film with James Stewart?"

"Why would I know that?"

"Might be something you want to freshen up on since you'll be living in a year-round Christmas town, trying to sell Christmas to everyone who stops by your wannabe farm. It's one thing to create a business. It's a whole other thing to try to sell an experience, and that's the difference between a successful business and one that crashes and burns after the first year."

My words quickly erase the smarmy look on her face, and in its place is an almost . . . distraught look, like I said something that struck a nerve.

"I . . . I need to go," she says, pushing past me.

Unsure of what just happened, I say, "Yeah, uh, that's right. You have to go. And I better not find you here again. You hear me?"

When she doesn't look back, my brain wants to tell me that I did it, that I scared her away, but my heart is telling me that this very well might be the beginning.

CHAPTER NINE
BETTY

NARRATOR: MAX DOESN'T KNOW JUST how deep his words cut.

But Betty does.

Instead of going to her cottage, she drives into town to Dwight's real estate office, where she parks her car, wipes her tears, and gathers herself. She thought she could handle this. With Joyful Ring Farm could be the new direction she needs, but it is also a stark reminder of the darkest moments in her life.

Max was right—she has no idea how to sell an experience. He hit the nail on the head. And Betty, despite her prior excellent Christmassy ideas, might be looking for her white flag of surrender sooner than she wanted.

———————

Composed, I open the door to Uncle Dwight's real estate office and wave hi to his receptionist, Harry.

"Is Uncle Dwight in his office?"

"He is," Harry says. "I think you can go back there."

"Thanks." I nod.

Uncle Dwight's office is festive on the outside. The windows are lined with artificial pine garland and lights, and the paper advertising the different properties for sale in town is printed out and taped, but it's cleverly lined with miniature garland to keep it Christmassy as well. Did Uncle Dwight think to do that, or is it a requirement?

Either way, it is a nice touch.

And inside the building, there's a Christmas tree in the corner, some green and gold fabric bunting hung around the perimeter of the room, and Christmas knickknacks displayed on every surface.

And it's like this year-round.

I head down the hallway to Uncle Dwight's office, and when I see he's on the phone, I hold my hand up in apology, but he waves me into his office and tells me to take a seat.

So I sit as he finishes up his call.

"Yes, 671 Lincoln Avenue just went under contract. Mr. Kevin, that's right. He wants a thorough inspection done. Yup. Okay, thank you." Uncle Dwight hangs up the phone and then leans back in his chair. "Wasn't expecting to see you today. Everything okay?"

Here goes nothing.

"Um, I, uh, I wanted to talk to you."

He leans forward, placing his forearms on the desk, looking determined. "You can't quit on me."

How did he know?

I let out a breath as tears start to well in my eyes. "I don't think I can do it. He was right. I'm going to fail."

He straightens up. "Who was right?"

"Maxheimer," I say. "And he didn't directly or intentionally try to hurt me, but he said something that really hit me hard and—"

"Hold on. First of all, why is he even talking to you?"

"I went to the farm to check out one more thing. I wanted to make sure they weren't using multiple suppliers for trees, because I had one that I really liked and then second-guessed myself. Well, I ran into him there. He's clearly on edge now with me being around. And we got into it a little. He was telling me that the difference between a successful business and one that crashes and burns in the first year is selling the experience, something I didn't know. And he's right. I have no idea what I'm doing. I'm the girl who crashes and burns in the first year."

He slowly bobs his head and then leans back in his chair. "You are not that girl. You are smart, Betty. You know how to put together a successful business plan, and yes, maybe you weren't able to see it through, but we talked about the reasoning behind it."

"I wasn't able to sell the experience, Dwight," I say, skipping the *Uncle* part this time, because at this point, it just feels silly.

"Which is something to be aware of, something to know now rather than later on down the road. But I don't think it's about the experience. I think you just need to immerse yourself more."

I shake my head. "I'm not going back to that farm. I don't want to see him again."

"You don't have to go back there. You have plenty of resources outside the farm."

"Like where?" I ask.

He spreads his arms wide. "This entire town. Each business has found a unique way to sell the Christmas season to each customer. I think you take the next week, and study each business and see how they do it. Take in every moment, every decoration, every interaction. Study the proprietors; watch and see what might work for you and what might not work, then apply that to the plans you've already drawn up."

"I don't know. I feel like I'll fail you."

"With that attitude, you could. And you have to stop thinking about this being a me thing. This is a you thing. I'm not investing in a farm; I'm investing in you. So have some pride in the fact that I trust you with this project. And honestly, you're the only one that I trust. I've built a small empire here, Betty. I've invested in real estate around town, I'm a landlord of several apartments and houses throughout this area, and I want to expand now. I want to invest in something that really is for the betterment of the town. I want to endorse Kringle's Christmas spirit, and I know you're the one to help do that."

I let out a large sigh and stare down at my hands, not sure I believe him.

"At least just take a week," he says. "Give me seven days of research, and see if watching the other proprietors around town sell the experience invigorates you to do the same. Can you at least give me that?"

Ugh, I hate to admit it, but it's the least I could do for him after everything he's done for me. And even though I'm feeling at my lowest right now, he's right. I should at least observe and see how everyone else is doing it.

Because if there's something I learned from my first business venture, it's that I didn't do comprehensive research on *why* other Christmas stores thrived in certain areas. I was just so determined for my store to succeed. *And here, in this town, I will be able to analyze so many different ways to "sell" Christmas.* I owe it to myself and Uncle Dwight to do that.

"Okay," I say. "I'll take a week to research."

"Really?"

"Yeah, really."

He smiles. "Good, and take the time to really immerse yourself, okay?"

I nod. "Okay."

Looking genuinely relieved, he says, "Thank you."

I lightly smile. "No, thank you for believing in me."

"You know I always will." He nods toward the door. "Now get out of here. I have work I have to do."

I chuckle and stand from my chair.

"Also, if you ever call me just Dwight again, I might very well have a heart attack."

I let out a heftier laugh. "Sorry. That mistake won't be made again."

"Good."

MAX

"Could you help us with our tree?" a woman in a snowsuit asks. Only her eyes are showing.

"Sure can," I say as I push up the sleeves to my flannel. It's a solid thirty-five degrees today, but I've been chopping down and lugging trees all over the farm, so I'm warm.

Can't imagine wearing a full snowsuit right now. I'd be drenched in sweat.

"Where is it?"

"Over there," she says, pointing to a tree that is right next to a green Buick Electra station wagon with wood paneling. Man, can't tell you the last time I saw one of those.

"Not a problem. Would you like it on top?"

"Inside actually. We have a tarp in the back, and the seats are down. The car's open. We're grabbing some cookies for the road if you don't mind just putting it in there."

"Not at all. Hope you had fun at the farm today."

"Uh-huh," she says and then takes off.

"Okay," I mutter and then head over to the station wagon. I pick up the tree and carry it to the back only to be startled right out of my fucking boots by Dwight, squatting down behind the car.

"Jesus fuck, what are you doing?" I ask as I attempt to catch my breath.

He pops up to his feet and gets close enough so he can whisper, "You listen to me, and you listen to me good. You are to leave my niece alone—"

"Dude, she's like a few years younger than you, so stop calling her your niece."

"I'm serious," he says, now poking me with his finger.

The nerve on this guy. I have about five inches on him and probably thirty pounds of muscle, and he's poking me. I can snap that finger in half by just using my index finger and thumb.

"She's not to be toyed with."

"I don't have fucking time for this." I reach for the back door to the trunk of the car, but he blocks me.

"I'm not fucking around, Maxheimer. Leave her alone."

"Uh, I'd love to, but she's the one who keeps popping up on my farm."

"Weren't you the one who visited her last night?"

I roll my eyes. "To make amends. To tell her that I wasn't some pervert trying to break into her cottage like you have made me out to be."

"You were creeping around. Is that false?"

I tug on my hair. "What's the point of this? You think I'll make a move or something?"

"Absolutely not. She'd never go for a guy like you. So don't talk to her. You hurt her today, and she's very fragile."

I hurt her? When? I can't recall a thing I said that would have been a direct insult.

"I don't need you saying things that bring down her spirit. With Joyful Ring is happening, whether you like it or not. So stay out of it."

This fuck . . .

"It will never do well. We have built the loyalty in this town."

"Something I'm not concerned about," Dwight says. "The town is small, numbskull, and I'm looking to snag all the out-of-towners who'll drive by my farm first. It will be an easy stop. Your farm will be a dying entity soon."

My anger surges, because how fucking dare he.

"What is your goddamn problem?" I ask, shoving his shoulder, and because he's a wafer of a man, he falls back into the car behind him. Great. With my luck, he'll start screaming *assault*.

He grips his shoulder and looks up at me. "You. You're the problem."

"Is this because I beat you at the Christmas Kringle competition last year? Dude, you're pathetic if it is."

"That is not the reason. It's because you are a fake. A phony. You parade around town like the lovable goof, preying on all the townspeople, getting them to fall for your sweet-talking, when in reality, you're a terrible person. You have been since high school, and it's about time someone does something about it." He straightens up.

"What the hell are you talking about?" I am truly confused.

"Naturally, you would forget." He rolls his eyes and adjusts the lapel of his jacket. "Just stay away from her. This farm is happening whether you like it or not. Enjoy this Christmas season, because next year, you're going out of business."

Then he bumps into my shoulder, barely moving me as he walks away.

I glance behind me and catch him getting into his BMW SUV, and music blasts out of the speakers before he takes off.

I scrub my hand over my face, so fucking confused. But then I think about his earlier words. His warning.

With Joyful Ring is happening, whether you like it or not. So stay out of it . . . The town is small, numbskull, and I'm looking to snag all the out-of-towners who'll drive by my farm first. It will be an easy stop. Your farm will be a dying entity soon.

Fuck, I want to punch the guy. Yes, we've been enemies for a long time, but would that mean I'd threaten his business and work hard to make it go under? Not a chance. We've worked for years to make this place successful. And he wants to fucking close our business? *Why?*

I'm fuming.

We rarely get complaints, so why are Dwight's words so foreboding?

"You haven't put the tree in the back of the car yet?" the woman says, stunned that I'm still standing there with her tree. She then turns to the woman next to her and whispers, "Told you this place isn't what it used to be. Last year we come here."

Fuck.

And that's the nail in the coffin of all rational thoughts and behavior.

Yup.

The world around me spins, dread fills my lungs, and I know there's only one thing I can do now.

Call the parents.

———————

I shut the door to my office in the reindeer barn and pull my phone out of my pocket. This was not what I wanted to do, but it seems like I don't have any other choice. I need help.

I dial my mom's number and squeeze my eyes shut as I take a seat in my office chair. This is what some might call rock bottom. I thought I could handle this on my own. I thought I'd be able to actually make improvements on the farm and impress my parents, but instead, I feel like I'm drowning, like I'm fighting a losing battle and there's nothing I can do about it.

The phone rings three times before it's picked up.

"Hello?"

"Hey, Mom, it's Atlas."

"What?"

"It's Atlas," I say, trying to fight the obvious background noise coming from her side.

"Who is it?" I hear Dad say.

"I don't know."

"Well, look at the screen."

"Oh, it's Atlas," Mom says. "Atlas, you there?"

"Yes," I shout, hoping that helps.

"What did you say?"

Sitting up, I press my fingers into my brow. "I said yes."

"Yes?"

"Yes," I shout.

"What does he want?" Dad asks.

"He's just saying yes."

Jesus.

Christ.

"Is he drunk?"

"I'm not drunk," I shout.

"Oh, he just said he's drunk," Mom says.

"No, I'm *not* drunk."

"It's okay. Sleep it off. Phone battery low. Don't call unless an emergency."

And just like that, she hangs up.

Mother . . . fucker.

Well, that was a completely useless idea. Glad it worked out.

I stand, pocket my phone, and then head out into the reindeer barn, where Cole is cleaning a brush.

When he spots me, he pauses and turns off the water. "Why do you look like that?"

"I need help."

I don't know if it's the seriousness in my voice or the dejection I'm portraying, but for the first time since the whole *invaders* conversation started, he takes me seriously.

"Dinner at my place?" he asks.

"Yeah, I'll be there at six."

CHAPTER TEN
MAX

NARRATOR: BOTH DOWN ON THEIR luck but for vastly different reasons. Betty's trying to find her worth, while our dear friend Max is trying to keep his. And unlucky for him, it seems like his parents aren't interested in hearing from him, which is not helpful, because this puts Max all on his own. But I think Max has a plan brewing, something he's been thinking about all day. Something that if done correctly could possibly win this battle of wits.

And not only will it help him keep the family farm, but it will also best Dwight.

And truly, who is rooting for Dwight in this situation? Raise your hand.

That's what I thought. Not a single soul.

A man as sniveling as him deserves to be put in his place, don't you think?

———————

"I agree. He does need to be put in his place. Because going after Evergreen Farm like he is, that's bold."

Narrator: Some might call him the antagonist of the story.

Raises hand "I would."

Narrator: And some might say you're the hero.

"Well, if that doesn't puff my chest out and reinvigorate me, I don't know what does. Give me a hint. Does the good guy win in the end?"

Narrator: You will just have to wait and see.

"Fair, but one more question. Cole said something about a narrator a few years ago, and I thought he was losing his mind. Are you the same one?"

Narrator: *That would be correct.*

"Cool. I don't know what he was talking about. You're pretty nice, other than this whole Evergreen-Farm-thing-going-out-of-business, but I'm going to trust the process."

Narrator: *And that is why you're my favorite. On with the story.*

"Thank you all for being here today," I say somberly as I dab my mouth with my napkin.

When I arrived at Cole and Storee's house, I told them that I didn't want to talk business until after dinner. Cole rolled his eyes, but Storee patted me on the shoulder. When Taran and Guy, Storee's sister and her boyfriend, arrived, I caught up with them. Taran has been working as a nurse in town, and honestly, I couldn't really tell you what Guy does.

"Almost feel like he's part of this story so people don't ask about any love interests for Taran, but I could be wrong. He truly adds no value."

Narrator: *Ahem . . . please don't critique the story.*

"Right, sorry."

Anyhoo, he did tell me about this book he's been reading, *Nobody's Angel*. I tuned him out when he mentioned the book, just did the whole fake-smile-and-nod-my-head thing. Then I chose to sit as far away from him as possible at the table. He cornered Storee and Taran's aunt Cindy, who lives next door, and bless her, because she listened to the entire plot and even asked questions.

She has better manners than I do, that's for sure.

"Storee, dinner was delicious, and thank you for hosting. I have some things I need to speak to you about, and since I don't trust my brothers not to run their mouths, I'd really like to keep this to the inner circle of this table."

Cole leans in. "Dude, you're not going to be dramatic about this, are you?"

"No." I shake my head. "I'm not. This is serious." I lean back in my chair and let out a breath. "Dwight Yokel is on a warpath to put Evergreen Farm out of business, and so far, I can't see how he could fail."

"What are you talking about?" Aunt Cindy asks. "Evergreen Farm has been around forever. There's no way it will go out of business, not to mention Dwight Yokel has no business in being . . . well . . . in business."

"I share your sentiment, Aunt Cindy," I say. "But here are the facts. The empty lot next to Evergreen Farm, it belongs to him. It's just outside the town limits, meaning he can do whatever he wants with the land, even a competing Christmas farm. He's hired his niece to take over the responsibilities, and she's done enough snooping around my farm to have a general understanding of how we work. Not to mention they're not targeting townies, who'd support Evergreen. They're targeting visitors. And since their property is before ours on the way to Kringle, there's a great chance they can succeed."

"Feels like a real *You've Got Mail* situation," Guy says from the other end of the table.

"That's what I said," I say, pointing to my chest. Okay, maybe this guy isn't so bad.

"Atlas, you can't possibly think within a few weeks, they'll put your farm out of business," Storee says in a calm voice.

"Honestly, I think they would do anything they can to make it happen. Even by planting people to say negative things to customers. Just today, this lady complained about the temperature of the hot cocoa and made a big deal about it. People crowded around as she showed off her tongue."

"Hey, she came into the doctor's office today complaining about her tongue," Taran says.

"Seriously?" I ask.

Taran nods. "She asked if she could file a lawsuit, but we told her it wasn't worth her time because the words on the cup were *Caution: hot.*"

"Jesus fuck," I whisper as I push my hand through my hair. "See, this is what I'm talking about. I swear, my parents leave for a month, and it feels like everything's falling apart. They'll do anything to take me down, so I need an action plan. And I think I have one."

"Is it having a civil conversation with Dwight and the girl—"

"Betty," I interrupt Cole. "Her name is Betty."

"Wait, is that the new girl that I met the other day at the farm?" Storee asks. "She was really nice. You can't possibly be talking about her."

"Blond hair, bright blue eyes?" I ask.

"Yeah, that's her," Storee says, looking defeated.

"Uh, I was saying," Cole continues. "Have you thought about having a civil conversation with Betty and Dwight? Maybe tell them that whatever beef there is between all of you, maybe you could work it out?"

"Ha!" I guffaw and then cross my arms at my chest. "You don't think I thought about that? When Dwight attacked me in the parking lot—"

"Attacked you?" Cole raises his brow. "You're, like, thirty pounds heavier than he is. There is no way he attacked you."

"You didn't let me finish," I say. "When he attacked me with his poking finger and words—"

Cole rolls his eyes, but I continue.

"—there was no reasoning with him. And Betty, oh boy, she's even more stubborn. Trust me, if this was talkable, I'd sit down, buy them a meal, and hash it out. But unfortunately, that is not an option for me. Therefore, we have to form a plan."

"I like plans," Aunt Cindy says, looking interested in the prospect of being involved.

"Feels like we're about to be part of a mystery novel or something," Guy says, adjusting his glasses on his nose.

Okay, dweeb, the excitement is a little much.

"What do you have in mind?" Storee asks. "Turn the town against them?"

I shake my head. "They don't care about that. Any other normal human living in a small town would probably hate being the object of everyone's hate, which is not the case here. Which is why they don't care about pleasing the townspeople. It's not like it will hurt Dwight's business, because he's the only Realtor in town and will own that title until he decides to retire, because as the town ordinance states, only one person in a single job within the town. So . . . that screws us."

"Okay, so what's your plan?" Cole asks.

I'm so glad he asked.

I place my hands on the table, and on a deep breath, I say, "We make her fall in love with me."

"Jesus Christ," Cole mutters.

"Dear God." Taran shakes her head.

"That . . . is an interesting idea," Storee says, looking anything other than supportive.

"Well . . . I don't know what to say to that," Aunt Cindy says, her smile wavering.

And Guy, over at the end of the table, avoids eye contact and sips his water. And here I thought he might support me.

Blowing out a heavy breath, I get ready to convince this table that I'm not only onto something but that this idea has merit. "I'm serious."

"We can tell," Cole says and then presses his fingers to his temple in annoyance. "Dude, you can't make someone fall in love with you, and also, how will that stop her?"

"I'm glad you asked," I say. I stand, grab a rolled-up piece of paper and white spatula from my jacket, and bring them over to the table. "Please make room."

Grumbling occurs, but plates and drinks are moved, clearing enough space for me to unroll my plan, which I drew up earlier with some crayons

I found in the tree shack. I pin the edges down with a few glasses of water and then slap my spatula on the table, using it as a pointer.

"Jesus, was that necessary?" Taran asks, her hand placed over her heart.

"Yes," I say. "Now pay attention closely, because this is vitally important to follow." I point to a picture of a sad stick figure with blond hair with the name *Betty* written above her. "This is Betty. Notice how sad and lonely she looks. And this is me." I point to a buff stick figure with an axe and my name. "Notice how proud I am to be standing next to this tree, a tree that has been a part of my family—"

"Spare us, please. Just get on with the plan," Cole groans.

"Fine. There was a whole backstory that would have really added to the plan, offering sympathy for me and hate for her, but whatever." I clear my throat and move the spatula down to a picture of me handing Betty flowers. "This is the target. Enemy number one, the single human who has turned the life of your faithful friend, the one and only Atlas Maxheimer, upside down. We despise her and hope for her to trip and fall into a snowbank . . . gloveless."

"Gloveless." Aunt Cindy *tsks*. "That's quite harsh, Atlas."

I nod. "I know, I know, but that's how much we don't like her. She is on a mission to put lovable me out of business, and the only way to change her vision is to woo her. To make her fall head over heels in love with me."

"I don't see how wooing her will help," Storee interjects, worrying her lip.

"Let me get there." I point to the flowers. "We go on a full-frontal attack. Hold nothing back. We're talking pulling out my best moves." I lower myself near Cole and smile next to his face. "I offer her the moneymaker, my smile." I then move to Storee and tickle her neck, causing her to swat me away. "I make her laugh." I stand behind Taran and wrap my arm around her shoulders. "I embrace her with my manly body." I move over to Guy, and I'm about to kiss his cheek and then

think better of it, instead patting the top of his head. "I kiss her wildly, using tongue."

"Glad you didn't show that as an example with me," Guy says.

"Same, dude." Then I clear my throat and continue. "I woo her, over and over and over again until she has no other option than to give in to this"—I gesture to my body—"sex machine."

"Jesus Christ," Cole says, shaking his head. "And what are you going to do when she throws up when you present her with your . . . sex machine?"

"She won't throw up," I counter.

"Really? Because I just thew up in my mouth," Cole replies.

"Cute." I give him a mocking smile.

"I'm sorry. I'm trying to grasp this concept," Storee says. "How do you expect to do this when she probably doesn't want to be anywhere near you?"

"Once again, glad you asked." I move back to my plan and say, "By setting up booby-trapped meet-cutes—if you will—all around town, possible scenarios where she runs into me and has no other option than to interact with me. Scenarios where I . . . I don't know, save a dog in front of her or, even better, save her from getting run over by a moving vehicle where she's forced into my arms—"

"And she can feel the manly body," Guy says.

"Precisely, my man. Little instances that grow her liking of me and that can then allow that liking to grow into infatuation." I move the spatula down to an image of her with hearts in her eyes and hearts floating over her head. "And with that infatuation, we start to see her second-guess herself. Second-guess her actions. This is where she starts to rethink her idea of taking me out of business. Where she starts to think, *Hey, what am I doing to this man with the manly body that I seem to like so much?*" Then in my best girly voice, I clutch my chest and say, "*Oh goodness, I love Max so much. He's my night and day and my moon, and I don't see how I could possibly continue with this farm idea, because I wouldn't want to hurt him. Oh,*

Uncle Dwight, count me out. I no longer want to go through with this asinine idea, because the man who has secured my love with his bulging biceps and frying pan pecs has captured my heart. Count me out." Then I dramatically take a bow and say, "End scene."

When I lift up, I find Guy clapping for me.

Aunt Cindy smiling.

Taran looking around the room, unsure.

Storee shaking her head.

And Cole . . . well, let's just say I think he's checked out.

"So what do you think?" I hold out my arms, welcoming all honest opinions.

"Frying pan pecs?" Aunt Cindy asks.

"Yeah, want to give them a poke?"

"That's . . . that's all right, dear."

"Well, anyone else?" I ask around the room.

"Uh, does anyone need water? I think I'll grab some refills," Taran says as she heads into the kitchen.

"I think I'll grab some dessert," Storee adds, removing herself.

When they leave, I glance over at Cole, who still looks checked out, Aunt Cindy, who is gathering crumbs on the table, and Guy, who is looking around as well.

After a few seconds of silence, Guy finally speaks up. "I don't know. I think it has merit."

Huh, that's surprising. Guy might be my number one fan.

I look down at Cole, and when our eyes meet, he says, "You're an idiot."

"Come on," I groan and then move down the diagram. "See, look. I even drew us holding hands and walking into the forest together."

"Your diagram is asinine, not to mention you're neglecting so many factors. For instance, what if she doesn't like you?"

"Pffft, everyone likes me." I point my spatula at the other end of the table. "Right, Gus?"

His face falls flat as he says, "It's Guy."

"Oh shit, right." I chuckle. "Sorry, man. Uh, don't hold that against me. I'm billowing with energy."

"Don't do it again," he says, changing his tune. Clearly his fandom is wavering.

"What if she has a boyfriend already?" Cole asks.

"She just moved to a new town and is starting a new life. Doubtful she has a boyfriend. Also, Dwight said I wasn't her type, which makes me think she's available, but I'm just not the one to fill the position of boyfriend."

"Uh-huh, and what happens if—and I mean if—she does find you appealing and you somehow find a way for this woman to fall for you? Then what?"

Taran and Storee walk back in with drinks and cookies just as I say, "Simple. I date her up until Christmas when my parents return; then they can take over, I dump her, she's too distraught to even be near me, she leaves town, and Dwight doesn't have someone to run his project anymore. Problem solved. Bing. Bang. Boom."

Taran and Storee glance at each other and then head back into the kitchen while Aunt Cindy stands as well. "I think I'll go help them."

Gus . . . I mean Guy. Fuck, what is wrong with me? Guy leans back and chuckles while muttering, "Bing. Bang. Boom."

Cole just stares at me, blinking.

After a few seconds, he says, "Like I said before, you're an idiot."

"I'm not. This is a great plan. This will work. And it's the only way to make sure they don't try to take over. In the meantime, while I work my wooing magic, I can have Martha and Mae Bawhovier go through the town records for me and see if they can find any sort of . . . clause or something that talks about businesses overlapping outside the town limits, but that will take time. And I need time. Therefore, let the wooing commence."

I sit and cross one leg over the other, completely pleased with myself and my well-thought-out plan I've conjured up. "Come on. You can't tell me this plan isn't bulletproof."

"It's fucking Swiss cheese," Cole says. "There are holes everywhere. It won't work."

"You have lost your mind," I say with a shake of my head.

"Dude, look in a mirror when you say that."

Storee reappears, and this time, she's without cookies. With an empathetic expression, she takes a seat on the chair next to me and reaches out for my hand. She gives it a gentle pat while she says, "Atlas, you know I love you and put up with a lot of your ideas, but I really think this might be something that you don't pursue."

"Why not?" I ask. "I need time. This gives me time."

"Because . . . what if she grows attached to you? You don't want to hurt her."

"I don't want to hurt her?" I ask, sitting taller, pointing to my chest. "I don't want to hurt *her*? Uh, absolutely I do. Let's think back to what has happened so far. She moves in next to me, attacks me with a two-liter bottle, gets me sent to jail, which I have a court hearing for, thank you very much, and then snoops around my farm, attacks me with another two-liter when I was bringing her a peace offering, threatens me with a gallon of tea, leaves me high and dry to wallow in pain in the parking lot, and has a master plan to put my family out of business. I don't want to hurt her? Uh, no, I want to annihilate her. I want her crying so hard, she's dehydrated. I want her to know what pain is, the same kind of pain I felt when a bottle of Coca-Cola smashed directly into my sternum."

"When he puts it like that, he might have a point," Guy says.

"Thank you . . . *Guy*," I say, making sure to enunciate his name.

"And frankly, I don't see why he doesn't at least give it a try. Who's to say she'll fall in love with him? If anything, he can make her realize he's a human, and maybe sufficient guilt consumes her and slows her plans, giving Martha and Mae enough time to look through the town archives. I see value in the plan."

I slowly clap. "And that's why Guy is part of the story."

"Huh?" Storee asks.

"Don't worry about it." I shake her off. "But see, it's a valid plan. I just need you guys to be on board."

"Why the hell would we need to be on board?" Cole asks.

"Because I need you to help set the booby-trapped meet-cutes. Or if you want, we can shorten it to *the BTMCs*."

"No," Cole says.

"*Booby-trapped meet-cutes* it is then."

"I mean no, we're not helping."

Guy raises his hand. "I don't mind helping."

"Guy," Taran says, entering the room now. "Please, don't get yourself mixed up in all this."

"Why not?" He shrugs. "I don't have anything better to do at the moment. Might as well help a man save his farm."

"Damn it." I smack the table, rattling the glasses and china. "You are an unexpected twist in all this, and I like it." I lean over the table and hold out my hand. Guy takes it and gives it a good shake. "Thank you."

"Any time."

"Anyone else want to join?" I hold out my arms, gesturing to the rest of the group. "This is the golden chance to take part in an inaugural opportunity, one that I'm sure will be talked about for decades to come." When no one offers to join, I say, "Anyone, speak now. We might not have openings later." Crickets. "No one else, okay, that's fine. Gus, it looks like it's you and me."

His face falls, and I realize my grave mistake.

"Guy!" I shout. "Fuck, I meant to say *Guy*. Please don't leave me. You're all I have."

His nostrils flare as he picks up his water glass, letting my plan roll back up. "I told you not to make that mistake again. I'm out."

Motherfucker.

Good-for-nothing friends.

Ha, I wouldn't even call them that.

More like frenemies.

Not a single ounce of help from any of them. I should have known better. They don't like to be involved in anything epic. Real bores.

I make my way down the steps of Cole's house, my plan rolled up under my arm, and head to my truck, where I open the door and shift inside, shutting the door quickly, because fuck, it's cold out.

No matter how long I've lived here, the cold night air still—

"Atlas," I hear someone whisper as I get into my truck.

What the hell was that? I glance around, looking for the voice.

"Psst, Atlas."

I turn to the right to find Storee tucked half on the floor of my truck and half on the passenger seat.

"Holy fuck!" I shout, nearly wetting myself. I lean back against my seat and take deep breaths. "What the hell are you doing, Storee?"

"I wanted to talk to you in secret."

I glance toward her aunt Cindy's house, which is next door. "Weren't you walking your aunt Cindy back?"

"Yes, but then I came here because I wanted to talk to you. Took you long enough."

"Why are you hiding?"

"Because I don't want Cole to see me talking to you."

"Why?"

"Because . . . I . . . uh . . . I want to help you."

"Wait. Really?" I ask, hope blossoming in my chest.

See, there are good people in this world.

"Yes, under two conditions." She holds up her finger. "You don't tell Cole that I'm helping you."

"That's easy. He's dead to me at the moment."

"And the second condition is you listen to me. If we're doing this, then we're doing this right."

Pretty easy conditions to follow if you ask me.

"Okay, I think I can manage that. Can I offer some input?"

"Of course, but you can't go rogue on me. There's a delicate process to wooing someone, especially when they're someone you don't get along with. Trust me, I have experience."

"Right, because you and Cole hated each other, but then you flipped the switch and are now married."

"Exactly, and I know how to get there. There has to be buildup. There has to be tension, and then there needs to be a moment when you become real. A moment when she sees you as more than just the man who lives on the farm next to her. She needs to see you for you, and that's how you get her to fall."

"That's what happened with you and Cole?"

She nods. "Yup. Happened after the candy cane–making class we went to. He dropped his guard, and I saw past the gruff exterior to recognize that he was hurting inside. It changed everything. But we have to build to that point. We can't just lay it out there for her, because she'll believe that you're just getting to know her—"

"To get her to back off."

"Precisely."

I rub my hands together, feeling the excitement come back into my body. "I knew I should have been talking to you this entire time. And you acted like you wanted nothing to do with me in there. You wily minx."

"Of course. To throw my husband off. Come on. The minute I saw the crayon drawings, I knew I was in."

"I'm so glad my best friend fell in love with you."

"And I'm so glad my husband is your best friend. I've been waiting for something like this. Get me out of my mom funk. Go undercover. Smell the action again."

I smirk. "Missing the Christmas Kringle competition?"

"Just a little." She holds up her fingers. "Okay, meet me at Warm Your Spirits tomorrow at seven in the morning, sharp."

"Seven?" I balk.

"It's when I go for my walk with Flo and Evelyn. It won't lead to any suspicion from the husband."

"Gotcha."

"Okay. See you then." She starts to leave, but I stop her.

"Hey, do you think we need a secret handshake or anything?"

"Absolutely." Then she holds her hands out together like she's saying a prayer and then says, "Lay a motherfucking bomb on this Christmas tree."

Laughing, I form a fist and then crash my hand on top of her fingers.

She deflates them and then says, "Consider her Christmas ruined."

CHAPTER ELEVEN
MAX

NARRATOR: WERE YOU EXPECTING SUCH *a turn of events? For Storee and Max to join together in cahoots? It only feels right—her random spirit and his insanity. Seems like a match made in heaven to me. Let's just hope that Cole doesn't find out.*

Or anyone else for that matter, because if there is one thing we know for certain about a small town? News spreads fast.

———————

"What are you wearing?" Storee asks as I take a seat across from her in Warm Your Spirits.

I glance down at myself. "I wasn't sure if I needed to be incognito."

"You're a six-foot-four mammoth of a man wearing a ski mask and sunglasses. You're anything but incognito at the moment."

"You think people recognize me?"

"You're wearing an Evergreen Farm crewneck sweatshirt, so yes, I'm pretty sure anyone would recognize you."

"Shit," I mutter as I remove the glasses and the ski mask. Storee winces when she catches sight of me without my disguise.

"God, the bruising is all yellow and gross now on your face. And your hair looks terrible."

"Wow, thanks. Good morning to you too." I take my reindeer hat out of my back pocket and I fix it on my head. "How's that?"

"Better." She examines me. "The scruff on your face is thicker."

"Because it's seven in the morning and I didn't get much sleep last night. The wheels have been spinning, Storee."

"Really? I slept great last night." She leans in. "Cole did this thing with his tongue—"

I hold my hand out, stopping her. "I will not sit here and listen to you talk about your sex life with my best friend. It's bad enough I know what you did in my barn with a candy cane. I refuse to hear about tongue action."

"Are you sure? Might be beneficial for you."

"Trust me, I know exactly what to do with my tongue."

"When was the last time you used your tongue in that way?"

"Uh, don't you think that's a little private?" I ask as Tanya, the blessed woman, sets down my coffee. Guess she didn't need me to take off the mask to know who I was. If she asks why I was wearing it, I'll tell her wind chill was hurting my face this morning. She'll buy it. "Thank you," I say to her. She nods and walks away.

"When have you ever been private?" Storee asks. "A few weeks ago, you were telling me about the boner you woke up with."

"Because it was so hard, and I was sleeping on my stomach. It practically jackknifed me off the bed. Like a spring letting loose from its coil."

"That right there. That is why Cole is not helping you. You say such ridiculous things."

"It's true," I whisper. "That boner levitated me."

"I can't." She tosses her hands up and starts to move out of her booth, but I stop her.

"Fine. It didn't levitate me, but it did in my dream."

She rolls her eyes and then sets her arms on the table. "Listen up. We're doing this the right way, okay? And we won't be ridiculous and hysterical and overthink and embellish. We have a job to do, and it's to save the farm. And the way we're doing that is by wooing Betty. Now, I was able to score her information from Martha, who asked for it from Dwight. I asked her to meet me here."

"What? Now?" I ask, looking over my back. "I'm not ready. I'm not prepped. I don't know what to say or do. This is an ambush."

"Shhhhhh," Storee says, tamping down my energy with a motion of her hand. "She won't be here for another half hour. I told her I wanted to meet up with her since she's new in town, and see if she needed a friend."

"Ooo, good one."

"Thank you." Storee smiles. "I met her at the farm and already put the offer out there, so this shouldn't come as a surprise. I'll get intel from her, and we can use that for the wooing."

"Wow, that's . . . that's really smart."

"And that's why you're working with me and not my grumpy husband."

"You're right about that." I take a sip of my coffee, feeling the caffeine spike through my veins.

"But I want you here when she arrives. We'll make it seem like you just ran into me. You'll pick up Flo and bounce her around a bit before shooting off for a day on the farm. We want to make you seem approachable, loving, a gentleman."

"Everything that I already am." I smirk at her, causing her to roll her eyes.

"But you can't be your outlandish self, okay? Reel that shit in."

"I'm not outlandish."

She levels with me, her brow picking up. "Minutes ago, you told me your boner levitated you off your mattress."

"That's not outlandish. That's just providing context."

"You know what I mean, Atlas. You have to be normal."

I let out a long breath. "I'm normal most of the time. But when the nervous energy takes over, that's when the lips start to fly."

"I know. So don't get nervous."

"Easy for you to say. I have to woo a woman who"—I lean forward and whisper—"if I'm honest, is extremely attractive."

Storee's eyes widen as a large smile passes over her ChapStick-covered lips. "Oh, well, this is a new development I wasn't aware of."

"Can you not?"

"Uh, no, I can. I've never heard you mention anything about a woman you find attractive. This is the first time. So I need to revel in it."

"No, you don't."

"Tell me what you like about her."

"Nothing," I say. "I like nothing about her. I didn't say I liked her. I said she was attractive."

"Okay, then what do you think is attractive?"

"The obvious things," I say, getting annoyed.

"And what would those obvious things be?"

"You're really going to make me say it?"

She smirks and brings her mug to her lips. "I am."

"Fine," I huff. "She has a gorgeous face. Symmetrical in all the right ways. Her nose is cute, with a bit of a swoop at the end that I find adorable. And her bow-shaped lips are not too big but not too small either, perfectly proportionate. I think the dimples she has add to the charm of her face, but it's her eyes that are simply stunning. Caught me off guard at first. And when they shine against the bright snow, they're incredibly captivating."

"Oh...my...God," Storee says, unable to hold back her smile. "I was so not expecting you to say that. I was expecting a simple *I like her eyes*, not a monologue about how they captivated you."

Passing it off as nothing, I say, "I'm one with the words. What can I say?"

She leans forward more and whispers, "Are you doing this whole wooing thing to get with someone? Like, do you want to date her?"

"Absolutely not," I say with a shake of my head. "No, not even a little. She has a beautiful face, I will give her that, but her personality does not match. I've talked to her a few times now, and let me tell you, a real trash bag, that one. All garbage. Bleh."

Storee chuckles. "It feels like you're overcompensating."

"I'm not. Trust me, we have nothing in common. I'm a cinnamon roll, and she's an overbearing oven ready to roast me to dust."

"Uh-huh . . ."

"Storee, I'm serious. I have no intention of actually becoming romantically attached to this woman. How could I? She's related to Dwight, red flag number one. She thinks she can waltz into town and put someone out of business, red flag number two, and she uses Pepsi as a weapon, red flag number three. If I presented this case to that guy on social media who runs giant green and red flags across a field, he would struggle having to cart around the red flag that is Betty. So in conclusion, no, not interested. Thank you for asking."

"Okay. Are you sure?"

"Positive."

"Just want to be sure, because if there are feelings there, then I don't want to move forward with this in case you get hurt more."

"Trust me, I won't get hurt." I wink and then take a sip of my coffee. "I'm iron, baby. Nothing penetrates me."

"You know, a lot can penetrate iron. Even oxygen, leading to rust—"

"You know what I mean," I say exasperated.

Sheesh.

BETTY

Is it weird that I'm nervous?

When I got Storee's text last night, I was thrown off. How did she get my number? Then again, it's a small town. I think if you know the right people, you could find out anything. But when she asked me to have coffee, I felt . . . excited.

It hasn't been easy, being here, not knowing anyone but Uncle Dwight, someone who I've started to notice isn't the most popular in town. Walking around, few people say hi to him, but I do see others waving and talking on the side of the streets. Maybe because he's not as chatty as others, but it will be nice to chat with someone other than him.

And Storee seemed really nice.

I also brought my notebook so I can sit and study the atmosphere of Warm Your Spirits, which has such a cute name to begin with. But also probably a wonderful place to start when it comes to my research, because if any place can sell a warm Christmassy spirit, it's the local coffee shop.

I open the door to the store, and I'm immediately presented with the smell of coffee and baked goods.

The register and where the coffees are made are in the center of the shop, which has a little 360 view of everything that's going on, leaving the perimeter of the shop for seating. Decorations are carefully hung, pine and cranberry garland draping from one end to the other, while numerous Christmas trees decorate the space. Fake candles are propped up on every frosted windowsill, a fire is roaring in the back with real firewood, and subtle Christmas music plays in the background, offering that cozy Christmas feeling.

I take a mental note of the fireplace, because it's real, not an electric one, no gas involved, something the owner must maintain throughout the day. That's a really nice touch. Something I probably would never have thought of, because even though it smells like coffee in here, there is a subtle smoky scent that adds to the welcoming ambience.

Wanting to order first, I walk up to the counter, and an older woman with blond hair greets me. "Hello, dear. What can I get you?"

"Hi, um, what's your coziest drink?"

"Our peppermint mocha. Do you like peppermint?"

"I do. It sounds perfect."

"Great. Are you going to drink it here?"

"Yes, I'm actually meeting Storee Black."

"Oh, how nice. She's over in the corner. I'll bring you your drink when it's ready so you can chat."

"Wow, thank you." I pay for my drink, and the woman gestures me in the right direction. I slip my card back in my purse, lift my head, and then stop when my eyes fall on a very tall figure holding a baby and talking to Storee.

No freaking way.

For a brief moment, I think about bolting and texting her that I'm not feeling well so I'm skipping out on our meetup, but unfortunately for me, her eyes meet mine, and her face lights up with a smile.

Crap.

With a brave face, I head in that direction only for Storee to stand and greet me with a hug.

"Betty, it's so great to see you. Thank you for meeting me."

"Thank you for the invite," I say, feeling all kinds of awkward as Atlas turns toward me, holding Storee's cute baby, while another baby rests in the stroller.

"I believe you know Atlas."

I give him a short wave. "Yes, hi. How are you?" My nice autopilot kicks in, because I couldn't really care less about how he is. I honestly hope his leg rots and falls off. That's how much I care about his well-being.

"Doing better." He presses his hand to his chest. "Sternum has healed."

"Well, good for you."

He smirks . . . actually smirks and says, "Then again, holding this little bundle of joy could pretty much heal anything." Atlas kisses Storee's baby— God, I can't remember her name, how terrible—and the baby giggles.

The baby looks like she's older than one, which means she probably doesn't take too kindly to strangers, leading me to believe that Atlas and Storee know each other well.

Wait, doesn't her husband work at the farm? If I recall correctly, he does, which means ... they probably are all friends.

"Are you okay?" Storee asks, reading the confusion all over my face.

"Uh, yeah, sorry." I shake my head. "Just, uh, just trying to figure out how you two know each other."

Storee glances at Atlas and then back at me. "The annoying best friend to my husband."

"Annoying?" Atlas says with a cute raise to his brow. "Just the other night, you were singing praises about how funny I am."

"Funny looking," Storee says with a heaping amount of charm.

Motioning between them with my finger, I say, "Oh, so you two are close?"

"Barely," Storee answers with a huff. "I put up with him."

I feel Atlas look me up and down, his studying eyes making me feel exposed. "I think she's worried to have a cup of coffee with you," he says, "because you have an attachment to me."

"The attachment is frayed at best, so you don't need to worry about him. He was just about to stop bothering me anyway." Storee takes her baby back and then shoos him away. "Don't scare her away. I need friends of my own in this town."

"You realize this is my enemy, right?" Atlas says in a lighthearted tone while thumbing toward me. "You can't make friends with my enemy."

"Fine, then I dump you as a friend, and I take her on."

His mouth falls open in shock. "You don't even know her."

"Which says a lot about you."

That makes me chuckle, because *good comeback.*

Atlas clutches his chest. "You wound me, Storee."

"Yeah, what doesn't wound you? Now get out of here."

"You're just going to kick me out like that? What if Betty wants to get to know me better? She hasn't seen my charming side yet."

"Yeah, only your Peeping Tom side," Storee says with an eye roll that makes me snort.

"Hey!" Atlas points his finger at her. "I was not trying to be a perverted Peeping Tom. I was attempting to find out who the resident was."

"And knocking on the door was too hard," I say, arms crossed over my chest.

"As a matter of fact, it was," he says with a smirk that feels very flirty. "Not to mention I did you a favor."

"How on earth did you do me a favor?" I ask.

"Well, for one, I've given you quite the anecdote. Can't put a price on that. And also, I helped you prove that soda can be used as a weapon, so . . . you're welcome."

"I didn't say thank you."

He winks. "Yeah, but I can tell you're grateful. Most women I meet are."

"Ew," I say while Storee chuckles next to me.

"Anyway, I'll let you two get to your coffee date." He lets out a sigh and starts to pull away from us but not before stopping next to me, lining up shoulder to shoulder. With a smirk and a timbre so deep, he says, "Always a pleasure, Betty."

The sound of his voice, in a tone that I haven't heard from him before, pulses all the way down my back and buries itself deep in the depths of my being.

I glance up at him, startled at the reaction his voice has given me, and when our eyes meet, he winks one more time before taking off.

What the hell was that?

I . . . I don't even know what to do with that. How to react.

How to process.

Because . . . what?

Thankfully Storee breaks me from my spell as she gestures to the seat across from her. "Sorry about him. Please don't run away. I'd still love to have coffee with you."

Taking a seat, still slightly shook, I say, "Oh, no need to apologize. It's fine."

"I just know that things are tense between the two of you."

I wave her off. "Seriously, no need to worry. We can be civil."

"That's what he informed me of when he bumped into me, and I told him you were on your way, so get the hell out of here. But of course Flo wasn't letting go of him."

Florence, that's the baby's name.

"You know, it's annoying when you feel your kid likes your husband's best friend better."

I chuckle. "Well, for what it's worth, I'd choose you over him."

She presses her hand to her chest. "At least I have you on my side."

"Sorry, ladies, don't mean to interrupt," Atlas says, coming back with that deep voice, startling me. When I look to my left, he's standing there with that freaking grin again, holding out a tray. "I went ahead and ordered you both the peppermint hot chocolate cookie, and I also have your drink here, Betty. Told Tanya I'd deliver it for her so she could take a rest. It's only going to get busier from here."

Umm . . . what's happening?

Why is he acting like a saint?

Like the jolly neighbor, ready to lend a helping hand when called upon?

He sets down two plates with giant cookies on them and then places my drink right in front of me. When he rises, he tucks the tray under his arm, and I don't know what comes over me, but I say, "Why are you being nice to me?"

My question catches him by surprise, because his brows raise as Storee chuckles.

"I don't mean that to sound rude, but seriously, why?"

"I'm more being nice to my friend Storee." He lifts his chin.

"That's so not the truth," Storee says as she crosses one leg over the other with a smirk.

"Yes, it is," he says.

Storee shakes her head and laughs. "No, it's not." Then she looks at me and says, "It's because he thinks you have really pretty eyes."

Uhh . . . what?

Excuse me?

Did I hear that right?

I turn my attention to Atlas for some sort of confirmation that she's joking, but when I read his expression, all I see is him staring daggers at Storee.

Wait . . .

Is she serious?

From his reaction, I'm assuming yes.

He thinks I have pretty eyes?

I . . . I really don't know what to do with that.

"Go ahead. Tell her." Storee nods in my direction. "You know you want to."

Lips pursed, he lightly shakes his head, which causes Storee to roll her eyes.

"Oh stop. You were just telling me yesterday how pretty her eyes are. Go ahead. She's here. Tell her."

The back of my neck grows hot as I glance toward him.

"I . . . uh . . ." He stumbles, taking a step backward, looking all sorts of uncomfortable.

It's such an intense and awkward reaction that I feel like I need to give him privacy but don't know how to.

If only my chair would swallow me whole.

Silence falls between us.

The awkwardness grows.

Until he clears his throat and looks at me, his expression serious. He wets his lips.

Clears his throat.

Then meekly says, "I . . . uh . . . I think you have really pretty eyes."

Oh God.

He means it.

And now things just took a turn, because I don't know how to react to that, and when I don't know how to react, my awkward instincts kick in, meaning . . . I'm about to ramble nonsense.

I know it's coming.

I know it's my only way to fight off the bumbling feeling pulsing through me.

And there's nothing I can do to stop it.

My cheeks flame. I look away and hear myself say, "Oh, uh, thank you. They're, uh, they're my dad's eyes."

They're my dad's eyes?

Who says that?

"Your dad's eyes? You don't say," Atlas says. "Well, your dad has really pretty eyes then."

I look up at him again, and he's blushing as well. Probably just as much as I am. "I'll, uh, I'll let him know you think so. I'm sure he'll appreciate the compliment."

"That would be great." He clutches the tray to his chest. "Because who doesn't like a compliment?"

"Some people might not, but my dad does."

"My dad likes compliments too."

"Oh really?" I ask, wanting to slowly melt into my chair from the awkwardness of this conversation. "Glad your dad likes compliments."

"He does. Would you like to, uh . . . would you like to pay him one as well?"

Absolutely not.

Don't know the man.

Just want this to be over.

But clearly, I have no ability to end this as I say, "Oh, uh . . . sure?"

I can feel Storee watching us, metaphorically with a bucket of popcorn in her arms, enjoying every second of this.

"Great. Umm, you might need some help unless you've met him before. Have you?"

"No, can't say that I have."

"Ah, so yeah, umm, let me think . . . He and I are both tall. If that's something you want to compliment. We also have the same eyebrows. And hands." Atlas holds up his hands. "Lots of things to work with."

"Wow, that's quite a lot." Swallowing the saliva building up in my mouth and wanting this nightmare to be over, I say, "Well, tell him nice eyebrows. Congrats on . . . on how bushy they are."

Just swallow me whole, world, please. Please end this.

Atlas smooths his fingers over his brows. "Uh, thank you. I'll be sure to let him know."

"Please do."

Then silence falls between us.

The awkward cringe of *no one knows what to say* takes over.

And I can feel the sting of sweat break out on my neck, urging me to do something, anything to end this.

To make him go away.

To pretend this interaction never happened, because dear God, this might be the worst conversation I've ever been a part of. And it's because he's trying to be nice? Why is he trying to be nice? It's better when he's peeping in my window and I'm chucking liters of soda at him.

"Well . . . this is fun," Storee finally says, breaking the silence with one leg crossed over the other and a smile on her face. "Are there any other compliments you want to throw toward each other's fathers, or are you set on that?"

"I think we're set," I say.

"Yeah, all set."

"Great. Well, if you don't mind, I would like to have coffee with my friend." Storee gestures to me.

"Right." Atlas nods. "Yeah, sure. Okay, well, have fun chatting." He looks between us, waiting one second longer than he should. He clutches his tray and then adds, "Yeah. Okay. Bye."

With that, he turns on a dime but unfortunately for him runs right into another table, tumbling over it, head over heels with an earsplitting crash. His body flips over the table, the chairs tumble to the ground, and he's left on his back, looking up toward the ceiling, his coveted tray flung halfway across the coffee shop.

Oh dear God.

"Oh my God," Storee says as she stands with a baby on her hip and rushes over to Atlas, who's writhing on the floor.

"Fuck," he groans.

"Are you okay?" Tanya asks as she rushes to his side.

Not wanting to look like a beast who doesn't care, I stand up as well and start righting the chairs. "Yeah, are you . . . are you okay?"

"Fine." He slowly stands, his large body taking up space. He pats down his sweatshirt and rights his reindeer hat. "Just a bruised ego is all." His eyes meet mine, and once again, for some stupid reason, I feel my cheeks blush.

"Do you need any ice?" Tanya asks.

"Nah, I'm good." He twists back and forth and then side to side. "Shit, my back will be fucked now."

"Language around Flo," Storee says.

"Sorry." He clears his throat. "Well, now that I've thoroughly embarrassed myself, I think I'll go bury myself in work. Ladies, good seeing you." He looks around and then finishes with his eyes on me. "Have a good day."

"H-have a good day," I say as he takes off, his giant feet stomping across the shop until he's gone.

"Well, he'll be thinking about that all day," Storee says while taking a seat.

"You think so?"

"Oh yeah." Storee nods and breaks off a piece of cookie for her daughter. "Atlas is the type of guy who thinks and rethinks things constantly. Bet you anything he'll be bothering Cole about it tomorrow as well."

"Are they . . . are they really that close?"

Storee nods her head. "Yeah, their parents were best friends, which of course caused them to play together as kids. They grew up together, and then when Cole was eighteen, his parents died in a tragic car crash, and Atlas was the first one at his side." She drops a piece of cookie in her mouth. "His family took Cole in as their own, offered him a job, helped him through the hardest time of his life. I honestly believe if it wasn't for Atlas and his family, Cole wouldn't be around either."

Wow, that's not . . . that's not what Uncle Dwight has said about him.

"But enough about him. I bet he's the last person you want to talk about right now. Tell me about you. Are you all settled in? Are you enjoying Kringle?"

"Umm . . . almost settled in," I say, trying to get comfortable, even though this new information about Atlas doesn't seem to settle well. "Just have a few more things to take care of. And I love Kringle. It's so picturesque and everything I would have dreamed about living in a small town."

"*Picturesque* is the perfect way to describe it. My aunt Cindy lives here, and when I was younger, my family visited all the time. I didn't appreciate it as much because I lived in Southern California and didn't love the cold winters. But now I couldn't imagine being anywhere else. I'm sure you'll get to that point too once you spend a little more time here."

"Yeah, I think I might."

CHAPTER TWELVE
MAX

NARRATOR: *THE BACK SPASMS HAVE not stopped since his trip over the table.*

The embarrassment he felt has yet to subside.

And the humiliation of Storee telling Betty he likes her eyes is the only thing that has kept him from sticking his head in a pile of snow, because he saw the look on her face.

He saw the blush in her cheeks.

He heard the compliment about his eyebrows.

It gives him hope. Hope that their plan might work. That he might be able to create enough time for Martha and Mae to find something, anything to block them from creating this farm.

Only time will tell.

———————

Storee: Reporting in.

Max: Christ, it took you long enough. I've been thinking about your talk with her all day.

Storee: I know. The seventeen texts asking were unnecessary.

Max: Sorry if I feel like you're the key to saving my farm. And it was sixteen texts.

Storee: Remember what I told you about being dramatic?

Max: You're right, I'm sorry. This morning was humiliating, and I think I was trying to see if I fucked it all up.

Storee: No, I think the trip over the table was perfection. She seemed genuinely concerned. I told her you would be thinking about it all day, and she was surprised by that. I then gave her a brief, and I mean very brief, snapshot of who you are and how you took Cole in but left it at that. Planted the seeds.

Max: And now I need to water them.

Storee: Please, let's not be corny.

Max: You're the one who said "planted the seeds."

Storee: And like always, you're the one who took it too far. You could have just left it at that.

Max: You're right. I'm sorry again. So it went well?

Storee: Yeah . . . she's actually . . . really kind of cool.

Max: Um, pardon?

Storee: I'm serious, she's cool. Sweet. Fun to talk to. Has a sense of humor . . .

Max: Are you sure we're talking about the same person, because the soda wielder I know has no sense of humor and is a beast when it comes to soft beverages.

Storee: We're talking about the same person. I could see you two getting along.

Max: Oh no, you don't. Don't be getting any ideas. This wooing is pure business. There is nothing personal about it.

Storee: I know. But just let me state it now: If you were to date, she'd be a great match. I could see you two having a lot of fun together. I don't think she's this hard-ass that you think she is.

Max: I don't think she's a hard-ass. I think she's a devil. The mistress of sin.

Storee: You're being dramatic, but I'll just let her change your mind, because mark my words, it will happen.

Max: Anyone trying to put my family out of business will always be the devil to me.

Storee: Very mature.

Max: We're getting off track. Enough about this stupid attraction thing. We're on a mission, and that mission is to bide time and make her feel guilty for what she's doing. So the seeds have been planted. What's next?

Storee: Another BTMC of course.

Max: And this is why I'm working with you.

Storee: No, you're working with me because I'm the only one who would.

Max: A simple "you're right" would have sufficed.

BETTY

Storee: I'm on the right-hand side of the bleachers. Got a spot for you.

Betty: Thank you, see you there.

Gosh, it's busy. I shut my car door and close my jacket tighter as I make my way through the high school parking lot toward the gymnasium. During my coffee with Storee, she was telling me all about the Christmas Kringle competition and how it's one of the best things to experience while living in Kringle. She said that all the competitions are open to the public. What better way to experience the town than with a Christmas competition? So she invited me to watch the fruitcake challenge with her.

Never had any serious thoughts about fruitcake—I always hear how bad it is—so it might be fun to see if these competitors can change my mind.

I open the door to the high school and follow the signs toward the Christmas Kringle competition, taking in how even the halls are decorated for Christmas. Is it like this year-round? Or just for the season?

What I like is that they made a garland out of cutout hands. It seems they traced every hand in the school on green construction paper, stapled them all together, and taped them to the top of the wall. It's a really festive and inexpensive way to decorate that adds character to the space. Not to mention every door is decorated as well but with different movie themes. The *Home Alone* one is my favorite because they have Harry sticking his head out of a fake doggie door.

Obsessed.

When I find the gymnasium, there's a coat check at the door.

Fancy.

I give them my coat and then make my way to the right side of the bleachers, where I see Storee, Cole, Florence, and . . . ugh . . . Atlas.

Why?

She spots me and waves, so I put on my smiley face and head on up to them. Storee offers me a hug, and I give Cole a small wave.

"Good to see you," he says in a generic way.

Atlas is next with his no-teeth smile. I return it and then take a seat next to Storee. Evelyn is with her sister. I know this because Storee said her sister wanted baby time.

"Wow, this is intense," I say as I take in the scene in front of me.

Rubber mats run along the gym floor while five individual cooking stations are set up, one right next to the other, equipped with a working sink, burners, and ovens. It's like *The Great British Baking Show*, but right here in Kringletown, Colorado.

"Oh, it's very intense. Just wait. They just did the intros, and they're about to start the competition. That man over there in the red Santa suit—that's Bob Krampus."

"Yes, I've seen him around a bit. He's like the town mayor, right?"

"Yup. He's a good guy to have on your side. You don't want to mess with him or his town, or Christmas for that matter. He takes it very seriously."

Noted.

"And that guy over there in the black galoshes, holding the shovel, that's his son, Bob Krampus Junior, or BKJ as everyone calls him."

"Yes, I've seen him around. Uncle Dwight has pointed him out."

"Very nice guy, but also serious about the work they do here in the town. And that . . ." She pauses and then swats her hand over her face. "Dear God in heaven. Cole, is that you?"

I lean over to look at Cole, who is holding Florence.

"Fuck no, that's your daughter."

"What is happening?" Storee asks.

"Do you want me to take care of it?" Atlas asks, about to take Florence.

"Uh . . . let me check." Cole pulls open the back of her pants and then snaps them back shut. "Nope, you'll gag like the last time you tried to help."

Atlas squeezes his nose with his fingers, making me smirk, because what a stupid and ridiculous thing to do. "Don't remind me."

"Babe, I think this might be a two-person job. Grab the diaper bag," Cole says.

"Uh, excuse me while I take care of my daughter's bowel movements."

Storee and Cole work their way past us, leaving a wave of stench in their path. Oof, good luck to them.

Atlas glances over at me, and I glance over at him, only to quickly turn away as an awkward and unsettling feeling sets in.

I hope they're back soon.

Because I can't imagine sitting here the whole time, with Atlas that close and having to—

"This your first time at a Christmas Kringle competition?" I hear him ask.

Great, let the awkward conversation commence. I'm not good at this. I'll ramble. I know I will. Not to mention I don't want to talk to him. I don't know what to say.

Maybe if I keep it short and sweet, he will get the hint.

"Yup," I say, keeping my eyes facing forward.

"Not mine. Been to many."

Good for him.

"Probably because you lived here your whole life," I say, and it comes off bitchier than I want it to. And even though I'm not a fan of Atlas Maxheimer, it doesn't mean I should make snide comments. So I look in his direction and attempt to adjust the tone of my voice and the sharpness of my words. "Which, you know, gives you time to attend such events like this all the time, but people who just come to visit, it's hit or miss, you know, but you live here so you get to go all the time, and that's neat."

That's neat?

Yup, let the rambling begin.

"It is neat," he says with a nod as his eyes dart away. "I was actually in the Christmas Kringle competition last year." He makes eye contact with me. "I won."

I don't know why, but the way he says it with such pride, like he's flashing a gold medal he won at the Olympics, makes me laugh. Which in turn causes his brows to turn down.

His bushy brows.

"I'm serious. I won. You can ask anyone around us." He taps the guy in front of us. "Who won the Christmas Kringle last year?"

The man with a rather thick mustache under his nose looks Atlas up and down. "I don't know . . . Santa Claus?" Then he turns around on a huff, causing me to laugh even harder.

"Clearly not a townie," Atlas grumbles. "I can look it up on my phone."

"It's fine. I believe you."

"But do you really?"

"Does it actually matter?" I ask. "Not even sure why we're talking to each other."

He shrugs. "Awkward silence."

"Not really silent. The competition has started," I say.

He glances out toward the gym and then back at me. "Guess so." Then he leans forward on his quads and focuses on the competition, leaving the awkward silence to fill up between us again.

I'll be honest, I don't like awkward silence either, but I know if I let myself try to fill it, I'll end up saying things that I shouldn't be saying or that I don't want to be saying to him.

Like . . . how when I was six, there was a brief, and I mean very brief, moment in my life that I would collect my hair from when I got it cut, and I would put it in a clear box as a memento.

That's not something anyone needs to know.

But that's what the rambling does to me.

After a few seconds, my phone buzzes with a text. I glance down to see it's from Storee, just as Atlas pulls his phone out as well.

Storee: Sorry to do this to you, but Flo blew right through her pants, and I forgot to pack a spare set of clothes. Mom brain. She's currently wrapped in a blanket on the bottom half. We have to head home. But have fun. It's exciting to watch.

Crap.

Seriously?

What are the chances?

I let out a sigh just as Atlas pockets his phone.

"Assuming you just got the same text," he says, seeming none too thrilled.

"Florence needs new pants?" I ask.

"Yup."

"Pardon me," an elderly man says on the stairs next to Atlas. "Are those seats taken? My wife and I'd love to sit down."

"Oh, sure," Atlas says as he scoots down the bleacher, sliding right next to me. "Do you need help? Want me to take your bag for you while you get settled?"

"That would be wonderful," the shaky elderly man says as he hands Atlas what seems to be a small cooler. The man and his wife get settled, and then Atlas hands them their bag.

"You all set?" Atlas asks.

"Yes. Thank you."

"I'm Atlas," he says, introducing himself. "And this is Betty."

What is happening?

Don't introduce me.

The old man leans forward and waves. "Nice to meet you. I'm Frank, and this is my wife, Leslie. We drove up from Idaho Springs for the competition."

"Oh, I love Idaho Springs," Atlas says. "Beau Jo's pizza is so good. That mountain pie with the honey to dip the crust in. So good."

"Our favorite place to have a date," Frank says. "Do you two go there often?"

"Oh, we're not . . . we're not together," I say, waving my hand between Atlas and me.

"You're not?" Frank asks with confusion. "Oh, I would have surely thought you were. Friends then."

"Nah, more like enemies, Frank," Atlas says with a gentle nudge of his shoulder. "Our friends had to leave, which left us here together, alone. What are the odds?"

Apparently, pretty high.

"Oh, what makes you enemies, if you don't mind me asking?"

Atlas shifts his large body. "Oh, you know, just can't seem to agree on the same things. Nothing too serious."

Wait, what?

He's not . . . he's not going to throw me under the bus? Tell these strangers that I'm attempting to put together a rival farm next to his?

Given how I've interacted with him in the past, I would have assumed he would freely announce that to anyone. I'm surprised he didn't bring flyers with him to hand out to the people around us, stating what's going on. Asking for support. Maybe trying to rally some sort of backing on social media. Really getting the word out.

"Well, seems like you need to have more conversations." Frank unzips his bag and hands us each a can of root beer. "Maybe this is something you can agree on." He winks and then turns toward his wife, putting his arm around her and blocking us out.

"Pretty sure she prefers Pepsi," Atlas says while rubbing his forehead.

"Huh?" Frank asks.

"Oh nothing. Thanks for the drink."

Atlas then shifts in my direction with what little space we have and says, "I want to offer you this soda, but I fear what you might do with it. A two-liter bottle did damage, but a close-proximity chuck of an aluminum can very well might knock me out for good."

"Don't be ridiculous," I say, taking the can. "I wouldn't do that in public."

"Ah, so you only hurl soft beverages on your porch."

"Correct." I fumble with opening the can, probably because of my nerves. And to my surprise, he hands me his open can before gently taking mine. "Umm . . . thanks."

"No problem," he says softly and then takes a sip. "Can't remember the last time I had a root beer. I was always a cream soda kind of guy growing up."

"Pepsi girl," I say.

"Really?" he says sarcastically. "Wow, that comes as a big shock to me."

I hate that I chuckle, because I'm not supposed to be charmed by him, and yet in the coffee shop and here, he's been able to make me smirk . . . even chuckle. God, what would Uncle Dwight say if he saw me talking to the enemy. He'd probably be as confused as I am and then disown me.

I take a sip of my drink and watch the people on the gym floor, running around, pulling ingredients from the "pantry," and going back to their stations. It's like watching *Chopped* but for baking . . . in a small-town Christmas competition.

"This gym is big," I say awkwardly, really unsure of what else to say to fill the silence.

"Yeah, a movie was actually filmed here, and they built an entire home inside the space. It was a big deal."

"Really? When?"

"Back in the nineties. Some Christmas film. They did the inside stuff here and then filmed around town. Can't remember the title though. I don't think it was much of a hit."

"Oh . . . interesting."

I purse my lips, looking around, trying to picture a house being built inside this space. My brain can't compute.

And after a few minutes of tense silence, silence that I can't take, I ask, "Were you good at this? The fruitcake baking?"

"The first year, when I was helping Cole? No, but last year when I went at it on my own, I learned quickly what the judges liked, so I added pineapple to my fruitcake and used the base recipe that Storee has, and I ended up winning this round. The secret is mashed potatoes, and from the looks of it, no one paid attention last year."

Mashed potatoes in fruitcake? Uh, that does not sound appetizing.

"Cole was part of the competition?" I ask, shocked. He doesn't seem like the kind of guy who would be a part of such a thing.

"Yeah, out of spite. That's how he and Storee fell in love."

"Oh right, Storee mentioned that. Said something about how you were the jolly helper or something."

"Holly jolly sidekick," he corrects. "Not all heroes wear capes, and let me tell you, in that tale, I was the hero wearing a pair of dog ears and shorts two sizes too small."

"Wait? What?" I ask, turning toward him.

Smiling, he pulls his phone out of his pocket, and he pulls up his photos. It takes him a second, and then he flashes me a picture of him and Cole, both shirtless. Both dressed up.

Oh.

My.

God.

"We did a scene from *The Grinch* but then put a spin on it. Cole was the Grinch, and I was, appropriately, Max, his dog. Cole's lederhosen were my idea."

And what an idea.

I've seen my fair share of male bodies, but oh my God, Atlas is ... He's a giant. Enormous pecs positioned right above a full stack of abs, with such a deep V cut in his hips that I fear the shorts he's wearing, even though small, might fall off.

And yes, those shorts are small. They're so small that I can visually see just how big of a—*gulp*—package he has.

"That's, uh . . . um, quite the outfit. I like the ears. Are those felt? Suede? If suede, they could shrink. Did you think about that? Shrinkage?"

I glance up at Atlas, who is beaming as he says, "Shrinkage in cold weather is always a concern, but I think I handled it well."

"Oh God, I didn't mean like . . . that kind of shrinkage."

He chuckles.

"I meant fabric. Fabric on the ears, not the crotch. Wasn't talking about the crotch area at all."

"Neither was I." He winks and then stuffs his phone away. "But if you want to go there, the shorts were incredibly uncomfortable, there was mild chafing, and afterward, I spent the day in pajama pants and nothing else, no underwear, just freeballing it."

"Oh, nice." I nod, unsure of how to react to such honesty other than begging my brain not to visualize it. "I like freeballing it. I mean . . . not that I have balls. Nope, I have a vagina."

Oh my God, stop talking.

"Wow, you do? I have a penis," he says. "What a small world. Although from the picture, you can tell there's nothing small about my world . . . err, I mean, my . . . penis?"

I rub my forehead. Is this what happens when two rambling idiots decide to have small talk?

"So to sum it up, I have a penis, you have a vagina, and we're aware of both things."

"I think that is correct," I say, looking for the emergency exit to throw myself out of.

Frank leans forward, joining in with a hand raised. "We have a penis and a vagina over here as well."

Dear God in heaven.

MAX

"So have you, uh . . . have you seen a Steller's jay on the property yet?" My palms are sweating dangerously against the root beer's metal sides, testing my grip strength. The last ten minutes have been torture.

Absolute torture.

Once we established the body parts we have—don't get me started on that—for some reason, I asked if she had any moles. Because I told her I thought I had a mole on my thigh this morning, but it turned out to be some of the oatmeal I dropped while eating.

She told me she had no moles, but she has a birthmark on her inner thigh in the shape of a seahorse.

To which I replied, "Fascinating," and then asked if it was a boy or a girl seahorse. She was unsure, so then I said maybe she'd show me sometime and I could be the judge. This caused her cheeks to flush, which made me think of what I said.

Then I backtracked and told her I didn't want to peek in her pants. She said she didn't want me peeking in her pants, and then Frank patted me on the shoulder and asked if I needed a lifesaver, because I was drowning.

When Storee set up this plan, I thought it would be easy. She gave Florence her favorite thing in the world, applesauce, which of course always makes her blow out her diaper. She purposely forgot the second outfit so Betty had to sit next to me. She set it up. Now I'm just crashing and burning.

For a second there, when I was showing her a shirtless picture of myself and I saw the way she took me all in, I thought I was wooing her successfully. I was giving her all the woo, but boy, did that quickly fail.

When I give Storee the recap, I'll tell her Betty stared at my pecs and leave it at that. Can't let her think a poop explosion went to waste.

"What is a Steller's jay?" she asks.

"A bird that has a black head but a bright blue body. They're really pretty." *Like your eyes.* But I will *not* be saying that. *Keep that to yourself, man.*

"Oh, uh . . . no. I haven't explored the property much."

"You haven't?" I ask, my brows turning down.

"Just a little with Uncle Dwight, but I've stayed pretty set in the cottage."

"But don't you think if you're going to build this amazing farm, you should know more about the property?"

Don't worry. I see where I'm going wrong here, picking a fight that I should not be picking.

But who says they're going to put another person out of business without even knowing the land they're planning to use? Makes no sense to me.

"The snow is a little much at the moment," she says.

"Aren't you from Colorado?"

"Yes, but I grew up in Fort Collins, where you don't get as much snow as you get here up in the mountains. Do you ever leave Kringletown, or are you permanently fixed here, looking to break into innocent people's cottages?"

My expression falls. Through a clenched jaw, I say, "I was not breaking in. I was merely taking a gander."

"With a crowbar."

Steadily, I reply, "Because of the murderous bears. How many times am I going to have to say that?"

"For life," she answers. "For life."

"Seems like a harsh punishment for a misunderstanding."

"That was not a misunderstanding. That was you being a creep."

"I wasn't trying to be a creep," I reply, exasperated.

"Uh-huh, and what if I was naked when you were peeking in?"

"You weren't."

"But what if I was?" she asks, turning toward me.

Rolling my eyes, because what-ifs never pan out well, I say, "I would've enjoyed the show," before I can stop myself.

Her expression morphs into disgust. "Excuse me?"

Oh shit.

"Umm . . . what?" I ask, blinking.

"You said you would have enjoyed the show."

Time to backpedal.

"What show?"

"The naked show."

"Not sure what naked show you're talking about," I say, playing dumb.

"My naked show."

"Are you inviting me to watch a naked show you're putting on? Isn't that a little brazen?"

Her brow contorts. "What? No. I wouldn't want you seeing me naked."

"Then why are you inviting me to see your show? And for the record, I wouldn't want to see it either."

Now she frowns, because that was an insult.

Uh . . . time to backpedal some more.

"I mean . . . I would want to see you naked, but only if you were offering to let me see you naked. I wouldn't want to see it if you didn't want me to see it. But if you were showing me out of free will, like you wanted me to see everything, I'd look."

"You would look?" she asks.

"Yeah, I would look. Up and down. Take it all in. Every last inch." My mouth goes dry. "But because you want me to."

"I don't want you to."

"Great, because I don't want to," I say. "Unless you want me to . . ."

"What is even happening right now? I'm not going to be naked in front of you."

"Great, because I wasn't going to show you my nakedness either."

"Ew, I don't want to see you naked."

Ew?

Ew??

Well, that's fucking insulting.

She would be so lucky to see me naked.

"I have it on good authority that I have quite the body," I say, chin lifted.

"Doesn't mean I want to see it naked."

"Why not? I see it naked every day, and I think to myself, *Wow, I'm lucky*."

"You're deranged."

I clear my throat and look away, mumbling, "Yeah, well, you're not much better."

CHAPTER THIRTEEN
BETTY

NARRATOR: PAINFUL, DREADFULLY PAINFUL.

Max thought all he had to do was show up and talk to her, but what he forgot was he didn't know what to talk to her about. Nor did he realize that he'd be talking to someone who rambles just as much as he does.

Leaving their conversation a painful experience.

However, Frank and Leslie are having the time of their lives, even recording some of the conversation to listen to on the way back to Idaho Springs. They came for the fruitcake and are leaving with an awkward conversation to relive over and over again.

———

I owe him nothing. I can leave.

I can stand up from these bleachers right now and just leave without a farewell. Without even a glance in his direction.

After the whole naked thing—still feel like I'm going around in circles over that—I don't think he'd blame me if I left. I think he'd probably welcome it, and then he could kick back with Frank and Leslie over there and talk about what a disaster the last twenty minutes have been.

I think if I just stand, say *excuse me*, and take off without looking back, this could all just change within a blink of an eye. I can run to the local Myrrh-cantile, grab some alcohol, and try to wash away this day.

Maybe some cookies from Warm Your Spirits.

Perhaps some ice cream as well.

And some more two-liters, just in case he plans to stalk me again.

So then it's settled. I'm going to put everyone out of their misery and make my move.

On a deep breath, without saying a word, I stand from the bleachers with all the fortitude I can muster, and I'm about to turn to walk past Atlas when, to my dismay, he stands at the same time.

What the hell does he think he's doing?

He glances at me, looks me up and down with a confused expression, and in that briefest of moments, we silently stare each other down.

An unofficial challenge settling in between us.

Is he . . . is he bolting before I can bolt?

Before I can even ask, he turns and says, "Excuse me, Frank."

Frank and Leslie move out of the way, giving him a clear path of escape.

Insult thrashes through me as I watch his retreating back.

Oh no, he doesn't!

He thinks he's about to just walk out of here without a word, without saying goodbye?

Sure, I was going to do the same thing, but let's call a spade a spade. He's been nicer in this entire situation, and therefore, I hold him to a higher standard. Yes, I know. I heard it too, but I'm outraged, and you can't reason with someone who's outraged.

So before I can stop myself, I follow right behind, taking every step down the stairs that he's taking until we're both on the gym floor, heading toward the exit.

When he turns around to find me, his pace picks up.

Therefore, my pace picks up.

Together, we walk shoulder to shoulder, heading straight for the exit only for him to say, "Are you following me?"

"No." I walk past him and make my way out of the gym and into the chilly air.

"Then what are you doing?"

"Uh, I should ask you the same thing. What are you doing?"

"I was going to grab us a treat from the vendors. What are you doing?"

He . . . uh, what now? "Ummm . . ."

Okay, so maybe he wasn't leaving.

Maybe I'm the ass in this situation.

But hasn't that been the case the entire time?

"Betty . . . what were you going to do?"

Smiling like I'm a freaking horse, showing off my teeth, I say, "I was going to . . . uh . . . help you?"

He tilts his head to the side. "You were going to help me? All huffy and puffy like that?"

"Puffy?" I ask, blinking.

"Uh, like breathing *puffy*, not like *puffy*, you know, *puffy* referring to size. Just *huff and puff, blow your house down* kind of thing." He scratches his jaw. "But bringing it back to you. Why were you leaving?"

"I wasn't leaving."

"Yes, you were."

I shake my head. "No."

"Then why did you stand up when I stood up?"

Great question.

"Getting a better view. Really wanted a look at those fruitcakes going in the oven, because after all, that's where the magic happens, isn't it? Some people say magic happens in the bedroom. Not me." I shake my head. "I say magic happens in the bedroom, I mean . . . oven. It happens in the oven."

"Is that the truth?" he asks, looking genuinely curious.

"About magic happening in the oven?" I ask.

"No, about wanting a better view."

"I want to say yes." He eyes me suspiciously, so I clear my throat and bring it back to him. "Were you honestly getting us a treat from the vendors?"

"I want to say yes as well ..."

I gasp and then point at him. I knew it! "You were going to leave, weren't you?"

Flummoxed, he shoots right back, "Uh, so were you."

"Only to give us a reprieve from the mind-numbing conversation."

"*Mind-numbing* is a little harsh, don't you think?" he asks.

"What would you have called it?"

"Awkward and painful."

"How is that better?"

"Because I said it with charm, whereas you said it with disdain." He crosses his arms over his chest.

"Wow, you're arrogant."

His eyes widen. "I'm arrogant?" He points to his chest. "I've been nothing but civil toward you. Besides"—he holds up his finger—"that night I was trying to peek in, but I learned my lesson. So drop that."

"What about chasing me around your farm?"

"My God, it's like talking in circles with you." He pulls on his head. "For the love of God, realize that you're the one in the wrong in this scenario."

"What scenario? The leaving unannounced or ..."

"The entire scenario that we're in." He flails his arms around. "The one where you're trying to steal ideas from my farm and use them as your own."

"I'm not stealing ideas. I'm making sure not to make the same mistakes."

"What mistakes?" he shouts and raises his hands in the air. "Please, tell me what mistakes we're making. Because as far as I see it, we've been in business for an exceedingly long time."

"Well, since you asked," I say, holding out my hand and ticking my fingers off as I list the mistakes I've seen. "First and foremost, not having a paved parking lot. Dirt and snow create mud. Mud gets everywhere, even on the tree when you're dragging it out to your car. Also, not having fully paved sidewalks. There are some but not a lot, and if you want people to be able to access everything, you should really pave all avenues. Not to mention your suppliers are robbing you blind with extra charges, which is why you have to up-charge the fake trees. That's fine now, because you're the only place to get them besides Baubles and Wrappings, but even they have to up-charge. There are other, more earth-friendly suppliers that will provide more profit margin. Also, you serve one treat. Gingerbread. That screams a lack of knowledge of the Christmas treat industry. Sure, your vendors have some baked goods, but as the owner and proprietor, you should treat it as a Disneyland situation, providing customers with several options. And make them seasonal." I cross my arms over my chest, proud of myself. "That's just to name a few things I've noticed so far."

He stares at me, blinking. Unsure of what to say, because he knows I'm right. I've looked at what Evergreen Farm offers, and although it's a cute farm, there's so much more potential. Not having competition has made them complacent and, dare I say, lazy. Why implement alternatives when what they're doing seemingly works? I bet they haven't done a market analysis or research into other Christmas markets in years. If ever.

"Well . . . that's . . . informative," he says, his eyes racing as I can practically hear his brain attempting to calculate everything I said.

"Brother, what are you doing? Didn't think we'd see the reigning king at a Christmas Kringle competition until the passing of the crown," a guy who looks nothing like Atlas says as he comes up behind him. "Oh, who is this?"

I can see Atlas grow tight in the shoulders as another man walks up behind him.

"Who is who? Oh." Weathered eyes land on me, and a smile passes over his lips. "Yes, who is this?"

Atlas shakes who I'm going to assume are his brothers off him. "Ansel, Felix, this is Betty. Betty, these two morons are my brothers."

"Betty, it's nice to meet you. I'm Ansel." He takes my hand and shakes it but lingers a little longer than normal, causing Atlas to tug his brother's hand away.

And it's odd, because the man I was just talking to—the man chatting about naked shows—is not the man that I'm looking at right now. There's a darkness in his eyes, strength in his shoulders, like someone stuck a rod down his back and straightened him up to his full height.

There's a protectiveness about him.

It's . . . God, I don't even want to say it, but it's extremely attractive.

"Don't fucking hold her longer than normal," Atlas says.

"I wasn't." Ansel winks, and Atlas catches it.

He pushes his brother to the side. "And don't wink at her."

"Oh . . . are you two an item?" Felix asks, moving his fingers between the two of us.

"No," Atlas and I say at the same time.

"No?" Ansel asks. "Then why so protective?"

"Not protective. Just don't be a fucking fool around her, okay?" Atlas tugs on his hair, looking irritated. "Anyway, come on, Betty."

Come on?

Are we going somewhere?

Somewhere I don't know about?

"Where you going?" Ansel asks. "And can I get your number? Wouldn't mind taking you out on a date."

Atlas pauses and turns to his brother. "She wouldn't want to date you even if you were growing on her ass. Now get the fuck out of here." Then he takes my hand in his, enveloping my palm, and tugs me toward the parking lot, not giving me much chance to keep up with his long strides.

Umm, okay.

What's going on?

Because I have questions.

First of all, why are you holding my hand, sir?

Second, why are you so protective?

Third, and this one is for me, why do you like it?

When we are out of earshot, he mutters, "Where's your car?"

I answer nervously. "Uh, the Honda, over there."

Without another word, he pulls me toward my car and then brings me to the driver's side before letting go of my hand. He glances over my shoulder, most likely looking for his brothers, and then I see him relax.

What was that about?

He drags his hand over his face and blows out a heavy breath. "I'm sorry. They're idiots. I hope they didn't say anything to offend you."

"No . . . it was . . . it was fine."

"Are you sure? Because I know how they can be. And Ansel held your hand longer—"

"Really, it's fine," I answer.

He nods and rests his hands on his hips. "Okay. You sure?"

"Positive." I twist my hands together, unsure of what else to say as he stares down at me.

And I stare up at him.

Our eyes locked.

His chest falling up and down faster from his irritation.

My heart rapidly beating in my chest from the confusion I'm facing.

And then after a few seconds, he tugs on his hair and says, "Um, well, okay. I'll let you go. Sorry about earlier and the yelling and the awkward conversation and just, fuck, everything. Sorry about everything."

Thing I never expected to happen today: Atlas apologizing to me.

It doesn't feel right, because in the grand scheme of things, did he really do anything wrong?

"You don't need to apologize." I thumb behind me. "I was a jerk back there too."

"No." He shakes his head. "I was a bigger one. I made it weird by showing you a shirtless picture of myself."

Wow, really going far back with the apology.

And to be honest, didn't mind the shirtless picture. I learned some things from that picture . . . so many things.

"It's fine. The picture was fine."

"It wasn't," he says.

"But it was."

He looks me in the eyes. "Betty."

"Atlas," I say as his eyes don't leave mine.

He wets his lips.

His hands fit into the front pockets of his jeans.

And as we stand there, staring at each other, a heavy tension starts to build between us.

My palms start to sweat, his gaze far too strong.

My brain fixates on just how attractive he is. There is a slight curl to the ends of his chestnut brown hair. It seems like he shaved, but it just grew right back into a thick scruff. How he towers over me, his shoulders bulky with power, but he doesn't have any resemblance of an intimidation factor. Like he presents himself as someone not to mess with, but deep down, he's just . . . he's . . .

"Fuck," he grumbles, looking away and then pulling on the back of his neck. He clears his throat, and when his gaze meets up with mine once more, he quietly says, "I . . . I feel all out of sorts around you."

"What . . . what do you mean?" I ask.

He turns away, hands on his hips, truly looking like he's in distress. "I'm just . . . I'm having a hard time dealing with all this stuff." His eyes meet mine again. "I'm clearly not a fan of what you're trying to do. I think it's wrong, I think it's vindictive, and I don't understand why you're doing it, especially since you don't really know me or my family, but . . . Jesus Christ, Betty. I'm so fucking attracted to you that it's . . . it's fucking with my head."

Oh.

That's, um, that's unexpected.

"And I don't want my brothers near you, and I just sort of lost it back there, so I'm sorry."

Doesn't want his brothers near me?

Attracted to me?

Uh, that's one way to catch me completely off guard.

Not sure how to really respond, I say, "It's . . . it's fine."

"It's not." He blows out a frustrated breath. "Unlock your car."

"Huh?"

"Just unlock your car."

I reach for my keys in my purse and unlock my vehicle.

He opens the door for me and then gestures for me to get in. "Sorry that your day wasn't what you expected."

I take a seat in my car and say, "I'm . . . I'm sorry if I was rude back there."

"You weren't."

But I was. "Your farm is—"

He shakes his head. "Don't, okay? Just . . . let's not go there." Gripping the top of the door, he gently says, "Have a safe drive back."

Then he shuts my door, leaving me alone in my car, feeling . . .

Confused.

Nervous.

Slightly turned on.

Flattered.

Guilty.

Pretty much a gauntlet of emotions.

Shaking the thoughts and feelings out of my head, I put the key in the ignition, turn it over, and when the car doesn't start right away, I pause. Then I give it another turn. And another.

And another.

Noooo, not now.

I lean my head against the steering wheel just as there is a knock on my window, startling me. Of course, Atlas is standing there, hands in his pockets, so I open the door, and he asks, "Not starting?"

"No," I answer. "Um, do you happen to know anyone I can call?"

"Yeah, I'll shoot Kieran a text. He can come by and check it out." He pulls his phone from his pocket and starts texting. And the irony is not lost on me how it's so easy for someone like Atlas to text another person in town to help him out, whereas I have no ability to do that.

And once I start this project with Uncle Dwight, I won't have that ability either—because everyone will be against us.

"He says he's out on another trip right now and won't be back for about an hour or so. Told me to send him a pic of the car, and he'll come by a little later when he's back in town. Does that work?"

"Um, sure. I should probably call for an Uber or something."

The smallest of smirks plays on his lips. "Good luck. Not sure you'd be able to find one." He stuffs his phone in his pocket. "Come with me. I'll give you a ride back to your place."

"Oh, you don't have to do that."

"I'm headed that way anyway." He nods. "Come on."

"Um . . . okay."

I grab my purse and get out of my car. He holds his hand out, and I take it, only for him to chuckle. "I was actually looking for your keys."

"Oh my God," I say, embarrassment washing over me. "Of course. I'm so sorry."

"It's fine. Simple mistake. Anyone could have made it."

I hand him my keys, and he slips them under the driver's seat and then shuts the door.

"You can take my hand now if you want."

He holds his hand out, and it's really tempting. Super tempting actually, because I remember how it felt when he held it, but I shake my head instead.

"I'm fine."

"You sure?" He wiggles his eyebrows in a teasing way.

"Positive."

"All right, then come this way." He leads me toward a dark green truck, something that looks like it's been restored and well taken care of over the years. With tall tires and a boxier frame, it's definitely something I could picture him in. He walks over to the passenger side and opens the door for me.

"You don't have to do that," I say.

"I might not get along with you, but I'm still a gentleman . . . contrary to what your relative believes."

It's a low jab, but it seems to be a deserved one.

Once I'm in the truck, which took a hoist from me, I buckle up and wait for him to join. I take in the pristine interior. Clean, not a scrape or a scratch. Barely a speck of dirt. How does he keep it so clean working on a tree farm? I'd half expect the cab to be full of pine needles.

Though it does smell like a freshly cut tree, and if I were honest with myself, that's the scent that Atlas carries around with him.

He gets in on his side, an easy step up for his size, buckles up, and then the truck roars to life. "You chilly?" he asks.

"A little," I answer. So he turns on the heat for me and then twists the vents in my direction. "Thank you."

Guilt consumes me.

Consumes me.

Because let's review this. Minus the peeking-in-the-cabin thing, he's been . . . nice. He's been cordial. He's been helpful. He's been a little goofy. Maybe I'm missing something. Or . . . he could be playing me. I don't like to be that person, the cynic, because I like to think the glass is half-full all the time, but it's hard not to consider the change of behavior as something strange. But then there's what he said moments ago too.

"I'm just . . . I'm having a hard time dealing with all this stuff. I'm clearly not a fan of what you're trying to do. I think it's wrong, I think it's vindictive,

and I don't understand why you're doing it, especially since you don't really know me or my family, but . . . Jesus Christ, Betty. I'm so fucking attracted to you that it's . . . it's fucking with my head."

Ugh, I don't know. *He's* attracted to *me*? All six foot four of striking manliness attracted to, well, me? I'm not exactly unattractive, but I could imagine a man as good-looking as Atlas doesn't have to look far for a woman to fall at his feet. *Why am I thinking about this?*

"Everything okay over there?" he asks as he pulls out onto the road.

"Oh yeah. Just thinking."

"I know. You were muttering to yourself."

"Oh my God, was I?"

He smirks and makes a right-hand turn. "Yeah, you were."

"Did you hear what I was saying?"

"No, but were you thinking about me?"

"What? No, never. Why would I do that?"

He shrugs. "Just seemed like you were reflecting, but I could be wrong. Am I wrong?"

"I think you're wrong."

"Then I'm wrong."

"Great, you're wrong." I nod, even though he's right.

After a few seconds, he asks, "Then what were you thinking about?"

Crap.

Think of something quick.

Something that would make sense.

And something that would completely throw him off.

"Squirrels," I answer. *That's the first thing that came to mind?* He's going to ask why.

"Squirrels?" he asks. "You know, I don't think I've ever thought about squirrels so hard that I started muttering. I'm intrigued. Tell me more."

And there it is.

Saw it coming.

Here we go with the rambling.

"They're...uh...they're big bulkers."

"That's what you were thinking about? You were thinking about how they're big bulkers."

Make it make sense, Betty.

"Yes, because it keeps them warm," I answer. "Bulking up on all those nuts, because, ah, did you know that they bury their nuts to distract their predators but then don't dig them all up? Therefore, trees grow from squirrels burying all the nuts. Fascinating. The forest we live in could be because of squirrels."

"Huh," he says, looking thoughtful. "I never thought about squirrels in that way."

Oh God, why is he so innocent and cute? *Buying my story about squirrels. Ugh, Atlas.*

"Yup and, uh, to bring it full circle, I thought about the squirrels because they wouldn't need to have the car vents trained on them because they're all bulked up for the winter. If they were driving in this vehicle, they'd probably ask for the AC."

He chuckles. "Probably. Maybe even want sunglasses."

"And a blue Hawaiian shirt with surfboards on it. Maybe a necklace that says *On vacation.*"

"That would be one badass squirrel. I'd be friends with him."

"So would I, and I'd thank him for planting all the trees and compliment him on his weight."

"The one time it's acceptable," he replies.

"He'd probably high-five us and then hightail it out of here, no pun intended."

"Shame. Kind of wish the pun was intended. I like a good pun."

"Really?"

"Yeah, I'm terrible at creating them, but I think they're funny when told to me."

"Me too. My dad is good at puns, real quick on the draw. I don't know how he does it."

"People like that intimidate me, because how do their minds work that fast?"

"No idea. As you could see, my mind doesn't work unless I mouth what I'm thinking at the same time."

He laughs. "I'm probably just one step ahead of you, because instead of thinking my thoughts to myself, I let them out in the wild, only to drive everyone around me crazy with what's going on in my head."

"I do that too. Makes my mom crazy. She always tells me to not speak it unless I actually mean it, but what if I have to work the nonsense out? How can I do that in my head, where it gets all garbled? It's best to just let it all out verbally."

"Are we the same person? Because I see it the same way. Cole hates when I let loose on my thoughts. Then again, he's more of the quiet type and would rather sit in silence than have a conversation."

"I get that feeling from him. Funny that he and Storee are together, because she seems outgoing."

"Yeah, she brings it out of him. They're perfect for each other." He turns down the road that leads to both of our properties, a giant sign promoting Evergreen Farm on the right, reminding me of what I said.

"Um, sorry about the things I said about your farm back there. I know I apologized earlier, but it wasn't nice of me."

"Don't sweat it," he says as he passes his driveway and then turns down mine.

"I know, but I'm sorry."

He puts the car in park and then looks over at me. "Thanks, I appreciate it." He nods toward the cottage. "Need help getting out? I know it's a high step."

"No, I got it." But I don't reach for the door. Instead, I turn slightly toward him, a question on my mind that I can't seem to shake. "Why are you being nice to me?"

"Why am I being nice to you?"

"Yeah, I feel like . . . there's no reason to be nice to me given how I came into this town."

He shrugs. "It's who I am, Betty. I think maybe if you got to know me better, you'd see that." Then he gets out of the car, moves to my side, and opens my door for me. His eyes lift up to mine, and he holds his hand out.

Feeling breathless and guilty simultaneously, I take his hand, and he helps me down. When I look up at him to thank him, I notice how much taller he is. Probably about a foot, and yet he's not as intimidating as you'd think, given his height.

He's gentle.

"Thank you."

"Yup," he says, sticking his hand in his back pocket. "Okay, uh, see you around."

"Yeah, see you around."

And then he takes off, getting back in his truck and pulling away.

What happened between him and Uncle Dwight? I feel like I'm missing something, because the impression Dwight gave me compared to the way Atlas really is, well, it's confusing.

MAX

Storee: Meet me in the tree house. Be there soon. Be stealthy!

I glance over my shoulder, making sure no one is watching, and then I climb the ladder to the tree house that Cole and I have been working on for Florence. We're almost done; we just need some wallpaper on the interior, because if we're going to build one, we're doing it right. And sure, she's too young right now to be in here by herself, but when she gets a little older, it's going to be her clubhouse, and I'm glad I could be a part of putting it together for her.

I make my way into the clubhouse and then sit up against the wall to stay out of view. It's only a minute or so of waiting before I hear Storee approach. I hold my breath, hoping it's her and not Cole, because I would need to do a lot of explaining if he found me in here. My brain is too maxed out to offer up any lies.

Thankfully though, Storee pokes her head up and over the side, and then climbs in.

"Is this our secret hideout?" I ask as she takes a seat in the back with me and pulls out two small bags of Crunch Tators, handing me one before also pulling out a juice box. "Wow, look at you bringing the snacks."

"I was hungry, and I didn't think you'd appreciate me eating in front of you." She glances around the tree house. "This could be our secret hideout. Works for me. Cole thinks I'm over helping Aunt Cindy right now."

"Is she your excuse for everything?"

"Pretty much," she answers. "He doesn't even second-guess it."

"Sometimes, I feel bad for how clueless he is," I say as I pop a Crunch Tator in my mouth.

"Me too." She smirks and then says, "So tell me everything."

"First of all, is Flo okay?"

"She's great. Cole, though, is slightly traumatized from the blowout, but he always is. He was asking why I'd give her applesauce before we left for an event, and I said because she loves it. He couldn't argue with that."

"Very calculated."

"Did it work?"

"Ehhh, I don't know. I have to tell you, we're both awkward."

"Yeah, I know. It's why I think it's so funny that you're trying to woo her. It's like wooing yourself."

"To woo myself would be easy. I'd stick a gingerbread house in front of me and tell me to go wild. Done and done."

"I think it would take more than that, but we won't get into it. Tell me how it went."

"Crash and burn at first. I won't bore you with the details, but fuck, was it painful. I happened to show her a topless picture of myself in my short shorts right off the bat, which made things weird, and we didn't talk much. I couldn't think of things to say, and when we did talk, it was some random off-the-wall rambling. To the point that I was like, *Let me just get out of here and end it for the both of us, reset, and try again.* Well, she happened to have the same thought, and we left at the same time. Then we got in a fight about it, which then led to us running into my idiot brothers. Ansel immediately started hitting on her, I got pissed and jealous, and then I took her hand and led her to her car."

Storee is eating her Crunch Tators and listening intently.

"I told her I found her attractive, shocked her completely, and then she decided to leave. Only her car wouldn't start, so then I called for help and then took her back home in my truck. She apologized, I think I said it was okay, she asked why I was nice to her, I told her she should get to know me, and then I peaced out."

"Um, wow, that's . . . that's a lot to take in. And you think it went well? You'd call that a success?"

"Absolutely," I say with a positive smile. "First, she saw me with my shirt off, and she saw my package, so she knows I'm big everywhere."

"Gross."

"Hey." I point at her. "My body is something I can offer. I'm not ashamed to use it. And you should have seen her eyes. Wide and fixated on the goods. Proud to say, I impressed. Then she saw my protective side. Saw how nice I was. Saw how I could take care of her. I held her hand at one point. I was all over the place with the wooing, but the wooing happened. And it was great. She was so into it. Smiling, and let me tell you, when she did smile, fuck, it was gorgeous. She has this little crinkle in her nose when she smiles. But she also gets it when she's angry too. And . . .

sometimes when she's trying to think of what to say. Oh, and get this, when she's thinking, she mouths what she's thinking. Isn't that funny?"

Storee's smile grows even wider as she wipes her fingers on a napkin she brought. "That is funny."

"Yeah, I thought so." I look off through the window, thinking about Betty muttering about squirrels. "And did you know she knows a lot about squirrels? I thought that was fascinating. I mean, you see squirrels every day, but you never truly think about the impact they have on the world until someone educates you on them, and consider me educated."

"Oh?" Storee asks, still smiling.

"Yeah, we have them to thank for partial planting of our forests. They're doing the real work out there, and we're not even offering them an appreciative nod. Well, next time I see a squirrel, I'll be sure to thank them for their service in reforestation." I let out a sigh. "Anyway, I think I made progress."

"I'd say so," she says as she pops her straw in her juice box. "Great progress."

"Yeah, so what's next?"

"I mean, we should definitely get you some more face time with her. Like you said earlier, she needs to get to know you."

"She does. I think the more she gets to know me, the better off we'll be."

"Could not agree more. So here's what I have planned . . ."

CHAPTER FOURTEEN

MAX

NARRATOR: *DO YOU SMELL THAT?*

Is love possibly in the air?

The beginnings of a budding relationship?

From the hearts in Max's eyes when he was recollecting his time with Betty, I'd say there's a budding relationship, even if he's clueless about it at the moment. He'll get there, trust me, he'll get there.

But Max isn't the only one playing a ruse. No, now with Storee's firsthand observation of how Max talked about Betty, she's on a mission of her own. A mission to get the two together. Because she's known Max for a few years now, and she's never seen him talk about someone the way he spoke about Betty.

Because squirrels, really? He was gushing about squirrels?

Our boy has it bad.

Let's see what Storee has planned.

Max: I'm sweating. Cole's going to be pissed.

Storee: I'll handle him. You worry about yourself. Bring your A game. Got it?

Max: I will, but . . . Cupid Christmas Night? This is your sacred night with Cole.

Storee: I wouldn't call it sacred. Now stop worrying. See you in a few.

I pocket my phone and sit on a bench in Ornament Park. The exact bench Storee told me to sit on to wait for Betty to show up.

I can see this being a disaster. The other night, we went over a few ideas, and she was stuck on this one, said it would be perfect, but I had my doubts, still do. Cupid Christmas Night is a special night Kringle puts on every year. The date varies depending on the calendar and vendors, but it just so happened to land on tonight.

Every year, the town comes together and centers the event around the theme of love during Christmas It's for couples only, no kids, and there are themed cocktails, mistletoe everywhere, shareable foods, and even a walkway called Lovers' Lane.

I've brought a few dates over the years—no one too serious—but this was the night that Cole and Storee kissed—reluctantly—for the first time, so I'm not sure how my best friend will feel about this.

Hands stuffed in my jacket pockets, I watch couples walk hand in hand around the different vendors set up in Ornament Park. It's a little different this time. In the past, they've made maps to direct individuals to each business in town, which was great, because it brought in an impressive amount of business. But from what I've heard, there's been a lot of overcrowding in the past few years, given the popularity of the event with people coming from out of town, so they've brought some of the businesses into Ornament Park. They've each set up a booth to represent their business and offer a few different options from their offerings rather than all of them, which is harder work in a temporary site.

From what Tanya was telling me, everyone likes this format better.

"Oh, Atlas, what are you doing here?" Storee asks, startling me out of my thoughts.

"Hey, you two," I say, standing from the bench. "My brothers told me to meet them down here." I look around, playing up my acting skills. "But it seems like maybe they were teasing me and have left me alone on Cupid Christmas."

"Were you going to romance the night away with your brothers?" Cole asks, looking me up and down.

"No." I adjust my reindeer hat. "They were bringing dates and were going to bring one for me."

"Ouch," Storee says. "Stood up by someone you don't know."

"Yeah, kind of afraid she got one look at me and bolted."

"I could believe that, since you're wearing that hat," Cole says.

"Cole," Storee chastises him. "Be nice. He's clearly upset."

"He doesn't look too upset," Cole says, studying me.

"Trying to keep it together, man, but thanks for the concern."

"Do you want to join us?" Storee asks, right on cue.

"Uh, no," Cole says, shaking his head. "Not happening. He *does not* want to join us."

"Cole, he's your best friend."

"Yeah, and this is not the first time he's been stood up," Cole says.

Uh, I beg your pardon.

"He'll be fine. This night is about us."

"When have I been stood up before?" I ask, offended.

Cole shrugs. "I don't know. Just seems like something that would happen to you."

Fucking rude.

"I think you're remembering your past dating life, not mine." I rock on my heels. "This fella is a real ladies'—Betty," I say, surprised to see her this early in the night as she approaches Storee, looking cutely confused. "You're . . . you're here, in Ornament Park. That's . . . uh, that's swell. Great to, uh, see you. Looks like you're all bundled up and warm, which is important because it's a cold one. Very cold. Cold enough for shrinkage, you know?"

Betty looks at me, a little frightened, slightly startled. I don't blame her, because shrinkage? Really, man?

"You know, because we talked about shrinkage last time we saw each other. Just bringing it full circle." I loop my finger around and let out a whistle. "Um, anyway, comedians do it, but I'm not much of a comedian, are you? Eh, don't answer that. Anyway, um . . . hey, nice shoes."

As a group, we all glance down at her boots and then back up at each other.

"Umm, thank you."

Cole leans in and whispers, "You were saying something about being a ladies' man?"

"Shut . . . the . . . fuck . . . up," I whisper through clenched teeth.

Betty glances around our small circle and asks, "Uh, did I get the night wrong? As I was walking over here, it seems like this is a special night for couples?"

"Oh my goodness, did I tell you to meet me tonight?" Storee asks. "Ugh, I'm sorry. I meant tomorrow. Gosh, the lack of sleep is getting me these days. I'm sorry."

"Oh. That's okay. I can, uh . . . I can meet up tomorrow."

"No, no, don't be silly. You look so nice," Storee says. "Why don't you stay? Atlas was actually just telling us how he was stood up . . ."

"What are you doing?" Cole asks, leaning toward his wife.

Ignoring the looming ogre at her shoulder, Storee claps her hands together and says, "Ooo, maybe we can all hang out together."

Cole's grumpy expression deepens.

"I would hate to have wasted your night, and Atlas is feeling kind of glum from being stood up. Might be fun."

"I could think of something more fun," Cole adds, not being subtle at all. What a friend. I've been stood up, and he doesn't seem to care.

"I mean, I wouldn't mind some company," I say, joining in on the plan that Storee and I worked up together in the tree house. Everything seems to be falling into place. Just need Betty on board. It's a long shot, but there might be a chance she stays, and if she doesn't, I know Cole is kicking my ass to the curb.

Hell, I think he wants to do it right now, by the way he's looking at me. He's trying to communicate silently, telling me to go home and leave him to a peaceful night with his wife, child-free. *Sorry, man, a guy's got to do what a guy's got to do.*

#MustSaveTheFarm

Betty glances at all of us, but then her eyes land on me. "Were you really stood up?"

I shrug, trying to play it off as if I'm not too hurt about it. "Yeah. My brothers were playing a trick on me. Should have known. Told you they weren't fun to be around."

"Oh, that's not very nice."

"Yeah, they're not very nice guys," I add. And then just to really pull off the sad-guy effect, I toe the ground with the tip of my boot.

"So what do you say?" Storee butts in. "We can all walk around, make a night of it. I can treat you both to some dinner since we had to ditch you last time we were all together."

"I mean, I don't want to intrude," Betty says.

"Me either," I add, attempting to portray a solemn appearance.

"Oh, you're not at all." Storee waves us off. "It'll be fun. Come with me, Betty. We'll start the night with some drinks."

She takes Betty by the arm and directs her toward the Prancer's Libations booth. It's the local bar in town run by one of the beloved couples, Frank and Thachary Lamb—and no, not the Frank from Idaho Springs.

When they're out of earshot, Cole gets really close to me. He could practically lick my neck if he wanted. "What the fuck was that?"

Taking a step back, because, *dude, personal space,* I answer, "What was what?"

"That ambush."

"What ambush?" I play dumb, and trust me, I'm good at it.

"The one where I'm about to enjoy a nice evening with my wife, and then you go and show up."

"Uh, excuse me, I didn't show up. You two ran into me while I was licking my stood-up wounds. I'm sorry if my brothers are dicks and set me up for failure. You know how they can be."

Cole sighs, because he does know. Cole has always been more of a brother to me than my actual brothers. They're closer in age, they started a business together, and they've always been two peas in a pod, while I've been the outsider. I truly believe it's one of the reasons why I attached to Cole the way that I did, because he felt like the brother I was always looking for.

"Yeah, I know." He drags his hand over his face. "Can you at least . . . depart after, like, an hour? Give Storee and me some time alone?"

"I can manage that."

"Thanks." He sticks his hands in his pockets and then asks, "What was all that rambling about shrinkage?"

"Dude, don't ask."

BETTY

Okay, this is awkward.

This is a night for couples—it clearly states that on the signs I saw when I was walking toward Ornament Park. Cupid Christmas. And from the drink themes alone, I know this is a night for lovers, and I really shouldn't be here, but Storee clearly wouldn't let me just walk away.

"Are you sure you want me to stay?" I ask Storee as she takes our drinks from the bartenders and hands me two cups.

"Of course. I feel so stupid that I mixed up the nights. I think I was just thinking, *Oh, I get to get dressed up for two nights,* and completely forgot what I was doing."

"It's fine. I seriously can just meet up tomorrow."

"Don't be silly. This will be fun."

She leads the way back to the men, who seem to be joking around, because Atlas laughs at something Cole says while Cole smirks. I don't know much about them, but from an outsider looking in, their relationship seems special.

Really special.

There's a connection there that you don't see very often, something I don't see Uncle Dwight have with anyone.

I met up with him yesterday, and I talked about how I was impressed that even the high school was decorated. I failed to mention the whole bumping-into-Atlas thing, because I'm sure he wouldn't be happy about it. We talked about a few other things, like decorations that could be displayed year-round and could bear the harsh Colorado winter in the Rockies but also the blazing sun in the summer. I avoided all conversation about Atlas, even though I had a bunch of questions I wanted to ask.

Like . . . where did the hate stem from? What did he do to him?

Has he thought about possibly doing something else with the land other than a competing farm?

"Thanks, babe," Cole says, taking his drink from Storee and kissing her.

"Um, here you go," I say to Atlas, handing him his drink.

"Thanks, babe," he says with a wink, clearly mocking Cole, but it doesn't stop my entire body from heating up and reacting to the term of endearment.

"This is the best mulled cider you will ever have," Storee says as she cuddles into Cole. He loops his arm around her and holds her in tight. It's so cute, it makes me yearn for something like that. "The first time I had it was on Cupid Christmas Night with Cole, but technically we weren't together. We were pretending to be together."

"Really?" I ask, amused. "Why?"

"Long story, but it was for show. Let's just say the night was not enjoyable."

"Until they kissed," Atlas says, gently bumping my shoulder with his arm. "And they did it in front of the two biggest gossips in town, who of course went around and told everyone."

"Who are the two biggest gossips?" I ask.

"Martha and Mae Bawhovier," Atlas answers. "The sweetest sisters you will ever meet, but you have to watch what you say around them, because it will be repeated to everyone in town."

"It wasn't planned to kiss in front of them," Cole says after taking a sip of his mulled cider.

"Uh, they were the ones who egged us on," Storee says and then leans toward me. "Let me tell you, he was desperate to kiss me."

I turn to Cole for his rebuttal, but he just shrugs. "Yeah, I was."

Atlas chuckles. "He was desperate to kiss her for a long time. He saw his moment, and he took full advantage."

"That's sweet," I offer.

"It was." Storee stands on her toes and then kisses Cole, clearly so happy and so in love.

I've had my fair share of boyfriends, but I don't think I've ever looked at someone the way they look at each other. Something to strive for when I have my life on track. Right now, it's all kind of up in the air.

"What about you? Ever kiss under the mistletoe?" Storee asks.

I shake my head. "Never. Though I don't think I've ever been around mistletoe before. It wasn't a thing my family did, and I love Fort Collins, but it's not small and quaint like Kringletown, where you can hang up mistletoe and people would find it charming. It would probably go undetected there."

"Yeah, must be more of a small-town thing," Storee says. "Be careful though. It's everywhere here, especially on Cupid Christmas, and if you're caught under some and someone says, 'Kiss,' you have to kiss. Which is why this big guy got a chance at these lips."

"Oh, really?"

"Yeah," Atlas chimes in. "One year, I had to kiss Cole, and honestly, all I can say is that I was very underwhelmed. I can't believe Storee fell for him after their kiss, because what I experienced was stiff and lacking in passion."

I chuckle while Cole rolls his eyes. "You wish you kissed me."

"Don't tempt me," Atlas says. "I might pull you under some mistletoe and knock those boots right off your feet."

"Would love to see you try."

"Challenge accepted."

"Please don't," Storee says. "I don't need my husband falling for your luscious lips."

I glance at his mouth, and yeah, she's right. He does have some very nice-looking lips.

Atlas playfully brings his hand to his chest. "'Luscious lips'? Wow, Storee, you're going to inflate my ego."

"Yeah, please stop. We don't need him suffocating us all, especially if this was supposed to be a night for us alone."

"Wow, way to guilt-trip Betty and me," Atlas says, thumbing toward me. "I get stood up, and your wife confuses the nights. You would think we'd receive a touch of understanding, maybe a sprinkle of coddling."

"I've coddled you enough over the years."

"Yeah, maybe that's why I'm so sensitive."

Cole shakes his head. "No, you were sensitive when I first received you."

"Received me, huh?" Atlas asks with a smile written all over his face as he takes a sip of his drink. "And how did you enjoy . . . *receiving* me?" The question is full of innuendo and makes me chuckle.

"What is wrong with you?"

"I ask myself that in the mirror every day."

MAX

"Okay, I never thought Christmas nachos were a thing, but oh my God, they're a thing," Betty says as she takes another chip from the big platter we ordered to share.

High-top tables have been set up all around Ornament Park with the intention that people spend their money at the vendors and then take a walk down Lovers' Lane. So far, we're spending money.

We're on our second cup of mulled cider, we're devouring nachos, and honestly, I'm having a great time. Storee is leading the conversation like she said she would, so I wouldn't have to think of stupid things to say to fill the awkward silence, and it's all running very smoothly. I'm adding little anecdotes here and there, coming off as a great person to be around. Cole seems to be enjoying himself, and Betty has laughed quite a few times.

If I didn't know any better, I'd say she's having a good time.

"They're more like Thanksgiving nachos if you ask me," Storee says. "But they work."

"The sausage and stuffing and cranberry make it more like Thanksgiving, but the wreath shape, that screams Christmas," Betty says, sounding more . . . loose than normal.

I don't blame her though; the mulled cider is strong. I'm feeling a little loose too.

"I like the sausage," Cole says. "Not too spicy."

"No one likes a spicy sausage," I say with a smirk.

"In fact, they don't." Storee chuckles. "I mean, I certainly don't. What about you, Betty? Do you like a spicy sausage in your mouth?"

Betty picks up another chip and shakes her head. "I don't. I once had a spicy sausage in my mouth that made me gag."

The table pauses, all staring at her, wondering whether that was an innuendo or not.

When she looks up, seeing all of us staring at her, she clamps her hand over her mouth and then chuckles. "I mean like an actual sausage, not like, you know . . . a penis sausage. Not that I'd ever call a penis a sausage. I haven't seen any in real life that really resemble the kind of sausages I've seen, in the girth department at least, but you didn't ask that, so I don't know why I'm saying it." She looks away and sips her drink.

"I'm sorry that you gagged on a sausage," I say, trying to make her feel less awkward.

"It was really big. Hard to get my mouth around."

"I understand that completely," I say. "I've had a hard time getting my mouth around some sausages as well."

She looks up at me, confused.

"Uh, like actual sausages, not . . . the penis variety, just want to keep that clear. Just talking about food, because if we weren't, then I'd have to say I prefer tacos, if you get my drift. Yup, a taco guy over here, and you're a, uh, a sausage girl?"

"Yes, purely sausage, although I once kissed a taco."

"Really?" I ask, feeling Cole and Storee watching us.

Betty's eyes widen. "I mean, ugh, not like *taco vagina* or the food *taco*, I meant *taco* as referring to a woman. Like a woman can have a taco, and a man can have a sausage or vice versa or whatever part you want. Ugh, I shouldn't assign genders to food . . . To clear things up, I've kissed a woman before. It was a dare in college."

"What is happening?" I hear Cole mutter.

"Magic," Storee says, clasping her hands together.

"Are they the same person?"

"Yes," Storee answers.

"I kissed a woman too, a few times," I say with a nod. "And I've kissed

Cole on the cheek, not on the lips, even though I joked about it. And you've kissed a man . . ." I gesture to Betty.

"Oh yes, lots of times. I've touched many lips with my lips."

"Hey, so have I!" I say, pointing to my chest.

Cole rubs his temple. "Please, someone change the subject."

"So to sum it up, you once gagged on a spicy sausage, you haven't experienced a girthy penis, you kissed a girl once, but you prefer a man's lips on yours," I say.

"Yes, that pretty much sums it all up. And you've kissed many a woman but only Cole on the cheek."

"Yup," I answer. "Wow, we're good listeners."

"I'd say so." Betty nervously smiles and then takes a sip of her drink. I join her while silence falls among the group.

Well, that was going well for a second.

BETTY

I'm very aware right now of just how large Atlas is.

Like . . . very aware.

I don't know whether it's the mulled cider, or if I've just finally given myself enough time to pay attention, but man, is he large. Those shoulders, they're like two sets of mine put together. And his legs, they're nearly busting out of his jeans. Like tree trunks sprouting from his hips. Not to mention his chest. It's so expansive. How does one grow themselves to be that big? Does he have a hard time finding clothes to fit him?

In reality, he's not that much bigger than Cole, but to me, Cole feels like a good size, and Atlas is like . . . the giant who fell down from the beanstalk and has decided to live among the peasants.

And sure, I might be on my third mulled cider, and things are feeling a little hazy, slightly distorted, but I'm still very much aware . . . aware of his size.

"You're so big," I say, looking up at him as we all share some cookies that Cole grabbed from a local vendor.

Atlas glances down at himself and then back at me. "I grew myself."

"It's very impressive. You did a wonderful job."

"Thank you. You didn't grow that much."

"I know." I lean my chin on my hand. "Can you believe that? What was I thinking?"

"I don't know. Maybe you were concerned about other things . . . like . . . like growing that pretty face."

I smile. "Aw, was that a flirtatious compliment?"

"I'd say just a compliment. How could I ever flirt with the enemy?" He winks.

"You're right. You could never flirt with the enemy." I sigh and then turn to Cole and Storee. "Do you guys think I'm a jerk?"

"Yes," Atlas says.

I shove at his rock-hard chest, not even moving him a millimeter. "I wasn't speaking to you."

"Don't stifle my opinion like you're trying to stifle my farm." He chuckles, but I ignore the deep rumble and focus on Storee and Cole.

"I'm not trying to be a jerk."

"I don't think you're a jerk," Storee says, causing both Cole and Atlas to stare her down. "What? I don't." Storee shrugs. "She's clearly hearing information from someone who's not telling the truth, and she's trying to do right by them. I think she just needs to situate herself in the town a little more, and then she'll make the right decision." Storee winks at me.

"You see, I was thinking the same thing," I say, pointing to my chest. "I don't want to say it, because I'm supposed to not like this guy right here"—I jolt my thumb in Atlas's direction—"but I don't see why Uncle Dwight hates him so much."

"Thank you." Atlas slams his hand against the high-top table. "I'm a delight, right?"

"You're . . . you're nicer than I thought you would be," I say. "Then you could be being nice to me because you think you can change my mind about the farm."

"Can I?" he asks, so much hope in his eyes that it's actually cute.

"I don't know." I sigh. "I don't even know what I'm doing to be honest." I lift up my cup and take a sip. "This is getting depressing. Maybe I should leave."

"No, don't leave. We want you here," Storee says. "Right, boys?"

"I wouldn't mind if both of them left," Cole says, clearly wanting alone time with his wife.

"That's fine. I can take off." I down the rest of my cider. "Umm, perhaps there is a shuttle service off to the farm?"

"How about we get some water and walk it off?" Atlas suggests.

I look him up and down. "Just you and me?"

"I'd love that. Great idea," Cole says and then takes Storee by the hand. "Have a great night."

And before Storee can even get a word in, they take off, leaving me alone with Atlas.

"Wow, that was . . . that was a quick exit," I say.

Atlas's gaze trails after them. "Yeah, I don't think I've ever seen him move that quickly before." He brings his attention back to me. "Well, shall we?" He gestures to a booth that's selling water, and I nod.

He purchases us a bottle each, even though I tried to pay, and then together, we head toward the river that runs behind Santa's house and butts up at the base of the mountainside. I believe they call it the riverwalk. But it's lit up this evening with even more lights than usual, forming a long tunnel of all different colored lights.

It's beautiful.

"You grew up with this?" I ask, marveling as we approach the tunnel.

"I did," Atlas says. "And oddly, it never gets old."

"Really? You never get tired of all the Christmas decorations and music and the holly jolliness?"

He shakes his head. "No, because it's a special time of the year. It's when the most magic happens, and I like seeing everyone experience that magic. It's one of the pleasures of working on the farm. Watching families pick out their perfect tree, making gingerbread houses, going on sleigh rides . . . petting the reindeer. I might live in that element, but for some people, it's their first time seeing it, experiencing it, and I just love experiencing their joy."

That makes me stop because . . . how?

How is this the same man that Uncle Dwight has said is a horrible human being? I don't get it. The stories don't align.

"You okay?" he asks.

"Just . . . confused," I say.

"Why?" he asks.

"Because you're just . . . you're not what I expected."

"I told you, you need to get to know me."

"Yeah, you did."

"And now that you are, what are you finding?"

I take a sip of my water and tilt my head as I look up at him. "That you're sweet. That you're goofy. That you and I seem like the same rambling person."

He chuckles. "Yeah, that's true."

"That you're sensitive, a good friend, someone who is welcoming to all."

"I mean, I'm not going to steer you wrong on that."

I chuckle. "You're making it hard not to like you."

His brows raise, and he leans in a little. "Are you saying . . . I'm not on your hate list?"

"I don't have a hate list, but if I were to have a hate list, your name would not be on it."

The smile that crosses his lips nearly makes me weak in the knees. Consider me almost fainting. What did they call it in historical times? Swooning?

Yup, I'm swooning.

"Well then, I think that's cause for celebration." He holds out his hand, and I stare down at it for a moment. When I don't take it, he reaches for my hand and interlaces our fingers together.

Nervous, I ask, "What kind of celebration?"

"A true Kringle celebration."

"What does that entail?"

"Well, you want to learn what this town is about, right?"

"Yes." I nod.

"Then it's time to experience it, but you have to give in to the entire experience. Think you can do that?"

I wet my lips, knowing if Uncle Dwight ever knew about this, he'd probably murder me, but then again, the temptation is real. I can always pass it off as research, getting close to the enemy. He doesn't have to know it's because I truly, desperately want to see Atlas smile again.

"And what constitutes the whole experience?"

He smirks. "Everything. Traditions, food, music, shopping…everything."

I mull it over, giving it some thought, only for him to squeeze my hand.

"Come on. Say yes. I promise it will be fun."

I have no doubt about that.

He's a fun guy. I can see that already from the time I've spent with him.

"You know you want to," he jokingly says, and he's right.

I do.

I really do.

I oddly want to see where this night could take us. I want to learn about the Kringle traditions. I want to spend just a touch more time with him, even though Uncle Dwight would probably have a heart attack, but he's not here.

It can't hurt, right?

"Okay, yeah, let's do it."

A large smile stretches across his lips before he nods toward the sky and says, "Then look up."

My eyes trail up his body, past his face, and right up to the sky where a bundle of greenery hangs over us.

But not just any bundle of greenery.

No, it's mistletoe.

How on earth did I miss that?

Before I can ask, he pulls me in by the hand, wraps his arm around my waist, and then tilts my chin up. Warmth spreads through me as his beautiful eyes connect with mine, anticipation and promise beaming from them.

"Tell me no," he says, his hand carefully sliding up my neck.

Oh God, this . . . this was not what I was expecting, but . . . tell him no?

He wants me to tell him no?

How could I possibly tell him no?

Ever since Storee mentioned his lips, it's what I've been thinking about all night. It's what I've been stealing glances of.

And in my semidrunk state, there's no way I'd be able to turn him down.

"Why would I say no?" I ask, making that smile reappear again, right before he grips my cheek and lowers his lips to mine. On a sharp intake of breath, our mouths connect, and I feel myself melt into him.

My hand to his chest.

His thumb pressing my chin up.

My legs feeling wobbly beneath me.

And just as I settle in for more, he pulls away.

It was just a peck, loose-lipped and no tongue, but the damage has been done, because as he releases me, my eyes slowly open back up. When my gaze meets his, I know for a fact that I'm in a whole lot of trouble.

Because that kind of kiss is not something I will forget anytime soon.

CHAPTER FIFTEEN
MAX

NARRATOR: THE SETTING WAS RIGHT, *the mood was perfect, and it was a moment that he—*

"*Hey, pardon me, sorry to interrupt this storytelling of yours, but dude, major props to you for letting me get a kiss in at that moment. Honestly, wasn't sure where you were going with that whole taco-sausage thing—it was looking really downhill there for a bit—but fuck, a kiss. That was amazing.*"

Narrator: I'm glad you appreciated it.

"*Great timing. No one likes waiting until the end of a story for a kiss. Think you can squeeze in some more? Her lips are fucking amazing.*"

Narrator: I will see what I can do.

"*Okay, no pressure or anything. You do you. You're at the helm. I'm just here, waiting for your command.*"

Narrator: And with every compliment you give me, your chances of having a really good time with Betty are increasing . . . drastically.

"*Really? Did I happen to mention I was into food play like Cole? Though can we do something different, something that's not a candy cane? That's so last year.*"

Narrator: We have some time before that. Just . . . hang in there.

"*Right, sorry. Getting ahead of myself. Sorry to interrupt. Just wanted to say, awesome job.*"

Narrator: And once again, this is why you're my favorite.

"Which one?"

"I don't know," Betty cutely says as she scans the wooden ornaments in BKJ's vendor booth. "They're all so good."

"You can take all of them, but that might cost you a pretty penny," I say.

"Yeah, which I don't have." She examines the one of a house with a wreath carved above the front door that she keeps going back to. "This one is just so intricate and beautiful, and this will sound lame." She turns to look up at me. "But buying a house ornament the first year I'm in Kringle for the Christmas season feels symbolic in a way, like I'm accepting this town as my new home."

"Yeah, I like that, and not lame at all," I say as I move in behind her and pluck the ornament I was looking at from the booth. It's of a Christmas tree in the back of a truck that resembles mine. I swear he carved this ornament just for me. "I think this is the one I will go with."

"Ooo, I like that one. It's very . . . you."

"That's what I was thinking as well," I say and then gently take her ornament from her hand.

"What are you doing?" she asks.

"Buying them."

"You don't need to buy my ornament, Atlas."

"I told you we were going to experience this town, right?" I ask.

"Yes, but how is that experiencing the town?"

"Because in Kringle, you will find that we're all giving and welcoming, and we want people to find joy in the season, so this is a way for you to see that." From the curve in her lip, I can see she is barely buying my load of crap, but hey, she doesn't stop me as I carry the ornaments over to BKJ.

With a jolly smile, he takes them from me and asks, "Having a good night, you two?"

"I'd say so. What do you think, Betty?" I nudge her playfully.

"I am," she says softly, smiling.

"I'm glad. Nice to see you two enjoying each other." He rings me up, I pay, and then he hands me a small paper bag with both ornaments. "I thought of you when carving that ornament, Max."

"I was wondering."

"Glad it found its way to you." He offers us a wink. "Taking them to the tree?"

"Yup," I say. "Got to teach Betty about the town."

"Couldn't think of a better person to do that." He looks at Betty and says, "You're in good hands."

"I hope so," she says as she looks up at me with those soulful eyes.

I smile down at her and say, "You are." Then I turn to BKJ and say, "Have a good night, man."

"You too. And merry Christmas." He offers us a wave with his meaty paw, and I take Betty's hand again and direct her toward the center of Ornament Park.

"What tree is he talking about?" Betty asks.

You know, I have to admit, she's extremely cute, especially when she's not grumbling at me. When she's in a good mood, her personality shines through, along with her smile . . . and those lips.

Those lips that I want more of.

And thankfully, this town is presenting me another opportunity to indulge. Before I answer her about the tree, we walk through a gate and pause. A confused expression crosses her face right before I pull her in at the waist.

"Wh-what are you doing?" she asks, her hand falling to my chest to catch her balance.

Feeling like a lucky motherfucker, I point up, showing her the mistletoe.

"Oh," she says right before another smile tilts her lips up.

I take that as a go-ahead, and I bring my mouth back down to hers, letting myself relish in her lips again.

Fuck, they're so goddamn soft. So tentative. So fucking perfect that if I wasn't afraid that I'd push her too far, I'd spend hours under every goddamn sprig of mistletoe in this town, making out with her, exploring her mouth, and only letting up for air.

But because this is all new, I pull away quickly, reluctantly. This isn't about me. This is about her, giving her a taste, showing her the kind of man I am.

When her eyes slowly open—again—her gaze finds mine, and she slowly tastes her lips. "That was . . . unexpected."

I smile down at her. "Just giving you the experience."

Hand in hand and telling myself not to take her mouth again even though I want so much more, I guide her toward the large town tree, which is propped up and decorated in the middle of Ornament Park. Colored lights glitter up and down the branches with an oversize, glittery star on the very top that shines from all directions. And then scattered throughout are ornaments from all over.

"It's such a beautiful tree."

"It's from the farm," I say proudly. "There's a section in the back that customers are not allowed to pick from. We reserve it for the town. Bob Krampus will come out with his wife, Sylvia, and BKJ, and they will hand-pick the tree together. It's been their family tradition ever since BKJ was a little guy, so my dad has told me."

"That's . . . that's really sweet."

"Yeah, it's one of my favorite traditions we have on the farm because there is fanfare behind it. People from the town will watch the tree get chopped down, and then it's a tradition, watching it get raised up in Ornament Park."

"That's really sweet. Who hangs the ornaments?" she asks, walking up to the tree. "I'm surprised they don't have a fence around it."

"People from all over town hang the ornaments, from all over Colorado. Tradition says you come here, make a wish in front of the tree, and then hang an ornament that is meaningful to you. Then, if the ornament is still there the next morning, your wish will come true."

"Is that really the case?" she asks. "What if the wish doesn't come true and the ornament is still there?"

I move in right behind her and lean down to her ear, letting my hand rest on her hip. "Well, from what I've been told, Bob Krampus has been known to say that sometimes it takes many years of hanging the ornament on the tree for those wishes to come true. So every year, the tree committee will gently pack up the ornaments that were not collected, and when the next year comes and we do a new tree lighting, they hang all the wishes back up on the tree for the people who are still looking for their wish to come true or who are still looking to enjoy that Christmas magic."

She presses her hand to her heart. "That's . . . that's really sweet. Have you ever hung an ornament on the tree?"

"First time," I say.

"Seriously?"

"Yeah, seriously," I say. "I've never thought of something that was important enough to wish for. But this year, I have something." I can see the wheels turning in her head, figuring out what exactly I'm not saying. Without saying much, I'm saying a whole lot.

I take out our ornaments and gently hand her the one she picked out. I fold the bag, stuff it in my pocket, and then move in behind her.

"From what I've been told, you're supposed to hold the ornament in your right hand, look up at the wishing star on the top of the tree, and then make your wish. When you're done, hang the ornament, and then walk away. Are you ready?"

"Ready," she says softly.

"Then go for it."

I look up at the tree, hold the ornament in my right hand, and then in my head, I wish for Evergreen Farm to be safe for many years to come.

Then I hang my ornament on a branch just as Betty does the same.

For a moment, I soak in the feeling of putting my very first ornament on the tree, the meaning behind it, and the impact it will hopefully make on my life.

Together with our wishes now held in the universe, we walk away, and I lead her to the kiosks in Ornament Park. There is one where you can rent blankets, so we head in that direction, and I lay down my credit card as a deposit, grab two extra-large ones, and loop them over my arm.

"This way," I say, nodding toward a less crowded space in the park.

We head off to the right so we're closer to where the river is trickling over the almost iced-over rocks, and I lay out the blanket. She takes my hand right before I help her down.

I lie all the way down, and she joins me before I drape the second blanket over us.

"Are you cold?"

"I'm okay for now," she says.

"Let me know when you get cold, but this is what my parents did after they made a wish on the tree. They lay down and stared at the stars."

"Did their wish come true?"

"It did," I say. "They never told me what it was, but they said it fulfilled their life, so I'm taking their advice and staring up at the stars like they did."

"Do you know anyone else who had wishes come true?"

"Yeah," I say. "My brothers. They wished for their business to take off, and they've done really well. They own Toboggan Tours in town. Not sure I mentioned that. Martha and Mae both had wishes that came true. Bob Krampus said Bob Krampus Junior came along after a wish. And a few others. I know it's hard to believe, but there's something about being in Kringle that makes you believe in Christmas magic."

"Yeah, I'm starting to understand that." She looks up at the sky. "Anyone you know who didn't have their wish come true?"

"Not that I know of," I say. "Then again, not sure anyone would admit to their wish not coming true." I let the sounds of people walking by fill the air as I stare at the twinkling lights. They're not as bright here as they are on the farm because of light pollution in town, but they're still pretty enough to marvel at.

"Have you ever seen the northern lights here?" she asks. "I know the last few years, they've been visible in certain spots in Colorado. Seems this would be a magical place to see them."

"Yes, a few times. The town gathers together, we turn off all the lights, and we just sit back and enjoy the moment. No cell phones, no cameras, just our eyes and our memories. It's been some of my fondest memories here."

I hear her turn toward me, so I glance to the side.

"Is that what it's like here? The camaraderie? People helping people? Acting as a community?"

"Yes," I answer. "It's kind of like an unspoken rule: You help your neighbor. Over time, you get to know everyone and their backstory. Sure, there is a lot of gossip, but that's what you get with a small town, and the return is so much better. The friendships I have here fulfill me so much, and not just with Cole and Storee but with people like Tanya, who owns Warm Your Spirits, or Sherry Conrad or even Martha and Mae. There are inside jokes among the entire town. There is bickering like family, but there are also joyful moments, like when someone we've seen grow up gets married or has kids, like Cole and Storee. We're just one big family."

She lies back down, quiet for a moment, before she says, "I'm jealous of that."

"You are?"

"Yeah," she says quietly. "I am."

I haven't spent a lot of time around Betty, but I can recognize that she seems subdued all of a sudden. It makes me realize that I know little about *her* backstory. Her family, her previous job, her relationships. Does she have siblings? Is her uncle her dad's only brother, or are there more

Yokels out there? Is she closer to her mom? What occupation did she leave to come here?

In so many ways, she's still a stranger to me. But I do know that I want her to experience the *true* home that Kringle offers. "You know you can be a part of it, right? Making Kringle your home, you can make so much of it. Get to know people—"

"Atlas, you know my situation is different."

"How is it different? We always welcome new people to town."

"Granted, everyone has been so nice to me, and I'm really appreciative of that, but when your relative in town is Dwight, it makes fitting in harder. I know he's not a favorite among the town, but he's a really nice guy, and he picked me up when I was . . . well, when I was at an all-time low." Her eyes meet mine. "He gave me an opportunity I'm still not sure I can handle."

"I don't know; seems like you're doing a good job, scoping out the competition," I tease, but it seems to fall flat as her eyes remain focused on her lap. Clearing my throat, I say, "So Dwight, he means a lot to you."

She nods. "He's the sibling I never had. When our families would get together, he was the one that I always trailed behind. He would sit and play card games with me when no one else would. He's just . . . he's special to me. And I know he's tough to get along with. Trust me, I'm well aware of that, but I feel bad for him sometimes because I don't think people give him a chance."

Yeah, because he's a fucking dick.

But clearly I can't say that to her, especially since it seems like she really relies on him.

"Listen." I tug on my hair. "He . . . he isn't all that bad." I nearly gag on the words. "He's just . . . he's not around everyone as much, and he can be difficult at times."

She nods and then sits up abruptly, letting the blanket fall to her lap. She rubs her hands over her arms and says, "Sorry, um, I think I should go. I'm getting a bit chilly."

Shit, not the right thing for me to say.

Is she chilly, or are we crossing over to conversational territory that she doesn't want to be in?

I'm thinking the latter.

But I don't want to push her; I've already tested her enough tonight with the kissing.

"No need to apologize," I say and then sit up as well. "I'm feeling pretty good right now. I think the alcohol has worn off if you want me to take you home."

"No, that's okay. I might grab a hot chocolate, hang out a little bit longer on my own, and then drive back."

"I can stay with you," I say.

She shakes her head as she stands. "That's okay. I've taken up enough of your time."

"You say that as if hanging out with you is a chore. Because I need you to know, it's not. I've really had a good time tonight, once we got past some of the awkwardness."

"I had a good time too," she says and then looks away.

"Then what's wrong?"

"Nothing," she sighs, her leg bouncing, her mind reeling.

"Betty, seriously, what's going on in that head of yours?"

Her lips clamp shut, and she looks anywhere but at me, so I stand as well and grip her chin so she has to look at me.

"What's bringing on this abrupt change? Wanting to leave all of a sudden?"

She wets her lips, her eyes connecting with mine. "Umm...maybe... maybe you'll enjoy a hot cocoa with me before you go?"

Not ready to speak about it just yet?

Okay, not a problem. If anything, I'm patient.

Wanting her to realize that, I answer her. "I'd love that."

BETTY

The guilt I feel around Atlas is overwhelming.

Debilitating.

Like all I can think about is how I'm supposed to be finding a way to put this man out of business. And for what?

Because of some vendetta my uncle has?

I just don't see the point of it all.

Wouldn't it be more beneficial if we find a way to somehow work together?

Given all the talk of the community and how they work together, seems like a more intelligent plan.

God, when I had my shop, I would've loved to have had a community like Kringle. A whole bunch of small businesses that relied on each other, that sought help from one another, rallied together. Just walking around Ornament Park and seeing all the vendors network, it's . . . it's unlike anything I've ever seen before. No wonder the town is thriving, because everyone is working together.

And it seems more productive to be in everyone's good graces than to go against them.

It's a conversation I'll need to have, because when I was lying down on the blanket with Atlas, it hit me all at once: this is what I want, and there is a roadblock in the way. That roadblock is Uncle Dwight.

"Did you know there's something special about this hot cocoa shack?" Atlas asks as we step to the side and wait for our cups to be prepared.

"What?" I glance at the shack, but it seems like all the others.

He tugs me to the right and then points up.

I look toward the overhang, and of course, there's more mistletoe.

When my eyes meet his, he's smirking, and God, I can't resist it. I don't even know what's happened tonight. I went from not liking him to awkward encounters to kissing him under mistletoe. Not sure how that all happened, but here I am, standing on my toes to reach him better as his lips gently press against mine.

It's short and brief like the others. There's no holding the back of my head, keeping me in place, or open-mouth action. Just a brief kiss, but it packs one of the biggest punches to the gut that I've ever felt. Like a zap of electricity pulsing through me.

It's been like that all night.

With each kiss, I've felt more connected, more desperate . . . more guilty.

"Max, your order," a man calls out.

Atlas moves away and grabs our drinks; then he hands me one. "Warm those lips up. They're a little cold."

"Why? Do you expect to run into one more sprig of mistletoe before the end of the night?"

"You never know where you might find one."

"Are they hiding in your pocket? Is that how they keep showing up?"

"If they were, we'd have had more than three kisses tonight, that's for damn sure."

I feel my cheeks flush, despite the chilly weather.

With his hand on my lower back, he guides me toward an empty bench on the perimeter of the park, offering a stunning view of the lights bouncing off the mountain right behind the river.

"So how did Cupid Christmas treat you?" he asks before taking a sip of his drink.

"Well, I thought I was hanging out with Storee, and instead, I kissed the enemy." I smirk. "Kind of liked it."

"'Kind of'?" he asks, his brows shooting up. "Only kind of?"

"Yes, because I fear if I say that I really liked it, you'll gloat, and I don't think I can handle the gloating."

"I'm not the kind of guy that gloats."

"Oh please, Atlas."

He chuckles. "Yeah, you're right. Best to keep me humble."

"Something we can agree on."

"Yes, the one thing." He sips his cocoa but keeps his eyes on me.

"What?" I say, feeling my cheeks blush again.

"Nothing."

"No, you can't get away with that. What were you thinking?"

"Ah, you know, just how when I first saw you, that brief glimpse of time before the Pepsi bottle hit my head, I never would have thought that I'd be sitting on a bench, having a normal conversation with you."

"Another thing we can agree on, because as you were being driven off in the back of a cop car, I never would have thought that I'd end up kissing you three times in one night."

"And here we are now. I think some people call that growth."

"Some people might," I say as I glance out toward the lights. "So"—I clear my throat—"are there any other activities you take part in during the holiday season?" I ask as I hold the cup of hot cocoa with both hands, keeping my fingers warm.

"I like going to the Christmas Kringle competitions. I think those are fun. We do ice-skating out on the farm, so when I'm not working, I like to take a few laps around. Breakfast with Santa is enjoyable, because I like seeing Bob in his element. He really is one of the best people. The way he speaks with the children and asks for their names before they sit down so he can play the part. I don't sit down to eat, but I volunteer."

He volunteers? God, is there anything else that he might want to tell me to really dig the dagger of guilt into my heart?

"There are some snow castles I like to go look at up in Breckenridge. Have you seen them before?"

"Oh my gosh, yes. We went a few years ago. They were amazing."

"My mom and I have gone a few times. One year, we were able to drag

Cole along with us, which was surprising. He was fascinated by how they were engineered. Even got a picture of him examining them."

I chuckle. "I could see that. He seems like the kind of guy—oh hey, is that Cole and Storee over there, hanging an ornament on the tree?"

Atlas looks out toward the tree, and I catch the smile that tugs on his lips. "It is. Surprised that Cole is participating."

"Let me guess, not something he used to do before Storee?"

He shakes his head. "No, he thought it was stupid and childish. Though he was in a very dark place for ten years, so I'll give him a break. Glad to see him finally starting to live again. It's great seeing him as a father, as a husband. Seeing him smile and laugh again. It was something I missed. That night when he lost his parents, the light vanished from his eyes. Storee and the girls have slowly brought it back."

"It's sweet, seeing the way you care for him."

"Truly, the brother I always wish I had," he says.

And that speaks volumes.

CHAPTER SIXTEEN
MAX

NARRATOR: THE SNOW IS CRISP, *magic is in the air, and Max spent the night scoping out every single sprig of mistletoe that he could find so he could spend a little more time tasting Betty.*

Granted, this started with his desire to save the farm, and he swore up and down about not having any intimate interest in her, but I think we all knew where this was headed. Because despite her intentions for being in Kringle, he sees something else in her. And the more time he spends with her, the more he's starting to realize just how much he could like her.

———————

"Crunch Tator for you, Crunch Tator for me," Storee says as she takes a seat in the clubhouse and then hands me another juice box. "Shall we start this meeting with our secret handshake?"

"I think we shall," I say as I steeple my hands together, making a Christmas tree shape.

Storee bombs the tree with her fist, and then we open up our Crunch Tators.

"How much time do you have?"

"Like five minutes," she answers. "Cole was wondering why the hell I had to go see Aunt Cindy on Cupid Christmas Night. I told him to warm up the pineapple candy cane and I'd be right back."

"Eck, gross."

"Don't knock it until you try it, Atlas," she says while popping a chip in her mouth. "So how did it go?"

I can't hold back my smile. "We kissed three times."

"What?" Storee whisper-shouts. She turns to me and pushes at my shoulder. "That wasn't part of the plan."

"I know. It just happened. Mistletoe really worked, and then we hung an ornament on the tree together, stared up at the stars. It was . . . it was nice."

Storee slowly nods and then points her chip-coated finger at my mouth. "You're smiling. What happened to 'I don't like her, and this is all to save the farm'? That smile and the hearts in your eyes you have whenever she's around suggest something different."

I set my bag down and turn toward Storee as well. "I don't know what's happening to me, Storee. I shouldn't like her. She's trying to take out the farm, and she has all the ways to do it, but for some reason, when I look at her, I don't see that person. I see someone else. I see someone who is looking for a fresh start. Someone looking to set down some roots. Someone looking for joy. She doesn't seem like she has a vindictive bone in her body. You know?"

"I get the same feeling from her. And I don't know. I feel bad deceiving her, because I really like her. She's sweet and funny, and I could see us being good friends."

"Yeah, I don't like deceiving her either. Then again, I think the BTMCs haven't really been booby traps at all, just opportunities for me to grow fucking feelings for her. Like . . . when we were saying goodbye tonight, I was desperate to find another sprig of mistletoe, any excuse to kiss her one more time. I wanted to drive her home. I wanted to walk her up to her door. What is wrong with me?"

"Nothing. You found someone you're interested in."

"I know, but I feel like I booby-trapped myself. It wasn't supposed to go this way. She was supposed to fall for me, and then I was supposed to pull the old switcheroo on her. Now I'm starting to like this woman, and I'm pretty sure she's still set on taking my family and me down."

"Do you really think that?"

I tug on my hair. "I don't know. It just seems strange that she had an instant dislike of me, and I can't help but think that Dwight is behind that." She had such a negative view of me, and that was just so foreign.

"Because you're just . . . you're not what I expected."

"And now that you are, what are you finding?"

"That you're sweet. That you're goofy. That you and I seem like the same rambling person."

"I think her opinion of me is changing. But I don't truly know where she stands when it comes to me."

"Well, there is a way to find out."

"Ask her?" I shake my head. "What am I going to do? Go up to her and say, *Hey, Betty, are you having feelings for me? If so, could you not try to build that farm next door? Thanks.*"

"No, that's not what I was going to say."

"Then what?" I ask.

"Time to commence phase three."

I sit back. "What's phase three?"

"See if we can make her jealous."

———————

"This is stupid, Storee. She's not going to fall for it."

"I know what I'm doing," she says as she adjusts a hat on one of the six mannequins we brought over from the farm storage.

"A fake party to make her jealous? You really think that will work?"

"We're trying to gauge her reaction. And then we'll know what you mean to her. If she acts sad or upset that maybe you didn't invite her, then we know she shares your feelings. If she couldn't care less, then that's when we have to reassess our entire approach. Because if you're starting to grow feelings and she has none, this could end very horribly. You could end up with a broken heart and a run-down farm."

"Wow, thanks for that." I look around at the way Storee has set up the house.

Old mannequins from when my mom used to sell vintage Christmas-themed dresses on the farm are decked out in holiday outfits, also pulled from the archives. They are all lined up along the windows. Lamps without the shades are positioned to light up the mannequins and cast shadows against the curtains—she saw it in a movie once. She mixed some Christmas music with background noise of people chatting for me to play, and there are two revolving fans that have strings tied to them to move three of the mannequins' arms, which we had to lubricate with WD-40, which, have you ever smelled that shit? Woof.

"I'll text you when we hit the stop sign right before we get to your driveway. It will be a simple emoji."

"What emoji?" I ask.

"I don't know, just any emoji."

"Any? Don't you think that's confusing?"

"How is that confusing?" she asks. "It doesn't matter what emoji. It's just a symbol to say, *Turn everything on and get ready.*"

"Okay, so we're not doing different emojis for different signals?"

"No," she says with force. "The emoji I choose means nothing other than *Get the fuck ready.*"

"Okay, whoa, no need to swear."

She rolls her eyes and then checks around the room again. "Now don't fiddle around with this stuff. I have it set perfectly."

"What if something needs to be adjusted?"

"No fiddlin' around," she says, pointing at me. "If something goes wrong, it's because you touched it. Everything is set perfectly. Let it be."

"But what if a head falls off? These mannequins are old. We can't have a headless person gesturing to someone with a head."

"Obviously put the head back. But do not touch anything else, got it?"

I nod, not feeling confident about this. "Are we sure this is the right move?"

"For the love of God, yes." She blows out a breath.

"Only one more question for you."

"What?"

"I'm having a party at my house . . . but where are all the cars?"

"That . . ." She pauses and then presses her lips together. "Huh. You know, great point." Then she snaps her fingers. "I'll tell her you bring people in on a party bus so they can drink and have fun."

"You think that could work?"

"I can be pretty convincing. I mean, I convinced Cole to wear a thong and you to throw this ridiculous fake party."

She has me there.

Knowing she's right, she heads toward the door and then turns toward me. "This is it, Atlas. Don't get scared."

"Why am I going to get scared? You're just doing a drive-by, right?"

"Noooooo, she's coming to your door, remember? I'll have her pick up the ornaments off the tree, and we'll bring them to you. She'll be excited that the ornament was still there, and you'll answer the door but keep it partially shut so she can't get in, and then talk to her. It's in the script."

"What script?" I ask.

"I texted it to you."

"No, you didn't."

"Yes, I did," she counters.

I pull my phone out of back pocket and flash her our text chain.

She clamps her hand over her mouth, and her eyes widen. "Oh my God, did I send it to her?"

My stomach drops and panic ensues. "Holy fuck, Storee. Did you?"

She fumbles for her phone, her hands shaking as she unlocks it. I look at her screen, my heart pounding as she pulls up her text thread with Betty.

Together, relief washes through us as we see the last texts were about them meeting up at Ornament Park.

"Jesus Christ," I say, hand to heart. "I think I almost had a heart attack."

"That's so weird. I typed it up. I swear I did. Oh God, did I send it to Cole?" Once again, my anxiety skyrockets only for her to say, "Nope, not Cole. Oh shit, it was Tanya."

"What?" I say, turning to her.

"Oh, not her either."

My expression turns to irritation. "Who the fuck was it, Storee?"

She clicks around, saying, "No, nope, not them." And then finally she clicks on my name and starts laughing. "Oh, I typed it up to you and just didn't press Send. Isn't that funny?"

I stare at her, sweat now pooling in my armpits from the stressful emotional roller coaster she just sent me on. "Yeah, fucking hysterical."

"Well, anyway, take a gander at that, and let me know if you have any questions." She twiddles her fingers at me. "See you later."

When she shuts the door, I drag my hand down my face and then lean against the wood. I should have picked someone else to help me. I really should have.

———

"I'm dreaming . . . of a white . . . Christmas," I sing as I tap my foot, waiting for a text from Storee.

God, this is boring.

I'm too afraid to move, too afraid to touch anything, too afraid to not be ready since I've been catatonic ever since she left, and I fear I might lose my mind soon.

If only Cole were here.

If only he knew.

If only—

Beep.

I nearly jump out of my pants as I retrieve my phone and look at the text from Storee.

Storee: The package has been secured.

I stare down at the text.

We didn't talk about a text about a package being secured. Does that mean she and Betty are on their way?

I scroll through the script, looking for any indication that there will be a package secured, but when I come up short, panic starts to set in.

Was that supposed to be the emoji text?

She made it quite clear that it would be an emoji. That she wouldn't say anything, but she'd just send a random emoji, which was when I needed to turn everything on.

So is the *package secured* the new emoji?

Should I flip the switch?

This is why we should have done another run-through, because now I'm panicking.

I don't know what to do.

Now—

Knock, knock.

I whip around to look at the front door.

She's here?

Holy fuck, she's here.

What?

There was no emoji!

The music isn't on.

The people aren't moving.

The lights are not shadowing.

All rational thought processes jump out of my head, and like a family running through the Chicago O'Hare airport trying to catch their plane, I sprint around the living and dining room, flipping on switches, turning on music, and making the lights as bright as they can be, casting shadows onto the curtains.

The house is buzzing with a fake party that just so happened to have an uproar when there was a knock at the door.

Fuck, she's so not going to believe this.

Putting on a brave face, I go to the door, open it slightly, and stick my head out of the parted slot only to find Ansel standing on the other side.

Mother.

Fucker.

"Whoa, what the fuck was that?" he asks. "It's like someone banged the jukebox and it came back to life. What's going on in there?"

"Nothing," I say, closing the door even more.

His brows pinch together. "What are you doing while Mom and Dad are gone?"

"Nothing. Mind your own business. Now . . . now go away."

That doesn't help my cause, because his curiosity is piqued.

"Let me in."

"No," I say.

"Atlas, let me in."

"I said no. Now . . . leave. You need to be gone, like right now."

He folds his arms across his chest. "Not until you tell me what you're doing."

"I'm not doing anything. Therefore, I have nothing to tell."

"Says the guy who has someone talking to another person with their head off."

"What?" I pull away from the door. "The fucking head fell off?"

Ansel takes that moment to push inside the house and nearly knocks over one of the fans that's been meticulously set up.

"Whoa, what the fuck, dude?" He glances around, taking in the half-dressed mannequins, the strings, the lights. "This is some creepy-ass shit."

I find the head that rolled off the mannequin under the table.

"Get out. I'm doing something, and I can't have you here." I snag the head and bring it back to the mannequin. I think about what to do, how to rectify this, and then remember Dad's gum, which he keeps in his office. Forgetting about Ansel, I run to the back of the house into Dad's office and then squat down to his trunk. I flip open the top and start digging.

"What are you doing?" Ansel says. "Dad will pound you if he knows you're looking through his stuff."

"Pound me? Really? Dad doesn't even know what a fist is," I say as I move aside a *Playboy* from November 1990, thankfully wrapped up in cellophane, and that's when I find his stocked up Fruit Stripe gum. I pull out three strips, shove them in my mouth, and start chewing. I'll take care of the trunk later.

I rush back to the dining room and chew like I've never chewed before, my jaw growing tired. Ansel simply stares at me. Just when I feel like the gum is ready, there's a ding from my phone.

Full panic sets in.

I pull my phone out, and there's a text from Storee.

It's two emojis.

Two?

A tooth.

And a gold medal.

Why did she send two?

Two is not what we agreed on.

And why a tooth and a gold medal?

Jesus fuck.

I take the gum out of my mouth, place it on the bottom of the neck of the mannequin, then slam the head onto the body, run to the door, slam it shut from where Ansel left it open, grab my brother by the sweater, and bring him over to the stairs.

"Hey, watch it. What are you doing? You're going to stretch my sweater."

I get right in his face and say, "You're going to sit the fuck down, shut the fuck up, and not mutter one goddamn word, or else I'm telling Felix that you're the reason Jim dumped him. Got it?"

That clams Ansel up real quick as he sits down and remains silent.

I have about two seconds before I see lights come down the driveway.

This won't work.

This is so stupid.

Why did I agree to do this?

When I hear a door shut, I turn to Ansel and point my finger at him, and he zips his mouth shut.

When there's a knock at the door, my body feels like it's broken out in hives. I count to five and then walk over to the door and twist it open.

Betty is standing on the other side, worrying her lip and looking adorable in a pair of black skinny jeans, snow boots, and a puffy jacket.

"Oh, hey," I say, my hand propped up on the door, already starting to sweat. "Sorry about the noise. Uh, good to see you. I like your, uh, I like your jacket."

She glances down at it and then back up at me. "It's the same one I wore yesterday."

"Really? Ah, must be different in the light. So what's going on?"

She glances past my shoulder. "Um, well . . . I didn't mean to bother you and your, uh, your party."

"Not bothering at all," I say as my mind goes back to the script that Storee provided me. "Just a little fundraiser I do for families who need funds during Christmastime."

Okay, that's not a lie. I do donate money to families who need a

little supplementation, but it's money of my own, and my parents match it.

"That's . . . wow, that's really sweet." She glances down at her hands, where she's holding our ornaments. "I feel kind of silly coming over here, interrupting you."

"You're fine. It's good to see you."

"Yeah?" she asks as her eyes meet mine again, but this time, they stay on me longer, allowing me to read her. And in a snapshot of a second, I see everything that I need to see.

The uneasiness.

The uncertainty.

The . . . longing.

Unmistakable. I can see her *want* mirror my *want*.

It's right there.

Clear as day.

"Yeah," I answer, trying not to get too excited. "Did you have a good time last night?"

She nods and then softly says, "I really did."

"I did too." I wet my lips and lean ever so slightly forward, just enough that our conversation feels more intimate. "What are you up to?"

"Um, well, you know." She clears her throat, seeming far too nervous, so I try to help her.

"Are you hanging out with Storee tonight?"

"Yeah, we, uh, we're going to get lost in Baubles and Wrappings and then grab a bite to eat. But I thought that I would, uh . . . bring this over first. It feels kind of silly now but—" She lifts up the ornaments, and I smile as I take mine from her.

"It stayed overnight?"

She smiles. "It did."

"Yours too?"

She holds hers up as well. "Mine too."

"Well, if that's not a good sign, I don't know what is."

"You think our wishes will come true?"

"I'm really hoping mine does," I say, looking her dead in the eyes.

The corners of her lips tilt up as she smiles back at me. "Yeah, me too." She clears her throat. "Well, uh, I'll let you get back to your party. I don't want to keep you long. Or Storee for that matter." She takes a few steps back. "I hope you raise a lot of money and have a fun time." Another step back, growing too close to the steps.

"Hey, be careful," I say.

She takes another step back. "Yup, be careful. Always have to be careful. Funny thing about being careful."

She takes one more step, and I see where this is going, so I rush out the door and snag her by the waist, right before she tips backward down the stairs.

"Oh!" The surprise in her voice is cute, but then her eyes fall to my mouth. "Uh, sorry, did I . . . did I forget?" She nervously laughs, making no sense at all.

"Forget?" I ask.

"Yeah, you know, the tugging at my waist and all. I get it, no big deal. We did it before."

What on earth is she talking about? Before I can ask, she lifts up on her toes and presses a kiss to my lips.

Christ.

Her fucking lips.

Unsure why this is happening, my grip on her grows tighter, my mouth wanting to explore, but she doesn't even give me a second before she's pulling away and starts looking around. "Where's the mistletoe? That's number four, right?"

"Huh?" I ask, feeling dazed.

"That's why you snagged me, right?" She gulps. "For a kiss? Because of, you know . . . some mistletoe hanging?"

I swallow and catch my breath. "Uh, no. You were about to fall down the stairs backward. And I didn't want that to happen."

She glances behind her and then back at me. "Oh dear God, you weren't wanting to kiss me?"

"I mean, yeah, I want to kiss you, but I don't want to kiss you if you don't want to be kissed. I was just trying to help you so you didn't fall."

"That's why you said, 'Be careful.'"

"Yeah, that's why I said, 'Be careful.' What did you think I meant?"

"I really don't know. I'm just . . . ah, I'm sorry."

"You don't need to apologize."

"No, I'm bothering you and then kissing you—"

"You're not bothering me." I push a stray piece of hair behind her ear. "I'm glad you brought my ornament over. It's special. Thank you."

Her panic pauses for a moment as her eyes connect with mine. "Oh, um, you're . . . you're welcome."

Then I right her back on her feet and let go of her. "It was really good to see you, Betty."

She shifts, and I can see her nerves really take hold of her. "Are you sure you're not just saying that to be nice and make me feel better because I randomly kissed you with no mistletoe?"

I reach up and pinch her chin with my forefinger and thumb, making her feel just how serious I am when I say this. "I mean it."

She gulps and her eyes search mine. "Okay, that's, uh, that's good to know. Thank you for the information. I'll just, uh, plug that away as noted." She nervously laughs. "Atlas Maxheimer thinks it's good to see me. That's just great."

"Any reciprocation on that thought?" I ask as I release her and stick my hands in my pockets.

Her eyes widen. "Oh, yes, uh, great to see you . . . pal." She playfully punches my arm.

"'Pal'?" I raise a brow at her.

"Comrade?" she asks with a wince.

I chuckle. "Sure. After you hit me with a two-liter, at this point, I'll take *comrade*." I rock back on my heels. "Well, I hope you have a good night with Storee. Baubles and Wrappings seems like the perfect place to get lost in."

"Oh yeah, should be fun. I'm excited."

I nod, knowing this needs to end at some point. "Okay. Well, have a good night, Betty."

"Yup." She awkwardly waves. "You too." But then she doesn't move. She remains still and just . . . stares. Since it seems like she's waiting for something, I take that moment to see just how far I can go with this.

I take a chance, close the space between us, and wrap my arms around her, giving her a warm hug. And she returns it immediately, melting into my body and pressing her face against my chest.

I hold her for probably longer than I should, reveling in how she feels so . . . right in my arms.

When I finally let go, she smiles up at me, waves, and then takes off toward Storee's car, nearly skipping away. I let out a deep sigh, knowing that I just got the confirmation that I needed.

She feels the same way.

She feels the same exact way.

With a chest full of pride, I head back into the house where Ansel's still sitting on the stairs, mouth shut. When I shut the door, I say, "You can speak now."

As if he's been holding in his breath, he exhales loudly and then asks, "What the hell was that?"

"Nothing you need to worry about," I say as I turn off the music but leave the mannequins in place, just in case Storee and Betty decide to come back.

He follows me. "That was weird."

"There was nothing weird about it."

"There was so much weird about it," he says.

"Can you just leave me alone."

"Not after that. Dude, that was a full-on party you faked."

"Leave, Ansel."

"Like, a full-on party. I'm worried."

"Well, don't be," I shout, getting irritated with him.

"Whoa, okay. Sheesh, you're wound tight."

"I'm just trying to figure some things out, and I don't need you harping on me about what I'm up to. Just let me do my thing, and don't worry about it, okay?"

Might be a little harsh, but the last thing I need is for my puke of a brother to find out about Betty and Dwight and what they're trying to do while also realizing that I'm starting to like this girl when I have no right liking her at all. Because here's the thing: If Ansel finds out how I feel about Betty, there's no way he's going to just drop it. No, he'll annoy me incessantly until I lose my goddamn mind, and then that's when he'll strike by spreading the news around town, because that's the kind of guy he is.

Always the instigator.

I still don't understand how Felix puts up with him on a daily basis, but then again, they've always been closer.

"Okay." Ansel brushes off his shoulders.

"Why are you still here?" I rub my forehead, wishing he'd just vanish.

"I came over because Mom texted me that you called, and she couldn't hear you and hung up. She wanted me to check on you because she was worried that something was wrong. Took me a few days, but I'm here."

Wow, a few days. What a brother.

"I'm fine. I called to see how their trip was going," I lie.

"Was that all? Everything fine at the farm? Because if you need Felix and me to pitch in since we know how to run a business, we can do that."

Of course he would say that. What a dick.

My irritation grows as I look my brother in the eyes. "I don't need your help. I'm fine. The farm is thriving. Everything is good."

"I mean, you say you don't need my help, but then I come here, and you have Mom's old mannequins dressed up and talking to each other, so I'm sorry if I feel like something's a little off."

"I'm fine. Now get the hell out of here. I need to clean up."

"Okay, but you know where to find me if you need anything."

Yeah, over my dead body would I ever go to him looking for help.

BETTY

"I feel bad," I say, as we make our way down a row of dishes.

Baubles and Wrappings is a very interesting store, almost like a mini-Target but without the food. Instead of all new clothes and products, it's a combination of new products, thrift store items, and vintage finds. Naturally, every last item is geared toward Christmas.

When Storee asked if I wanted to get lost in the store, she really meant it.

"We went over this, Betty. He was probably excited to see you. He even said it."

"I know, but I just . . . I don't know. Was that stupid to drive all the way over there to give him an ornament? That was stupid. Like clingy. Did it look clingy?"

She smirks. "Not at all. You said he appreciated it, right?"

"He did. He was excited to see that our ornaments made it through the night."

"See, there you have it. He was excited. That's all you need to worry about, okay? Atlas is a genuine guy, so he won't lie to you. When he says something, he means it."

"Yeah, I'm starting to see that." I pick up a dish that's in the shape of a Christmas tree with a green truck piled with unadorned Christmas trees painted on it. It reminds me of Atlas, and for a brief second, I think about getting it for him but then remember that would be weird. We're not really close enough for me to buy him a Christmas plate and tell him that it reminded me of him. Especially when I'm also in the process of devising a business plan that's supposed to put him and his family out of business.

Speaking of said business plan, I have yet to put one together. Uncle Dwight texted me this morning to see how it was going, and I told him that I was still immersing myself and needed some more time. It's the second time I've canceled on him, and if I do it again, I know he'll think something's up. I don't have it in me to meet with him at the moment, not when I'm feeling so confused inside.

I'm picking up signs that while Atlas is generous to Kringletown, community focused, kind, and thoughtful, and therefore perceived so well here, my uncle doesn't have that same . . . esteem. People don't light up at the mention of his name. They respect him, there's no doubt about that, but they don't seem to hold the same level of admiration for him. *And yet I'm expected to destroy the Maxheimer family business.* And that's getting harder and harder to want, the more I feel for Atlas.

"This might be me overstepping, and please tell me if I'm wrong," Storee says, "But it seems to me like maybe you might like Atlas."

I run my fingers over the edge of the plate, taking in the embossed pattern. "Yeah, I, uh, I think I might, and I don't know what to do about it. I don't even know him that well still, but . . ." I sigh and put the plate down. "Can I tell you this in confidence?"

Storee nods. "Of course."

"Thank you." I turn toward her and say, "He doesn't seem like the guy that my uncle has portrayed him to be, and that's really confusing. I thought that he was this bad guy who hurt my uncle, and taking over his farm would be so easy—remorseless—but the more time I spend with

Atlas, the more I realize that he's really not that guy. And I don't know, maybe my uncle has experienced something different with him, but the whole plan just seems . . . off."

"Well, I don't know what Dwight has gone through when it comes to Atlas, and I haven't lived in this town long enough to even pretend to know, but what I can tell you is that what you see with Atlas is all real. Every single bit of it. He's a good guy, inside and out. It doesn't get more genuine than him. And I'm not just saying that because I want you to change your mind. I'm saying that because I mean it."

I nod and then move down the aisle. "I kind of wish that wasn't the case."

"Why?"

"Because." I spot a pickup truck with a tree in the back of it, and my mind goes right back to Atlas and his ornament. "It would be so much easier if he was a jerk, but now that I know a little bit about him, it's making it harder to consider my uncle's offer."

"I can understand that." Storee thinks about it for a second. "Why don't you give it some thought, sleep on it, and maybe start drawing up ideas of something else you can do with the land? Something that you think would be a great contribution to the town, something the whole community can get behind, rather than trying to take out an already existing business?" She shrugs. "Then you can present it to Dwight. When he's happy, you can move forward with seeing where things can go with Atlas. Just my two cents."

"That all seems pretty bold, and I'm not that bold of a person," I say, hating that I even said the words myself. I wish I was bold. I wish I was more take-charge, but at the end of the day, I'm a people pleaser, and I make decisions based on how people will see me, not what's best for me. It's something I've been working on. Clearly not doing a good job so far.

"I understand that. Sometimes it's hard to find your voice, but if you keep working at it, you will find it at some point when you need it the most."

I turn toward Storee, so happy that I ran into her at Evergreen Farm. "Thank you. I feel really lucky that I can call you a friend."

"So do I."

CHAPTER SEVENTEEN
MAX

NARRATOR: *OKAY, I KNOW WHAT you're thinking. How can Storee still put on this show for Betty, playing the trickster behind the scenes, and act like they're friends?*

Well, here's the thing you need to know: The moment Storee noticed Max had heart eyes for Betty, she threw his stupid plan—drawn-out diagram included—right out the window. She has a plan of her own, and it's called being the Cupid Christmas matchmaker.

Max might be busy trying to save his family farm.

Betty might be busy trying to figure out her feelings for Max and what to do with the land.

But Storee . . . she has a bigger plan, and it seems like it's going like clockwork.

Storee: Don't come to the clubhouse tonight. I think Cole is onto me. I can't keep visiting Aunt Cindy at night. Want to meet up at Warm Your Spirits tomorrow morning?

Max: Of course he's sniffing us out. Tell him to mind his own business.

Storee: I don't think he's completely sniffed us out yet, but he's cluing in, so it's best not to lead him anywhere, you know?

Max: Oh, I know. I can meet tomorrow morning.

Storee: Good, we can discuss your next move.

Max: Do you think there needs to be another move?

Storee: Uh, did you think you'd simply stop after tonight?

Max: I don't know. What did you think about tonight? Did she say anything to you?

Storee: She did, but she said it to me in confidence, so I can't repeat it.

Max: Are you being serious right now?

Storee: Very much so. She's my friend, and I want her to be able to trust me.

Max: Wait, hold on. So you're telling me you obtained information about Betty but won't share it with me, even though you're the one who came up with the plan tonight?

Storee: Correct.

Max: Uh, whose side are you on? You're supposed to be helping me.

Storee: And I am, but I've also become friends with Betty, and I don't want to break that trust we've built.

Max: You became friends with her because you were trying to help me. Don't you remember the plan? Woo her, get her to fall for me, then devastate?

Storee: I'm quite clear on the origin of this entire situation. I don't need the reminders. But I'm reminding you that I met her before all this went down and told her if she needed someone to chat with, I was her girl. Therefore, I'm playing both sides, and if you make me choose a side, I'm choosing her side purely out of spite.

Max: Wow, just wow. And we even had a secret handshake. You're just going to throw that all away?

Storee: No, you are if you don't understand the position I'm in.

Max: Jesus . . . I feel bad for Cole if this is what he married.

Storee: EXCUSE ME?!

Max: I mean . . . way to have morals. Proud of you, sis.

Storee: Don't call me sis.

Max: Can you at least tell me if you got good vibes from her, like that she might like me? Because I got those vibes, but now I'm questioning everything.

Storee: I think she likes you, which is why we need to meet tomorrow, because if she likes you and you like her, you can't blow this.

Max: How can I possibly blow this?

Storee: Many ways, Atlas. Many ways.

———————

BETTY

I stare into the mirror while applying my mascara, my mind going a mile a minute. To slow down, I take a calming breath and then talk through what I'm feeling.

"I have to run into town today and grab a few things from the store. Bread, peanut butter, salad fixings, and some more Pepsi because I have a problem. Then I want to pop into Baubles and Wrappings again, because last night, Storee's words made sense. I need to start tinkering around with another business idea for Uncle Dwight." I fit my mascara brush back in the tube and then pick up my hairbrush and start combing out my curls and turning them into soft waves. "A fresh notebook always brings new ideas."

I pick up my hair spray and lightly douse my hair.

"But first stop is Warm Your Spirits, because I've been wanting to try that coffee cake, and I believe today is the day. I also think it would benefit me to start chatting with more townspeople. If more people know me, the easier it might be to convince Uncle Dwight to take his idea in another direction."

I set down the hair spray and pick up my perfume.

"And maybe I can swing by Evergreen Farm." I wince at myself in the mirror, already hating how desperate I seem. "Just to apologize for interrupting his party. That would be the proper thing to do." I spritz myself on the neck and then lightly drag the perfume over my jaw and just below my cheek. "And if Atlas happens to invite me—AHHHHHH!"

I jolt to the side when Buzz, my tarantula, falls into the sink.

"Dear God in heaven," I say, hand to heart. "I thought you were a rat." I chuckle and then carefully carry him back to his aquarium.

I sometimes let him out of his cage but put him in a well-contained area. Seems like he broke out this morning. What a tricky fella.

When he's secure, I go back to the bathroom, check myself one more time, and then grab my coat. Today is going to be a good day.

———

"Good morning," Tanya says as I approach the counter. I've come to know her a little since I've moved here, and she seems pretty nice, a little nosey, which I kind of like, and protective of her town. Then again, that seems to be everyone who lives here. "Nice to see you this morning, dear. What can I get you?"

"I've been eyeing that coffee cake for a while, Tanya, and today is the day I give in to temptation."

"Ooo, great choice. This is fresh from the oven as well." She takes the silver tongs positioned in front of the bakery case, pulls out a hefty piece of coffee cake, and places it on a plate. "And would you like your normal coffee as well?"

"You know my order?" I ask, surprised.

She winks at me. "That's my job. Of course I know."

"Oh, that's ... that's kind of cool."

She chuckles. "Does it make you feel at home?"

"Yeah, it does."

She nods. "Then I'm doing my job. I'll also start a tab for you if that works. That way, you don't have to keep paying every day."

"Oh, are you sure?"

She waves her hand at me. "Of course. That's what we do here, help each other out." She winks and then starts making my coffee.

I pick up my plate and turn toward the seating perimeter where I spot Storee and Atlas in the corner, both looking at me with smiles.

Oh, I didn't know they were here.

Storee waves me over, so with my coffee cake in hand, I walk over to where they're sitting. Atlas scoots over on his bench, making room for me, because Storee has her double stroller, both girls happily content.

Seriously, she either has the best, most chill kids ever, or she's a miracle mom.

Probably both.

"Hey," Atlas says as I sit down. God, he smells so good. I could just bury myself in his scent. "Storee was just telling me how much fun you guys had last night."

I glance up at Storee, who offers me a wink, which I take as assurance that she's kept what I said close to her. "Yes, it was so much fun."

"Did you happen to pick up any Christmas presents?" He playfully bumps my shoulder. "Possibly for someone who you might be trying to put out of business?"

I glance in his direction, his deep brown eyes sparkling with humor. "I was unaware that you put yourself on my Christmas list."

"Your Christmas list?" he asks with a raise of his brow. "Are you going to ask Bob Krampus for me for Christmas? Because you don't have to ask

Santa. You can just ask me." He winks, and a thrill of lust and excitement shoot through me at the same time.

"I meant my list of people I buy things for Christmas. Not like . . . my present list. I wouldn't ask for a human for Christmas. That's . . . that's absurd."

He chuckles, and so does Storee. "I don't know." Atlas rubs his hand over his jaw, seeming way more playful, way more flirtatious than normal, and it's slowly breaking down my walls. "I wouldn't mind sitting on Old Krampus's lap and telling him I'd like a beautiful blond with bright blue eyes to be set under my Christmas tree."

"Ooo, good one," Storee says, leaning in.

Atlas smirks. "Thanks." And then he adds, "Do you think she got it that I was talking about her?"

Storee nods. "I think so." Then she turns to me and whispers, "Did you understand that he was asking for you for Christmas?"

I feel my cheeks blush. "Yeah, I think so."

Atlas then turns to Storee. "Can you make it clear to her that I was talking about her, because I don't want her second-guessing what I said."

Tanya quickly drops off my drink, and I thank her as Storee cheekily says, "He was talking about you, Betty. He really wants you for Christmas. I even saw drool come out of the corner of his mouth when he asked."

Now Atlas turns to me. "Can you please let Storee know that there was no drool?"

This is so stupid and so ridiculous, but I can't help but play along. "Storee, Atlas wants to be clear. There was no drool."

"Can you please tell Atlas that there is drool right now?"

Laughing, I turn to Atlas. "There is drool right now."

"Where?"

Keeping up the charade, I lightly brush the corner of his lip with my thumb. "Right there."

His eyes are burning into mine as he lightly wets his lip. "Oh, my mistake. It's probably because you smell like fucking heaven this morning."

Storee leans in even closer. "If you didn't catch that, he thinks you smell good."

I turn to Storee and say, "I think he smells better."

Storee rolls up her napkin and tosses it at Atlas. "Atlas, she thinks you smell better."

Atlas smirks and turns to me, tucking some hair behind my ear. "Yeah, well—"

"What the hell are you doing?" I hear someone roar behind me.

And I don't have to turn around to know who it is. I can hear it in the voice, and I can see it in the way Atlas reacts.

Before I can answer, I'm yanked out of the bench by my arm.

"Hey, don't fucking touch her like that," Atlas says.

I look over my shoulder to find a steaming uncle.

"Excuse me?" he asks. "Don't touch her like that? Want to explain to me why he feels like he can speak to me in such a way?" Uncle Dwight asks.

"Dwight, I think . . . I think you should lower your voice," Storee suggests.

"Don't tell me what to do." He then whips me around to face him. "What are you doing? Why is he touching you like that?"

"I . . . um." I'm tongue-tied, unable to answer.

He leans back, his eyes searching mine, and then he starts shaking his head. "No, no, Betty. Please don't tell me you like him."

Guilt once again consumes me.

"I . . . I don't . . . I don't know."

It's a lie. I do know, but I can't get myself to say it out loud.

"You realize what he's doing, right?" Uncle Dwight gestures to Atlas. "He's acting like he's interested to deter you from putting him out of business, because he's desperate and he knows that's what we can do. So he's resorted to this."

"Dwight, I really don't think this is the place—" Storee starts, but Uncle Dwight ignores her.

"He's horrible," he continues. "The things he's done to me."

"Dwight, come on," Atlas says, causing Uncle Dwight to eye him angrily.

"Tormented me in high school because I was different."

"What are you talking about?" Atlas asks.

"You've seen it around town," Uncle Dwight continues. "The way everyone seems to like him, but no one likes me. He's been a master of manipulation since high school, and now he's turned you against me."

"No, that's not what's happening," I say.

"It's not?" he asks. "So you're just over here, letting him touch you because..."

I bite on my bottom lip, because I really have no answer to that.

"I see. Well, I heard rumblings that people have seen you two together, but I didn't think much of it. I thought they were talking about you being at the farm, but now I know." He nods and lets go of my arm. "Well, let me leave you with this." He blows out a heavy breath. "Remember when my girlfriend in high school was fighting cancer?"

I nod. It was a terrible thing. The whole family knew about it because we donated and raised funds for her cancer treatments, but sadly, she lost the battle.

"I made a wish that Christmas," he continues. "I made a wish on the Ornament Park tree with a very special, near and dear to me ornament. I wished for her to battle, to fight." I see tears start to well in his eyes. "And when I went to go look for it the next day...it was missing."

I gasp, my heart pounding a mile a minute.

No.

There's no way.

Atlas wouldn't do that.

Uncle Dwight looks Atlas in the eyes. "I later found out it was

Maxheimer who took it down." He wets his lips. "Jessica passed a few days after Christmas."

"Oh my God," I say as I turn to Atlas. "That's . . . that's horrible."

"And the only reason why he's talking to you, why he's trying to get on your good side is to not only save his farm but to try to take you away from me as well. When you first got here, I told him to stay away from you. I told him to not even look in your direction, and he took that as a challenge."

"Dwight, that's—"

"Don't," I say, backing away. "Please don't say anything."

"Betty," Storee says, looking confused. "Atlas wouldn't do that."

"How do *you* know?" Uncle Dwight says. "You've only been around a few years, but you saw the Christmas Kringle competition last year, how he got everyone to turn against me. The entire town doesn't like me, and it's all because of his manipulation." He shakes his head. "I've always been different from you, Maxheimer. Shorter, weaker, not as talented or well-connected, but I'll be damned if you try to take Betty away. Your little game is over. The challenge is over. Leave her alone."

And with that, he turns away and starts heading toward the exit.

Not even thinking about it twice, I leave my coffee cake and drink on the table and chase after my uncle until I reach him just outside the coffee shop. "Wait," I say, tugging on his arm.

"How could you do that to me?" he says, looking so disappointed. Angry. "How could you . . . embarrass me like that?"

"I wasn't . . . I didn't mean to embarrass you."

"The entire town is probably laughing at the fact that my own family member would rather hang out with a Maxheimer than me. Is that why you kept canceling? To hang out with him?"

"No," I say out of desperation. "No, I've just been . . . I've been confused."

"Because he's preyed on you."

"He didn't prey—"

"Let me ask you this," he says. "Didn't he try to break into your place? Then he chased you down at the farm. There was hostility between the two of you, right?"

"Yes," I say, feeling skeptical.

"And then he just started . . . being nice to you out of nowhere?"

I pause, thinking about it, trying to recall the moment when the switch flipped. He tried to bring me that popcorn, and then I was supposed to be hanging out with Storee, and he was there . . .

"I can see the wheels starting to turn in your head. This is all part of his manipulation, Betty. He's done it for years, but I'm the only one who calls him out on it. The reason he has this entire town eating out of his palm is because he's been able to manipulate their opinion, just like he did with you. He's not a good person. I've told you that from the beginning, and you chose not to listen."

"I just . . . I got confused," I say, feeling incredibly stupid. "I didn't mean to embarrass you. I'm ashamed to say that I felt like I was maybe helping in a way."

"Helping?" he asks. "How would cuddling up to Maxheimer be helping?"

"I . . . I thought that maybe we could come up with another idea," I say, feeling really ignorant and guilty. "An idea that the entire town could get behind. You know, so we had support."

"Did he suggest that?"

"No." I shake my head. "We haven't really talked about the plans—"

Uncle Dwight grows closer. "How often do you talk?"

I bite on the corner of my lip, knowing he won't like the answer. "I don't know, a few times a week."

"What?" His eyes go wide. "Jesus Christ, Betty." He takes a step back. "You've been talking to him a few times a week? Just letting him play you like that?" He lets out a disappointed sigh. "He deliberately took away my wish. He knew how important that was to me, and he took it away. I don't blame him for her death, but I blame him for diminishing my hope."

"I'm so sorry. I had no idea."

He looks away. "I was searching for you because I have to head out of town for a week. I have to attend an end-of-the-year business conference in Aspen."

"Okay, do you . . . do you need anything from me?"

He shakes his head. "No . . . just . . . just don't let him fool you, Betty. He's only going to hurt you in the long run like he's hurt me." Then with that, he takes off.

I turn around, not sure what to do now, and spot Atlas standing inside the doorway. Part of me wants to go straight to him and be held in his enormous arms. But then I think about Uncle Dwight's words.

Let me ask you this. Didn't he try to break into your place? Then he chased you down at the farm. There was hostility between the two of you, right? And then he just started . . . being nice to you out of nowhere?

I don't know who you are, Atlas Maxheimer.

I wouldn't mind sitting on Old Krampus's lap and telling him I'd like a beautiful blond with bright blue eyes to be set under my Christmas tree.

Did you mean that? *Or are you capable of lying so masterfully that you even have your best friend's wife convinced?*

I can't face him right now, so I turn on my heel and head back to my car.

CHAPTER EIGHTEEN
MAX

NARRATOR: WELL, THAT WAS NEARLY *unbearable to witness. If it wasn't for the tea being spilled about the feud, I might have looked away, but there was too much drama to keep me from leaving.*

What do you think?

Does Max have it in him to take someone else's ornament off the tree?

He's no saint, that's for certain. With the way this started between him and Betty, his intentions weren't pure, but can we trust that he's a genuine guy?

Or is there a secret side of Max that we don't know?

———————

"Max, open up." Cole bangs on my front door.

Grumbling, I peel myself off the couch and open the door for him but leave it as I go back to my comfort zone. I've been sitting here ever since this morning, when I decided not to partake in farm duties today and opted to catch up on some admin work. *Thank God for competent staff who can pick up the slack when I'm not there.*

Cole shuts the door behind him and then joins me in the living room. He studies me for a second and then says, "Everyone has been sent home."

I glance at him. "Why?"

"The storm," he says. "Have you not been paying attention?"

"There's a storm coming?" I noticed the winds have picked up, which causes power outages out here on the farm, but a storm?

"Yes. They're calling for over a foot of heavy snow. Jesus, man. What the hell has been going on? You don't show up to work today; you're clearly not paying attention to the weather; you're sulking around; you've been having secret meetings in the tree house with my wife—"

I sit up. "You know about that?"

"Yeah, of course I do, as it's hard not to hear you two out there chomping on Crunch Tators. And then Storee's been a mess, saying she's worried about you. So . . . what's going on?"

I drag my hands over my face as I say, "You don't want to know."

"Clearly, I do if I'm here."

Yeah, and I know he's not going to leave me alone until he finds out. Well, he's going to regret it, because I'm a mess too, and I have no problem unloading all my problems on him.

"Remember the plan?" I ask, defeated.

"What plan?"

"The one I laid out in my diagram?"

"The one you drew in crayon?" he asks with a raise of his brow.

"Yes, that one."

"Yesss," he drags out skeptically.

"Well, Storee and I sort of got together and put it into action."

"Jesus Christ." He shakes his head, looking extremely frustrated when he sits in the chair opposite mine. He rubs his temples and asks one simple question, "Why?"

"Because I was desperate. Because I thought it would work. Because I thought I was being really smart and intelligent and stealthy. But the problem is I didn't think I'd start liking her while putting the plan into action, which I did. And I didn't think Dwight would get in the way, which he did. And now it's all a mess. She's mad at me. Won't talk to me. And worst of all, she thinks I'm a barbarian bully who tormented Dwight in high school." *Something I definitely did not do.*

"Why would she think that?"

"Because that's what he told her this morning. He told her that I bullied him. Tormented him. That I was the one who took his wish ornament off the tree, the one for Jessica."

"What? He's blaming that on you?"

"Yeah. And I have no idea why. First, he was the one who started being a fucking dick in high school, and instead of taking it, I just gave it right back, but I didn't torment him. Second, I'd never take an ornament off that tree. It's sacred. My parents taught me that from an early age. But now Betty is under the impression that I lied to her, that everything I did was all about manipulating her opinion—"

"I mean . . . wasn't it though? Wasn't that the plan?"

I look up at my friend. "It was until it wasn't. I liked her far too quickly to even try to manipulate her, and the wooing wasn't out of revenge, it was out of interest. I can admit that now."

"And did you woo her?"

I look my friend in the eyes and nod. "I fucking did."

"Wait." He pauses and then sits up. "Is that why you were there at Cupid Christmas Night?"

I smirk. "Yeah, dude. It was all planned."

"You fucker. That was my one night out with my wife."

"It was her idea." I hold my hands up. "And you still had your night out. It just started with me, but it ended with her."

"So what now? You like her, and she thinks you're an ass?"

"Pretty much," I say.

"So tell her you're not."

A gust of wind blows, and the lights flicker. I glance around the room, knowing exactly what's going to happen. "Not that easy, man. Dwight convinced her that I'm a con artist, so anything that I say to her will be perceived as disingenuous." I glance outside, taking in the snow that's starting to blow around. "Dude, you should get home before it gets bad."

He looks out the window as well and nods in agreement. When he stands, he asks, "Want to come with me? Pack a bag real quick. You know you're going to lose power."

"It's fine. I have the Yeti battery packs and the generator, plus I stocked up on wood. I'm good."

"Food?" he asks.

"Good on that too."

"What about your mental health? Will you be okay alone? Maybe you should just come with me so you can at least . . . chat with Storee about this mess you guys got in."

And see, he is a good guy. It's times like this when I want everyone to see that my best friend isn't a complete grump and that he really does care about me.

"I'm good," I say. I head over to him at the door. "Seriously, you don't want me sulking around your house. Plus I can check on the reindeer if I'm here."

"I gave them extra feed, so they should be good, but yeah, I appreciate that." He heads toward the door and grips the handle. "You sure?"

"Positive," I say.

"Okay." He lets out a deep breath and then turns toward me. "You're a fucking moron for getting yourself into this disaster. Let it be known that I truly believe that."

"Uh . . . thanks?"

"But," he continues, "if you like her, then you have to set the record straight. Not sure how you're going to do that, but you need to."

"Yeah, thanks for stating the obvious."

He pats my shoulder. "That's what I'm here for. Let us know if you need anything. Stay warm."

"I will," I say, and then he takes off.

I grab my phone from my pocket and pull up the weather app. I quickly look over what's coming my way and mentally go through the routine. It's going to be a long, cold night.

BETTY

"Fuck, fuck, fuck," I say as I try flipping the breaker again, the wind whipping around me, snow getting thrust in my eyes. My nose is nearly freezing off my face.

When nothing happens, I realize that I'm absolutely fucked. I shut the panel and then head back to the front of the cottage, where I knock the snow off my boots and then get back inside.

When I shut the door, I shed my winter jacket and snow pants, drape them over the back of a chair, and rub my hands together, looking around my small cottage.

What the hell am I going to do?

Panic sets in because I have no electricity. Not even a backup battery anywhere. Believe me, I checked. My heat source has turned off. There is no way I'll be able to drive anywhere, and even if I could, Dwight isn't home. He left. So it looks like I'm hunkering down through this storm.

Since it's colder in the loft area, I grab my blankets and bring them down to the living room, where I set them up on the couch to form a cocoon, wishing I had more blankets right about now.

I slip on a pair of leggings, then some sweats on top of those, double-sock my feet, and put on a long-sleeved shirt and a sweatshirt. I grab my winter hat and slip that over my head, and then put on my bootie slippers as well. I glance at Buzz. Worried about him, I cover his aquarium with a few towels, hoping that will keep him warm.

When that's settled, I sit on the couch, wrap myself up, and then just stare out the window, watching large flakes of snow rapidly fall to the ground while the wind picks them up and moves them around at the same time, like some sort of snow tornado.

And because my heating source is turned off, I can feel the immediate effects of it. The heat is seeping from the cottage while the cold moves in.

It's going to be a long, long night.

MAX

Cole: Electricity turn off?

Max: Yup. But I have a fire going in the fireplace. Set up the air mattress down here and brought all the blankets. Generator is on hold. Yeti's ready to charge anything I need. I'm comfortable.

Cole: Good.

Max: Is it bad over there?

Cole: Yeah, the lights are flickering, but I doubt we'll lose electricity. We don't tend to like you do.

Max: Which is why I'm prepared.

Cole: Storee wants to know if you've heard from Betty at all.

Max: No. Definitely don't think I'm who she wants to talk to at the moment.

Cole: Not about that, about the storm.

Max: Oh . . . no . . . wait, fuck, I bet she lost power too. I wonder if she has any backup options. I haven't been in her cottage, so I don't know what she has going on in there. I doubt Dwight would leave her without the ability to keep the place warm if the power goes out.

Cole: Maybe you should check with her.

Max: Doubt she'll respond.

Cole: Still check with her. Storee will send her contact information to you.

My phone beeps with another text message, and it's from Storee.

I click on the contact and then pull up a text thread to type out a message.

Max: Hey, Betty. It's Max. I know I'm the last person you want to hear from right now, but since the power went out, I wanted to check in on you and see if your power went out or if you need anything. The storm is pretty brutal, and this will continue through the night. Temps as low as five degrees.

I hit Send and then call Cole and put him on speaker.

"Hello?"

"I sent her a text," I say. "Doubt she'll respond."

"I sent her a text too," Storee says. They must have me on speaker-phone as well. "But it's not saying *delivered*. Does yours say *delivered*?"

I glance down at the text and then answer, "No."

"Let me try calling her," Storee says.

I reach for another log and then poke the fire with the fire poker to get the log deeper into the embers.

"The phone went directly to voicemail. I think her phone is off," Storee says.

"Do you think she's with Dwight?" I ask.

"I have no idea. Things kind of blew up after the coffee shop," Storee answers. "I tried talking to her, but she didn't reply. She could be with Dwight."

I tug on my hair and look out the window at the blizzard-like conditions. "What if . . . what if she turned her phone off to save power? Do you think she's in her cottage all alone?" My stomach churns at the thought of it.

"I don't know," Storee says.

"If she is, does she have heat?" Cole asks.

"I have no fucking clue," I answer. "Fuck, do you think I should go over there and check on her?"

"Have you looked outside?" Cole says. "It's nasty, man. And now that it's dark, it will only get harder to get to her."

"But what if she doesn't have heat? It's going to be really fucking cold tonight, man. If she doesn't have heat, she could freeze."

"If you think you can make the trek, I think you should check on her," Storee says. "But if you can't make it, if it seems too hard, then just turn around. Maybe send some crews out there to check on her."

I let out a sigh. "Yeah, let me, uh, let me bundle up and at least try."

"Okay, let us know how it goes."

I say my goodbyes and then hang up.

Christ.

The last thing I want to do is go outside with the wind whipping around like it is, but I also can't sit here and wonder if Betty is in her cottage without any heat. I know it won't settle well with me. So I suit up, slip my boots and my reindeer hat on, and grab a flashlight.

This is going to fucking suck.

I open the back door to the house, and I'm immediately whipped in the face with snow.

Fuck.

Me.

Tilting my head down and pulling my hood up and over my head, I turn on my flashlight and head out, immediately regretting my decision when my leg sinks into at least half a foot of snow already.

This is going to be hell.

I trudge through the snow, getting smacked in the face with cold, frozen flakes, the wind a constant irritant and villain during the trek. Limbs of trees are weighed down by the fresh snow, clearing a better path for me as I make my way through the woods, trying to create the most direct route possible.

It's moments like these that I'm glad I know my land so well, as each familiar-shaped tree is keeping me heading in the right direction. Snowstorms can be so dangerous, because it's easy to fall and lose your sense of direction.

"Fuck, I have to be close. I've been going for about five minutes, so—" *There.* Her car. And behind that? Her cabin . . . without any lights.

Fuck.

I hurry as quickly as I can, and when I reach her porch, I shake off the snow before knocking on the door.

"Betty. You in there?"

I don't hear anything, so I knock again.

"Betty."

Nothing.

In case she possibly left the door open, I twist the handle, and to my surprise, it is unlocked, so I push the door open and flash the light inside, only to find a lump on the couch, covered in blankets.

I rush over to her and squat down.

"Betty . . . hey, you in there? It's Atlas."

I pull down the blanket to see her scared face look up at me, her teeth chattering.

"Fuck," I whisper.

I need to get her out of here.

BETTY

I can't feel my body.

My toes are numb.

My hands are numb.

I know my heart rate is low as I try to still my body, but it's useless.

I need to call for help. I need to . . .

Bang, bang.

My heart startles from the knocking on my door.

"Betty. You in there?"

Atlas?

Bang, bang.

"Betty."

After a few seconds, the door opens, and a rush of cold air flows into the house, eliminating any heat that I might have had left.

Heavy footsteps approach, followed by a body nearing me.

"Betty . . . hey, you in there? It's Atlas."

Blankets are pulled away from my face, and his eyes come into view.

"Fuck," he whispers, taking me in. "We have to get you out of here."

"C-can't m-move," I say, my teeth chattering so much that I can barely get the words out.

"I got you. Don't worry. I've got you."

He removes the blankets, but I protest. "C-cold."

"I know," he says softly. "You have winter gear on, good."

Yeah, I put it on when I realized the blankets weren't doing the job.

"I need you to climb on my back, okay?"

"W-what?" I ask.

"Betty, climb on my back."

"I . . . I can't."

He turns to look at me and then sighs. "Okay." He then wraps me up in a blanket and picks me up himself, holding me like a baby.

"Come on."

"M-my B-B-Buzz."

"Huh?" he asks.

"B-blankets. P-put blankets." I gesture to Buzz's tank, and he glances over at it. He sets me down for a moment, lifts up the blankets, and then nods.

"Okay." He puts more blankets on the aquarium and then scoops me up again. "It's going to be rough, okay? Put your hood up, and bury your face in my chest. I'll be as quick as I can."

MAX

I clutch Betty close to my chest as I follow my tracks back to the house, my flashlight barely dangling from my hand, lighting the way.

The only thing propelling me forward through the snow and my aching back is pure adrenaline, because the moment I saw her under those blankets, I went into protection mode. Why didn't she call someone? Why didn't she ask for help? Was she just going to stay there and freeze to fucking death?

Jesus Christ.

And why isn't fucking Dwight checking up on her?

Why didn't he give her a backup power option?

Because he's a dick, that's why.

I make it back onto my property and thankfully use the light on the back porch to guide me. I move up the stairs, open the door, and then bring her inside the den, where I gently set her down, only for her to crumple to the floor.

"Fuck." I quickly shed my jacket and boots and then do the same for her, pulling her out of the snow-covered clothes.

She's practically lifeless as I carry her into the living room, where the fire is still going.

Her body is freezing. Her legs, her arms, even though she's wearing

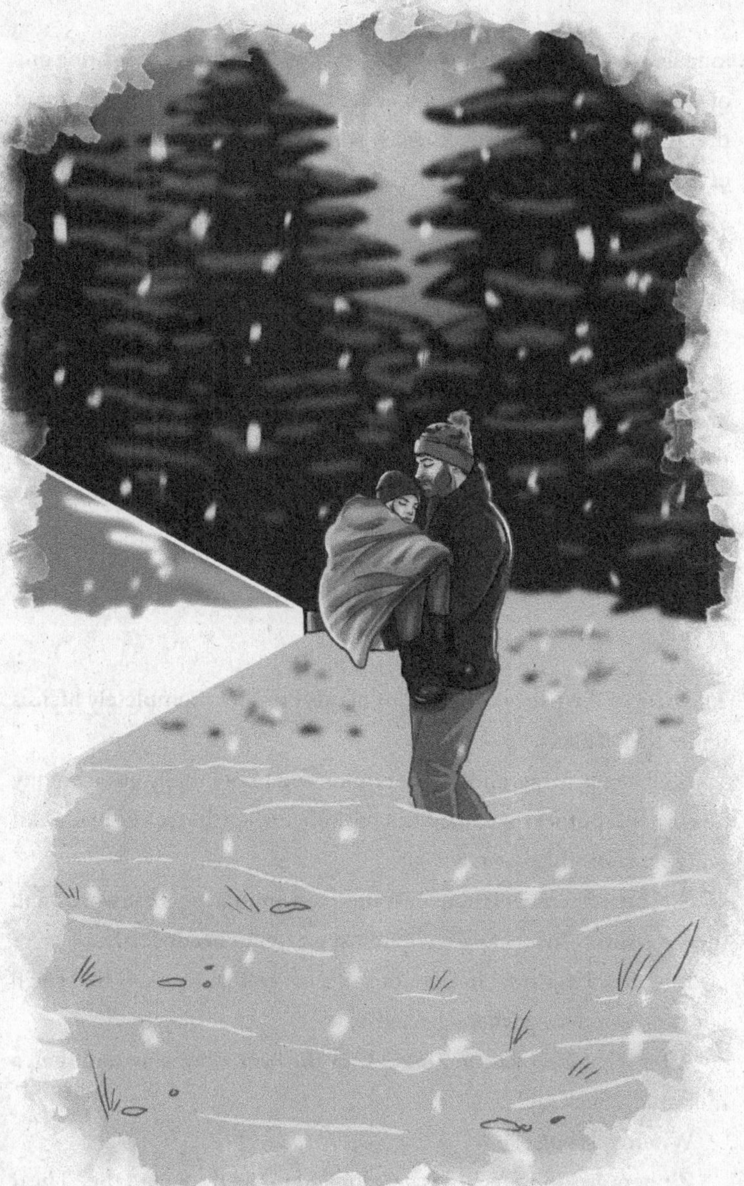

long sleeves, are freezing. I set her down on the couch and then bring one of the wingback chairs close to the fireplace. I pick her up and put her in the chair and then start covering her with blankets. Then I squat in front of her and run my finger over her cheek.

"Betty, you okay?"

Her eyes lightly open, and it takes her a second, but she nods.

"Okay." I put another log on the fire to increase the heat and then say, "I'll be back. Don't move, understood?"

She just nods and closes her eyes. I wait a moment and watch her breathe, making sure she's okay, and when I think that she'll be fine, I go to the back of the house again, suit up, and then trek back out to her place.

BETTY

The heat of the fire blazes in front of me, but I feel completely lifeless under the blankets.

My head is fuzzy, and I'm not quite sure how I really got from my house to here other than Atlas. But the in-between, the trek he made, not quite sure how that went.

All I can remember is him breathing hard, muttering curse words, and then reassuring me that we were almost where we needed to be.

And now I'm sitting in front of a fire, covered in blankets that smell like him, wondering where the hell he is.

After what feels like an hour, I hear the back door shut and then a muttered, "Fuck me."

Where was he?

Zippers are undone, boots are clunked to the floor, and then I hear him approach, only to see him come up beside me and squat down again.

His nose and cheeks are bright red, his eyelashes and eyebrows have droplets of moisture clinging to them, and his hair is wet and curled in the cutest way.

"How are you?"

"O-okay," I say still shaking.

"I'll make you some tea." He stands again and then moves off toward the kitchen, where I hear him move around, opening cabinets and shutting them.

Why . . . why is he doing this?

Why is he being so kind? I shift in my seat, not wanting to ruin my cocoon, but I want to be more comfortable, and that's when I see Buzz's aquarium on the hearth.

Wait . . . did he . . . did he go back for Buzz?

I mean, of course he did. I don't remember much from my cottage to his house, but I can tell you right now, he didn't carry that aquarium and me together.

But why?

After everything that happened this morning . . . why?

CHAPTER NINETEEN
MAX

NARRATOR: WHAT A KNIGHT IN *shining armor, a true hero some might say. If I could, I'd have stripped him down to just a pair of jeans and a reindeer hat, letting you watch in slow motion as he trekked across the snow, his nipples hardening, his muscles flexing, turning into our very own Jack Frost and making that snow his bitch.*

But of course, we must be realistic here. Instead, he was a knight in shining snowsuit . . . and a reindeer hat.

But now that he's back and trying to warm up, do you think we should have them get naked for body heat?

Ehh . . . I think I might edge you a little bit more.

Fuck, it's cold.

I shakily place two coffee cups on the counter and wait for the kettle to heat up. Thankfully, it doesn't take long. This isn't my first time losing electricity out here, so we have stocked up on items that can utilize batteries or don't suck too much power from the Yetis. This teakettle is one of those.

The water starts to boil, so I pull it off the warmer and pour it into the mugs. Then I dunk two peppermint tea bags into the water and carefully carry them to the living room, where Betty is still a lump on the chair.

She seems to have a little bit of color in her face now, but when I first set her in front of the fire, I swear she was ghostly white. Freaked me the fuck out.

I set the mugs on the hearth next to her fucking tarantula—that fucking thing was a surprise. "Can you sit up a little more and stick your hands out? It will really help to drink something hot."

She shifts, but it's slow, and when she sticks her hands out, I test them. Still cold. Christ. How long was she in there without any heat?

I gently hand her the mug and then notice how hard it is for her to hold it, so I wrap my hands around hers, helping her.

Her eyes meet mine, and I say, "Go ahead. I'll help."

We bring the cup to her lips, and she blows on the hot liquid a few times before taking a sip.

"That's it. Take another one for me."

She sips, and then I take a sip too, letting the hot liquid pool in my stomach, instantly defrosting me. We spend the next few minutes sipping the cup together until it's gone. Then I pick up my mug and do the same thing, wanting to warm her up as quickly as I can.

When that mug is done, I bring my hand to her cheeks and feel that there's some warmth spreading through her body now.

"I'm going to change out of these clothes and wash up a bit. Do you need anything?"

"N-no," she says, her voice still weak.

"Okay." Unsure of what else to say, I grab my phone from the coffee table behind her and head upstairs, where I don't plan on being very long because it's cold. I have to get out of these clothes.

When I get up to my room, I close the door, dial Cole's number, and put it on speaker as I take some baby wipes that we keep for instances just like this and start stripping down to clean up.

"Hello?" he answers.

"She was in the cottage, fucking frozen, man."

"Are you serious?" Cole asks.

I wipe down my body, even though I took a shower before the power went out. "Yeah. No lights, no heat source, nothing. Found her in a pile of blankets, barely any life to her face."

"Jesus, fuck. Do we need to send paramedics?"

"No." I slip on a new pair of boxer briefs and then socks. "She's in front of the fire right now with a lot of blankets, and she just drank some tea. I had to help her, of course, but she drank it. She's warming up, but I'm keeping an eye on her."

"Okay, do you need us to do anything?"

"I don't think so. Not like you can do anything anyway. It's brutal out there." I slip on a pair of blue-and-green-plaid flannel pants and a white long-sleeved shirt.

"Are you okay?"

"Yeah," I sigh as I take a seat on my bed. "I went back out after I brought her to my house, because she has a tarantula."

"What?"

"Yeah, my thoughts as well. And since the heat went out, I didn't think it would survive, so I went back and got it."

"I would have let the spider die," Cole says.

"And that's why people say I'm the nice one between the two of us."

"Yeah, I guess so. Okay, so you're safe then?"

"I'm good. I'll keep an eye on her, and I'll let you know if anything changes."

"Okay, sounds good. Be safe, man."

"You too."

I hang up the phone and then head down the stairs with the long-sleeved shirt that pairs with my pajama set. I set it next to the fire to warm up. Then I sit across from her and take her in.

Her eyes are closed, the blankets are up to her chin, but she's stopped shaking, and she definitely has more color in her face.

I can't believe she thought she'd just stay there all night. The thought of it makes me physically ill, because she wouldn't have survived.

Not a goddamn chance.

Wanting her to rest, I add another log to the fire, and then I set the bed up. It's going to be a long night.

BETTY

I can feel my toes.

My fingers.

My limbs.

Everything is . . . warm.

And as I open my eyes, comfort spreading all through me, I notice that I'm no longer in the chair in front of the fire but rather on a bed in front of the fire.

I look around, confused, and that's when I find Atlas off to the side in a chair, watching me.

"You're awake," he says, leaning forward by resting his forearms on his legs. "How do you feel?"

"Warm," I answer, my voice normal now.

"Hungry?"

"Um . . . a little," I say.

"Good. I have some soup for you. I planned to wake you up in a bit."

He gets up from the chair and then brings a plate to the coffee table, which he's moved to my side, and puts it down. There is a bowl with soup in it, steam coming off the top, and a piece of bread on the side.

"Let me grab you some water."

When he heads toward the kitchen, I attempt to sit up but feel weak. Incredibly weak.

"Hold on. Let me help." He moves in behind me and sets some water on the coffee table. He helps me lift up and then, to my surprise, takes a seat behind me, letting me use him as a backrest to lean against.

He speaks softly as he says, "Want me to help you with the spoon?"

"No . . . no, I'm okay."

"You sure?"

"Yeah. Thank you." I dip the spoon in the tomato soup and then blow on it a few times before bringing it to my mouth. Warm, creamy, delicious.

I lean against him, allowing him to prop me up as I devour the soup like it's my first meal in a week. The heat of the soup warms me up even more, to a point that I'm starting to feel comfortable again, not like I have to keep shaking to get my body temperature up.

"Want me to break apart the bread for you?"

"That's okay," I say, feeling all kinds of awkward because . . . once again, this is not the man that Uncle Dwight told me about. I couldn't be more confused.

He traversed through a snowstorm to help me, then went back to help my tarantula. He's kept me warm, fed me, made sure that I had everything I needed, even helped me drink, and is now letting me use his body for my own comfort.

There has to be a mistake.

There's no way he would do all this just to manipulate me, right?

I finish up my soup, and when I'm done, he softly asks, "Do you want to lie down?"

"Can I sit on the couch?"

"Of course." He stands from the air mattress and, to my surprise again, bends down and hoists me into his arms as if I weigh nothing. He carries me to the couch, blankets and all, and sits me down. He drapes a few blankets over me and positions a pillow behind my back, propping me up. "Comfortable?" he asks.

"Yes," I say softly, my mind running a mile a minute.

He takes a seat on the opposite side of the couch and faces me. "I, um, I set a long-sleeved shirt next to the fire to warm up if you want to wear it. Keep you warmer."

I glance over at the plaid pajama top and find myself nodding.

I don't know whether it's because it's warm or because it's his, but I want to wear it.

He grabs it from the hearth and then helps me put it on before covering me in blankets again.

God, it feels so good, and it smells just like him.

When he takes a seat again, he stares at the fire.

"Thank you . . . for coming to check on me," I say.

He still stares at the fire as he nods. "Of course."

"And for bringing me here and bringing Buzz. And taking care of me. You . . . you didn't have to—"

"I'm not that guy, Betty," he says, startling me. He slightly turns his head so he's looking at me. "I'm not the guy Dwight paints me as. And I know he's done a pretty good job making me look like the bad guy, but I promise you, I'm not that man."

The way he looks at me, like he's pleading for me to believe him, it nearly splits me in half.

"Bringing you here, it wasn't so I could manipulate you, so you could believe that I'm some kind of good guy when I'm not. I brought you here because the moment I thought that you might not have a backup power source, I felt this deep-rooted panic inside me. I tried texting, Storee tried calling, and when no one could get to you, I knew I had to go to your place. And when I saw you in the dark, freezing, my stomach dropped. I was . . . I was fucking terrified, Betty." He pushes his hand through his hair. "Seeing you, lifeless like that . . . it terrified me. And it terrified me because I care about you. Genuinely, from the bottom of my soul, I care about you. This isn't an act. This isn't some revenge on Dwight. This feeling I have, in my goddamn chest, this thumping, pulsing feeling, it's me caring for you." He stands from the couch. "And I can't . . . I can't just get over it. It's why I've tried to get close to you as you've tried to come up with ways to harm my farm. It's why I've spent countless hours thinking about you, why I spent a night looking for every sprig of mistletoe I could find so I could kiss you, and it's why this morning, when I saw you walk toward me in the coffee shop, my heart skipped a beat. I like you. It's as simple as that. I like you."

And before I can even respond, he takes off toward the kitchen, leaving me with a heavy heart full of guilt.

Because I believe him.

MAX

I press my hands into the counter, taking a few deep breaths, trying to calm my racing heart.

I've never done that before.

Ever. I've never put my heart on the line like that, told a woman how I feel, and fuck, it's terrifying but also freeing.

There's only so much I can say to convince her, to let her know that I'm not the person Dwight portrays me as. I just hope . . . I hope she can possibly believe me. I stand taller, looking around the kitchen. It's fucking late, I'm tired, exhausted, and honestly, I just want to go to bed, so I lock the back door, straighten the dirty dishes—I splash a little water on them so they don't crust overnight—and then I walk back into the living room, where she's still seated on the couch, staring at the fire.

"Um, I'm going to go brush my teeth. I should have grabbed some items for you when I went back to your place, but I'll pick out some clothes and bring them down for you."

She absently nods, so I take that as my moment to leave. I head upstairs and grab my toothbrush, a brand-new toothbrush for her, and some toothpaste. Then I rifle through my pajamas, looking for something that might fit her, but they're all huge. I consider grabbing a pair of my mom's, but that seems even weirder to me, so I take my smallest pair of pants downstairs along with the wipes in case she wants to wash up.

I bring everything to the downstairs bathroom and quickly get ready for bed, glancing in the mirror occasionally to see that my hair has curled in weird ways and my eyes look tired and worried.

A real treasure.

Shaking my head, I go back to the living room and say, "Uh, bathroom is all yours. There's some water in there, so when you go to the bathroom, just put water down the toilet, and it should do the trick. I left a flashlight on in there for you, so you don't get lost. And, uh, there's a brand-new toothbrush in there as well, dentist approved if you're worried. Oh, and some pajama pants if you want something to change into. They're flannel but will probably be huge on you." I tug on my neck. "I can sleep on the couch, and you can take the air mattress so you're close to the fire. I wasn't planning on having a guest, or else I'd have blown up another air mattress, but I'd have to go digging for it."

"It's fine," she says and then scoots to the edge of the couch.

I'm quick to rush over. "Do you need help?"

She shifts the blankets off her, and a chill takes over her entire body, causing her to shake. "No . . . I'm good."

"You sure?"

She nods, but I still take her hand in mine and help her to her feet. When she's fully standing, she looks up at me, those ocean eyes of hers nearly splitting me in two.

"Um, let me get out of your way," I say. I step to the side. "Bathroom is down the hall on the right. Yell if you need anything."

"Thanks," she says softly and then heads that way . . . slowly.

I waver between helping her to the bathroom and holding back. She's weaker than I thought she'd be. Then again, being that cold for that long, it takes a toll on the body. She's probably exhausted, so I should make her a comfortable place to rest.

While she's in the bathroom, I set up the bed so there's a fitted sheet and top sheet on the mattress, something I planned to bypass because I was by myself, but now that she's here, I want her to be as comfortable as possible. I place a few blankets down, then fold it all at the top, and put a pillow down as well. When I'm happy with it, I place another log on the fire, take the spare pillow and blanket, and toss them on the couch just as she comes back into the living room. She's wearing my pajama top, which she put on earlier, but it seems like she took her sweatshirt off, and she's wearing the pair of pajama pants I let her borrow, but they're dragging on the floor.

Fuck . . . it's adorable.

When she sees the bed that's set up, she glances over at the couch, and she makes a displeased expression. "Is that what you're sleeping with?"

I glance back at the single blanket and the pillow. "Yeah, it's fine."

"You won't fit on the couch, Atlas."

"Eh, I'll curl up."

"I can take the couch," she says as she slowly moves toward it.

"No," I say, sounding more forceful than I want to. "I mean, no, please, take the air mattress. You're already cold. You need to stay close to the fire. I'll manage it throughout the night, but it might die down a little, and I don't want you getting any colder than you are. You're taking the air mattress."

She looks at the air mattress, studying it, and then says, "Share it with me."

"No, it's okay. You take it."

"Do you not want to share it with me?" I swear her pupils grow larger than normal as she stares up at me.

I mean, yeah, I want to fucking share it with her. That would be amazing, but I don't want to make her uncomfortable. "I, uh, I don't have any problem sharing it. I just want to respect your space is all."

"Please share. I might need your body heat during the night anyway."

I mean, valid point. "Okay, yeah, I can share with you."

"Thank you," she answers quietly and then moves toward the bed.

"Do you need help?" I ask, pausing her from getting down on the mattress.

"Atlas?"

"Hmm?"

"I really can do this myself."

"I know." I push my hand through my hair, feeling awkward and nervous. "I just . . . I don't know. I want to make sure you're okay."

"I appreciate that, but I can handle this."

And then I watch her climb on the air mattress and slip under the covers.

Okay, she can handle this.

I check the front door one last time to make sure it's locked, grab my phone and a flashlight, and set them next to the bed in case I need them in the middle of the night, put one more log on the fire, and then move down to the air mattress and slip under the covers as well, making a deliberate point to stick to my side of the bed.

"Are you, uh, are you comfortable?" I ask.

"Yes," she says with a shiver.

"Want another blanket?"

"No. Can you . . . can you come closer?"

"Oh sure," I say on a gulp as I slide closer to her.

And then to my utter surprise, she closes the distance and plasters her body right against mine. And it's awkward, because my arm is against my right side, and she's up against my arm. I want to put my arm around her. I want to have her close, but that's pretty presumptuous—

"Can you hold me?" she asks, causing a sweat to break out on my upper lip, because was she just reading my mind?

"Are you sure?" I ask.

"Positive," she says.

Well, she doesn't have to ask me twice. I loop my arm around her, and immediately, she snuggles in close, resting her head on my shoulder and placing her hand on my chest. Her faint scent of lavender filters up to my nose as she fits perfectly into my side.

Well, motherfucker . . . this is . . . this is more than I could have asked for.

At first, I can feel my body grow stiff, unsure how to handle this, but as she melts into my side, nuzzling her head against my shoulder, the tension wears off, and I ease into the hold, allowing myself to spread my hand along her hip and get comfortable.

"That okay?" I ask.

"Perfect," she says, her answer so quiet, so . . . relaxed that it actually makes my heart beat faster. Knowing I can make her feel comfortable with me, that means so much.

I close my eyes, allowing myself to revel in this moment because I can't really recall a time when I felt this attracted to a woman, when I waited with bated breath to see if she'd give me her time. And right now, she's giving me her whole night.

She sighs against me, and her hand splays out across my chest, warming my body, as my imagination starts to play with me. What if her hand moved down an inch or two? What if it traveled to the hem of my shirt and her fingers toyed with the idea of touching my bare skin?

What if—

"Atlas?"

"Hmm?"

Her thumb strokes my chest, spreading another wave of warmth through me. "I need you to know something."

"What's that?" I ask.

Then to my surprise, she sits up and stares down at me, her beautiful face half-lit up by the fire.

"I, um . . . I want you to know that I . . . that I believe you."

"You . . . you do?" I ask, feeling my chest fill with relief.

She nods. "I do, and I'm sorry if . . . if I've seemed ungrateful tonight, because I'm not. I'm so grateful for you. I don't know what I would have done if you didn't come and rescue me. Rescue my tarantula. You . . . you put your life on the line for me, and I don't think I'll ever be able to repay you for that."

"You don't need to," I say, my pulse picking up, my body tingling.

"I can at least tell you how grateful I am," she says as her thumb continues to stroke my chest. "And I'm sorry it took me so long. I was just processing."

"Processing what?"

"All the things you were doing. I have . . . I have one person telling me one thing about you, but then I see your actions, and your actions speak so much louder than your words, and I want to believe that you're not doing it to manipulate—"

"I'm not," I say quickly. "Fuck, I'm not, Betty. I genuinely care about you, and what I said earlier, it's all true. I like you. I don't know how it happened, maybe when we were awkwardly talking about penises and vaginas in the gym, I don't know, but I felt like I knew you on a deeper level, like we're the same person, and fuck, you're hot and funny and cute—"

She places her finger over my lips, quieting me. With a smile tugging on her lips, she says, "I believe you, Atlas. I don't know why Dwight said those things, I truly don't, but I do know that you are not the same person he speaks of."

"I swear to you, Betty." I wet my lips. "I swear to you that I didn't touch his ornament. You know me. You know how sacred that tree is. I wouldn't do that."

She nods. "That's what I was trying to process, because it didn't make sense. None of it makes sense. I really hope I'm not being blind about all this and it's not one big ruse, but I believe you. I trust you. I think . . . I think Dwight is placing the blame on you when it was maybe someone else."

That's what I've been thinking about today too. *Who did that to him?*

Was it intentional? If so, it was truly unkind. But hearing that Betty believes I wasn't an asshole to Dwight, well, it feels as though I've been validated. And I didn't realize until this moment how important that was to me. *Betty approving of me.*

I let out a long pent-up breath and drag my hand over my face. "Fuck, I'm so glad you said that. Because it wasn't me. I promise you, it wasn't me."

"I know." Her hand slides down my stomach. "I know wasn't you." And then her hand slips under the hem of my shirt, and just like that, her fingers are touching my skin. "And I'm sorry that for a moment, I believed you were capable of doing that to him."

It's extremely difficult to think right at this moment, but it's not lost on me that her trust in me could all come undone if she finds out about the wooing plan. Even though my intentions weren't honorable initially, I'm honestly into her now, and I loathe the idea of Betty finding out about the ways Storee and I *did* manipulate situations. *I want her to trust me. I want her to choose me.*

"You . . . you don't need to apologize," I answer as her hand travels up my stomach. My teeth tug on my bottom lip as she drags her finger across my abs.

"I just want you to know that I trust you, that I'm grateful for you."

"I really appreciate that, Betty. Probably more than you know."

She smiles softly. "It's the truth. And also, thank you for tonight. For coming to get me, housing me, keeping me warm. For everything."

"You're welcome," I answer softly while her finger circles my stomach, creating a type of heat deep inside me that will keep me warm all night. "Thank you for giving me a chance."

"Hard not to." She shivers, which concerns me.

"Here, let's get you under the blanket." I start to adjust the blankets, but she stops me as she worries her lip. "What?" I ask.

"Um, I was kind of wondering, and please feel free to say no, but maybe, to keep me warmer and maybe you warmer, that possibly you would consider, only if you want to . . . if you could maybe sleep with your shirt off?"

Fuck, how cute is she, asking all shy like that? Sleep with my shirt off so her hand is constantly on my skin all night? As if she has to ask fucking twice.

"Is that what you want?" I ask, and she responds with a timid nod. I'll make this easy on her. "Then yeah, I can." I sit up, and she moves to the side as I reach behind my head and pull my shirt off. I toss it to the side and then lie back down.

I watch as her eyes take me in. Talk about a fucking ego boost.

"You won't be too cold?"

Too cold? My body is a fucking inferno right now, especially with the way she just wet her lips while checking out my chest.

"Nah, I was probably going to get too hot with it on."

"Okay. Um, well, thank you."

And then she lies back down, resting her head on my shoulder and snuggling in close, her hand back on my chest, and that's about it . . .

Not that I was looking for more.

This is perfect.

This is all I need tonight.

Nothing else.

CHAPTER TWENTY
BETTY

NARRATOR: *THAT'S ALL HE NEEDS tonight?*

Who is he kidding?

I think we all know where he thought that request was going. He was probably thinking an innocent request to take his shirt off could lead to so much more, especially after those finger swivels on his abdomen. Surprised he didn't go hard just from her slight breath on his chest.

I don't think he's content with just holding her.

I bet he would at least want a kiss.

Then again, it's Max. He tends to live in a land of delusion.

———————

Oh God.

Oh God.

Oh God.

I'm resting my head on his naked chest.

I can't believe I was bold enough to even ask him to take his shirt off. The request fell past my lips, and I immediately felt my cheeks go red, but then he took his shirt off without a problem, and now I'm lying here, plastered to his naked torso, my hand on his chest, and I have no idea what to do.

Do I tell him the dentist-approved toothbrush was one of the best I've ever used? Because it was.

Do I tell him that his clothes smell like a mixture of Tide laundry detergent and pine trees? Because dear God, it's the best smell ever.

Do I tilt my head up, lightly kiss him on the jaw, and say good night? Because that seems like something that I could make happen, but I don't know if we're at a kissing point right now.

Sure, we've kissed before, under mistletoe and mistakenly on his porch, but there is no mistletoe in this room; I've looked around. And of course, he said things to me tonight that have led me to believe that if I did kiss him, he'd kiss me back, but if he wanted to kiss me good night, wouldn't he have done it already?

God, why is this so hard?

"Are you warm?" he asks, startling me out of my thoughts.

"Yes," I squeak. "I mean, yes, I'm warm. Thank you. And thank you for caring for me."

"Thank you for letting me care for you."

"Thank you for even thinking about caring for me."

He chuckles. "Are you as nervous as I am?"

I sit up again, shocked. And this is why I like this man so much, because he's not afraid to say how he feels. He's not trying to be some macho alpha male, walking around town, staking his claim. No, he can admit to his feelings. He can be goofy. He can lie here on this mattress and feel just as many nerves as me—at least I hope he is.

"You're nervous?"

He chuckles again. "Yeah, I'm fucking nervous."

"Why are you nervous? I know why I'm nervous, but you . . ."

"Because, Betty, after this morning, I didn't think that you'd even talk to me, and now you're here, in my house, sharing a bed with me. I don't . . . I don't want to fuck this up."

And the genuine look of insecurity that crosses his expression just about does me in.

I don't care what Uncle Dwight says—he's wrong. There is no way

Atlas had any part in the torment that he experienced. Can't be. This man who's staring up at me, I don't think he could hurt a soul. He's funny and goofy and sexy and caring. He cares so much that he saved a tarantula he's never met in a snowstorm.

And the thought of that puts me at ease as I trace my thumb over his scruff. "You're not going to fuck it up."

His hand on my hip tightens, tugging me in closer.

"Promise?" he asks, his eyes growing dark.

"Promise," I say as I lean forward, hoping that this is what he wants too, and I lightly press my lips to his.

He groans and then brings his hand to the back of my head, holding me in close as his mouth parts and he kisses me harder.

Lust beats through me as I turn more toward him, lining up my chest with his while I grip his face and match the intensity of his kiss, parting my lips, letting my tongue peek out ever so slightly, causing him to groan even louder. And it's the sexiest sound, hearing the way that I can turn him on.

And we stay like that, kissing, making out, exploring with our mouths for I don't know how long, but it settles me. It feels like I was meant to do this all along. Warmth and comfort and everything you'd expect from a kiss with the right person, it all swirls around me, telling me this is it. This is who I should be kissing.

When I pull away for some air, I stare down at him and the heaviness in his eyes as he looks back up at me. There's happiness there, satisfaction, and it's so freaking thrilling.

"Imagine if we did that under some mistletoe," he says in a lazy voice.

I chuckle. "It would have been the talk of the town."

"It would have set the standard for all other couples."

"We would have made history. They would write Kringletown history books about us."

"It wouldn't be Cupid Christmas Night anymore. It would be the Christmas Cosmic Kiss Night."

"Ooo, that has a nice ring to it."

"I thought so too." He cutely smiles up at me.

I rub my thumb over his cheek. "I don't think I've ever told you this before, but you're very handsome."

"Thank you. I grew my face myself."

I laugh. "I'm very impressed. It's symmetrical with a great nose, sharp jaw, and beautiful eyes. Oh, and I can't forget the bushy eyebrows."

"I could say the same thing about you. I mean about the symmetrical face, not the bushy eyebrows. You have nice eyebrows and a nice face. All in all, really fun to look at."

"It's astonishing you don't have women hanging all over you from the way you so effortlessly compliment me."

He chuckles. "Yeah, I would like to think that I'm smooth, but I'm really not. I'm fucking awkward."

"Yeah, I've noticed, but I find it endearing and comforting, because I'm the same way."

"Which I like a lot."

I smile softly and then kiss his lips one more time, just a feather of a kiss though, before I pull away and lie back down, but instead of resting my head on his shoulder, I turn away.

"Uh, what do you think you're doing?" he asks in a cute protest.

"Hoping that you would get the hint and spoon me."

"Oh, right." He chuckles and then turns as well, and he scoops me into his large arms and plasters me against his heated chest. "There. Comfortable?"

"Very."

"Warm?"

"Yes," I answer.

"Good," he says as he buries his head in my hair.

"Thank you again for tonight, Atlas."

"You don't have to keep thanking me," he says as he nuzzles me.

"I keep thinking about what would have happened if you didn't come and get me."

"Well, I wouldn't be wrapped around you right now, that's for damn sure."

"I'm being serious," I say.

"I know," he whispers. "But I honestly can't think about it. I just . . . I just want to hold you, knowing that you're not in your cottage, nearly freezing to death. I like knowing that you're here, next to me. Safe."

"I like it too," I say as I sigh into him, wanting him closer.

So much closer.

For a moment, I consider maybe having some skin-on-skin contact, allowing myself to truly feel his warmth, but that seems bold.

Isn't that bold?

His hand moves across my stomach as he shifts behind me, getting even closer. My skin prickles, my heart hammers, and for a moment, the movement leads me to believe that maybe . . . maybe he's feeling the same way.

So on a deep breath, I decide to take a chance and slide his hand under my shirt so he's pressing his palm against my skin.

He clears his throat, and immediately, insecurity consumes me.

"Oh, um, is that . . . is that okay?" I ask. "I thought that maybe, um, that possibly—"

"Betty, trust me, I'm more than okay with this."

"Are you sure? Because if you weren't, I wouldn't be offended. You could just pull your hand right back out."

"Not happening."

"Okay, because the option is there. I just thought that it might be nice to have some skin-on-skin contact, but you know that's presumptuous of me—"

His hand slowly slides north until his thumb connects with the underside of my breast, stealing all the air from my lungs.

Oh God ... oh God!

"I'm perfectly content," he whispers, his breath caressing my ear as he keeps his hand firmly in place.

My skin prickles.

A dull throb erupts between my legs.

And my staggered breath shifts my chest just enough that every time I breathe out, my breast skims across his thumb.

I try to steady my breathing. I try to calm my raging pulse, which seems to be hammering in my ears, but I can't because, God, he's so close.

No longer am I cold.

No longer do I need all these blankets.

No, I just need him, because one little pass of his thumb has my body heating like an inferno.

"Are you okay?" he asks, his mouth still right next to my ear.

No, because I want more.

Need more.

"Umm, slightly turned on," I say, unable to stop the truth from coming out.

"Yeah?" he asks, and I can hear the smile in his voice. "Only slightly?"

And then he drags his thumb over my breast, and I nearly wilt from the feel of it. I can't tell you the last time I was with a man or even had a man cop a feel; it's been a long time. So to have someone like Atlas—so handsome, so consuming, so overwhelmingly sweet—even be interested has me nearly panting.

"Maybe a little more than slightly."

"Was it from the kiss ... or was it from this?" he asks, swiping my breast again.

A moan falls past my lips. "A combination."

"Good answer." Then to my chagrin, he moves his hand back to my stomach, to a more suitable place.

I steady my breath before I ask, "You're, uh, you're not going to—"

He removes his hand completely from my shirt, and hope falls as he places his hand on top of the fabric.

"Oh," I answer. "Did I make you uncomfortable?"

"No," he answers casually but then starts to unbutton my shirt. Beginning with the bottom button, he works his way up, using one hand and freeing the fabric all the way until he gets to the top.

I can't breathe.

I can't focus.

This can't possibly be happening...

And then he gently tugs me to my back so I'm staring up at the ceiling right before he hovers over me, his handsome face coming into view. In a deep, sultry voice, he says, "That's better."

I stare up at him, anticipation and nerves coursing through me as he slowly parts the shirt, one side at a time, exposing my breasts.

My chest heaves.

My mouth goes dry.

And my nipples pucker as he stares down at me.

"Fuck," he says, dragging his hand over his mouth, a look of awe crossing his expression. "Jesus, Betty. You're so fucking hot."

It takes all but two seconds before he brings his mouth back to mine, but this time, he's greedier. And I fall into his desire while his hand drags up my side, against my ribs, where he holds me in place. I squirm, wanting more, but he keeps still, taking charge of my mouth instead, owning me in this moment, not letting me lead but instead demanding that I follow and...I love it.

I love being possessed like this; I love his strong hold and his demanding kisses. I love the way his jaw scrapes across mine and how he nibbles ever so slightly on my lip. I love that he kicks my legs open with his knees, parting me to make room for his pressing body. And I love that when he allows some of his body weight to crowd against mine, I can feel exactly how turned on he is against my leg.

His lips move across my jaw and to my neck, where he licks the column and then kisses the spot just below my ear. A chill breaks out across my skin, and my nipples go hard as he travels lower to my collarbone, where he kisses, nips, and sucks.

My hands glide across his back and down to the waistband of his pants, where I slip my fingers past and under his boxer briefs.

"Fuck," he breathes before lowering his mouth farther while his hand slowly cups my breast.

"Please," I say, my voice sounding distant as this out-of-body experience happens to me.

He kisses my sternum, then my cleavage, and then he glides his cheek across my breast, my nipple passing over his lips before he squeezes my breast and then sucks my nipple into his mouth at the same time.

My hand tangles in his luscious hair as I hold him in place, wanting him to continue to play with me with his mouth. And he does.

He tugs on my nipple with his teeth, sucks, licks, nibbles. He makes me so wet, so turned on, that I want to shed my shirt, push my pants down . . . and push his pants down as well.

"God, Atlas," I say, my hips now thrusting against his leg, seeking out any friction to relieve some of the built-up tension that he's created.

But he doesn't give me what I want. Instead, he moves to my other breast and starts playing around with it, driving up my need, making me writhe beneath him, to the point that I move my foot to the hem of his pants and push them down. I can feel him smile against me before he lifts up and quirks a brow at me. "What do you think you're doing?"

"The same thing you're doing."

He shakes his head. "No, I'm playing with your tits. You're trying to strip me down to nothing."

"Um, you unbuttoned my shirt. I think it's only fair that I push your pants down."

"Nah, I'm in control." He pulls his pants back up and then goes back to sucking on my breasts, nibbling across the sensitive flesh, making me so crazy with desire, I swear I might just come from him doing this.

And that has never happened before, but he's teasing, playing with me in all the right ways. He's making me needy, desperate, to the point that I let out a long moan and then move my hand between us to find some relief, only for my hand to be snatched away.

"No fucking way are you about to do that," he says against my chest. "No fucking way."

"I need relief. Please."

He lifts up to stare down at me, his chest heaving slightly. "You want relief?"

"Yes," I say.

"Betty, I haven't even begun playing with you. This is just the beginning."

"I need the end," I say, a plea of desperation coming from me.

He rolls his teeth over the corner of his lip, considering my plea. "Then use me."

"Huh?"

He rolls off me and lies on his back. "I don't have condoms, but . . . use me. Get off on me. Make yourself come."

Really?

Just . . . just use him?

I don't think that has ever been offered to me.

But I want to. Bad.

Smiling, I move on top of him and lower my throbbing center over his erection. "Oh my God," I say as I feel just how large he is. "Atlas . . ."

His hands fall to my hips and his eyes focus on my breasts, which peek out from my open shirt. "Ride me, Betty."

Needing more contact, I slip off him and then take my pants off, only to lower myself back down on top of him, leaving me in nothing but my thong. His hands move up my legs and to my backside, where his fingers dig into my ass.

"Christ," he says as he pushes me forward over his length. "Ride me, Betty. Come on me, baby."

I plant my hands on his pecs and start rotating my hips, making my weight sink on top of him as the friction between us builds.

"Fuck, that's it," he says as his muscles strain beneath me.

It's so incredibly hot. I let my hands travel over his thick pecs, reveling in how muscular he is . . . all over. I've never been with a man like him, with such a strong, burly stature.

I rotate my hips to the left, to the right, and then thrust up and down, allowing my clit to run along his length, over and over again until I feel my orgasm build at the base of my spine.

"Shit," I whisper as my fingers dig into his skin.

"Getting close?" he says, his breath labored.

"Yes." I nod and then pick up my pace. "So . . . close."

He helps me, moving my hips along his cock, making sure I don't slow down but continue to pick up speed, rubbing me over and over until . . .

"Oh fuck, oh God, Atlas." My head flies back, and a long loud moan falls past my lips as every muscle in my stomach pulls together and my orgasm skyrockets through me, pulsating and throbbing. I ride it out, feeling every last glorious sensation until I'm completely spent.

I let out a long breath and then open my eyes to find him staring up at me, looking crazed and hungry all at the same time.

I don't have a moment to even ask him if he's okay before he's flipping me to my back and pulling his cock out of his pants.

"Oh my God," I whisper as I watch him stroke himself.

So thick.

So long.

How . . . how could that ever fit?

Precum runs down the tip to his hand, where he uses it for lubrication, picking up speed as he lowers closer to me.

"Squeeze your . . . tits," he says, the muscles in his neck straining, the sinew in his forearm flexing. "Fuck, I want to come on them."

I part my shirt, then push my breasts together, only for him to lower some more and pump harder until he lets out a feral moan and busts all over my chest. It's easily the hottest thing I've ever experienced, watching this breathtaking man unravel before my eyes.

"Fucking hell," he mutters as he strokes himself lightly and then opens his eyes to find my gaze on him. "Christ."

I wet my lips, his hot cum decorating my chest. "No one has ever done that to me."

Catching his breath, he asks, "Did you like it?"

I nod. "More than I probably should have."

He smirks and then leans down and places a kiss on my lips. "I'll keep that in mind."

MAX

Desperately, I want to text Cole like a giddy schoolgirl and tell him that I just came all over Betty's delicious tits, but it's past midnight, and I'm sure that's the last thing he wants to be woken up by. Or told for that matter.

But fuck. What was that?

I wasn't expecting to even share a bed with her, let alone get the opportunity to play with her. And yet here I am, waiting on the mattress for her to finish cleaning up, fresh from an orgasm and riding on cloud fucking nine.

And the best part about all of it is that she believes me.

She actually believes me.

I wasn't sure that would happen. It still angers me that Dwight has held a grudge for all these years over something I didn't do. *Why not just ask me?* And although I haven't been completely honest with Betty, I'm glad that she's seen the parts of my character that *show* her that I'm not cruel and thoughtless. Vindictive.

Betty comes back into the living room, her shirt buttoned up but nothing on her legs. She tiptoes across the hardwood floor, and then quickly shimmies under the covers and attaches herself to my side, cuddling in close.

Fuck, I like this.

I like her.

I place my arm around her and keep her close as I kiss the top of her head. "Are you cold again?" I ask.

"Yeah," she says, placing her feet up against my legs.

"Fuck, your feet are cold."

She chuckles. "I'm sorry. Let me grab my socks."

"Do you want me to grab you a new pair? Or maybe warm them up by the fire for a moment?"

"Maybe the fire," she says.

I lift up, find her socks, and lay them out on the hearth. "Let those warm up for a second." Then I lie back down and pull her against my chest again, hoping my body heat helps. "You want to put your pants back on?"

"No, they'll just fall off anyway. I just need my feet covered, and then I should be good."

"I can add another blanket," I suggest.

She rubs my chest with her hand. "Really, this is good. Stop worrying about me."

"Yeah, easy for you to say. You didn't see what you looked like when I plucked you off your couch." I let out a heavy breath, still thinking about it. "What the hell were you thinking?"

"Honestly . . . I thought that I could hunker down, but right before you came, I was thinking that maybe I'd have to call 911 because I could feel myself starting to slip. You . . . you saved me." She kisses my chest, and I grip her tighter.

"You could have called me."

"After what happened this morning? I didn't think that was an option."

"It wouldn't have mattered. I'd have been there so much sooner. And not to be a dick or anything, but where the fuck is Dwight, and why isn't he checking in on you? Is he really that mad?"

"He's out of town for a conference," she answers. "I don't think he even knows that the power went out."

"Well, he knows there was a storm. Hell, why didn't he provide you with any backup batteries or heat sources?" I grind down on my teeth. "He should have taken care of you."

She rubs my chest. "Hey, maybe we don't talk about the what-ifs and just focus on the fact that I'm grateful you came and got me and I'm grateful that I'm here, with you, in front of this fire . . . fully satisfied."

That brings a smile to my lips. "Well, I wouldn't say 'fully satisfied.' If I had condoms, this would have been a different night."

Her thumb rubs against my skin. "You know, I'm on birth control and I haven't had sex since the last time I got tested. You wouldn't have to use them if you didn't want to."

That makes my breath catch in my chest, because I've never gone without a condom . . . ever.

I swallow the saliva building up in my mouth from the mere thought of it. "Probably, uh . . . probably not the best thing to say to me."

She chuckles. "Why not?"

"Because I've never . . . I've never gone without a condom, and after the way you just humped the fuck out of my dick, I'll probably paw at you way too much."

"You say that as if it's a bad thing."

I tug on her shirt, pulling it up so my palm meets her skin, and that's when I feel that she's not even wearing her thong.

God, she's going to kill me.

"Better watch what you wish for." I kiss the top of her head. "But I'll be good. I don't want you too cold. Your body is worn down. I probably shouldn't have even started . . . touching you, but Christ, I couldn't stop myself."

"Well, I'm glad you did. I really liked how you played with me, how you took charge."

"Yeah?" I ask, surprised that she's talking about it. Also something I've never had, communication after sex. Every woman I've been with has been on the shier side. Which is fine, no judgment, but Betty is different. In an extremely positive way, that's for sure.

"Yeah." She kisses my chest again.

"Good to know. Let me check on your socks." I lift up and pat them. They're warmed but not too hot, so I lift the blankets and put her socks on for her. When I glance up and find her smiling at me cutely, I know I've hit the goddamn jackpot.

"Thank you," she says as I lie back down. "Now stop getting up. You're letting the heat out, and you keep disturbing my comfort."

I laugh. "Sorry, babe."

"Babe, huh?"

I shrug. "Do you prefer *darling*? *Sweetie*? *Tantalizing tits*?"

"*Tantalizing tits*?" She laughs out loud. "Never been called that before."

"Well, you should have, because your tits are easily the sexiest I've ever seen."

"Stop," she says, nudging at me. "That's not true."

"Betty." I sit up, disrupting her comfort again. I bring my fingers to the buttons of her shirt, undo the top few, and open the shirt, revealing her chest, and I love that she lets me. "They fit perfectly in my palm." I grip one and run my thumb over her nipple, hardening it. "Responsive, slightly firm, and your nipples, so goddamn hard, like little pebbles. Jesus, they're so fucking hot."

"So you coming on them"—she swallows—"was that you claiming them?"

My temperature spikes from that one word: *coming.*

"Yeah," I answer, my mouth going dry. "You okay with that?" I run my finger over her nipple again.

She bites down on her lip and nods.

Christ.

Let go of her breast, dude.

Lie back down.

Take a few deep breaths.

Do not overwork her.

I clear my throat and start to button her shirt back up, but she stops me. "What are you doing?"

"Trying not to take advantage of you."

"It wouldn't be taking advantage if I want it," she answers.

Fuck. Those eyes, the way they're pleading.

"Betty." I clear my throat again. "It's been a rough night, and I think—"

I go still when her hand connects with my half-hard cock.

"Fuck—" I whisper, trying to take a deep breath. "Betty, I really think—"

Her hand slips inside my boxer briefs, and I grow hard in her palm.

"Jesus."

She pushes me to my back and then undoes the rest of her buttons, letting the shirt flap open again, giving me a perfect view right before she dips down and starts kissing my chest, grazing her lips over my pecs, her tongue lapping at my nipple, and then moving down to my stomach.

Fuck, I should stop her, I really should, but for the life of me, I can't as her tongue runs over my abs, farther down, kissing, nipping, until she gets to the waistband of my boxer briefs where my cock is straining to be released.

Seriously? Seconds. It took her goddamn seconds to get me to a point where I'm sweating, needing her to do more.

She lifts up, gives me the most telling smirk I've ever seen, and then lowers my boxer briefs down my legs, leaving me completely naked to her.

"Oh my God, Atlas," she says as she takes me all in. Her satisfied expression turns me on even more, because I can see genuine appreciation and excitement in her eyes. Wetting her lips, she leans down, her hard nipples dragging along my legs as her mouth kisses just below my belly button, right next to where my cock is straining, twitching, begging for her touch.

But she doesn't give me what I want. Instead she kisses and licks around me while I feel her nipples scrape along my skin at the same time.

It's torture.

But it's so fucking good.

"Touch me," I say. "Fucking touch me, Betty."

I see her smile as she continues to kiss around me while her hand moves between my legs and her thumb lightly caresses the seam of my balls.

Immediately, my legs spread as I let out a large sigh. "Christ."

It's gentle.

It's purposeful.

It's driving me fucking mad.

She's touching me in just the right spot to keep me turned on without giving me what I want.

I sit up on my elbows, taking in the scene before me, her beautiful face millimeters away from my dick, her lips torturing me, her thumb playing with me, precum slipping across my head.

"Betty. Fucking touch me."

Her eyes glance up at me. Her sinful smile grows even larger as she keeps her gaze fixated on mine and peeks her tongue out, slowly licking the precum off my cock.

"Jesus fuck," I growl, the faint stroke nearly making me come.

Her thumb strokes my seam one more time before she encircles my cock, applying pressure right before her mouth closes around the head.

"Fucking hell," I yell as I fall back to the mattress and drape my arm over my eyes, my hips pumping gently into her mouth from the invasion of warmth that just surrounded me. "Fuck, I can't . . . I need more."

Her mouth tightens around my cock, her lips sucking as she moves me in and out, and it's the best fucking feeling of my life.

"That's it, baby," I say. "Harder. Suck me harder."

She squeezes my cock, pumping as she laps my head and then sucks again, applying such strong pressure that my orgasm starts to tingle up my spine, my legs going numb as all the muscles in my body begin to contract.

"Fuck, close."

My balls tighten as she sucks even harder, really pulling.

"Betty, I'm . . . I'm . . ."

Her hand pumps me faster.

Harder.

Her lips cinch around me like a vise, and before I can move her away, my balls tighten, my cock swells, and I come inside her mouth with a roar.

"Fuck," I shout, tipping over the edge. Pure euphoria. She finishes me off, taking every last drop before I'm completely sated.

And as I lie there, trying to catch my breath, Betty licks me, fucking cleaning me off, and it's so goddamn surreal.

"Come here," I say, still lying down, floating back from the pleasure she just shot through me. "Sit on my face."

"What?" she says, her eyes widening.

"You fucking heard me. Sit on my face."

"Atlas—"

"Now," I say with force.

She wets her lips and then straddles my chest, nervously moving forward. I offer her assistance, grab her ass, and pull her forward until her pussy lines up with my mouth.

And just from one deep breath, I know I'm going to be in fucking heaven.

I peek my tongue out and gently take one lap against her exposed clit. Fuck, she's so wet.

"Oh God," she says as I look up at her, her beautiful tits on display, her nipples hard, her teeth pulling on her lip. So I watch her as I swipe again . . . and again . . . and again, taking long languid strokes, loving how her breath changes.

I move my hands up her sides as the shoulders of her shirt fall, only hanging on by her elbows now.

Sexy.

So fucking sexy.

I drag my hands over her stomach, then cup and squeeze her breasts while swiping at the same time.

"Oh yes," she whispers, her hips rotating over my tongue. Any insecurity she might have had is completely gone as she falls into the moment with her eyes squeezed shut and her head slightly tilted back.

I drag my thumbs over her firm nipples, pinching them ever so slightly while I flick at her clit faster with short, concise strokes, sending a wave of vibration through her. Her legs tighten around me, and her hands fall to mine as I continue to play with her nipples.

Her breathing sharpens.

Her body contracts.

And her mouth falls open as a feral moan falls past her delicious lips.

"Oh God, oh God . . . oh . . . f-fuck," she screams as I continue to flick over and over, watching her build up to the point that she screams my name. She tightens around me, her orgasm rocketing through her beautiful body. "Fuck . . . fuck, Atlas," she yells as she comes all over my face.

I'm obsessed.

I want her coming on my face every goddamn day.

After a few seconds, she unclenches and then rolls off to the side, her hand covering her eyes in disbelief as I move over to her, kissing along her neck until I reach her mouth and lightly kiss her on the lips.

When she moves her hands, letting me see her satisfied eyes, I smile down at her and say, "Stop tempting me. We need to sleep."

"You're the one who opened my shirt."

"A shirt I'll never be able to look at the same again. That's yours from now on."

She smiles. "Consider it taken."

I lean down to kiss her again. "Okay, Christ, maybe I should sleep on the couch."

"No, please don't." She clings to me. "I'll be too cold without you."

I press my forehead against her. "Okay, but seriously, we sleep now."

"Okay."

"Let's . . . clean up again, and then I'll put another log on the fire. You get fully dressed, and we can sleep."

"Cuddle and sleep."

I kiss the tip of her nose. "Yes, cuddle and sleep."

CHAPTER TWENTY-ONE
MAX

NARRATOR: WELL . . . WHO KNEW ATLAS Maxheimer had it in him?

I mean . . . I did. The man might look and act like a cinnamon roll, but there's a secret side to him only a few people know about . . . not even Cole.

Though I think Cole is about to find out.

Betty is sleeping, wrapped up in a swath of blankets with the fire still blazing in front of her. I woke up during the night to feed it, keep it going, but I need to bring more wood from the den into the living room because we're starting to run low. I have plenty of wood but just need to rotate it.

With my phone in hand, I move toward the kitchen, where I start boiling some water for some instant coffee. Not my favorite, but it will do.

Leaning against the counter, I turn my phone on after powering it off late last night, and I go straight to my text messages, where I text Cole.

Max: She sat on my face last night, and I made her come.

There, that should get his attention.

Next, I go to the weather app to see what the day has in store for us. More snow this morning, but then it should lighten up in the afternoon. I glance out the window and see that we probably did get about a foot of snow. Still no power, but I know the crew will be working on it as soon as they get to the roads, which will be cleared sooner rather than later. I heard the plows working hard last night.

The one good thing about living in the mountains is that even though it snows a lot more than, let's say Denver, we have a better plow system, and we can usually be out and about on the roads faster.

My phone vibrates with a text, and I smile as I open up Cole's response.

Cole: Jesus, dude, the details.

Max: You want the details? Oh, okay. It started with her snuggling into me at night, a real one-bed situation, and then she stuck my hand up her shirt, and I caressed her breast. She has the sexiest fucking tits ever. I was hard as a stone.

Cole: NO! I DON'T want the details. Stop . . . just . . . stop.

Max: Well, that wasn't very clear. If you plan to use sarcasm in your messages, you'll have to be more direct.

Cole: It's too early for this. Is the farm okay?

Max: That's what you care about? The farm? I just told you she sat on my face, and you're not going to say anything to that?

Cole: I don't know why you're telling me this. Storee is the one you're in cahoots with.

Max: Huh, you're right. Let me text her. BTW farm is closed today. Take the time off, I'll let the employees know, and don't worry, I'll check on the reindeer. Also, maybe let your wife sit on your face today.

Cole: I don't need your advice on where my wife fucking sits. She knows exactly where to sit when it comes to me.

Max: Yikes. Maybe have some coffee. You're coming off grumpy.

I switch text threads and send a text to Storee.

Max: She sat on my face, and I made her come.

It takes about two seconds for Storee to respond, which is another reason I probably should have texted her first.

Storee: OMG!! SHE SAT ON YOUR FACE!!!! That's so exciting. Was it the best thing ever?

Max: I want my face to be her seat for the rest of time.

Storee: You know, Cole has said something along those lines to me. Looks like you two have a lot more in common than I thought. Man, I didn't think you'd be a face seater.

Max: Is that the proper term?

Storee: I'm making it. Seriously, I guess I never thought about how you would perform in bed. Let me ask you this . . . did you perform well?

Max: Can I be detailed?

Storee: Please.

Max: Clearly, I'm best friends with the wrong person. *Clears throat* I made her come twice last night. First time she dry-humped the fuck out of my cock, and then I came all over her tits.

Storee: Ooo, a dry-hump, cum-to-tit shot. That's amazing. Did she like it?

Max: A lot. Even asked if that was me claiming her, and I said yes.

Storee: OMG, this is the sweetest thing.

Max: And then of course right after, I couldn't contain myself and started playing with her again, but then she went down on me, and, Storee, I've never been sucked like that before.

Storee: I'm so happy for you.

Max: And then that's when she sat on my face, and I played with her tits while fucking her with my tongue.

Storee: That's so hot. How did you finish the night?

Max: Satisfied.

Storee: No, like . . . what did you do after you had her sit on your face?

Max: Oh ha-ha. We cuddled and now she's still sleeping while I'm making some instant coffee and texting you.

Storee: Wow, what a night.

Max: The best part of it all is that she told me that she believes me, that she doesn't believe what Dwight said. She doesn't believe that I'm the man Dwight has said I am.

Storee: Wow, that might be better than the sitting-on-the-face situation.

Max: Ehh, I don't know, I really liked her coming all over my tongue like that.

Storee: You dirty, dirty man. I had no idea. If you need some pointers, I have some good ideas . . .

Max: I'm not doing anything with a candy cane!

Storee: You say that now.

Max: No. But thank you for helping me. I really like her, Storee.

Storee: Aww, I'm so glad. What are you doing today?

Max: In my mind, hanging out, getting to know each other more. Checking on the farm. I first need to see if she wants to stay.

Storee: Pretty sure she's going to want to stay.

Max: I hope so.

Storee: She will. But to secure the deal, bring her breakfast in bed.

Max: Do you think Pop-Tarts and instant coffee will be good enough?

Storee: What kind of Pop-Tarts?

Max: Cherry, of course.

Storee: Then yes, I think it will be good enough.

Max: Okay . . . off to please my queen.

Storee: AHHHHHHHH! Good luck.

———————

BETTY

The crackling of the fire is the first thing to wake me up.

The second thing is a thump sound, followed by Atlas swearing.

"Motherfucker," he says under his breath.

I open my eyes and see him leaning over, wincing in pain.

Wrapped up in an immense number of blankets, I wiggle my head out just enough to say, "Are you okay?"

His eyes meet mine, and he replies, "Shit, did I wake you?"

"No, I was waking up," I lie, because I don't want him to feel bad. "What did you do?"

"Stubbed my toe on the coffee table," he answers and then takes a seat next to me on the air mattress. "How did you sleep?"

I smile up at him. "Wonderfully."

"Yeah?" His hair is askew, his scruff is thicker, and he looks all kinds of adorable in the morning with that smirk of his.

"Yeah, I did. You're really good at spooning."

"I taught myself."

I chuckle. "Wow, you grew your face yourself, and you taught yourself how to spoon. Looks like I hit the jackpot."

"Glad you see it that way, because you did." He winks and then says, "I brought you breakfast in bed. And before I hand it over, I don't want you to get your hopes up that banana pancakes and bacon are about to be placed on your lap. I might have a fire going and a generator warming up some hot water so we can take quick showers, but that's the extent of the luxury while the power is out."

"I'm just grateful I'm not a Popsicle frozen to my couch this morning."

"Me too." He nods. "Sit up for me."

I untangle myself from the blankets and sit up only for him to place a cookie sheet lined with a dish towel on my lap. On top of the dish towel is an unwrapped Pop-Tart arranged on a plate, a cup of coffee, and a banana.

God, he's so cute.

I smile up at him and say, "Cherry Pop-Tarts are my favorite."

"Wait, really?"

"They are. Clearly the best choice out of all the options."

He presses his lips together and then looks away. "That . . . that makes me want to have you sit on my face all over again . . . with said cherry Pop-Tart in your mouth."

I laugh. "An odd fantasy, but I'd be game."

"Don't tempt me." He gets up and heads back toward the kitchen.

"Where are you going?"

"Grabbing my tray. You're not the only one eating a cherry Pop-Tart this morning."

He heads back to the kitchen, and I start peeling my banana. Clearly, Atlas has been looking after the fire overnight, because there's a fresh log on it. *And he made me breakfast.* It's so thoughtful, especially considering reserves must be low. I've had a few boyfriends here and there, but they've never treated me like this, and Atlas isn't even my boyfriend, just a guy who likes me.

"Not going to stub my toe this time," he says as he comes around and takes a seat on the air mattress next to me. "How's the coffee? Instant isn't always the greatest, but it's the best I could do."

"Haven't tried it yet. But I bet it's not as bad as you think it is." I lift the mug up to my lips and take a sip, only to shiver from the muddy taste. "Oh . . . oh my God." I cough and he takes the mug away from me as I quickly take a bite of my banana to get the taste off my tongue. "That's . . . that's horrendous."

He chuckles. "Sorry. Should have warned—it's an acquired taste. I can grab you something else."

"No, it's fine. Don't get up again. I have some water that you brought over from last night."

"You sure? I can make you some tea."

"I'm sure," I say, placing my hand on his leg. "Seriously, you don't have to cater to me, Atlas."

"I just want to make sure you have everything you need."

"I do," I say with a shy smile.

He points at me. "Are you . . . are you flirting with me?"

I push at his hand, causing him to laugh. "Not anymore."

He takes my hand and brings it to his mouth, where he presses a sweet kiss to my knuckles. "I'm glad I can fulfill everything you need."

"You're ridiculous."

"So are you."

"How am I ridiculous?" I ask as I wrap my lips around my banana— seductively—and take a bite.

His lips purse as he stares at me. "For the love of God, don't make me hard when there's a Pop-Tart on my lap. I'll never be able to look at them the same."

I let out a low laugh and then repeat, "How am I ridiculous?"

"Well, I'm glad you asked, because last night, I experienced something that was utterly ridiculous, and I have questions."

"Oh, I can't wait to hear this."

He takes a bite of his Pop-Tart—a huge bite—chews, and then says, "That thing you did with your thumb on my balls last night—that should be illegal."

"You've never had that done to you before?" I ask, kind of shocked.

"Uh, no. Never."

"Have you ever had your balls played with?"

"Not so much," he answers. "I mean, a little bit of a brush here and there, but you were all in last night."

"Uh, yeah, because that would be like . . . you going down on me but then touching nothing else. Sure, it would feel nice, but to have you playing with me in other ways is what heightens the orgasm. Sheesh, that's like . . .oral 101."

He snorts and then covers his nose. "Shit, I didn't know there was a class. Let me guess, you aced it?"

"Aced it and started teaching."

"Well, aren't I a lucky guy? So glad I fetched you from your cottage."

"Fetched me? Is that what we're calling it now?"

"I don't know, has a nice ring to it."

"I prefer *saved*," I say. "Because that's exactly what you did."

"I was worried," he says, growing serious. "Glad I checked, because last night . . . it was special, and not because of what we did but because of what you said to me." His eyes meet mine as he speaks his truth, which is so refreshing. "It means a lot to me that you trust me, that you believe what I told you last night. I don't know why Dwight thinks I did all those things to him, but I didn't, and I'm grateful that you believe me."

"I'm sorry that I second-guessed you—"

"Don't." He shakes his head. "Don't be sorry. You didn't know. You just believed what Dwight told you, and that's fair. He's a relative and the person who helped you move out here. Why wouldn't you believe him?"

I stare off into the fire. "I'm just wondering where he came up with that. I mean, does he really not like you that much that he would make up lies?"

Atlas scratches the side of his cheek, his nails rubbing against his jaw creating a sandpaper-like sound. "I don't know where he got that from. As far as I can remember, there was beef when we were on the basketball team together, and it just seemed to grow. We weren't friends. He was a dick to me, and I'll be honest, I was a dick right back. I'm not proud of it, but I was also a high school boy with nothing better to do than puff my chest and try to have the upper hand. But I never did anything maniacal like he's saying. So, fuck, I don't know where it comes from."

"Definitely something I want to figure out, but maybe not when things are so . . . raw."

"Yeah, probably best." Atlas picks a crumb off his plate. "How long is Dwight gone for?"

"A week," I answer.

"A week, huh? That brings us right up to a couple days before Christmas."

"It does."

He nods. "Do you, uh, do you have any plans?"

"Not really. I was actually kind of thinking about leaving Kringle."

"Leaving?" His head pops up. "What do you mean?"

I sigh and set my tray to the side. "When I first came here, I was struggling with my confidence, with friendships, with what to do with my life, and . . . well, do you, uh . . . do you remember the conversation we had on your farm? It was outside the gingerbread house. You were talking about how if, as a proprietor, you don't sell the Christmas experience, you're out of business within a year."

"Vaguely. I think that was the same day Dwight came up to me and told me to stay away from you or at least shortly after that."

"Well, what you said actually hit me hard, and I know I shouldn't be looking for any sympathy, given the circumstances, and I guess I'm not, but more so looking for you to understand." I fully turn toward him and cross my legs. "Umm, I had to shut down my business this year. It was a year-round Christmas store in Fort Collins."

"Oh shit, Betty. I'm sorry."

I shake my head. "Please don't apologize. You didn't know."

"Still, I can't imagine what that must have felt like."

I offer him a shrug. "It wasn't fun. I sank everything into it, including all my hopes, money, and relationships, and it didn't do well, and I had to close down. It was really hard. The people who I thought were my business friends turned their backs on me. I had to sell inventory at near cost to try to get a semblance of money back, and the embarrassment of not being able to successfully keep a business open plagued me. So when I came out here for Thanksgiving, Dwight, or Uncle Dwight as I call him, told me he had a piece of property he wanted to show me. He had all these plans of me growing the land into something special. I was apprehensive at first, but somehow he encouraged me to give it a shot. So I started to dream up ideas, ideas that I had no right dreaming up, and then, well, our conversation on the farm brought me back down to reality, and I told Uncle Dwight I couldn't do it. I couldn't be a part of his plan." I look Atlas in the eyes and say, "I was scared to fail again."

"Because of what I said?"

"Because of everything. Please don't hear what I'm saying as this being your fault or anything like that, as you had no idea. It was just a culmination of our conversation, my already battered ego, and a lack of confidence and direction on my part." I blow out a heavy breath. "Anyway, Uncle Dwight convinced me to stay and give my decision a week. He wanted me to soak in the town, and that's when I started hanging out with you and Storee."

"I'm glad you did." He takes my hand in his.

"I'm glad too, because now I'm here . . . with you."

"You *are* here." His smile is so sweet. So genuine. He squeezes my hand and asks, "So what do you think you'll do now? Do you want to go back to Fort Collins?"

I pull my legs into my chest and stare out the window at the wintery, snowy day, thinking about the time I've had here and how I've felt more alive in the last couple of weeks than I have in a while.

"Not really. I like it here. I like the community. I like Storee . . ." I meet his eyes. "I like you." That makes him smile. "I just don't know how to navigate the Uncle Dwight situation, especially since he's done so much for me."

"Yeah, I can understand that." He lets out a sigh. "As much as it pains me to say this, because the last thing I ever want to do is something nice for Dwight, but why don't I bounce some ideas around with you? We can come up with alternate plans for his property that will not only benefit him in the long run but also . . . benefit the town."

"You would do that?"

"If it means you stay longer, yeah. Yeah, I would."

I smile at him. That's extremely kind *and* selfless. Have I ever had a new friend be so generous with their time? Where were my friends when my life imploded recently? *Silent.* Which explains why I haven't made an effort to keep up with them since I moved here. *Which is kind of sad.* All I can do is thank him, as this sort of thoughtfulness is a rare gift. "Thank you. You've no idea how wonderful that sounds."

He pushes some of my hair behind my ear, gazing at me with such an adoring look that the tension I was feeling quickly eases. "Tell me about the store you had. What was it called?"

I smile sadly, thinking about the store I put so much effort and thought into. "It was called the Christmas Box, and it was a collection of everything you could think of when it comes to Christmas. I specialized in ornaments, because those are always a big seller. But then I would sell items from crafters, personalized printed wrapping paper, just a conglomerate of things that I loved so much. It was like joy when you walked into the store. And I had this idea to do wreathe-making classes and never got the chance to see it through, but I know it would have been a hit. I also had a workshop in the back where you could make your own Christmas sign. That was my favorite."

"That's a really good idea," Atlas says. "Maybe that's something fun you can offer in some way."

"Maybe," I say.

"And what about these so-called friends? Where are they now?"

I shrug. "Long gone. I met them at a small business meetup. They were super-supportive at the beginning, but I think it's because they were trying to grab on to the success of something to help their business, you know? Like if I succeeded, they would have succeeded. But once things started to take a turn, they jumped ship, and I really didn't hear from them."

"Which makes them not friends at all."

"I see that now."

"You need people in your life who will help you no matter the ups and downs you're going through." He takes my hand in his. "You can count on me to be that person."

"Yeah? Are you saying that only because of what I did with my thumb on your balls?" I ask, lightening the mood.

He chuckles. "Clearly. You opened a new world for me. Consider me your number one fan."

CHAPTER TWENTY-TWO
MAX

NARRATOR: LOOK AT MAX MATURING *before our eyes. Didn't know if he'd be able to set aside his hate for Dwight, and yet all it took was a great set of breasts and a little thumb-to-the-balls action to get him to sing a different tune—and boy, did he sing a different tune last night.*

I think feral dogs heard him howl from miles away.

Since Betty isn't leaving town will she stay with him through the week? Or is she going back to the cottage with Buzz? I bet I know what Max wants, but we will have to wait and see.

———————

"This is your story, but I wouldn't hate it if it snowed some more or if the power stayed off. The air mattress escapade was a nice touch."

Narrator: Always with the compliments. Keep this up, and I might grow you a few more inches if you know what I mean.

"If you make me any larger, I'm going to fuck her pussy and her throat at the same time."

Narrator: Exaggerate much?

"I mean, I knew I was packing, but my dick was huge last night."

Narrator: Are you complaining?

"Fuck no. Just worried about our heroine is all. Can she take it?"

Narrator: Trust me, she'll be fine. You just worry about yourself and keeping up your stamina. You'll need it.

"Aye, aye, captain."

———————

"Are you sure you want to come?" I ask Betty as she puts on her boots.

"Positive."

"You won't be too cold?"

She finishes tying her boot and stands straight. She walks up to me and places her hand on my chest. "You need to stop worrying about me."

"Impossible. You shivering on your couch will forever be branded on my brain. There will always be worry."

"You're sweet." She lifts up onto her toes and attempts to kiss me but doesn't reach. "Ugh, you're so tall. Help a girl out." She then steps up on a box that's next to the back door and becomes more level with me, giving me a kiss on the lips. "There, that's better. But yes, I'm coming. I want to see the reindeer."

"Okay. But follow in my footsteps, because it's deep."

"That I think I can do."

Decked out in snow gear, we head out the back of my house, and I start the path for us, reaching behind me to hold her hand. It's a bit of a walk through a lot of snow, and when I step into it, I realize just how deep it is.

"Shit, I don't know if this is a good idea." I glance behind her. "It's really deep."

"Let me see," she says as she steps into the snow, and it goes up over her knee. She looks up at me, little flecks of snow falling on her cheeks, making her look far too beautiful. "Seems fine."

I shake my head, laughing. "It's not fine. Here, I'll give you a piggyback ride over there."

"Oh my God, Atlas, not necessary."

"It's either that or I pull you in a sled. Take your pick."

She sighs and then checks out the toboggan next to the house. "Fine, piggyback ride. I refuse to be pulled around in a sled."

"That's fine."

I back up to the stairs and turn around so she can hop on. It takes her a second in her snow gear, but once she's on my back, I start making our way through the snow and out toward the reindeer barn.

"Are you sure you can handle this?"

"I lift trees for a living and work on a farm. Carrying you on my back through over a foot of snow really is nothing."

"Well, it seems like a lot to me."

"Just remember this when I attempt to undress you later but get a cramp."

She chuckles. "Let's make sure you have some electrolytes in you then, because I wouldn't want you cramping up while thrusting."

"Yeah, nothing erases a boner more than a charley horse."

She laughs, her chest bumping against my back. "Ever have a boner erased?"

"Twice," I answer with no shame. "First one was when I was enjoying myself in the shower and my mother walked in, needing to grab the hair dryer. She rummaged around for what felt like an hour, which deflated the dick rather quickly."

"I could imagine."

"And then when I was mid-thrust after a long day on the farm, I cramped up, and yeah, things softened really quick. I ended up finishing the girl off with my tongue, but it was embarrassing, and we never went out again."

"Wait, seriously?" she asks.

"Yeah, I think the whole softened penis inside her wasn't her favorite thing."

"Yeah, but that's no reason for her not to see you again."

I shrug. "Wasn't the right person for me. That was more of a *we're single and need to get out some energy* thing."

"Oh. Does she still live here?"

"No," I answer. "She's over in Aspen now, making hats for rich people."

"Do you have any past lovers who still live here?"

"Nervous?" I playfully ask.

"I mean, just nice to know."

"Uh, a girlfriend from high school, but she's married now with kids."

"Is it . . . is it Storee?"

I let out a huge laugh. "No. She didn't grow up here."

"Oh, that's right, duh. But wouldn't that be awkward if she did?"

"Awkward? No. I'd have way too much fun with that, bugging Cole all the time that she was mine before his."

"I could see you doing that."

"It's who I am. Not ashamed. Kind of proud of it."

"Aren't instigators always proud of themselves?"

"I think they are. What about you? Any past lovers I need to worry about, driving up here and saying, *Don't touch my woman*?"

"Your depiction of my love life is comical," she says. "They wouldn't say, *Don't touch my woman*. They would say, *Let go of my wench*."

I laugh as I cross over to the farm property, the reindeer barn in sight. "Did you date pirates in your past?"

"Yes. You might not know this, but there's a whole gaggle of pirates in Fort Collins, and I blew through them like a cold breeze on a wintery day. Eye Patch Ezekiel was my most intense lover. He's the one that I'd worry about."

"Eye Patch Ezekiel, huh? I'll be on the lookout for anyone making me walk the plank."

"He might disguise it under glasses, so I'd be careful."

"Oof, good point. I'll just be prepared at all times."

"Probably best."

I make the last few steps to the back, and then I grab the shovel that

Cole left out. I set Betty on the ground and then shovel around the door so I can get it open.

When everything is clear, I take her glove-covered hand, and we make our way into the reindeer barn, where everything is calm. It's not warm at all, but they can handle the weather. Cole has draped them all in their blankets, and they seem to be comfortable.

"Wow, why did I think it would be warm in here?"

I chuckle. "Power's out, babe."

"Right, that's still something I'm forgetting. Will they be okay?"

"Yeah, they're fine." I move over to their stalls and start checking their feed and water. The water is starting to freeze over, so I take a pick and break it up.

"What can I do?" Betty asks.

"Introduce yourself to the reindeer. Pet them, give them some love. I'm just making sure their water is good. I have to clean out some of these pens, despite hating doing it, and then I'll top off their feed."

"I can clean the pens."

I straighten up. "Over my dead body will you pick up reindeer shit. Jesus Christ, Betty."

She chuckles. "Why so offended?"

"Because do you really think that's something I'd allow you to do? No, you're too goddamn pretty to be picking up shit."

Her smile grows. "I'd counter that by saying you're too pretty as well."

"I know I am. That's why Cole's ugly mug usually does it, but he's not here. Therefore, I have to take care of it."

She presses her hand to her heart. "You are so brave."

"Thank you."

I grab the scoop for poop from the wheelbarrow—ugh, the worst part about snow days—and take it to the first stall.

"Were you ever interested in taking care of the reindeer?" Betty asks as she pets Cupid on the nose.

"I mean, not really. Cole always liked them, and then when his parents passed, it seemed like an easy job for him to take over from my dad, who had gotten older. Carrying around sacks of feed and cleaning up crap has worn on him. It was a great transition."

"Oh, so your dad took care of the reindeer before Cole?"

"Yeah, and if he were here right now, he would probably do it, even though I'd fight him about it and say I could do it."

"Where are your parents right now?"

"Europe. My dad surprised my mom with a trip to the Christmas markets."

"Ah, so you're watching the house for them?"

I wince, because yikes, this is embarrassing. "I appreciate you thinking that, but I actually moved back in with my parents a few years ago. I wanted to save up to build a house of my own on the property. I'm just about ready to start the process. I think in the new year, I'll start looking at plans."

"Oh wow, that's pretty cool. Do you want a log cabin like your parents?"

"I think so." I finish cleaning the first stall and then move over to the next. "I'd want it to fit in with the style of the buildings on the property, not be an eyesore. There is a pumpkin farm that we went to this past Halloween, Cole's family and I, and it's a family farm like this, and all the houses are in the back, but they all have their own style, and I don't know. It just looked off."

"I think I know the farm you're talking about, and I thought so too. Are your brothers doing the same thing?"

"Fuck, I hope not," I say, causing her to laugh. "They have their own place in town, close to their business, and I hope it stays that way."

"So they don't have any interaction with the farm at all?"

"No." I shake my head. "None. What about you? Do you have siblings?"

"No," she answers. "Only child."

"Oh, that's right, you said that. And Dwight was the sibling you never had."

"Yeah, Dwight was the closest thing to a sibling I had growing up. We'd always have holidays together. And I called him Uncle Dwight as a joke and it's stuck, so when he came up with this idea, I almost felt like . . . I had to at least give it a try."

"The pressure of family is fun, isn't it?"

"Did you get pressure to stay and help with the farm?"

I move into the next stall, making quick work because I can see that she's starting to get cold. "Hey, if you want to scoop some feed into their buckets, you can. The scoop is in that green bin over there."

I see a smile cross her face, clearly happy to help.

"I wasn't really into the farm thing growing up. I knew in high school that I'd be joining the family business, and there were times that I was resentful about that, because in a way, a job defines who you are, and I didn't want that definition to be laid out for me. But as I started working more and more with the people in town and the tourists, seeing the smiles on their faces, it just . . . it made sense to me. I saw why my parents did it, and I saw the purpose behind the farm and why my parents wanted to keep it in the family."

"That's . . . that's really sweet." She holds out the scoop. "Is this enough?"

"Two of those," I answer.

"Did you always want to be a shop owner?" I ask her.

"I majored in business, so I thought that I'd do something in that realm, and when I saw the storefront one day on a walk, I had this entire vision come to life in my head, and I just . . . I went for it. My parents were supportive and helped me put the whole thing together. It went great for a while, but then it just sort of crashed and burned." She sighs. "Doesn't feel right getting this second chance to help Dwight, because what if . . . what if I mess it up?"

"You will if you think that way," I say honestly. "You need to have confidence that you will succeed, especially with the right idea, and I'm telling you right now, the best idea is not competing against an already established business in town."

"Yeah, I can see that. Dwight didn't think it would be a problem, not having the town behind him, but I don't know. After being here for a while and observing the way everyone supports everyone, I just can't see how it wouldn't be an issue. And plus, wouldn't you want that support? Like ... it feels almost like a circle of help. You pick up a coffee at Warm Your Spirits, and Tanya tells you about a shirt that would look perfect on a person and tells them to go to Baubles and Wrappings, and they tell them to go visit Santa, and then Santa asks them if they've visited his reindeer, then they come here, and you say they should ... I don't know ... stay another night—"

"Eh, that's not entirely possible. There isn't a lot of lodging here."

"There isn't?" she asks.

"No, we have the inn in town, but that's pretty much it. Because Kringle saddles up against the mountain, there isn't much land for housing, which is why people stay outside town and then come in for the day."

"Oh."

I glance back at her, watching her mind start to turn. Her eyes find mine.

"What if ... what if I came up with some sort of housing idea for the town? Do you think that would be stepping on the inn's toes?"

I stand up and lean on the shovel, thinking about it. "You know, I don't think so, as long as it's a different type of idea than what they have. Plus, they're overwhelmed all the time, and I know Crystal and Tim over at the Roasting Chestnut have been wanting to do renovations but have been struggling because they're constantly booked. It might be helpful. What are you thinking?"

"I'm not really sure, but what if ...?" She pauses and places the scoop back into the feed. "What if it was something like the cottage that I'm in?

But a ton of those? All throughout the woods. The cottage is really nice, and Uncle Dwight had it set up very quickly. There could be a main lodge with a general store, almost like a KOA campsite, but instead of camping, it can be individual cottages."

"That's a brilliant idea," I say.

"But would you hate to have a campsite next to you?" she asks.

"Trust me when I say there's enough room between the properties that I don't think it would be a big deal. Also, you have a lot of acreage, so you could have the cottages on the other side, which would give more room in between. And you can have it so they're more like two-person cabins—like an adults-only setup, because the Roasting Chestnut is geared toward families. A lot of family suites."

"Oh really?" she asks.

I nod. "Yeah, you can focus on the adults-only experience. Hot tubs, spas, a bar . . . things like that."

"That's really smart." A large smile crosses her face. "Oh my God, did we just come up with an idea together?"

"Nah." I wink. "You did. I just offered some support."

BETTY

Curled up on a chair, Post-it notes and a pen in hand, I continue to write down idea after idea while Atlas prepares us a delectable lunch of peanut butter and jelly sandwiches.

The power hasn't come back on yet, but Atlas thinks it should be coming back soon. He says it's not usually out that long, which has made me realize if Uncle Dwight and I were to open up adults-only cottages, we'd need a solution for the power outages, because that's a guaranteed way to a one-star review.

Which of course got me thinking, I know nothing about hotel management, and sure they're not hotels, but they're similar, just individual cottages. There's so much that goes into it that I'm unaware of. And I've made a ton of notes on things that I need to look into when the power is back and I have internet again.

"Why is it so smoky in here?" Atlas asks as he walks in with two plates.

"What do you mean?" I say, looking back at the fire.

"Oh, it's just your mind working overtime."

"Oh my God."

He laughs and sets the plates down on the coffee table, which he brought closer to the couch after we moved the air mattress to the side. "Too cheesy?"

"A little," I answer and then set my Post-it notes and pen down. When we got back from the farm, I asked if Atlas had anything I could write on, and that's what he gave me. I thought it was cute, so I used them, even though I was looking for something more along the lines of a notepad.

I take a seat on the couch next to him, and he hands me a plate. "Thank you."

"You're welcome. I hope you like—"

The lights flicker, and then the room is illuminated, the Christmas tree in the corner lighting up in a multitude of colors.

Atlas glances around. "Well, looks like the power is back. Maybe I should have waited a second to make lunch. I could have made something a little more appealing."

I chuckle. "Why, I love peanut butter and jelly. This is great. Thank you."

The sound of the furnace kicks on, and the entire house seems like it's in reboot mode as it tries to catch up with the time it has lost being out of power.

"So . . ." he says, chewing on his sandwich. "Do you want some mood music?"

"What kind of mood are you trying to set?" I ask with a raise of my brow.

"A Christmas one." He pulls his phone out of his pocket and presses a few buttons, then from a speaker in the living room somewhere, "White Christmas" by the Drifters starts playing. "How's that?"

"Perfect." I turn toward him and cross my legs on the couch. "I know I've said it a million times, but thank you for bringing me over here."

"You're welcome."

I nudge him with my foot because I can see that his demeanor changed the moment the lights came back on. "What's wrong?"

"I don't know, was just kind of excited to have you to myself again, but then the stupid lights came on, and I have no excuse to hold you hostage now."

I laugh. "Oh, is that what this has been the entire time? A hostage situation?"

"A sexy hostage situation."

"Uh-huh. Does adding *sexy* make it better?"

"In my head it does."

I chuckle. "You won't want me hanging out here, bothering you."

"Says who?" he asks, looking around. "As far as I see it, I'm good with you just staying here, preferably naked."

"You know, Atlas, you never struck me as a horny man."

"Yeah, well, you're to blame for that." He takes a bite of his sandwich. "You stuck my hand up your shirt. Therefore, it's your fault you unlocked this beast."

"I don't recall sticking your hand up my shirt."

His jaw drops, and it makes me laugh. "Uh, let me just go back to the moment when you changed everything between us." He sets his plate to the side. "I believe this is how it went. You asked to cuddle. I said yes because I was desperate and needed to be close to you. You turned away, and I spooned you; then you took my hand, put it under your shirt, and asked if it was okay. I said, 'Uh, yeah,' because what kind of fool would I be if I said no?"

"I did that because I thought your hand was cold, but you're the one who caressed my breast."

"That's because you put my hand up your shirt. You think I'd lie there and act like my hand needed to be warmed? Fuck no. I was getting a feel in."

"Either way. You're horny."

"So are you! I touched your breasts for a few seconds after you already orgasmed, because I just wanted to tell you how great they were, and then you were like, *Don't stop*, and started doing things to my dick I've never felt before." He leans in closer, weirdly examining my mouth.

"What are you doing?" I ask, palming his face and pushing him away.

"Seeing what kind of suction you have on those lips, because it felt like a goddamn vacuum when you were wrapped around me."

"Oh my God, Atlas." I shake my head in mirth.

"If awards were given out for hardest suck, you would have won gold."

"I don't know if that's something I should be proud of or not."

"Yeah," he says on a sigh. "You should, Betty. You absolutely should."

"Either way, you're horny, and I think out of self-preservation, I should go back to my place." The minute I say the words, I see his entire demeanor fall, like I just told him his puppy died.

"You really want to go back?"

"I mean . . . I don't want you to get sick of me or anything. We just started . . . doing things," I say awkwardly. "Don't you think there should be some separation?"

"Uh, no. I think there should be more connection."

"I'm being serious, Atlas. There's a lot of moving parts between us, and I just want to make sure that we're doing this whole thing . . . right. You know? And I don't want to come off as ungrateful or anything like that—"

"I don't want you to stay because you think you owe me," he says, looking insulted.

"No, I wasn't saying that."

"I want you to stay because you want to hang out."

I let out a heavy sigh, knowing I'm not expressing myself the way that I want. "I do want to hang out with you and not because I feel like I owe you but because I like you. But I also have a lot I need to do in order to prove to Uncle Dwight that I have a better idea than the one he initially thought of. And I have less than a week to do that."

He nods. "I get it." He wets his lips. "Can I at least take you out on a date?"

I feel my heart beats quicken. "I hope that you do."

"Tonight?"

I nod my head. "Tonight. I can meet you in town because I have some things I want to do."

"I can bring you into town and drop you off, because I need to pick up some supplies and go gush to Cole about a girl that I like."

I snort and cover my nose. "Oh my God, please tell me you're really doing that."

"You don't know me that well if that's a question you even have to ask."

"You're right. My apologies."

He leans in and grips my chin with his forefinger and thumb, bringing me in close. "Then it's a date." He kisses me gently, and I melt into his touch, letting his lips linger longer than I probably should.

CHAPTER TWENTY-THREE
MAX

NARRATOR: A DATE, A DATE, *he has a date!*

Can you see it? Him skipping about, unable to control his excitement? Well, I saw it and spared you the details. Might have lost a little respect for him, especially because after she left, he skipped around and then ran into the coffee table again, causing him to go headfirst into the Christmas tree.

He took a giant hit to the ego and scratched up his face, but other than that, both eyes are intact, which was a win in the end.

Let's just hope he can keep it together tonight, as the last thing he needs is another blow to the head ... or ego for that matter. Then again, the blow to the ego might have helped after the willy he was wielding. Whenever a man has a penis that big, you have to humble him somehow.

―――――――

"What are you doing here?" Cole asks on a groan after opening the door and finding me on the other side.

"Wow, what a greeting." I push past him with my change of clothes in hand and take off my shoes. "Where are my favorite girls?"

"In the living room." Cole shuts the door, and I move into the living room, where Storee is nursing Evelyn and Florence is playing on the floor.

"Why are you here?" Storee asks, taking the wind out of my sails.

"You know, I expect that kind of greeting from him, but from you?"

I take a seat on the floor next to Florence and pick her up to give her a hug.

"I didn't mean that in a mean way. I just thought you would be at your house . . . with Betty."

"Yeah, you and me both."

"Fuck the whole thing up already?" Cole asks as he takes a seat next to Storee.

"No, you dick," I say as I cover Florence's ears. "Betty just had some things to do, and we're going on a date tonight."

"You are?" Storee asks, excited. "Where are you taking her?"

"I was going to take her to the deli."

Storee's face falls while Cole shakes his head. "You can't be serious."

"Of course I'm not serious." I roll my eyes. "Honestly, that's something Cole would do, not me."

"They have an amazing chicken parm sandwich," Cole defends himself.

"Eh, it's okay," I say.

"Bullshit. I watched you lick your fingers several times after eating one," Cole says, calling me out.

It's true. I'm a finger licker.

"Either way, I'm not taking her there. I honestly was thinking about meeting her at Antlers Antiques and then taking her to Prancer's Libations for dinner."

"Why Antlers Antiques?" Cole asks.

"Thought it would be a fun place to wander around. She's on a new journey and needs inspiration, and it's a great place for that, especially since the store's main focus is Christmas antiques."

"I think that's a sweet idea, actually," Storee says.

"Thank you."

"Has she decided to do something else with the land?"

I nod. "We talked about it today when we were checking out the reindeer. She was the one who brought it up. I didn't pressure her or anything, as I really wanted her to want to make that change. Anyway, we talked about her putting cottages on the property and making it an adults-only retreat."

"Oh." Storee brightens up. "That's actually an ingenious idea. Sherry Conrad was telling me the other day how busy the inn is, especially during the holiday season."

"Yeah, that's what I said too. I think it's totally feasible. But the idea is just at the beginning stages. I think taking her to Antlers will help her see some of the history of the town and maybe spark some ideas."

"Thoughtful," Cole says with a curt head nod.

"Is that me getting your approval?"

"If you need it."

"I don't."

Cole rolls his eyes. "I still can't believe you two morons tried to pull a fast one on me."

"Oh please. You had no idea," Storee says as she hands Evelyn over to Cole, who starts burping the baby. I look away as she adjusts herself.

"I could hear the consumption of the Crunch Tators from inside the house. Hell, I think Bob Krampus heard it from his house."

"Dramatic much?" Storee asks. "You had no idea until recently, so stop acting like you did."

"I knew something was going on. You don't go visit your aunt Cindy when I'm naked in bed."

I cover Florence's ears again. "Uh, hello, you have an impressionable child who can hear you."

Cole waves his hand. "She only says *Dada, ball,* and *no.*"

"If that's the case"—I lean forward—"you should have seen the size of my boner last night."

"Jesus . . . Christ," Cole says while Storee laughs.

"It was—"

"Bo-na," Florence says, causing all of us to stop and stare down at her.

"What did she just say?" Cole asks through a clenched jaw.

"Bo-na," Florence repeats while waving her hands.

Uh-oh.

I slowly set her down as she continues to say it over and over again.

"You know, I think I'll head to the bathroom while you take care of . . . that . . ."

Without looking back, I grab my bag of clothes and run to the bathroom, fear consuming me that Cole is right behind me, ready for murder.

"Well, I haven't seen you around much," Bob Krampus says as I spot him on his way to his house in Ornament Park.

"Hey, Santa," I say with a wave. When in public and Bob is dressed in his red suit, like he is now, we're to always address him as Santa. "Yeah, I've been sort of busy."

"Word on the street is you've been pursuing Dwight's niece. Is this true?"

Hands in my pockets, I nod. "Yeah. Dwight is not fond of the idea."

"So I've heard. Martha and Mae filled me in when they came to talk to me about the situation over there. Odd that you want to date someone who wants to put your family out of business."

"Yeah, that's not the case anymore," I say. "She's coming up with a new idea, and she'll present it to Dwight when he gets back."

"Oh really?"

"Yup. She's a smart woman, but that's her information to tell, not mine."

"A good man, I see. Looking past the differences and still finding good in her."

I shrug. "She's a good match. She's quirky and goofy like me. She's also beautiful, and it's really easy to talk to her, even if we're both rambling."

"Well, I'm glad to hear it." Bob claps me on the shoulder. "I've been waiting for you to find someone. Thought maybe you were waiting for Cole to find love first, since you're so protective of him."

"Nah, I think I was just waiting for the right one to come along."

"Think she's the right one?"

"I think she *can be* the right one," I say. "We'll see. Kind of have to jump the hurdle that's Dwight."

"Yes." Bob strokes his beard. "What is the feud between the two of you?"

"I honestly don't know. But I found out the source of the animosity comes from something that I didn't do, but he's convinced I did."

"What is it?"

I shift on my feet and look to see if Betty is headed my way, and when I don't see her, I say, "He claims I took his ornament off the town tree after he'd made a wish to help save Jessica from her cancer."

"Oh dear," Bob says with a shake of his head. "I remember when Jessica was sick. Just a terrible thing. I didn't know about the ornament though."

"Neither did I until I was blamed for it. Anyway, I need to find a way to bridge that gap with Dwight, because I really like Betty, and if I want any shot with her, then I need to figure out a way to get along with him."

"Yes, you do. And while you're at it, maybe encourage him to be more of a friend to the town. He seems to isolate himself, and it's one of the reasons why I think he lost the Christmas Kringle competition last year."

"Umm, the reason he lost was because I was superior at everything."

Bob lets out a hearty laugh. "Yes, and humble too." He looks to his side. "Oh, your lady friend is approaching. Here." He reaches into his pocket and pulls out a container of spearmint Tic Tacs. "Have a few."

"Oh shit, does my breath stink?" I hold my hand out, and he plops three into my hand.

"No, but it's nice to be minty fresh." He points at me. "Don't spoil your dinner with those."

"I won't."

He clasps me on the shoulder one more time and then takes off. I turn toward Betty and watch her approach in her camel-colored coat, looking so fucking beautiful with her hair down and curled at the ends.

"Hey." She places her hand on my chest and stands on her toes so she can kiss me briefly. "Did Santa tell you if you're on the nice list?"

"He did," I say as I take her hand in mine. "But he did warn me that you seem to be on the naughty list after sitting on my face."

Her eyes widen, and she pokes me in the side, making me laugh. "You did not tell him that, did you?"

"No, but I did say *boner* in front of Florence, and let's just say, it's her new favorite word."

Betty covers her mouth with her hand. "Oh my God, why did you say that in front of her?"

"Cole made it seem like I could say whatever I wanted and she wouldn't retain anything, so I was telling him about how huge you made my boner, and she repeated it."

"First of all, what is wrong with you? Why would you talk about that?"

"It was impressive, was it not?"

Her smile tells me everything I need to know. "Doesn't matter if it was impressive. You should keep that stuff between you and me. Also, don't talk about boners in front of children. Dear God, Atlas."

"Yeah, I see where I made a mistake. I apologized a lot, but Cole still wants to murder me."

"Because his baby girl is saying *boner*."

I chuckle and then lean in close. "Honestly, it was hard to control my laughter. I went into the bathroom after it happened to change for our date, and I couldn't stop chuckling. I almost had to punch myself to get rid of the giggles."

"And here I am, ready to go on a date with you. There might be something wrong with me."

"Nah, you're making all the right choices." But just to be safe, I tug her toward the antique store so she can't change her mind. "How was your thinking session?"

"Could have been better," she admits.

"Why? Couldn't stop thinking about me?" I obnoxiously bat my lashes at her.

"Actually, yes."

"Really?"

"Yes, and please don't make a big deal about it, okay?"

"As if I'd make a big deal about something like that."

"Atlas," she deadpans. "You were just making a big deal about your boner. You make big deals about everything."

"Uh, because that boner was the size of a log."

She pauses our stride and turns toward me. "You know what? I don't think I can do this." She lets go of my hand, and before she can even move, I wrap arm my around her waist and pull her into my chest, making her laugh.

Whispering into her ear, I say, "I know it's intimidating, babe, but it will fit."

"Oh my God, I really can't stand you right now." She laughs as I kiss her neck. She turns and loops her arms around my neck as we stand on the edge of Ornament Park. She pulls me down and kisses me on the mouth, letting her lips part and teasing me so goddamn hard that it takes me a second to steady myself when she pulls away. Whispering, she says, "It might have been a log, but I'm the one who knows how to make said log grow, so don't forget that."

"Babe," I say in a daze. "Trust me, I'll never be forgetting that."

Then I take her hand, and we cross the street together.

Subtly, over the town speakers, "Have Yourself a Merry Little Christmas" by Mel Torme plays in the background while families and couples walk out of the Polar Freeze, heading right to Santa's house. The faux gas streetlamps are lit up, and there's a briskness in the air and not a cloud in sight as stars glitter above us.

It's the perfect night in Kringle with the fresh snow still covering the trees and the colored lights bouncing off the white of the snow. We couldn't have asked for a better evening.

"Where are we headed?" she asks, pulling me in close.

"Antlers Antiques. Thought it might give you some inspiration for your cottages."

"That's sweet."

"And then I thought we'd head over to Prancer's Libations. I have a table reserved for us. It can get busy at night, so I wanted to secure a place in the back."

"Thoughtful. Thank you."

"Of course. Had to impress you on our first date."

"Would you call this our first date?" she asks as we walk past the post office. "You wouldn't consider Cupid Christmas Night our first date?"

"No." I shake my head. "I didn't ask you out. We just happened to hang out that night."

"And kiss."

"Yes, and kiss, thanks to the mistletoe. But that wasn't a date. Neither was last night at my house. This is a date. I asked you out, you said yes, and now we're doing something together."

"I see. Well then, I'm excited to be on our first date."

I lean over and kiss the top of her head. "Me too."

BETTY

"Okay, I already love it in here," I say as we step through the door of Antlers

Antiques. The first thing that greets us is a gaggle of old animatronic Santa Clauses, all with their fair share of wear and tear . . . and charm.

"It's a pretty unique place," Atlas says as he places his hand on my lower back. "My mom has found quite a few things here that she's used on the farm for decoration. Sherry Conrad owns the store. When she first opened, she'd scavenge garage sales and online forums looking for vintage Christmas decorations, and then as her reputation grew, people started bringing their items to her to sell."

"Wow, I'm impressed," I say as I run my hand over a vintage sign that says *trees*. "This would look cute on your farm, right next to the old red truck you have on display that people take pictures in."

He takes in the sign. "You know, you're right. Adds a hint of green to the picture. I think I might grab it, surprise my mom."

"And if you moved the truck over to that grove of trees that points you toward where to cut, it could be a really great photo opportunity that includes the entire farm, not just the truck. With the sign addition, I can see people using that as their Christmas card picture."

He slowly turns to look at me. "Well, isn't that a good idea?"

I smile. "I think it is."

"Me too."

"Give me one second." He heads over to Sherry Conrad, who's sitting at the cash register, reading on an e-reader. "Hey, Sherry, think I can have some *sold* stickers?"

She glances up at Atlas, and I watch as she smiles brightly when her eyes meet his. "Of course, dear. Goodness, I didn't even see you come in—" She glances in my direction and then looks back at Atlas. "Oh my, did you bring a lady friend with you?"

"I did," he says. "A lady friend who is on a first date with me."

Sherry presses her hand to her chest. "And you brought her here?"

"Yeah, trying to spark some inspiration in her, and it seems like I already have." He holds up the stickers she gave him. "We'll be around.

Might have a few purchases today; we'll see. That *tree* sign I'm already claiming."

"You know, you're the first one I thought of when I saw it," she says. "So glad you can give it a home." Then she turns to me and wiggles her fingers. "Hello, dear. Have a look around and let me know if you have any questions. I added a new room in the back, all vintage gifts. Might be one of my favorite additions."

"Looking forward to it," I say as I move over to a section of old boxes and milk crates, my mind starting to run wild with ideas. Atlas joins me, placing his hand on my back again as I move around the crates. "These are so cool."

"My mom uses those for display."

"Yes, that's where I've seen them before. I thought it was a cute way to add height to shelves."

"Where would you use them?"

"I don't know, but I definitely want to take a picture, maybe add it to a vision board."

"Good idea," he says as I snap a picture, and we move down the aisle.

"From the small ideas I had today, one of the things I thought about was having an overarching theme for the cottages. Like . . . the Candy Cane Cottages, something like that."

"Cole and Storee would enjoy that idea," Atlas says with an eye roll.

"Why do you say that?" I ask, confused.

"Do you not know what they've done with a candy cane?"

"No," I say on a laugh. "What did they do?"

He leans in close to my ear and whispers, "Sexual things."

"Oof." I clench my legs together. "Wouldn't that burn?"

"You would think, but they at least had the intelligence to do it with a pineapple-flavored candy cane. I didn't ask for specifics. All I know is that it's something they have done more than once, the first time being in the reindeer barn, and that it gets . . . sticky. So yeah, they would like your Candy Cane Cottages."

I sigh, thinking about it. "Ugh, does it make the idea weird now?"

"No." He shakes his head. "They made it weird with pineapple candy canes. You can keep it classy with the classic peppermint. Plus, you could find a lot of cool stuff here to help decorate. Not to mention *Candy Cane Cottages* has a really nice ring to it."

"I was thinking the same thing," I say, feeling giddy about it. "And I actually took a look at my cottage's brand, and they have smaller versions that are made from logs but painted in red."

"I like that," he says. "I really like that actually."

"They'd pop beautifully against the trees, and with some lit paths with red and white lights, it could be a really pretty place to stay."

He smiles down at me. "I could not agree more."

"You mean that?"

"Listen, I won't lie to you. This idea is awesome and something we need in this town. I want you to succeed, so I wouldn't lie about thinking you have a strong idea."

That brings a smile to my face, because I want to succeed too.

We keep walking down the aisles, picking out some things that could possibly work for the main house, such as decorations and signs. Sherry lets me know she has no problem putting some things on hold for me until Uncle Dwight gets back, so I place a few sold stickers on some signs that I think would be perfect, one in particular for the hot tub area I'd love to set up.

When we reach the back, we head into a separate room that must be the new one Sherry was talking about, because it's decked out in toys and gifts, and a life-size cardboard cutout of Michael Jordan.

"Christ, I'm surprised that's here and Ansel hasn't purchased it yet," Atlas says, pointing to Michael. "He's a huge fan of Michael. I was more of a Shaquille O'Neal kind of guy."

"Because he's tall like you?" I ask.

"Well, Shaq has quite a few inches on me, but yeah, I was center on my team and towered over a lot of my teammates and opponents."

"Were you any good?" I ask as I pick up a clarinet with *Kenosha Kickers* engraved on the side. I set it back down, wondering who would want someone's used clarinet. Those things are slobbered on.

"I was all right. I think I still hold the record at the school for most rebounds."

"Ooo, stud," I say with a wink and then move over to an old plastic case with a snap button. I open it up to find a collection of Micro Machines, all dented and looking like they've had better days. "Looks like someone either got their collection donated or donated it themselves."

"Felix used to collect these," Atlas says, picking one up. "He had a whole lot of them. Ansel would fuck with him and hide one every once in a while. Drove him nuts."

"Ansel seems like a troublemaker."

"Yeah, to say the least." Atlas sighs and then picks up a snow globe. "Hey, look at this." He shakes it up and brings it toward me. In the center is a red cabin with large candy canes on the side of the house. "If this isn't a sign, I don't know what is."

"Wow," I say taking the snow globe from him. "This is … this is exactly what I envisioned."

"Perfect." He lifts my chin and then gently kisses me. "Then I'll get it for you, something to remind you of the vision and goal."

"Oh, you don't have to do that."

"I know I don't, but I want to."

He takes the globe from me and then grabs my hand, leading me around the rest of the room. But instead of taking a look at everything else around me, I can't stop looking up at him, and of course, he catches me.

"What?" he asks.

"You're really sweet. Probably the sweetest guy I've ever met."

"My parents raised me well," he says.

"I can tell. You're really supportive, and I appreciate that. When I was starting my other business, my boyfriend at the time really didn't get it. It was one of the reasons why we split up. He said I was spending too much time thinking about the store, and I didn't understand why he didn't comprehend the importance of how much time and effort I put into it."

"Sounds like an inconsiderate douche. You're better off without him."

I squeeze his hand. "I think I am."

CHAPTER TWENTY-FOUR
MAX

NARRATOR: WORD ON THE STREET is Florence is still saying boner.
  Just thought you might want to know that.
  Really got nothing else to say.
  Shall we carry on with the story?

Ornaments, garlands, and lights dangle from the ceiling, the mood's set with dim lighting throughout, and the subtle sound of instrumental Christmas music playing in the background brings the entire space together.

Betty sits across from me, sipping her cranberry martini, while I can't help but stare at her and the way she takes in the decorations, how she delights over her drink and exudes pure joy with every little detail that she sees.

"This might be one of my favorite places ever. Reminds me of one of those bars you see on social media that people are always showing off during the Christmas season. You know, the ones shrouded in Christmas decorations."

"That was the inspiration, actually," I say. "With the added elements of tartan and reindeer."

"I seriously love it. Makes me rethink my entire candy cane theme."

"Don't," I say. "Your candy cane theme is perfect."

She twists the snow globe I got her and says, "It is, isn't it?"

"I love it. Also really liked the idea of getting a candy cane when you check in."

She smirks. "One to eat, not to play with."

"You might need to add a note that says, *Please use candy canes responsibly.*"

She nods. "You know, not a bad idea, followed by *Peppermint stings.*"

I laugh. "Yeah, cover all your bases." I lift my drink—went with a soda since I'm driving—and I take a sip. "So tell me something about you that I don't know."

"There's a lot that you don't know."

"Well, give me a quick rundown then. What are your interests, your dislikes, pet peeves, comforts? I want to hear it all."

She sips her drink and then sets it down on the table. "Interests . . . well, I like to crochet, even though I haven't done much since I've been here. I've been kind of busy with this guy stalking me."

"Guilty, not even ashamed of it."

She smirks. "I also like everything Christmas. It's one of the reasons why I liked coming here to visit. I love chocolate-covered cherries, like obsessed. Sometimes I get a few boxes during the season just so I can have them when they all go away after Christmas."

"I love a chocolate-covered cherry." I wet my lips, thinking over all the things I can do with that. "What else?"

"Umm, dislikes. Well, I don't like it when people lie. I don't like mean people. I think there's enough rudeness and lack of empathy in the world that there's no need to feed it."

"Could not agree more."

"And I really don't like chocolate oranges."

"Wait . . . really?" I ask. "You mean the ones wrapped in foil that you crack?"

"Yeah, hate them."

"Okay, so you are obsessed with chocolate-covered cherries but hate chocolate oranges."

"Correct."

"Got it. What else?"

"You said *pet peeves*, right?"

I nod, so she thinks on that.

"Um, well, isn't that lying?"

"Umm, I see a pet peeve as something that's unusual that you can't stand. Like . . . people taking pictures of babies in cutout pumpkins." I lean forward and say, "Cole did that with Florence, and I couldn't get on board with it."

She laughs. "Okay. Hmm, let's see. Well, working in retail for a bit, I realized there is a proper way to hand back change."

"Oh yeah? How does it go?" I ask.

"Coins first, then dollars, receipt in the bag."

"Why that order?"

"Well, the coins first so people can hold on to them, then bills so they can stick them in their wallet, receipt in the bag so they don't have to fumble with it. The worst is when they do receipt, bills, and then coins on top of the bills, so the coins go spilling everywhere. It's inefficient and frustrating."

"I can see your point. Okay, great pet peeve. Last one is comfort."

"Hmm, comfort." She sips her drink again, and as I watch her lips curl over the edge, the temptation to pull her across the table becomes very strong. "Ooo, I have one. Whenever I'm not feeling well or just need that comfort food that makes me feel better, I always grab a microwaveable mac and cheese."

"For me, it's a frozen pizza," I say.

"Do you eat the whole thing?" she asks.

"Have you seen the size of me?"

"Right." She chuckles. "You definitely eat the whole thing."

"That would be correct."

"So how about you? What are your interests and dislikes? I already know the comfort and pet peeve. Noting not to put babies in pumpkins around you."

"Smart." I tap my head and then give it a thought. "I obviously like basketball. When it's summer, I join a three-on-three league, and that's pretty fun. I like the outdoors, and I like to sometimes get metaphorically lost in the woods. I know our forest so well at this point that I'd be able to find my way no problem. I also really like forestry. One of my favorite things to do is to walk along our property and clean up the forest."

"Is that a thing?" she asks.

"Yeah. It's how you keep your forest thriving. You have to take down the dead trees, make room for new. We get all our fireplace wood from cleaning the property. You have to renew the space to keep it growing, something you'll have to do on your land. It probably hasn't ever been cleaned out and could really use it."

"Oh, I had no idea."

I wink at her. "I can teach you. As for dislikes, same as you, lying is not my favorite thing. Also I hate when the big pick on the little, or anyone picks on anyone for that matter. When I had more spare time on my hands, I'd help out at the school with after-school activities, and I found that there still are a lot of bullies out there, and I hated it. I made sure to point it out and teach those kids a lesson."

"You helped out at the school? That's really cute."

"Yeah, there are days I miss it and days that I don't. Like when the kids come to the farm and I teach them about forestry, I really miss working with them. But then they go and spit on a tree because they think it's funny, and it makes me want to punt them across the yard."

She laughs. "Spit on a tree? Really?"

"Yeah, fucking punks." I shake my head.

"Why would that even be a thing they think to do?"

"Great question. And of course they're from out-of-town schools, so it's not like I can address it with their parents. Instead I just threaten them while holding an axe."

"Oh my God, like you threaten to chop them up?"

Now it's my turn to laugh as I shake my head. "No, I just grip my axe tightly and stare them down. They get the picture. Do it again, and they very well might be chopped up."

"I bet you can be very intimidating."

"I can. I've practiced the look in my mirror."

"Have you really?"

"Oh yeah. It's a look I learned from my dad and perfected. You have to let these youth know that you mean business. Good thing you're going to create an all-adult resort, because then you won't have to deal with punk-ass kids."

"I mean, I like children, but yeah, you're probably right about that."

"I like kids too, mainly my two nieces. They're fucking adorable . . . when not in cutout pumpkins."

"Heaven forbid they're in cutout pumpkins."

"The nerve of Cole and Storee." I shake my head with mirth.

———

"The most awkward date I've ever had? Hmm." Betty cutely taps her chin as she thinks about it.

Our food has been delivered and devoured. She got the fish and chips, and I got the burger. She had some of my brussels sprouts, and I had some of her fries. It felt like we've been sharing meals for years.

There's an ease when I'm around her, a comfort, like I've known this woman my whole life and I'm finally able to hang out with her.

Not to mention she told me when I had ketchup on my nose, and I told her when there was something in her teeth. There was no embarrassment, just laughter and gratitude. And to me, that's a true testament to how you get along with someone.

"Well, there was this one guy that I went on a date with—he was a train conductor."

"Like an actual train conductor?" I ask, because that's a job you don't hear about someone having very often.

"Well, he was one in training. And all he talked about was all the bodies he witnessed getting run over by the train."

"Wait . . . seriously?" I ask.

She nods. "Yeah, it was depressing and disgusting, and at one point, I asked him to stop because I couldn't take it anymore, so then he went into animals. Needless to say, there wasn't a second date."

"Jesus. Maybe the guy didn't get the memo on how to properly act when on a date."

"Yeah, he definitely didn't. My mom set him up with me as a favor to a friend. I told her I wouldn't be doing any more favors for her friends."

"After that, yeah, I'd be the same way. Are you close with your parents?"

"Pretty close. I'm the only child, but they also aren't the type of parents that attach to me and revolve their lives around me, you know? I chat with them, catch them up on my life, and they go off and do their own thing. I'm assuming you're close with your parents."

"Maybe a little too close at the moment," I answer. "I wish I wasn't sharing the same living space as them, especially since my brothers tend to rub it in a lot, but I know it will pay off in the long run."

"It will. Building your own house will be worth it."

"Yeah, I agree."

"Do you have any awkward dating stories?"

I tug on my hair and lean back in the booth. "I mean, where do I begin? Being a guy in a small town with not a lot of options, you tend to date a few people who are in and out of the town, and there can be some real weirdos."

"Really?" she asks, her expression emitting intrigue. "Tell me some."

I heave a sigh. "There was the girl who wanted to try to have a conversation without using the letter T in any of our words." I clear my throat and say, "Ee was he worse nigh of my life."

Betty bursts out in laughter. "Why on earth was that a thing she wanted to do?"

"I have no goddamn clue. When I asked her out, she was normal, but then she sprang that on me, and let's just say I faked intestinal issues and fled."

"Did you have to say *intestinal* without the T?"

"I believe I said, 'Oh no, my belly is ouchie. Bye-bye.'"

She chuckles some more. "I guess I'm pretty normal compared to her."

"Betty, you are easily the most normal. I was just thinking about how it feels so easy with you. Like I don't have to think too much. We just work together."

She tilts her head cutely to the side. "I was thinking the same thing."

"Really?"

She nods. "Yeah, this is easily the most entertaining, thoughtful, fun, comfortable date I've ever been on."

Leaning forward, I take her hand in mine and entwine our fingers. "You know what that means, right?"

"If you say we're destined for each other . . . I couldn't agree more."

I laugh. "Holy shit, you know me too well."

"Do I know you too well, or are we oddly the same person?"

"Yeah, I've considered that as well. Maybe we should do a rapid-fire round, see how similar we are."

"Ooo, I like that idea." She rubs her hands together. "On three, favorite month of the year."

"December," we say together.

"That was an easy one," I say.

"Yes, but if we couldn't match up on an easy one, do we even dare on the hard?"

I point at her. "Good thinking."

She playfully fluffs her hair. "Thank you."

"Okay . . . if you were a misfit toy in *Rudolph the Red-Nosed Reindeer*, which toy would you be?"

"A water pistol that squirts jelly," we say together, making us laugh.

"Because squirting jelly is way more fun than water," she says.

"Fuck yeah. Honestly, Pistol has it easy. Charlie-in-the-Box, on the other hand, what a major disappointment." I stab my finger into the table playfully. "I don't know one single child who would play with a Charlie-in-the-Box. It's either Jack or get it away from my face."

"Whoever thought of a Charlie-in-the-Box is deranged. An absolute menace to society."

"Lock them up," I say.

"Throw away the key," she adds, making me like her that much more.

And it must be obvious, because I have a smile stretching from ear to ear as I look back at her.

"Okay, here's a question for you." She wets her lips. "If eggnog was the liquid, what would you dip in it? On the count of three. One . . . two . . . three."

"A dick," we say at the same time, only to bust out in laughter so loud that the entire bar turns to look at us.

But we don't care.

We continue to laugh until we both have tears in our eyes.

After a few seconds, I take a deep breath and say, "You don't even have a dick."

"True, but I'd find one and dip it," she answers. "I'd dip it until it was fully coated."

I wipe at my eyes. "Fuck, you were made for me. Any other normal person would say a cookie or a cinnamon stick or something food related, but no, not you. You're dipping a dick."

"Or a dong, some might say. A new Christmas tradition, dipping the dong."

I snort. "It's not really Christmas until Granddad dips his dong in the eggnog."

She winces. "Did we have to get Granddad involved?"

"He's people too."

"True," she says with a nod. "Just because they're old doesn't mean that they're dead."

"That's right. Granddad deserves the dip."

"And Grandma deserves to dip too."

I raise a brow. "Are you talking . . . maybe a nip dip?"

Her eyes light up. "Oh my God, what if . . . the key to Christmas magic is a dong dip and a nip dip in eggnog, only for the tip of the nip and the tip of the dong to connect, coated in eggnog, and that's what sparks a Christmas miracle."

I sit back and start to slowly clap. "Holy shit, Betty. I think we just cracked the code." I lean forward again and whisper, "We know the secret to Christmas."

She smirks. "I dare you to ask Bob Krampus."

"Ha!" I guffaw loud enough for the sound to echo through the bar. "If I asked Bob Krampus if he and Sylvia dip their nip and tip in eggnog to form Christmas magic, you can bet your cute fucking ass that I'd be exiled from town, never to be seen again."

"You think so?"

"I know so. Bob Krampus doesn't take kindly to tomfoolery when it comes to his—"

"What doesn't my father like?" A large figure presents himself at the end of our table.

I look over, taking in unbuckled black galoshes, a black snow shovel, and a long black jacket. When my eyes make their way up to his face, I know I better watch what I say next, because it's none other than BKJ.

"Um, milk and cookies," I say and then clear my throat. "BKJ, great to see you. Umm, out shoveling?"

"Cleaning up some of the sidewalks, making more room. Dad was saying the walking spaces were looking tight, so you know, want to make sure no one gets hurt." He looks between the two of us. "Dad told me you had a date today. It's good to see you two together . . . laughing and having a good time."

"Yeah, a very good time." Betty bites down on the corner of her lip and then glances at me, her gaze fleeting.

Uh-oh.

I know that look.

I recognize that feeling.

Hell, I've felt it. She's uncomfortable.

She's awkward.

She's about to ramble.

"We're talking about dipping penises in eggnog."

And yup, there it is.

Christ. Now I know how Cole feels.

"Pardon me?" BKJ says, tugging on his ear.

"And nipples. Penises and nipples in eggnog," Betty continues.

"As a joke," I say, wanting to help out, because wow, probably not what BKJ was thinking he would hear when he walked up to us. "And we weren't talking about your dad and mom using eggnog in that way. Not even a little."

"Nor did we say it was how Christmas miracles happen," Betty continues. "Not one mention of your parents. None at all. And definitely not about how a nip and a tip would connect and make magic. Nope. Not even a little. Because that's inappropriate and would be way out of line to speak about your parents in such a way, so we would never."

BKJ raises his brow, his mustache twitching while he stares us down.

I can see Betty's gulp.

I can feel the back of my neck sweat.

"Yup, nary a mention of them," I add for good measure.

He studies us for one more second and then says, "You know, you very well might be a perfect match." He taps the table. "Have a good night."

Then he takes off, clomping his boots across the hardwood floor until he leaves the bar.

I turn to look at Betty. "Wow, you are not smooth at all."

Her mouth falls open, mirth all over her expression. "As if you are."

"Uh, smoother than you."

"You're the one who brought up his parents."

"Well . . . you brought up the penises, which triggered me to talk about the parents. I wasn't going to say anything about the eggnog."

"Oh . . . you were. It would have been a few seconds, but you would have. Guaranteed. I could see your mind twirling. I honestly think I said that to protect you."

"Oh, bullshit." I laugh. "His boots scared you, and therefore you started rambling. I was holding it together."

"If you call that holding it together, then I fear for you." She crosses her arms. "Let's call a spade a spade. We were both folding under his stare. Admit it."

I scratch my jaw and then say, "But I don't know why. He's a nice guy, and I'm taller than him—I shouldn't be frightened."

"It's the boots and shovel, simple as that."

BETTY

"Okay, this is amazing," I say as I take a bite out of a Junior Mint ice cream cake while sharing a booth with Atlas at the Polar Freeze.

I've never been to the local ice cream shop because every time I've visited, it's been cold, and ice cream doesn't really scream *Christmas* to me, but I've been missing out. First of all, the entire place is set up as if you stepped foot into the Arctic tundra. The walls are coated in plaster and shaped to form caves, coves, and arches that are painted in white and covered in clear glitter. The floor is concrete with icebergs painted like stepping stones leading up to the counter. An old soda shop-type bar spans across the right side of the store while iceberg-blue and white leather booths flank the other side, offering a great deal of seating. My favorite parts are the snowflakes, icicles, and lights that dangle from the ceiling, adding that last piece of whimsy to tie everything together.

"My favorite treat. They only make it during the Christmas season."

"Really?" I ask, taking another bite while Atlas has his arm around me, keeping me close to his side. Yes, we're that couple, sitting side by side in a booth rather than across from each other. "Why would they keep such a delicious thing as a seasonal dish?"

"I think it's to get more people through the doors during the Christmas season. It's so cold, ice cream really isn't someone's go-to treat."

"Oh, yeah, that makes sense."

"They actually do a monthly special to keep people coming in. The Junior Mint is by far the best." He takes a bite, and I watch as his mouth wraps around the fork, his expression suggesting he's truly enjoying the dessert.

I've shamefully watched him enjoy his food all night.

I've watched him suck, lick, chew—it's been a cornucopia of turn-ons,

and now that we're here eating dessert, I'm starting to get the impression that he's not the only horny one in this duo.

"Hey."

"Huh?" I look up at him.

"You're staring at my mouth."

"Am I?"

"You are," he says, smirking.

"Umm, I don't think I was."

"Uh-huh, so then what were you looking at?"

"The, uh, penguin behind you. Bold choice since penguins and polar bears don't live in the same habitat."

"We're getting back to you staring at my mouth in a second, but . . . they don't?"

"Nope, it's a misconception," I answer. "Penguins live in the Southern Hemisphere, and polar bears live in the Northern Hemisphere."

"Huh, I didn't know that."

"Well, you're welcome for educating you. Anyway"—I take the last bite of the ice cream—"we best be going home now." I attempt to get up, but he holds me down by the waist.

"No way. I told you we'd be going back to the whole staring-at-my-mouth thing."

"Ugh, you're insistent." I turn toward him and sigh. "Yes, I was staring at your mouth. I've been staring at it all night. I've envisioned what you can do with that mouth, and I've thought about how you can use it on me. Okay? So yes, you're not the only one who apparently has a horny mind. Happy?"

His smile grows wider. "Yes, very happy." He tugs me in even closer, so my hand falls on his chest.

"I . . . I want you to know something though," I say as he leans forward and kisses my neck right in the middle of the Polar Freeze, like two high schoolers who just shared a mud pie. "I have no intention of . . . of doing anything tonight. We shall go our separate ways."

"Okay," he says simply. "If that's what you want." He kisses the spot below my ear, and I lean into the touch.

"Yes, that's, um, that's what I want."

"If that's the case, then let me get you back home. Don't want to keep you from a good night's rest."

I pull away from him and pat him on the chest. "That's very respectful of you, sir."

"Sir?" He quirks a brow, making him look almost irresistible.

"Yes, well, I grow formal when nervous. Now, shall we be on our way?" I gesture toward the door, causing him to chuckle.

"We shall."

I head out of the booth first, and Atlas follows closely behind. When I reach for his hand, he doesn't link our palms together. Instead, he grips the back of my neck possessively and guides me out of the ice cream shop.

Dear God.

We make it down the sidewalk to where his truck is parked, and he brings me to the passenger side. Before he opens the door, he gently places me against the vehicle and tilts my chin up. "Did you have a good night?"

"A really good night," I answer. "Thank you for taking me out, making me laugh, and creating an environment where I can be creative and think things through."

"I want you to succeed, and I love seeing your mind work. It's really hot."

I smile. "You're really hot."

"I know." He smirks and then bends down and presses a very light kiss to my lips before pulling away, leaving me wanting so much more. "Let me get you home."

He moves me to the side, opens the door for me, and then helps me into his truck. I buckle up while he shuts the door and then goes around to this side. When he gets in, he glances at me and then back at the steering wheel.

"What?" I ask.

"Just thought that you'd sit in the middle, but that's fine. I can still reach you from here."

He buckles up, turns the car on, and then places his hand on my thigh as he pulls out onto the road. My eyes immediately fall to where his hand is . . . his very large hand. I've had a man hold my thigh before, but for some reason, this is different. There's a more poignant connection between the two of us, so when he does place his hand on my thigh, an addicting electricity bounces through me.

"So unlike the train conductor, do you think I can score a second date with you?"

I glance over at him and place my hand on top of his. "There will be a second date for sure."

"See, when you don't talk about running over people with trains, you can grant yourself a better chance at a second date. Someone should really talk to that guy."

"Maybe he's learned his lesson by now," I suggest.

He shakes his head. "Once a train talker, always a train talker. He needs to find a match who doesn't mind such conversation."

"And what kind of match would that be?" I ask.

He gives it a thought and then says, "A mortician."

"You know, that's actually probably a good pairing."

"I thought so." He turns out of town and heads down Route 25 toward our properties.

"Is the town always this busy during this time?"

"Oh yeah, gets even busier as we near Christmas."

"I'm sure you all love and hate it."

"Yeah, you could say that. It's nice having the business, but there are times when you just want to walk around the town during Christmas without droves of people getting in the way. Thankfully all the proprietors in town will hold space for townies. Which is why I was able to get a table at Prancer's Libations."

"That's actually pretty cool. Do you think I should have some sort of eatery at the cottages?"

"I think it's something you should definitely consider," he answers. "Gives everyone more options."

"That wouldn't be stepping on anyone's toes?"

"The menu would have to be approved, but I doubt anyone would be upset about it, especially since it gets really busy with reservations this time of the year."

"Hmm, something to think about." I rub my thumb over his knuckles. "Thank you again for tonight."

"Thanks for saying yes," he says and then turns down my driveway.

When he puts the truck in park, he unbuckles his seat belt, but I stop him from leaving the truck. I unbuckle my seat belt as well and scoot toward the center of the seat.

I move my hand up his cheek, loving the rough texture of his scruff, and then I bring his face down to mine and kiss him.

At first, it's gentle, soft, nothing too overwhelming, but the moment he reciprocates with his slow, drugging kisses, something in me goes feral, like if I don't drink this man up right now, I might fall apart.

So I open my mouth, letting my tongue collide with his, and the touch of his tongue against mine sends a shock wave of lust through my body, lighting me up and creating a desire so much greater than I ever expected.

He settles into the kiss, allowing me to take control while his hand lightly caresses my backside, keeping me in close but not forcing me— just a hint of possession. Just enough possession that I swirl my tongue around his, dancing, melting into the moment as my hand slides down his chest and to his lap, where I glide my palm over his bulge.

He groans into my mouth, his possessive hold on me growing as he turns even more toward me. I apply more pressure, letting my palm feel his growing erection and the way that I can turn him on with just my mouth.

His kisses grow more intense, moving past my mouth and across my jaw as he angles my head. His other hand parts the buttons of my jacket and finds my sweater, slipping his hand underneath. When his palm connects with the cup of my bra, I undo his pants, pulling down his zipper and slipping my hand inside, causing him to pull away and look at me.

"Fuck... what's happening?" he asks, breathless.

"I don't know," I answer, looking him in his beautiful dark eyes. "I should... I should go to my cottage."

"Yeah. Maybe you should."

Smiling, I open up his side of the car and climb over him, where I pause for one second, trying to tell him exactly what I want in this moment. His eyes gleam with intrigue as I hop out of his truck, grab him by the hand, and tug him toward my cottage with me. He has just enough time to lock up before I have him on the porch behind me, waiting for me to open the door.

With shaky hands, it takes me a few seconds to make the key work, but once it does, I barge in and strip out of my coat. He does the same, and then pushes me gently against the wall and starts attacking my mouth again, swooping down and claiming me.

I paw at his sweater, wanting it off so I can feel his warm skin. I tug on it, pushing it up until he reaches behind him and pulls it all the way off, leaving him in undone jeans. I sigh as I let my hands explore the contours of his muscles, from his flattened, thick pecs to the muscles along his ribs and the V in his hips. My fingers don't let one inch go untouched as he continues to own me with his mouth.

"I fucking love kissing you," he says as he gets even closer, tugging on my sweater. I raise my hands above my head, and he quickly pulls it off, revealing my red lace bra. "Get rid of this." He reaches behind me and quickly releases the clasp of my bra with one flick of his fingers. He tears it off me and then grips my right breast, letting it rest in his palm before he squeezes. "Fucking gorgeous."

Then he reaches between us and undoes my pants, pushing them down as well. I make quick work of them and my boots, while he takes off his boots as well, and when we meet back up, he lifts me up against the door, and I wrap my legs around him as his mouth claims mine once again.

His hands move up to my breasts, and his thumbs rub over my nipples, while I tangle my hands in his hair and rotate my hips against him.

"I want to feel you," I say, trying to push at his pants.

He gets what I'm after and pushes his pants down, then lines my center up with his erection.

"God, yes." I start to grind against him. My hips have a mind of their own. "You're so huge."

He grumbles something against my skin as his lips kiss down the column of my neck and then back up, both of us in a frenzy as we attempt to satisfy this burning need between us. But it's not enough, the friction. It's not what I need.

I need so much more.

I pull away and look him in the eyes as he catches his breath. "I want you inside me."

His eyes go hungry as he wets his lips. "You sure?"

"More than sure. I want you filling me up . . ." I pause and then finish, "With your cum."

"Fuck," he growls before carrying me over to the couch.

He sets me down and then pushes his pants and boxer briefs off, freeing himself from his confines.

"Take your thong off," he says as he grips himself and starts to pump.

I watch in fascination as the muscles in his forearm fire off with every movement. "Now, Betty."

The tone of his voice snaps me out of my haze, and I remove my thong and toss it to the side, leaving myself completely naked.

"Stand up."

I stand from the couch and wait for the next command.

"Turn around and bend over."

Oh God, is he going to take me from behind? Nerves shoot through me as I turn around and bend over.

"Lower. I want to see how wet you are."

I bend lower and wait.

"Spread your legs, Betty."

I spread and then feel him come right up behind me, and with the head of his cock, he strokes my entire length, letting my arousal drench him.

"So wet. So fucking wet for me."

With his other hand, he palms my ass and then, to my surprise, spanks me.

"Oh God," I cry out as he smooths his hand over the sensitive area.

He strokes me again with the head of his cock, relaxing me, and then spanks me again, sending a jolt of lust through me this time and causing me to moan. I surprise myself with the sound, but when he strokes me one more time with the tip of his cock, I *need* another spank, and he delivers, this one a touch harder.

"Yes, Atlas," I cry out and then feel him bend over me, his chest to my back as he speaks softly into my ear.

"It's taking everything in my goddamn body not to bend you over my knee and spank you until you come. You hear me? Everything."

I wet my lips and nod.

"That will happen. Not tonight, but it fucking will."

And then he lifts up and takes a seat on the couch, spreading his legs. He starts stroking himself, using my arousal as his lubrication.

"Come here," he says, holding his hand out.

I take his hand and allow him to pull me to his lap, where I straddle his legs, his cock between us.

He runs his hand up my side and to my breast where he gently plays with my nipple, making me even more wet, even more needy. "I want you to take control. Fill yourself up on your time. Tell me what you need. Got it?"

I nod.

"I have protection in my wallet. Do you want it?"

I bite on my bottom lip and shake my head. "I want you bare."

His chest heaves a little harder as he nods. "Your choice."

"I want you . . . bare, Atlas."

"Then have me," he says as he positions his cock for me.

I sit up on my knees and tilt to the side so I can find the right angle to have him enter me. And because he's so long, I have to take a couple of inches at first. My mouth falls open in surprise from the feel of him, the initial sink causing me to squeeze around him tightly.

The muttered curses falling out of Atlas's mouth are the greatest things I've ever heard.

"Fuck, so tight. So goddamn tight. Jesus Christ," he says, placing his hands behind his head and breathing heavily.

I rest my hands on his shoulders and lower another inch.

"Motherfucker," he says, his stomach hollowing, his neck straining.

I move down another inch, and he's practically panting now.

The sight of him holding back, slipping inside me, it's such a turn-on, making it easier to slide down on him until I'm fully seated, bottomed out, so full that I feel like I might burst.

"Oh God," I say, my fingers digging into his skin. "Oh fuck, Atlas."

"Jesus Christ." He takes a few deep breaths, and when his eyes connect with mine, they're dazed, hazy, like he's in another world and unable to focus. "Fuck, baby, stop . . . stop squeezing."

"I can't," I say, contracting around him. "You're so big."

"I know, but I'll . . . Fuck, Betty. I'll come too fast. Please stop squeezing."

"I can't," I say as I shift, causing him to groan even louder.

"Fuck." His hands fall to my sides, and he lifts me up ever so slightly and pushes me back down, the feeling of him bottoming out again hitting me in a spot I've never felt before and sending a jolt of pleasure through me.

"Yes, Atlas." I lift up, replicating the movement and slamming down. "Oh God, it feels so good."

He groans again, not doing much, just letting me take control. But I don't like it. I want to feel possessed by him. I want to feel him lose control.

So I lean forward and press my mouth to his ear as I say, "Fill me with your cum."

It triggers something inside him, because he lifts me off the couch, still inside me, and lays me down on the rug, shoving the coffee table to the side and spreading my legs wide.

"Eyes on me, got it? Don't fucking close them."

I do as he says, and with his hand pressing down on my abdomen, making the pressure of him inside me that much stronger, he starts to move in and out. It's slow at first, testing me, but then I grip his ass, encouraging him to let loose. Pulling nearly all the way out, he slams back into me, and I swear, I can taste him in my throat as he does it over and over and over again.

Stretching me.

Making me breathless.

He's creating such a fullness inside me while hitting my G-spot that I start to unravel, my orgasm at the base of my spine, building and building.

"This fucking cunt," he growls. "Fuck, I'm going to come."

I feel him grow tense, his body shifting, pumping faster,

relentlessly, until everything starts to fade to black. My body tingles, and I can't hold off anymore as I tip over the edge, my orgasm rocketing through me.

"Atlas, oh fuck, yes," I scream as I come all over his cock.

"Motherfucker," he grinds out as I contract around him. He punches the ground, stills, and then comes hard, his cock swelling before he fills me up. He bows his head, takes a few deep breaths, and then mutters, "Jesus Christ."

Slowly, his eyes part open, and when they fix on me, a look of disbelief crosses his expression.

Catching my breath, I bring my hand to his cheek and let my thumb caress his scruff. He leans down and lightly kisses me while we come off the high of our orgasms. After a prolonged moment of our mouths matching up, he pulls away and slowly removes himself, leaving me feeling so empty.

"Wait right here," he says and then stands from the floor, his cock still erect as he walks to the bathroom.

I drape my arm over my eyes and try to hold back my smile, but it's nearly impossible because, oh my God, that was easily the best experience of my entire life.

How is it possible that I've gone this long without experiencing a true orgasm, one that takes over my body and rocks every inch of it?

How?

I hear him in the bathroom using the sink, and I consider joining him, but he told me to stay, so I do. I wait for him, thinking back to all the other guys I've been with and how lackluster those experiences feel now. And not just because Atlas is clearly bigger than all of them but because of the connection I feel with him. Because of the undeniable attraction. Because of how well we fit together.

He comes back into the living room and surprises me as he takes a warm washcloth that he must have found in my cabinet and helps me clean up. Then he lifts me up off the ground and carries me to the bathroom.

He sets me down, grips my chin possessively, his thumb angling my lips up, and he kisses me one more time before shutting the door to give me some privacy.

I lean against it, catching my breath and telling myself that this is the real deal.

There's nothing fake about the way we feel for each other, and there is no way I'll let Uncle Dwight ruin this. No, we have to find a way to make this all work, because I can't give him up.

I won't.

CHAPTER TWENTY-FIVE
MAX

NARRATOR: OUR DEAR FRIEND MAX *just found a land where kitten kisses are payment and unicorns rain candy down on all the peasants. Where rainbows are real-life slides and Brenda Lee is constantly rocking around the Christmas tree, never getting tired.*

Yes, he's hit the apex of all orgasms.

He's seen the light.

He now knows what it means to touch heaven but not fully accept an invitation.

Don't let me bore you with the summary. How about we let him explain it instead?

———————

This is what euphoria is—the feeling after being inside Betty.

It's like my dick is being carried around on a velvet pillow in a parade of sex where all the luckiest of people get to experience raw joy.

Yes, that's what this is. Raw joy.

Nothing is better.

Nothing is more satisfying.

Nope, it's my dick and Betty's pussy that's the combination. I feel really bad for all of you sad motherfuckers who don't have that combination, because wow.

She thought I was horny before, well she better look out, because after being inside her, fucking bare, there's no looking back now. Hell, as I wait for her to be done in the bathroom, I'm gearing up for round two.

I'm like a young man all over again, ready to wield my cock like a freshly sharpened katana and come all over the place.

Her pussy did that to me.

Her pussy and her eyes.

Well, her pussy, her eyes, and those tits.

Fuck, the way they bounced as I moved in and out of her.

And fuck, how she clenched around me. Like a goddamn vise down there.

She's perfect.

Everything about her is perfect.

And I'm so fucking lucky that she came to this town and tried to put me out of business. Something I wouldn't have thought a couple of weeks ago.

The bathroom door opens, and I look over my shoulder from where I'm sitting on her couch and watch her cross the room, her beautiful naked body swaying with every step.

When she reaches me, I pull her down on my boxer brief–clad lap, and she says, "Not fair. Why do you have clothes on?"

"So I didn't fucking jump you the minute you got out of the bathroom. Trying to tell myself to give you a break, that you might be sore. Are you?"

"I might be a little."

I smooth my hand over her soft skin. "Shit, I'm sorry. I sort of lost control—"

"Don't apologize." She cups my cheek. "I loved it. I loved everything about it. Don't second-guess a thing."

"Okay." I turn and kiss the palm of her hand. Her eyes glitter at me, her smile so sincere. God, I don't want to leave. I want to stay. I want to hold her tonight. I want to wake up in the morning with her in my arms. Make her breakfast again. Take a shower with her. Get her dressed.

Fuck her so many more times.

Looking her in the eyes and knowing I'm taking a chance, I say, "Can I stay tonight? With you?"

"You want to?" she asks.

"Desperately," I answer. And this is how I know that Betty is so special. I have *never* been so desperate to stay with a woman overnight. Yes, the sex may have been great, but this woman gets me like no other woman has before. I'm completely gone for her.

The corners of her lips turn up. "I'd love for you to stay. I even have a dentist-approved toothbrush you can use."

That makes me chuckle. "You make it hard for me to leave when you say things like that."

So these cottages were not made for people like me. For a little sprite like Betty, sure, it's perfect, but for a six-foot-four man with long legs and a barrel of a chest, not so much.

After we got ready for bed, Betty led the way up to her loft. I had to contort my body up the small set of stairs and then get on all fours to crawl to her bed because the ceiling is so low.

I can tell you right now, it's a good thing I fucked her on her living room rug, because if she watched me climb those stairs with an erection, she probably never would have stopped laughing.

"Are you comfortable?" she asks as she rests her head on my shoulder, cuddling in close.

"Now I am," I answer. I kiss the top of her head, perfectly content.

She lightly chuckles. "Good, because for a second there, I thought you were going to cramp up getting up here."

"Me too," I say, thinking about how my leg got caught in her sheet and I had a hell of a time getting it out. It's a shock that she finds me as attractive as she does, given my clumsiness. I'm just glad she wasn't witness to me tripping headfirst into the family Christmas tree.

"This was the perfect end to a perfect date. Thank you." She kisses my jaw, and I melt into her mattress, so goddamn content.

"And you thought you didn't want to spend the night with me again," I tease.

"Looks like I didn't know what I really wanted."

"Do you now?"

She nods her head. "I do." Then she's silent for a moment.

"Is there a follow-up to that? I'm sensing there is."

"I mean . . . I just, I think I'm getting in my head."

"About what?"

"I'm getting nervous, because I, um, I really have a liking for you."

I chuckle. "I really have a liking for you as well."

"You better." She pokes me. "But I'm also worried."

"Worried about what? Trust me, I'm not going anywhere. And tomorrow when I'm chopping down trees and helping families out at the farm, I'll be thinking about tonight the entire time."

"I'm not worried about you. I'm worried about Uncle Dwight."

"Oh, yeah, I've been thinking about that."

"When he finds out, he's going to . . . God, he'll be so upset with me. He'll think I betrayed him, that I'm purposefully trying to hurt him. That's not the case at all. I just think . . . I think he's wrong about you, and I need to find a way to make him see that, you know? But I don't know how when he's so mad, when he's so caught up in what he thinks you did."

"I know. I worry about it too. I want to find a way to talk to him myself, to maybe see what I can do to make it better. We've been feuding for years, but at this point, not only am I over it, but I don't want it to jeopardize anything I have with you."

"Same."

"I can talk to him when he gets back, have a serious conversation with him, and hopefully he can listen to me."

"Maybe I should talk to him first, let him know how I feel."

I shake my head. "No, I think that will put him on the defense. I think if I talk to him first and possibly clear the air, that might open his mind to the idea of you and me."

She thinks on that. "Yeah, maybe you're right." Then she clears her throat and asks, "On the subject of you and me, is there a definition there? Would you say we're dating?"

"Yes, I would," I answer honestly. "Together exclusively if you don't mind."

She chuckles. "I prefer the exclusivity part. I don't need some tree-chopping hussy coming into Evergreen Farm thinking she can proposition you."

"First of all, never seen a tree-chopping hussy other than you."

She gasps, making me laugh.

"And even if a tree-chopping hussy propositioned me, I'd say, *Sorry, lady, but this dick belongs to Betty.*"

"Pretty bold statement."

"A correct statement."

She kisses and rubs her thumb over my chest. "How did this all happen? How did we go from me nailing you in the head with a Pepsi bottle to this?"

"I think about that all the time."

"And seriously, why were you trying to break into my place?"

Groaning in exasperation, I say, "I was not trying to break in."

She chuckles and kisses my chest again. "Okay, but a crowbar, that's suspicious."

"And as a man who has now been to the jail in our small town, I realize it was not the wisest choice of weapon to keep me safe from murderous bears. But let the record state that I had zero intention of breaking into your place. I just wanted a peek inside."

"Do you regret peeking inside?"

"No," he answers. "But I do regret bringing chocolate-covered pretzels and popcorn over, because that two-liter to the chest was unnecessary."

She chuckles. "Self-defense is important."

"Yeah, I'd hate to meet up with you in a soda aisle at the grocery store, that's for damn sure. Imagine the carnage."

"I'd decimate everyone on that battleground."

I run my hand along her hip, loving this moment of levity, how I can joke around with her, tease her. There's nothing but joy here. I can't say that how Storee and I set out to woo Betty has completely disappeared from my mind. I'm sure Betty and I will talk about it sometime and have a good laugh at our ridiculousness. *That's for another day.* But this last forty-eight hours with Betty has given me a whole new perspective on relationships and what I want when it comes to the perfect person for me.

And right now, it's looking a lot like Betty.

BETTY

I set my coffee down and blow out a heavy breath before I pick up my phone. I stare down at the text thread with Uncle Dwight.

I don't know how to approach this. I know Atlas wants to talk to him and clear the air, but maybe I can lay a little groundwork.

I cross one leg over the other and look out the window of Warm Your Spirits, trying to come up with the right phrasing. Well, step number one would be to ask how his conference is going, so I lead with that.

Betty: Hey, just checking in. How's the conference? Had a pretty

bad storm here, lost some power at the cottage but made
it through.

Don't tell him how I made it through, because that doesn't really need
to be stated.

Coffee cake in front of me—I'm going to finally try it after my failed
attempt last time—I cut off a piece with my fork and place it in my mouth.

So moist.

The moistest.

So much of this cake is moist that I don't think I'll ever get over just
how moist it really is.

Love a moist cake.

Moist. Moist. Moist.

"How is it?" Tanya asks as she sets a napkin down at my table.

"Moist," I say with a smile, causing her to cringe.

"Such a cringe word."

"*Moist*?" I ask. "No, it's a perfect descriptor, especially for a cake. Not
too wet, just damp enough to not choke you out while eating."

She chuckles. "Well, I'm glad you're enjoying it."

I take another bite as my phone vibrates with a text. "So moist."

She shakes her head in mirth. "Well, enjoy."

I set my fork down and am surprised when I see a text from Atlas on
my phone.

Max: Wishing we had another snowstorm right about now. Just
watched Cole shovel reindeer excrement, and let's just say,
it did nothing for me.

I chuckle and text him back, feeling all kinds of giddy.

Betty: Does Cole shoveling usually do something for you?

Max: I mean, depends on whether I'm in the mood to marvel at
his forearms or not.

Betty: Didn't know I had competition. Is Storee aware?

Max: She's very aware of our sick and twisted relationship. Glad
you're starting to clue in. Also, how are you feeling?

Betty: Sore, but a good kind of sore.

Max: I'm sorry. I know you don't want me apologizing, but I am,
I'm sorry. I fucking lost all sense of control last night. I blame
it on how you wouldn't stop squeezing around me.

Betty: Blame that on your size.

Max: You know what? I will take the blame.

Betty: That's awfully big of you. What a true gentleman.

Max: I try. What are you doing later? Can I stop by? I have
something for you.

Betty: Really?

Max: Yeah, really.

Betty: Just working on my proposal for Dwight, but I'm open
to visitors.

Max: Good, because I'm a visitor and I want to see you.

Betty: Want me to cook dinner?

Max: If you want to, but you don't have to.

Betty: I'd like to do something nice for you.

Max: Then consider me your dinner date.

Betty: Okay, see you tonight.

Max: See you tonight, Betty.

I can't hold back my smile as I pick up my coffee and take a sip. How
Atlas was still available by the time I came along, I will never understand.

My phone buzzes, and when I think it's Atlas again, I smile down at
my phone only to see a text from Uncle Dwight. Oh, right.

I open up the thread and read his response.

Uncle Dwight: Conference is boring like it is every year. It's more of a way to network. You lost power? Huh, that shouldn't have happened.

I'm about to type back and say that Atlas says it happens when there are high winds, but I catch myself.

Betty: Well, I heard that it happens with high winds out here.
Uncle Dwight: Who did you hear that from?

Oh crap.

I waver on what I should say. I could tell him the truth, but I feel like that will end in him not talking to me. Or I can give him a little white lie so that he doesn't freak out and start building up ideas in his head that will only hurt my chances in the long run.

I choose the white lie.

Betty: BKJ

I wince as I press Send and hope that it doesn't come back to bite me in the ass.

Uncle Dwight: Oh, interesting. That's something that should be fixed. When I get back, I'll talk to a few people to ensure that doesn't happen again.

Huh, well, that's nice of him. I don't know why I have this inexplicable feeling that he's out to get me, because he's not. He hasn't been from the beginning. He's been helpful; he's wanted to see me succeed. And yet I have this doomsday feeling when I think about him. And I know it has to do with Atlas and the feelings I have for him. Uncle Dwight clearly won't approve of them. I just wish this entire situation was different. That there wasn't a rift between the two of them.

Uncle Dwight: Other than that, everything else good?

I roll my lips together and text him back as nerves bounce around inside me.

Betty: Everything's good. I have this new idea that I'm trying to flesh out, but I think it would be better than our initial plan. I've immersed myself in the town and I've found some areas where they're lacking, so putting that all together.

Uncle Dwight: That's great. I can't wait to hear it. I'll be back on the twenty-third. Talked to your parents, and I think they're coming for Christmas as well.

Wait, he talked to my parents? When did he do that? And how come my parents didn't say anything to me?

Uncle Dwight: Oh shit, wait, that was supposed to be a surprise. Fuck, when they come, you have to act surprised.

Oh, well, that makes more sense.

Betty: That's fun. I think I can manage acting surprised. It will be nice to have my parents here for the holidays.

Uncle Dwight: I thought so too. Hey, I have to get to another meeting. We'll chat later. Can't wait to see the presentation.

Betty: Okay, have fun.

I set my phone down as I absorb the information about my parents coming to visit. I'm excited to see them, excited to have them here in Kringle, but I just got a whole bunch more nervous. Uncle Dwight's *non-reaction* to my alternative development was odd. He'd been so determined to destroy the Maxheimers' farm and livelihood, so his jovial acceptance just doesn't ring true.

Ugh.

If only this was easier.

CHAPTER TWENTY-SIX
BETTY

NARRATOR: MAYBE IT'S JUST ME, *but things seem to be getting more intense, don't you think?*

How do you think this Dwight-Atlas thing will play out?

Are we in the trenches, barreling toward a third-act breakup?

Heavens to Betsy—or Betty—I hope not.

If this author is smart, they'll just play around with dipping the dong, shout out the I love yous with an epic tie-in to the town, and write an epilogue to inspire all other epilogues.

But that almost seems not their style, doesn't it?

———————

Soup is staying warm.

Bread is ready to be toasted.

And the drinks are chilling in the fridge.

When I got home after enjoying a long walk through the property, I took a shower, redid my hair with a blowout, and put on some mascara, but kept it at that. I had a hard time trying to figure out what to wear, because I didn't want to seem too fancy, but I also didn't want to come off too casual, so I chose a sweater dress but skipped the leggings. It's warm enough in the cottage with the heat from the furnace and the stove that I'm comfortable.

I also made sure to spritz myself with some perfume, a scent that I hope drives Atlas wild.

Nerves bounce around my stomach as I wait for him to show up, wondering what he might possibly have gotten me.

I lift up the lid to the slow cooker and give my cheddar broccoli soup a stir, the carrots and broccoli I added looking really good.

I hope he likes it.

I set the lid down just as there is a knock at the door.

Excitement pulses through me as I move toward it, adjust my hair and dress, and then open it up.

Atlas is standing on the other side, wearing jeans and a green sweater, his hair still wet because he's fresh from the shower.

"Hey, you." He steps in and wraps his arm around my waist, pulling me in close. "Christ, you smell amazing," he says right before he kisses me.

I smile into his kiss and loop my arms around his neck, so happy that he's here.

When he pulls away, he gives me a quick once-over. "You look fucking good, Betty."

"Thank you," I say, my cheeks burning from the compliment.

"I like this sweater thing you have on." He tugs on the fabric. "Easy access." He wiggles his eyebrows, and it makes me chuckle. "Now, close your eyes. I couldn't wrap what I got you, but I want it to be a surprise."

"Okay." I close my eyes and hear him step back out onto the porch.

"Open them."

I open my eyes and catch him standing on the porch, holding a mini-Christmas tree and a box of Queen Anne chocolate-covered cherries. "Merry Christmas," he says sweetly. "I noticed you didn't have a Christmas tree, and that tends to be my specialty, so I thought I'd bring you one."

"Oh my God, that's . . . that's really sweet."

"And the chocolate-covered cherries are because they're your fave, but there is a stipulation: You must eat them with me."

"I think I can handle that." I loop my arm around his neck while standing on my toes. "Thank you," I say softly before kissing him.

"You're welcome," he replies in the same tone before resting his forehead against mine. "I thought about these lips all fucking day."

"I thought about you too," I say, bringing him into the cottage because I'm starting to get a chill. "Maybe a little too much."

"There's no such thing." He sets the cherries down on the counter and then says, "Holy shit, Betty, it smells amazing in here."

"Thank you. I hope you like cheddar broccoli soup."

"Love it." He holds up the tree. "Do you mind if I find a place for this?"

"Not at all."

"I was thinking over here in the corner. It's not next to the heat, which won't dry it out, but it's still in a prominent place."

"I love it," I say as I lean against the counter, watching him set up my tree. It very well might be the cutest present I've ever gotten, especially given that it's coming from him, the guy who spends his life helping people find the perfect tree to create memories around.

He turns toward me, smiling, clearly proud of himself, and then walks up to me, placing his hands on my hips. "I didn't get you ornaments . . . yet. Wanted to make sure you liked the tree first. Next step would be decorating it together."

I smooth my hand up his chest. "I'd love that. Maybe we can make some."

"We have some popcorn garland kits at the farm that I can grab. Maybe you can come over to my place and we can make some popcorn garland . . . naked."

I laugh. "Obviously, it would have to be naked. I can't imagine making popcorn garland any other way."

"And this is why you're perfect for me," he says, lifting me up on the counter and moving between my legs. He glides his hands under my dress and moves his lips across my jaw to my ear, where he asks, "Is the soup okay for a few minutes?"

"Yeah, it's on warm."

"Good," he says, and then takes the hem of my dress and pulls it up, shimmying around until he pulls it completely off my head.

He tosses it to the side and then takes me in. I'm wearing a matching deep green bra and thong, both see-through.

"Christ," he says, moving his hand over his mouth. His fingers glide over the strap of my bra. "Did you wear this for me?"

"I did," I say as his hand travels to the see-through cups, his thumb running over my nipple. "Do you like it?"

"Like it?" he asks, looking stunned. "Babe, I fucking love it."

Then he reaches over his head and tugs his sweater off, giving me the view that I want, his expansive, well-toned chest, a view that will never grow old . . . ever.

He grips the back of my head and pulls me against his body only to claim me with his mouth, kissing me with force and possession, his fingers digging into my scalp as his mouth parts, allowing his tongue to dive against mine.

I moan against him, falling deeper into the feel of him as he cloaks me with his body, bringing me in close so our skin is touching. When his mouth leaves mine, he trails his lips along my jaw and down my neck.

"I can't get enough of you," he says as his hands move to my bra strap. "I fucking need you." He unclasps my bra, and then slowly slides the straps down my shoulders and pulls the fabric off. Then he lays me down on the counter, the cold surface shocking me for a moment, but he doesn't give me time to adjust as he licks his away around my breasts, lapping at my nipples and then sucking them in between his lips.

"God, yes," I say as I squirm beneath him. "I love how you play with me."

His teeth lightly nibble on my nipple, tugging ever so gently, just enough to elicit a yelp from me. He pulls up, worried. "Did I hurt you?"

I shake my head and pull him back down, *showing* him I want more,

and he does just that. He squeezes my breasts, playing with them, tweaking them, licking and sucking until I can feel my arousal start to grow wetter and wetter, my need for friction increasing. Something to ease the buildup of tension that's forming between my legs.

"Fuck me," I say. "Make me come."

"Not yet," he says and then reaches above me and grabs the box of chocolate-covered cherries.

With one hand and his mouth, he opens the box, while the other hand pulls down my G-string and tosses it to the floor.

He rips open the box, pulls back the cellophane, and then plucks a cherry out. Turned on and wondering what he's going to do, I spread my legs for him, which makes him smile.

"That's it, Betty. Keep them spread."

And then to my surprise, he bites off the bottom of one of the chocolates and tips it over, letting the cherry syrup land right above my pubic bone.

"Oh God," I say as he does the same to another cherry, but this time, he moves it lower, right on top of my pussy. He wets his lips with his tongue, his eyes growing heady as he stares at my spread legs.

Grabbing one more cherry, he tears off the bottom and lets the juice fall all over my arousal before bringing the cherry and chocolate up to my mouth where he feeds it to me. I let my lips linger on his finger, pulling and licking him clean, which only makes him crazier.

Leaning back, staring at the cherry syrup and me, he undoes his pants and pushes them down along with his briefs, freeing himself before he starts stroking his length.

I'm about to ask him what he's doing, but then he lowers his large body between my legs, still gripping his cock and stroking, and he juts out his tongue, licking the syrup off my pubic bone.

"Yes," I cry out, bringing my hands to my breasts, where I start playing with my nipples. I catch him looking at me as his tongue glides just below my belly button.

"That's it, Betty. Play with your tits." Then he kisses along my inner thigh, across my stomach, and to my other thigh, while I flick my nipples, making them into hard pebbles.

After a few seconds of him teasing and driving me mad with need, he releases his cock and parts me before bringing his mouth to my center. His tongue peeks out, and he laps up the syrup, causing me to cry out.

"Fucking delicious," he says and then continues to lick, flattening his tongue and lapping at my clit, cleaning every last drop of the syrup off me. "Jesus, I want you for dessert every goddamn day."

He spreads me even farther and rapidly strokes his tongue over my clit, over and over again, building up my pleasure and forcing all my muscles to contract.

He grabs another cordial cherry, holds it between his lips, and rubs it over my slit, running it up and down, across my clit, only to lift up and snatch it in his mouth.

His eyes on me, he says, "So fucking good." Then he bends down and licks me clean, playing with me, teasing me, refusing to give me the release I need.

"Please," I beg. "More."

He parts me with his fingers and drives his tongue against my clit with long slow strokes, making my chest arch off the counter, my heart beating rapidly, as my muscles start to tingle. But I need it faster. I want to feel him inside me. I want . . . I want so much more.

He lifts up and grabs another cherry. This time, he runs it across my stomach, up and over my breasts, and then holds it above my mouth. He nods at me, indicating he wants me to part my lips, so I do, and he crushes the tip of the cherry with his lips, causing the syrup to dribble into my mouth. He quickly swallows and then claims my lips, the cherry flavoring mixing between us while he kicks off his pants and briefs.

My tongue swipes against his, and he grunts as he gets up on the counter as well, straddles my body, and then, to my utter shock, turns around so his erection is right at my face. His head buries between my legs. His tongue fires off over my clit, heightening my arousal once more.

So I take that moment to grip his cock and bring it to my mouth, swirling my tongue over the head.

"Fuck," he breathes out, tensing over me.

Smiling, I gently start massaging his balls while I continue to swirl my tongue, around and around.

"Baby . . . fuck, that . . . Christ." He rests his forehead against my leg for a second, taking a few deep breaths. "Babe, suck . . . suck me in. Take me deep."

Wanting to please him, I do as he says and open my mouth wide, trying to take him as far as I can take him. When he hits the back of my throat, I gag, and he moans loudly.

"Shit, I'm . . . fuck, baby, do it again."

I take a deep breath, squeeze his balls just enough, and then take him to the back of my throat, swallowing at the same time.

"Mother . . . fucker," he growls, the sound so guttural that I repeat the motion, over and over again, causing him to stop what he's doing and focus only on his pleasure.

And I love it.

I love it so goddamn much, that I can distract him this much with my mouth, control him to the point of him forgetting what he's supposed to be doing. It's so hot.

So I pump his cock with my hand, play with his balls, rolling them in my palm, and I suck . . . I suck hard, giving him the best pressure that I can. And it seems to work as his hips shift, his body tenses, and he slams his fist against the counter as he stills. "Fuck, I'm coming."

He fills my mouth, and I swallow, taking all of him until there's nothing left.

"Jesus, fuck," he mutters and then pulls away, hopping off the counter. When he turns to look at me, I see a crazed expression cross his features. And I know he's about to rock my world.

He gets between my legs again, but this time, he drapes them over his shoulders, pulling me in close, and then slides two fingers inside me while he starts kissing, sucking, licking, attacking my pussy to the point that I can barely breathe.

It's such an onslaught on my senses that all I can do is brace for impact.

"Yes, Atlas, oh God, oh God, don't stop, right there."

He applies more pressure and curves his fingers up, stroking me in the way that he would if he was using his cock, and it ignites the fire, setting off my orgasm and sending me into a tailspin.

"Oh fuck!" I shout. I arch off the counter while he continues to pleasure me, over and over, my body shaking, convulsing, until my orgasm finally settles and there is nothing left for me to give. "Oh God," I mutter as I try to catch my breath.

He gently licks me clean and then rests me back down on the counter and disappears into the bathroom. I lie there, catching my breath and feeling just . . . wow.

I can guarantee I've never done anything like that before.

Not to mention, how did this counter hold up the both of us?

Impressive.

He comes back into the kitchen, starts wiping me down with a washcloth, and then pulls me up by the arms so I'm sitting.

"You're all sticky. I think I have to give you a shower."

I place my arms on his shoulders and say, "Why do I feel like that was all part of the plan?"

"Because maybe it was." He winks and then picks me up, causing me to wrap my legs around his waist while he carries me to the bathroom and turns on the shower.

MAX

"Fuck," I cry out while I have one leg propped up on the bench in her shower, the other anchoring me to the shower tile while Betty is bent over.

Her hair is tied up in a bun on the top of her head so it doesn't get wet, but if it wasn't, I'd be tugging on it, pulling so she knows who fucking owns her.

Instead, I slide my hand around her neck and gently grip her while I pulse faster, harder.

"Yes, Atlas. Yes, right there," she calls out, squeezing me so fucking tight.

"You have to come, Betty. Fucking . . . come," I say through clenched teeth, holding back as much as I can, but the pleasure is too strong, she's too tight, and before I can stop myself, my cock swells, and I start spilling inside her.

Thankfully, she goes over at the same time, calling out my name and contracting around my cock, prolonging my orgasm and providing me with the best feeling of my life.

It takes a few seconds for us both to come down off the high, but once we do, I slip myself out of her and then help her stand tall, keeping my hand around her throat and turning her around.

I let out a deep breath and capture her lips, kissing her for a few moments before I slide my hand down her backside and bring her in close for a hug.

"You make me come so hard," I whisper. "Almost blacked out."

She kisses my wet chest and then places her chin on my pec while staring up. "Same."

She's so fucking beautiful.

She's sexy.

She's funny.

She's awkward in the best way.

The entire package, and I'm so goddamn lucky.

We finish cleaning her off and then turn off the water. I wrap her up in a towel, and then she grabs one for me from her cabinet. As we dry off, we steal glances at each other, both smiling.

I slip my boxer briefs back on, and she heads up the stairs, where she slips on an oversize T-shirt and that's it. What I prefer.

"You know, I took time picking out my outfit for tonight." She grabs two bowls from her cabinet. "And I wore it for, like, five minutes while you were here."

"Which means you did a good job picking it out, because it made me want you that much sooner," I say as I move in behind her and kiss her exposed neck while she ladles soup into the bowls.

She sets the bowls to the side and turns to me, her finger going into my chest. "Listen here, Mister Kissy. We're going to eat this soup without any funny business, understood?"

"Where's the fun in that?"

"The fun is that I worked hard on this soup, and I want to show you that I can cook. Therefore, I need you to eat it."

I lean down and press a kiss to her forehead. "I appreciate you cooking for us, and I want to respect that. Is there anything I can do to help?"

Her expression is sweet as she says, "Can you grab us drinks, and I'll toast the bread? Do you want to eat on the couch or at the counter?"

I glance over at the counter and say, "The counter has too many memories at the moment, so couch."

"And the couch doesn't have memories?" she asks, a raise to her brow.

"You're right. How do you feel about eating outside?"

"Unfavorable," she says.

"Yeah, same. I'll stick with couch."

She brings the bowls over and starts toasting the baguette she got for us to dip into the soup while I fetch the drinks, going with iced tea for the both of us.

I bring the drinks over just as the bread is done toasting, and she joins me.

She takes a seat next to me, and I'd prefer for her to be on my lap, but then again, we're eating hot soup here, so best we stick to our own areas of the couch.

I blow on a spoonful of the soup and then taste it, impressed with the flavor. Cheese, garlic, broccoli—hell, it's really good.

"Betty, this is really fucking delicious."

"Really?" she asks, hope in her eyes.

"Yes, really," I answer. "Probably the best cheddar broccoli soup I've ever had."

"You're not just saying that?"

I shake my head as I eat another spoonful. "No, this shit is good." I blow through my first bowl, taking it down with ease, not even bothering to use the bread.

She's on her third spoonful when I get up and help myself to seconds.

She chuckles and asks, "How is your mouth not completely burned?"

"I have a metal mouth," I say as I ladle more soup into my bowl. I walk back over to the couch, and this time, I take a little more time, allowing the flavors to dance across my tongue rather than inhaling. "How was your day?"

"It was good. I took a long walk around the property, and I noticed what you meant by having to keep your forest clean. I've never thought about it before, but there were a lot of broken-down trees and dead logs all over."

"Yeah, you have to clean those out and make room for the new stuff to grow. At Evergreen, we plant and cut by section, meaning we have split the back property. Each section has a cutting year, where people come in to grab their trees; then we clean out, replant, and move on to the next section. We continue the process each year. It's how we can continue to be kind to the land but also provide trees for our visitors."

"I had no idea. That's fascinating."

"I agree," I say with a smile. I could talk about trees all day.

"When I was on my walk today—which, by the way, was a workout thanks to the snow—I found this little creek toward the back end of the property that I thought would be neat to have a small hiking trail to. It's maybe half a mile, so a whole mile to and from, but we could have a few benches there or even a picnic table and make it a quiet place for couples to go. It was really peaceful."

"That's a really good idea. Will you show me sometime?" I ask.

"I'd love to."

I break apart a piece of bread and dip it into my soup. "So are you going to add that to the proposal you plan on giving Dwight?"

"Yeah. I took pictures and added them to my presentation today. Not sure what kind of clearing or marking we're going to have to do for the trail, but I think it's a good addition to things we could offer."

"I'd definitely go there if I was staying at your cottages. See anything else fun?"

"Just some birds. I only spotted a few, given it's winter, but I can only imagine how many varieties there are in summer. It must be stunning. I thought about maybe putting out some bird feeders with cameras, so people can see them up close."

"Yeah, great idea if you want to attract those murderous bears to your property," I say with a smirk.

She pauses. "Oh, I didn't think about that."

"Yeah, you have to be careful around here with wildlife. We have cameras set up all around the property, and we're always catching bears skittering across it."

"Really?" she asks, her eyes widening.

"Yeah. Why do you think I had the crowbar?"

"I just thought you were being your dramatic self."

"I'm dramatic for a reason," I tease. "I know about the killer bears out there, and bird feed will bring bears to your cottages in droves. Unless you want to hand out crowbars at check-in, I'd avoid the bird feeders if I were you."

"I mean, the crowbars might be a fun way to spark some talk about the cottages, a real social media attention grabber, and if we painted them red and white like candy canes ... could be a novel idea."

"And bear attacks will also bring a lot of social media attention."

She chuckles. "Yeah, might not be the best idea." She scoops some soup into her mouth and then says, "This is why I need someone like you, to help me sift through things like this. If it were up to me, every cabin would have a bird feeder and probably be attacked by bears nightly while my forest died a slow death from not being cleared out."

"You can run anything by me. You know I'm here to support you."

"I appreciate the offer." She dabs at her face with her napkin. "Not sure how I can repay you."

"Really?" I ask my brow raising. "You don't know how to repay me?"

She chuckles. "Never mind."

"Not that you need to repay me, because you don't, but if you ever want to show appreciation, I wouldn't mind a repeat of the cherry cordial chemistry we had."

"Is that what you're calling it?"

I shrug. "Not really sure."

"Could be a new thing. Maybe instead of a crowbar at check-in, they each get a how-to tip sheet with a box of chocolate-covered cherries. We could call it the cherry cordial sixty-nine."

I let out a laugh. "Now that's some solid thinking. Maybe you should change the name of the cottages from Candy Cane to Cherry Cordial."

That gives her pause as she thinks about it. "You know, that might not be that bad of an idea."

"Are you seriously considering it?"

She shrugs. "Why not?"

"Babe, can you imagine explaining that name to Dwight?"

"Ha," she says. "Not really."

I chuckle. "Not only that, but it's a Christmas town. If you come in bringing the sex, not sure anyone will support you."

"Not even you?" she questions playfully.

"Oh, it would be you and me on an island, but that's an island I don't mind floating away on."

CHAPTER TWENTY-SEVEN

MAX

NARRATOR: THERE'S ONE THING FOR sure: I'll never look at a chocolate-covered cherry the same.

And rumor on the street is every time Max sees a chocolate-covered cherry, he gets hard.

Then again, would we expect anything else from him?

At this point . . . no.

———————

"Why are you looking at me like that?" Cole asks as I sit on a stool in the reindeer barn while he brushes Donner. "It's fucking creepy."

"How am I looking at you?"

"With your teeth hanging over your lip, eyes wide."

"What? No, I'm not."

"You were."

"You're delusional," I say. "I was looking at you normally."

"No, you're looking at me as if you want to say something, but you also think that you shouldn't say anything."

"Ha, as if I have something to tell you." I cross my arms at my chest, dying to tell him about last night. But you know how it is; I have to play hard to get.

"You have something to tell me."

"No, I don't."

"Yes, you do."

"You act as if you know everything about me." I scoff. "Clearly, you have no idea."

He sighs. "Just fucking tell me and get it over with."

"Fine," I say, dropping the act, causing Cole to shake his head. "You're not the only one who knows how to play around with candy when it comes to sex."

"Oh Jesus." He rolls his eyes, but I continue.

"Last night, I took a box of chocolate-covered cherries to Betty's place, and I dragged them all over—"

"I really don't need the details," he says, holding up his hand.

"We did a sixty-nine," I say, unable to stop myself.

"Come on, man," he groans. "Jesus, that's the last thing I need to think about."

"You think about me in a sexual way?"

Cole stands tall, points to the barn door, and says, "Just leave. I can't with you right now."

"You know, that seems to be what you say all the time now. Whatever happened to *best friends forever*?"

"You've been insufferable lately. Between your parents disappearing, scheming with my wife, and now telling me about cherry sixty-nine bull-shit, it's just . . . too much."

"First of all, you promised to take me with sickness and health."

"Uh, no, I didn't."

I steamroll him and say, "And I'd think after how I've stood by your side for so many years, you would at least let me gush to you." I stand from the chair and move toward him. "Dude, I'm not kidding you when I say I think she's it. I know it hasn't been long since I've known her, but I'm not kidding, man. I feel it in my bones. She's it."

That makes him stop what he's doing and turn toward me. About time he gives me some of that dark attention of his. "You're being serious? This isn't some joke?"

I shake my head. "Dead serious, man. I think..." I pull on the back of my neck. "Fuck, I think I'm falling for her."

"Jesus." He sets his brush down, finally realizing the importance of the conversation. "I knew you liked her, but falling for her?"

"Yeah, it happened fast. I just... I like her a lot. She's smart, creative, she knows what she wants, and she's not shy about it. Not to mention she's beautiful, amazing in bed, and she gets me. There's a connection between us that I've never felt before, and I plan on doing everything I can to keep her in my life, even burying the hatchet with Dwight."

"That's a must if you want to be with her."

"I know, but I need to figure out why he thinks I'm the one who took his ornament. I asked Tanya the other day, and she had no clue. She asked Martha and Mae, and they had no idea. I just... I can't figure it out, and I feel like if I had an idea about that, then I'd be able to come to him with answers rather than asking him to believe me that I didn't do it, you know?"

"Yeah, that would be helpful," he says, scratching the side of his cheek. "Let me see what kind of digging I can do."

"You would do that?"

Cole nods and starts brushing Donner again. "You might annoy the fuck out of me, but like you said, *best friends forever*."

"Dude." I spread my arms wide. "Bring it in."

He side-eyes me. "Don't make me take back my offer."

"You're right. Too much." Growing serious, I say, "Thanks though, for helping out."

He nods. "Anything for you."

And I know he means that.

———————

"Have you done this before?" Betty asks.

I pick up a piece of popcorn, poke my needle through it, and then drag it down the string.

"A few times. It's all about where you push the popcorn through. Too close to the edge, and it's just going to break off."

"I've noticed that," she says as she concentrates hard on her needle, threading her popcorn.

Tonight she chose to wear a low-cut long-sleeved shirt in a navy blue that makes her eyes pop and her tits look amazing. I told myself when she was coming over that we were going to string popcorn, have dinner, and then I was going to have her for dessert. I promised myself to be in control and not try to fuck her the minute she walked into my house. Because if anything, I don't want her thinking I like her just because of the sex. I like her for so much more than just that.

But with that shirt and the way her tits have been hanging out, I'm telling you right now, I should win a goddamn award for keeping my hands to myself.

"I can't believe people will do this every year." She sits back. "It's hard."

I can tell you something else that's hard: my dick and her nipples.

She has to be wearing one of those see-through bras again, because her nipples are poking against her shirt as if she's not wearing a bra at all . . . Wait . . . is she?

"Atlas."

"Huh?" I say, looking up to meet her eyes.

"You're staring at my boobs."

"Yeah, I know," I say, not being shy about it. "Just wondering if you're wearing a bra or not."

"Why would you think that I'm not?"

"Because of the way your nipples are pressing against your shirt," I answer.

"Oh." She glances down at her shirt and then, to my surprise, tugs on the front of it, revealing her bare breast.

"Fuck," I mutter.

She readjusts her shirt casually, as if she didn't just show me her entire boob. "I didn't wear a bra because I figured you'd strip me down the minute I walked through the door, but boy, was I wrong. We've been doing arts and crafts for an hour now, and not a single orgasm has been had."

I swallow the saliva building up in my mouth. "Um, yeah, because I told myself I wouldn't have sex with you until after dinner."

Her brow creases together. "Why would you do that?"

"Didn't want you to think I only saw you as a hole I can stick my dick in. I actually like you, more than just for sex."

She presses her hand to her chest, a look of appreciation on her face. "Aw, that's oddly crude yet sweet at the same time."

"Just telling you the way it is. I like you. I want you to know that. I want you to know that we can do more than just sex." I hold up the string of popcorn. "Like arts and crafts. And I wanted you to see that we can chat and have a conversation that doesn't consist of you telling me to fill you with my cum."

Her cheeks go red. "God, I did say that, didn't I?"

"You did. It was hot, and I hope you say it more. But say it after dinner, when the sex will commence."

"You've scheduled it?"

"Loosely scheduled," I say.

"How loose is that schedule?" she asks, moving in closer, causing me to gulp from the way her shirt dips in the front.

"Um . . . pretty loose."

"Like . . . almost nonexistent?" she asks as she straddles my lap, draping the popcorn strands to the side and making sure to stick the needle in the couch so as to not lose it.

I brace my hands on her thighs, already growing hard from just having her on me.

"Some might say *nonexistent*."

"Are you sure?" she asks as she leans forward and starts kissing my neck while her fingers play with the hem of my shirt.

"Oh yeah, pretty sure."

"Good." She lifts my shirt up and over my head, and I help her take it off, dropping it to the side. Her hands immediately drag down my chest, her fingernails scraping along my nipples, her lips following as she moves down my body and then between my legs, where she kneels on the floor in front of me.

Anticipation roars through me at what her mouth can do.

And her hands.

Eyes on me, she tugs her shirt up and over her head, leaving her bare, her nipples hard, her tits looking so damn good.

"Christ." I tug on her hand, trying to pull her up. "I want your tits in my mouth."

"And I want your dick in mine," she replies with an evil smirk. She stands and shimmies out of her pants, leaving her in just a black thong, her hair down, looking so goddamn good that it's going to take everything in me to let her take control.

She bends in front of me again and undoes my pants. I help her take those off as well, followed by my briefs, so I'm left naked on the couch, my hard-on stretching up my stomach, looking for her mouth.

"I love your dick," she says as she smooths her hands up my thighs, right to my cock, where she grips the base. "I love everything about it." Her tongue lightly swirls along the head, causing me to sink deeper into the couch. "And I love how you react to how I play with you."

"Because you're really fucking good at it," I say, letting out a deep breath as she wraps her lips around the tip and starts gently sucking while pumping her hand up and down my length. "Feels so fucking good." I move her hair out of her face so I can watch her better, see her lips play with my length, watch her small hand grip me tightly.

She pulls off and then licks up my length, tantalizing me, teasing me, giving me so little but also so much. And when she pulls her mouth away and smiles up at me, I feel myself fall more and more for this woman.

"I want you inside me, but first . . . I'm hungry."

"Oh yeah?" I ask, wondering where she's going with this. And then she grabs one of the finished popcorn garlands and starts to wrap it around my cock. "What are you doing?"

"Nibbling," she says as she leans forward and bites off a piece of popcorn like it's a piece of candy off a candy necklace.

"Jesus," I say, her teeth and lips scraping along my length as she takes off another and another and another. Occasionally she licks, gives me a little more of her mouth, but for the most part, it's her teeth. And when she clears off a good amount of popcorn, occasionally licking the head of my cock, she wraps more popcorn string around and then starts nibbling again. "Fuck, babe. You're . . . you're killing me."

She smiles up at me and swirls her tongue around the head again, causing me to groan and drape my arm over my eyes.

"Christ, you have to—"

A car door slams outside, followed by voices. What the hell?

I still.

"Wait, babe."

"Are you really going to come already?" she asks, smiling up at me.

"No. I heard—"

The front door handle jiggles, the lock is undone, and I have a second to cover Betty with the blanket on the couch before the door flies open and my parents come waltzing in.

"Oh," Mom says as she sees me on the couch in clearly quite a position.

The blanket is covering Betty and my popcorn-wrapped cock, but that's about it. Clothes are scattered everywhere, and you can tell that my bare ass is firmly planted on my mom's couch.

"Dear God." Mom covers her eyes.

"What's going on?" Dad asks, stepping in behind her where he spots me. "Are you naked on our couch?"

"Oh my God," Betty says from under the blanket. "Oh my God, Atlas."

"Is there a person under there?" Mom asks, pointing to the lump but then covering her eyes again.

This is . . . not ideal.

First of all, there was nary a mention of them coming home, so what the hell is happening right now?

Second of all, I'm naked, Betty just has a thong on, and my cock is still rock-hard with a popcorn garland wrapped around it.

Third of all . . . this is not how I wanted to introduce Betty to my parents.

And I really don't know how to handle this.

Kind of at a loss at the moment, because how does one recover from this?

Wish I could phone a friend, ask Cole what I should do, but since that's not an option, I go with whatever comes out of my mouth.

"Oh, hello, parents." I clear my throat. "Uh, wasn't aware of your arrival today. As a matter of fact, I'm naked, and yes, that's a person under the blanket. Her name is Betty. Hey, Betty, why don't you give a little wave to my parents?"

To my utter surprise, Betty sticks her hand outside the blanket and waves. "Hello, nice to meet you, Mr. and Mrs. Maxheimer."

"Umm, hello," Mom says awkwardly.

"Hello." Dad clears his throat.

"So anyway, we were just enjoying some, uh, arts and crafts." I gesture to the strings of popcorn. "As you can see, we're having a wonderful time doing it . . . I mean the crafts, doing the crafts, not it. We weren't doing it. Just crafting."

"Then why are you naked?" Dad asks.

I nod. "Yeah, it's how we do arts and crafts. In the nude. You, uh, you haven't done that before?"

"I prefer to craft with clothes on," Mom says.

"Solid choice." I nod. "I think most people also prefer to craft with clothes on, but I also don't think they're aware of the benefits of crafting with clothes off, so . . . you know . . ."

"And what are the benefits?" Dad asks, crossing his arms.

Why they haven't excused themselves and allowed us to gather our clothes and flee is beyond me. Instead, we're going to discuss the benefits of crafting while naked. Leave it to the Maxheimers.

"Glad you asked," I say, trying to come up with some benefits. "Well, it takes you back to the roots, our ancestors, you know, carving things in caves before clothes were invented." I scratch the side of my head as Betty shifts, her hair brushing along my thighs and still hard dick. Christ, you would think the thing would deflate at this point. Then again, it's Betty, there's popcorn wrapped around my cock, and I can feel her breath across my skin. "Also, clothes don't get in the way, you know, accidentally gluing a sleeve or sewing popcorn into your shirt. Really convenient to keep it naked."

"And airflow," Betty says from under the blanket. "Great airflow while doing arts and crafts. Never get too hot."

"Great point, Betty. Solid, solid point. So there you have it." I hold up one finger at a time as I say, "Ancestry, nondestruction of clothes, and airflow. Anyway, you're back."

"Hope your trip was great," Betty says in a muffled voice. "Always wanted to visit the Christmas markets."

"Yeah, did you, uh, did you enjoy yourselves?" I ask, crossing my arms now. *Why the fuck are they still standing there?*

"It was great," Mom starts but then looks between us. "Are you just going to let her stay under that blanket?"

"I am." I nod. "She's only wearing a thong, so you know, doubt she wants to greet you with her breasts."

"I prefer handshakes," Betty shouts.

"And I prefer her breasts to stay private to me."

"Well then . . . get dressed, for fuck's sake," Dad says.

Finally!

"Hard to do that when you're just standing there, staring at us. Perhaps you could turn around for a moment, and we can gather ourselves?"

Dad grumbles and turns around with my mom.

I whip the blanket off Betty and then stand, pulling her up with me. I don't have time to apologize before I press her back to my chest and then wrap the blanket around the both of us like a burrito. Covered—hopefully—I say, "We're, uh, we're going to make our way upstairs now."

"Are you decent?" Dad asks.

"We're covered," I say. "You can turn around."

They both turn around together as they take in Betty for the first time. Not just a floating hand and voice now.

Her hair is slightly tousled from the blanket, and her heated body is pressed against mine in all the wrong ways, her ass cheeks gliding against my cock, keeping me harder than I want to be with my parents only fifteen feet away.

"Well, hello." Dad waves. "Welcome to our home."

"Yes, welcome to our home," Mom says with a curt nod as we all awkwardly stand here.

"Thank you for having me," Betty says, keeping a cheeriness in her voice. She deserves a fucking award after this. "It's such a beautiful home. Very cozy and inviting."

"I'm glad you enjoy it," Mom says, looking like she's wishing she was still back at the Christmas markets.

I clear my throat, wanting to get a move on with this. "Well, we're just going to head on upstairs if you'll excuse us." We take a few steps forward, only for something to drop to the floor.

What the hell was—

Wait . . .

Nooooooo.

In an instant, I feel my entire face go red.

My expression grows stark.

My muscles twitch with regret.

Holy.

Shit.

I forgot to take off the fucking garland.

It's still attached to my goddamn dick.

"What's that?" Dad asks, pointing to the floor, between my legs. "It's moving."

"Moving?" Mom shrieks, clutching Dad like it's some sort of Christmas snake about to bite her.

Growing sweaty, I say, "That's, uh, that's a popcorn garland."

"Oh." Dad nods in relief. "It's just popcorn garland, Ida. Must have fallen when he got up."

"Oh." Mom chuckles. "I would have been horrified if it was some sort of mouse. Don't want our guest thinking our house is infested with mice."

"I would never," Betty says. "You have such a beautiful house. Very well kept. I would never consider that mice took residence here."

Mom smiles sweetly while Dad nods toward the second floor. "Well, go on, get upstairs. Put some clothes on."

Yup, well, easier said than done.

Keeping the blanket wrapped around the both of us, we shuffle forward, only for the garland to shuffle along with us, trailing between my legs.

What are the goddamn chances?

"Oh, I think the garland is attached to the blanket," Mom says, pointing to the ground.

Nope, not so much.

"I can grab that for you."

Mom heads toward us, reaching for the garland, but I squeeze my ass cheeks together and yelp, "No, nope, don't touch it."

"It's fine, dear. I can grab it for you."

She bends down, and I screech, "It's attached to my dick. Do not tug it. Do not pull. It's attached to my penis, so please for the love of God, just let it be."

Mom backs up, looking absolutely horrified. "Why on earth would it be attached to your penis?"

Great question, and I'm about to tell her when Betty steps in.

"Umm, is that not how you make popcorn garland?" Betty asks. "I could have sworn that was in the provided instructions."

"We absolutely did not write that—"

"Ida," Dad grumbles from the entryway, dragging his hand over his face. "They were clearly playing around with the garland in a sexual manner, and we walked in on them. It's got to be something the young people are doing these days. Probably saw it on social media somewhere."

"Actually, we came up with it ourselves," Betty says, and I can feel her wince even though I can't see it. "Actually, you're right, it was social media. Definitely not something I came up with on the spot. Nor was I eating the popcorn off his penis. I was just . . . um, wrapping it around his penis because we wanted to . . . uh . . . we wanted to see how much we could wrap around for scientific purposes, you know, because he's so long and thick—"

"And we're going upstairs," I say, moving her along, the garland trailing behind. "Please, remove this from your memory. When we return, we will have a normal conversation about your trip. Okay? Great. Thanks."

We start up the stairs, plastered to each other, and with every step I take, the garland bangs against the wood stair, slightly tugging on my cock, reminding my parents what they just walked in on.

Yup, this very well might ruin Christmas.

"Oh my God, oh my God, oh my God," Betty says as she flees from the blanket once she's in my room. Her fingers dig into her hair as she looks up at me. "What the hell was that? Did you know your parents were coming home? And why did I talk to your mom about your monstrous dick? She probably doesn't want to know that, but I couldn't think of anything else, and when I'm nervous, I ramble, and oh my God, why didn't you remove the string from your dick before you got up? You should have removed it, because then they wouldn't have known that I was eating popcorn off your penis. But now . . . now they probably think I was hoping for some . . . I don't know . . . some seasoning from your penis for my garland." Her eyes widen. "They must think I'm a floozy. A harlot. I mean, I was on the floor between your legs with popcorn garland. I was clearly sucking your penis, eating popcorn off it like it's my very own corn on the cob. I'll never be able to look at them ever again."

"Whoa, whoa, whoa," I say, coming up to her, the garland still attached. I pull her into my chest and wrap my arms around her. "They're not going to think any of those things, especially the penis seasoning thing, because honestly, I don't even know where you were going with that."

"Atlas, that was not how I wanted to meet your parents."

"Yeah, that's not how I wanted you to meet them either. I'd have preferred it if we were both wearing clothes and you weren't hanging out between my legs."

"Ugh, that's what happens when I try to be adventurous. We should have just waited until after dinner like you scheduled, but noooooo, I had to try to seduce you like you seduced me, and look what happened. Your parents caught me nibbling on your nether regions." She pulls away and sticks her hands through her hair again, clearly in distress. "Think I can sneak out the window?"

"Babe, we're in the attic."

"I know, but I can be ... agile. I can shimmy off a roof."

I walk up to her again and pull her close to my chest, kissing the top of her head. "No one is going to shimmy off the roof. What's going to happen is we're going to remove the garland from my dick; then we're going to put clothes on and go talk to my parents. Simple as that."

"What clothes?" she asks. "My clothes are downstairs, and I didn't even wear a bra over here because I thought it would be sexy."

"Trust me, it was sexy. Everything about what we were doing was sexy, up until the point that my parents walked in."

"You're just saying that to make me feel better."

"Uh, nope, it's a fact. Took my dick quite a long time to become flaccid, even with my parents standing in the entryway. I was turned on and ready to follow your direction. And I'm not saying that to make you feel better. I'm saying that because it's the truth. If my parents didn't show up, I'd probably have your legs wrapped around my head, my tongue lapping at your clit."

She sighs. "Don't say things like that. You're just going to turn me on, and I refuse to have sex with you with your parents downstairs, your naked ass print still fresh on their couch."

"When I say that we are for sure not having sex with my parents downstairs, I mean that. Any sex will now occur at your cottage, because I can't possibly do anything with you here while they're here. You're far too loud."

Her mouth drops in shock. "I'm too loud? This coming from the man who growls loud enough to shake the logs of this home."

"I'm not loud," I say.

"Uh, yes you are." And then in a deep voice, she says, "*Oh, babe, yeah, take this dick, fucking take—*"

Knock, knock.

"Sorry to interrupt but, uh, thought Betsy would like her clothes."

Betty clamps her hand over her mouth, eyes wide.

"It's Betty, Mom," I say. "And I'm sure she'd love her clothes." I move over toward the door and crack it open, keeping my naked self to the side so she can't see. "And thanks. We will be down in a second."

"Sounds good. I have souvenirs."

"Yup, can't wait." I shut the door and turn toward Betty, who is covering her breasts now, looking pale and horrified.

"Oh my God, Atlas, your mother thinks I want you to take my dick."

I press my hand to my forehead. "She definitely does not think that."

"She does." Betty nods. "Yup, she does. Well, this relationship is over now. It was nice while it lasted. Thank you for the orgasms, but we're done now." She heads toward the window, and I quickly run after her, the garland still attached.

"Do not go out that window." I tug on her hand, and she turns toward me, her eyes landing on my penis.

"For the love of God, Atlas, take the garland off your dick! Why is that still on you?"

"I don't know. You used some sort of wizardry tying it on." I unravel the garland and then toss it. I'll never look at popcorn garland the same. "There, that better?"

"No," she says, her eyes welling up. "This is . . . this is a disaster."

She covers her eyes, and I quickly pull her into my chest, rubbing her back.

"And I can't even put my shirt back on because it's way too inappropriate."

"Shh," I say. "I know it feels embarrassing right now, but I promise my parents are chill. We'll be laughing about this later. And you can wear one of my sweatshirts, okay?"

She looks up at me, a tear falling down her cheek. "Can this please not be spread through the town? I don't think I'd be able to survive."

"I'll make sure of it."

CHAPTER TWENTY-EIGHT
BETTY

NARRATOR: *CAN'T GET THE VISUAL of that garland attached to his penis out of my head. What about you?*

And the thunking sound it made while he walked up the stairs?

Answer me this: Why didn't he gather the garland and carry it up? Why did his penis have to do the heavy lifting?

Either way, I know one thing for sure. While Betty was going to the bathroom and gathering herself, Atlas ran downstairs, looked his parents in the eyes, and told them not to repeat a thing that they saw. Then he ran back upstairs before Betty came out of the bathroom.

If anything, our boy Max is a gentleman. He lets her come first—for the most part; sometimes he's quick on the trigger, but we'll credit our girl for that—and he protects his lady friend from salacious town gossip. What more can you ask for?

Maybe parents who signal a warning before coming home, eh?

————————

"Seriously, it will be fine," Atlas says as he holds my hand and brings me down the last few steps and into the living room, where his parents have draped a sheet over the couch and are now sitting, waiting for us.

Great.

"Hey," Atlas says with a wave. "Wow, you guys are home. When did that happen? I was just upstairs with my girl, Betty. This is her by the way, fully clothed."

His parents both wave at me with curt smiles, clearly feeling the awkwardness in the situation.

"Yup, I wear clothes," I say, because I don't know how to handle things like this.

"We do too. We really enjoy clothes" his mom says while I feel the urgent need to stick my head in a hole. "I'm Ida, by the way, and this is my husband, Otto."

"Very nice to meet you." I lean in closer to Atlas, using him as a guide so I don't say anything more ridiculous than I already have.

"Very nice to meet you too." His mom motions between the two of us. "When did this happen? I didn't think we were gone that long."

"Long enough," Atlas says. "And it sort of happened right after you left. Betty came into town, and she actually, uh, she's related to Dwight."

"Yokel?" Otto asks.

"Yeah. He owns the property next to ours."

"He does?" Otto's brow pinches together. "I didn't know that. I've been wondering who owns that parcel for a while. I'm surprised to hear it's Dwight."

"So was I," Atlas says. "Anyway, he brought in Betty to help figure out what to do with the lot."

I feel my nerves kick up, because is he going to tell them what the original idea was? What I had planned initially? I really hope not, because that would be a surefire way for them not to like me. To ask me to leave.

"Oh, that's interesting. What are your thoughts?" Ida asks.

Not trying to put you out of business, that's for damn sure.

"Umm, well, I haven't said anything to Dwight yet, but I was thinking of some sort of cottage rental, like an adult resort kind of thing, but mini-cottages rather than a large dominating hotel."

"That's a wonderful idea," Ida says, sounding like the sweetest lady ever, despite finding me practically naked, under a blanket, nuzzling against her son's bare crotch. "We could really use some more lodging in this town."

"That's what I told her," Atlas says. "She has some really good ideas. Why don't I order some pizza, and we can talk about your trip and what Betty has planned?"

"That sounds great." Ida stands from the couch. "And after Betty goes home, you can clean the couch with the carpet cleaner."

"Is that necessary?"

Ida smiles gently and folds her hands together. "Atlas, it is absolutely necessary. Now if you're going to be difficult about it, I can remind you how I really entered my house after a long trip in Europe, but being the gracious woman that I am, I'm choosing to push that aside with the knowledge that my son is going to clean the couch his bare ass was on."

Clean the couch, Atlas. For the love of God, clean the couch.

Atlas nods. "Of course, Mom. I'll clean the couch."

She walks up to him, pats his cheek, and says, "Such a good boy." Then she takes me by the shoulders and directs me to the dining room. "Otto, grab everyone drinks. There are conversations to be had."

"So how did this come to be?" Ida asks as she picks up a piece of pizza from the box.

We spent the last forty-five minutes talking about their trip and my plans for the cottages, Ida joining in and telling me what a great idea it was while Otto nodded. They're actually really nice, Otto being the quieter of the two and Ida being a direct replica of Atlas.

"What do you mean?" Atlas asks.

"You two. Who made the first move? Did my son ask you out? Was he a gentleman about it?"

I glance over at Atlas, who has cheese hanging off his lip. "Umm . . . how did this come to be?"

"I thought she was hot and asked her out," Atlas says with a casual shrug.

Dear God, Atlas.

Could we try to look somewhat respectable?

"Oh my God, I hope it didn't go like that," Ida says, looking horrified.

You and me both, Ida.

"It didn't," I answer and then clear my throat, ready to put on a show. "I actually became friends with Storee, and she mixed up a night that we were supposed to meet. Atlas was there too, and we all hung out along with Cole. That, I guess, was the start of it."

"Christmas Cupid Night," Atlas says with a dangerous smirk. "She lured me under the mistletoe and forced her tongue into my mouth."

What the hell is he doing?

"Oh goodness," Ida says, while Otto coughs out a laugh.

"What? No, that's not what happened." I flash a look of murder over at Atlas. "He was the one who lured me."

"Didn't have to try hard." He winks at his mom.

And I seem to black out in that moment when I turn toward him and push at his shoulder. "What are you doing? You're making me look like a hussy, especially after the way your parents found me in a precarious position when they arrived home. You know good and well you were the one putting on the moves that night."

He glances at his parents and then back at me. Talking through the side of his mouth, he says, "I'm sorry. I'm nervous. I've never had a girl really meet my parents."

Talking through the side of my mouth as well, as if his parents aren't sitting right in front of us, I say, "Well, saying that I'm the one who lured you under the mistletoe isn't painting me in a good light."

"I know but it makes me look desirable."

"You want your parents thinking you're desirable?"

"Can't be sure. Just putting on a good face."

"Making me look like I had an open kissing booth at Christmas Cupid is not the way to do it."

"I would have paid to kiss you at the booth."

My anger lessons as I tilt my head to the side. "Aw, really?"

"Yeah." He smiles. "I would have spent all my money at your booth." He cups my cheek, and I lean into his touch.

"How much?"

"Whatever was in my wallet, and then I would have paid in favors."

Forgetting about his parents entirely, I lean in closer and whisper, "What kind of favors?"

He smiles broadly and runs his thumb over my lips, lightly tugging on them. "The kind of favors that—"

Otto clears his throat, snapping us out of our haze.

Oh shit, right, we have company.

When we turn our attention to his parents, we both straighten, and my cheeks flush with embarrassment.

God, what is wrong with me?

"You were saying how you're not a hussy?" Otto leads.

Right . . .

Face flushed, I turn toward his parents completely and try to put on a smile despite the sweat building at the base of my spine. "Um, so there was Christmas Cupid Night, where we got to know each other better, but then there was a snowstorm here, and we lost power. Atlas came to check on me and found me on the couch, wrapped up in blankets with no heat. I think that night changed everything."

Ida presses her hand to her chest, thankfully moving past the awkward moment. "Oh my goodness. You poor dear."

"He brought me here and honestly probably saved me, because I was not prepared for the electricity to go out. My cottage only runs on electricity—"

"And Dwight didn't set her up with a backup battery, so she had nothing."

"That's dangerous," Otto chimes in. "That could have been serious. Atlas, I'm glad you checked on her."

"Me too," I say, looking in Atlas's direction, once again falling into his delicious gaze. "Then he took care of me after that, and, well, it was kind of hard not to grow feelings for him."

Atlas tugs on the corner of his lip. "Yeah, same. I couldn't let her out of my sight."

"Or your arms."

"Or my bed."

I truly never really want to leave his bed.

We gaze at each other, hearts sputtering from our eyes as his hand clasps mine.

"Well," Ida clears her throat, trying to draw our attention, but I can't tear my eyes from her son. "Isn't that, uh . . . sweet? Rescued in a snowstorm." Ida holds her hand to her heart. "I'm glad you went and checked on her, because if you didn't, we never would have known that popcorn garland could be wrapped around a penis. Something your father and I can try."

That snaps us both out of our haze as Atlas turns toward his parents, a pinch in his brow.

"For the love of God, no," Atlas says, causing his parents and me to laugh.

"That was an eventful evening," Atlas says as he pulls up to my cottage. It's started to snow, and instead of walking, he loaded his truck up with a Yeti battery just in case I lose electricity and said that he'd hook it up for me if I do.

"Yeah, not how I expected it to go."

He takes my hand and kisses my knuckles. "Sorry that my parents walked in on us. Really wishing I knew how the evening would have ended. Did I come with popcorn around my dick, or was I going to come inside you?"

I chuckle. "Something we will never know."

"Shame. Are you okay though? I kind of thrust you into a situation of meeting the parents, and I just want to make sure you're good. Not sure if that was too soon for you, or . . . or you're rethinking your decision to date me . . ."

"Never." I shake my head. "I didn't mind meeting your parents at all. It wasn't too soon for me. I just wish it was under different circumstances. You know, where I wasn't licking your dick."

He chuckles. "Trust me, so do I, because when I get home, I know I'm going to be spending an hour cleaning that couch, and it was just my bare ass, but you know my dad is going to be looking over my shoulder, making sure I get every square inch."

"The price we pay." I squeeze his hand. "They were awesome though. After the elephant in the room disappeared, I had a really good time. Your mom is really sweet, and your dad is funny. He doesn't say much, but when he does, it packs a powerful punch."

"He's always been like that," Atlas answers. "I'm definitely more like my mom. Felix has more of my dad's traits, and Ansel, well, not sure where he came from, because he's on a whole different level."

"It's nice that you have siblings though. Kind of wish I did. Uncle Dwight is the closest thing to a sibling that I have."

"Yeah, I've noticed that."

"And speaking of families, he, uh, he kind of let it slip that my parents are coming into town to celebrate Christmas with me."

"They are?"

"Yeah, I'm not supposed to know, but maybe . . . maybe you can meet them? That's if we get things straightened out with Uncle Dwight. But no pressure if you don't want to meet them. I don't want you to feel pressure or anything—"

"I'd love to meet them," he says.

"Really?" I ask.

"Really."

"Okay, yeah, that would be . . . that would be great." I smile at him. "Thank you."

"You don't need to thank me." He kisses my knuckles again. "It's getting late. We should get everything into your cottage so I can go clean the couch."

"Probably smart," I say.

He opens his door and tugs me in his direction. "Come this way."

I follow him out his side of the truck, and he picks me up by the waist and brings me to the porch, where I unlock the door. I'm about to ask him if he needs help with the battery, but he closes the door behind him and then tears his long-sleeved shirt over his head.

My sweatshirt is next, and then I'm pushed up against the door and his mouth is on mine.

Immediately, I melt into his grasp, moving my hands up his chest and to his neck. He lifts me up and plasters me against the wall, where he pushes his already hard erection against me.

"Fuck, I need to finish what we started," he says. "But we have to be quick."

That won't be a problem. Just from kissing him, I'm already turned on.

He massages my breasts, his mouth trailing from my lips to my jaw, to my neck and back up, marking me with his scruff, completely unhinged and taking everything he wants.

It's immediate, the way that I light up with him, the way that I grow wet, the way that I need him inside me.

"Chair," I say, breathless.

He pulls me away from the door and sets me down. I grab the single chair I have in the corner and put it behind him before stripping out of my clothes. He does the same, and then I push him back on the chair and straddle his lap.

His fingers glide between us and right over my arousal. "You're so fucking ready for me."

"I am," I say as I lift up and he positions his cock.

"Take me, Betty. Fucking take every goddamn inch."

I slowly lower over him, allowing him to feel me inch by inch and watching as his neck strains and he bites down on his lip, trying to hold on to whatever control he has left.

When I'm fully seated, I take a few deep breaths, because no matter how many times he's been inside me, nothing prepares me for the way it feels to be this full.

"Jesus, Betty," he says, his hands falling to my hips. "I fucking love being inside you."

"I . . . God, your cock." My head falls back, and his lips find my neck, kissing, sucking, leaving his mark as I rotate my hips, allowing him to stretch me and press into places that no other man has been able to touch.

"I need more. Fuck me, Betty. Fuck me."

I place my hands on his shoulders and use him as leverage while I start bouncing up and down on him.

"Fuck yes," he says, his eyes on me. "Let me see you come."

I bite down on the corner of my lip and continue to move up and down, him helping me, both of us moaning, both of us seeking pleasure. But it doesn't . . . it doesn't feel like enough.

"More, Atlas."

Grunting, he lifts us up and carries me to the couch, where he bends me over the back. He pushes down on me, then wraps his hand around my hair and tugs my neck back as he enters me from behind.

"Oh my God," I say just before he spanks my right butt cheek. "Oh fuck," I yell. And he does it again.

And again.

And again.

To the point that I'm dripping wet. So turned on, so needy that when he starts moving in and out of me, I squeeze his cock.

"Fuck, Betty. You're going to . . . fuck, babe, squeeze harder."

I squeeze again, but this time when he enters, it hits me in just the right spot so my orgasm shoots up my spine, surprising me. I start coming all over him, my moans mixed with calling out his name.

"Jesus Christ," he shouts and then stills as I feel him come inside me.

And it's the best feeling, knowing I have control over him like that and that he can make me come so easily. It's addicting, and I will continue to feed the addiction for as long as he lets me.

He kisses the back of my neck, then my back, and then slowly pulls out of me while smoothing his hand over my ass. Then he spins me around, picks me up, and carries me to the bathroom to clean up.

He gives me some privacy, and I hear him moving around in the living room followed by the door opening and shutting.

Confused, I wrap my robe around me and go out to the living room, where he comes through the door again, this time with a space heater and the Yeti pack. When his eyes meet mine, he asks, "What's wrong?"

"Oh, um . . . I thought that maybe you left without saying bye."

He chuckles. "Yeah, that would never fucking happen." He sets his things down and then walks up to me and tilts my chin up. "I don't want to leave, which means I'd never leave without at least kissing you goodbye." He kisses me softly. "I love these lips."

"I love the way you make me feel."

"Same, Betty." He then picks up his sweatshirt and hands it to me. "Keep it." Then he winks and heads toward the door. "I want to see you tomorrow. Make time for me."

"I will. I'll come by the farm."

"Good. Then I'll come by after work."

"Sounds good."

"Have a good night."

"You too," I say, feeling so giddy.

He winks again and then takes off, leaving me in a state of falling . . . and falling hard.

CHAPTER TWENTY-NINE
MAX

NARRATOR: *NOT SURE THE SPANKING was necessary but—*

"*Hey, excuse me, sorry to interrupt, but just wanted to say the spanking was necessary. She likes it. Also, shout-out to you for the giant erections. Real top-notch. Proud of the both of us.*"

Um, this is not the time where you butt in.

"*Sorry, apologies. Just had to let you know you're doing a great job. Spankings are necessary. Parents watching a garland hang from my dingle . . . not necessary.*"

I don't know. I think the readers and I think otherwise. Now, please, we have things to accomplish in this story. No more interruptions.

"*Right, okay . . . doing a great job. Two thumbs up.*"

Max: I think I might be in love.

Storee: Wait . . . are you serious?

Max: I mean, I think so. I can't be sure. There is a truckload of lust parked on my heart, that's for damn sure, but also, I feel different about her. Like, I need to protect her at all times. I need to be around her at all times. I think about her constantly. That's . . . that's love, right?

Storee: That's the start of it, yeah.

Max: Then I'm starting to be in love with her.

Storee: Oh my God, Max, that's . . . ahh my heart.

Max: I know. It feels crazy, but I swear to you, this is it. I've never felt this way before, and with Christmas coming up, I want to get her something really nice.

Storee: What do you have in mind? Chocolate-covered cherries?

Max: LOL. Obviously, but something else too.

Storee: Do you have any ideas?

Max: Well, I was sort of thinking about getting her something to do with the cottages, but then I thought that maybe Dwight might not go for the cottages, so I don't want to do that, plus I already got her a snow globe to represent the cottages.

Storee: Yeah, and you don't want to go all in on the business. What about some jewelry?

Max: I thought about it, but she doesn't wear a lot of jewelry.

Storee: Yeah, that might not be a good gift then.

Max: What about a map of the town? Do you think that's lame?

Storee: What kind of map?

Max: Well, what if it was a map that I get commissioned, and I have the artist put hearts where we've kissed or I've had moments with her, special moments?

Storee: OMG, Max, that's actually really cute.

Max: Yeah? Not lame?

Storee: No, I love that, and I think she will love it too, especially since she wants to make Kringle her new home.

Max: Okay, then I think I'll do that.

Storee: You have to pick a nice frame for it.

Max: Obviously. Jesus, do you think I'm just going to hand it to her in a manila folder?

Storee: I don't know. You're a question mark to me. Sometimes you do the right thing; sometimes you don't.

Max: I like to keep you on your toes.

Storee: Not necessary.

Max: Okay, if you think that's a good plan, then I'm going to go for it. Martha has a cousin who could commission the piece for me, and she said he works fast. He's done a map of the town before, so I don't think it would take too long.

Storee: Better not. You only have a few days until Christmas. Oh, by the way, my husband has information for you—he wouldn't tell me what it was, but he said he had to talk to you.

Max: Oh shit, really? Better head to the reindeer barn then. Thanks for the advice. You're the best.

Storee: I know.

Smiling, I lift my axe off the ground, throw it over my shoulder, and start walking toward the reindeer barn, but I shoot a quick text to Betty on my way.

Max: Hated not waking up next to you.

Thankfully, she's quick to respond.

Betty: I know. It was sad and cold in my bed. Do you think your parents will let you spend the night?

Max: LOL I don't need their permission.

Betty: Then why didn't you spend the night last night?

Max: Cleaning the couch, remember?

Betty: Oh right. Did your dad watch over you?

Max: Like a hawk.

Betty: Yikes. But did you get your ass print off the couch?

Max: There wasn't one to begin with, so yes.

Betty: Don't tell him about the air mattress.

Max: Fuck no. But should I tell them about your countertop?

Betty: NO!

Max: LOL! Okay, have to talk to Cole. I'll see you later?

Betty: Yeah, see you later. XOXO

I pocket my phone and enter the barn, where Cole is sweeping up some feed.

"Hey," I call out.

He doesn't lift his head to look at me as he says, "Hey."

"Uh . . . is everything okay?" I ask, feeling the vibe in the barn as morose. He's usually grumpy and not in high spirits unless he's around Storee or his girls, but this, this is different.

He sets the broom against a pole. "Let's go to my office."

Okay, this is very unlike him. I follow him into his office, and we both take a seat.

He leans back in his chair and rubs his hand over his forehead. "So I did some digging, and you know how the Dankworths have the surveillance cameras outside their shop?"

"Yeah," I answer, wondering where he's going with this.

"Well, they've had them up for years. Even before the statue. They made it seem like they were put up for the statue, but no, they've had them up way longer."

"Okay, where are you going with this?"

"They've kept all the records and archived them. I was talking to Martha and Mae about it. So come to find out they have surveillance from the night Dwight's ornament was stolen."

"Wait, really?" I say, sitting up. "They could see that far back?"

"Here's the thing. They don't have it of the person actually taking the ornament, but you see the person head up to the tree and then head back, holding an ornament in their hand."

"Holy shit. And clearly it wasn't me."

He shakes his head. "No, it wasn't you."

"Then, fuck, let's tell Dwight. This will clear everything up. This is exactly what I—"

"Dude, it was Ansel."

I pause, my heart stuttering in my chest. "Wait . . . what?" I tug on my ear. "Did you just say it was Ansel?"

Cole slowly nods his head. "Yeah. It was him."

"Are you sure?"

"I saw it with my own eyes, or else I wouldn't have believed it. Ansel took the ornament."

I feel all the blood drain from my head as I try to comprehend what Cole is saying. "Ansel, my brother, is the one who took the ornament?"

"Yeah, man."

"Fuck." I blow out a deep breath. "Fuck, that's . . . that's . . . what the fuck was he thinking?" I roar, anger taking over as I try to process this. "Why would he do that? He knows what that tree means to our family. Jesus Christ." I stand and start pacing. "I mean, it might as well be fucking me, because there is no way Dwight is ever going to be okay with it being anyone in my family. He will use that against us. He . . . fuck. FUCK! Why would he do that? I mean, I knew it wasn't me, and I could say that until I was blue in the face, and Dwight might have been able to believe me at some point, but knowing that it was Ansel? Someone in my family? I'm fucked. I'm utterly fucked."

I lean against the wall, my hopes crashing all around me as I think about the implications of this.

Defeated, I ask, "What am I supposed to do? She wants me to meet her parents when they come into town. I'm supposed to talk to Dwight . . . Fuck, man."

Cole leans forward, forearms propped up on his desk. "I don't know. Let me . . . let think about this for a second." He rubs his fingers over his brow. "You like her, right?"

"Yeah, I think . . . dude, I think I love her. I was just telling your wife that this morning."

"You were?"

I nod. "Yeah, I'm there, man. She's all I think about. She just feels so perfect for me. And I enjoy her company. I want to be around her. I want to talk to her. I want her to tell me about her day. I really fucking like her, and now I'm just going to have to let her go because of fucking Dwight? Because of Ansel and his moronic tendencies?"

"No, you're not going to let her go. We're going to figure out how to approach this. Let me just think on it, okay?" He blows out a heavy breath and then looks me in the eyes. "Sorry, man. I wish I had better news."

"Yeah, me too."

BETTY

I stopped by the farm earlier today, but Atlas was really busy given the time of the year—which is crazy, because shouldn't people already have their Christmas trees? Either way, I texted him that I'd be at Warm Your Spirits working when he was done with work.

Uncle Dwight comes home tomorrow, and my nerves are high because I know Atlas wants to talk to him, to settle things, but what if Uncle Dwight doesn't want to settle things? What if he wants to hang on to this feud? I could see it happening, because although I love him, he can be very stubborn.

And my parents are coming in soon too. It just all feels very stressful.

Maybe it's one of those things that we hold off on telling Uncle Dwight until after the holidays. It would be wonderful to see Atlas on Christmas, but if giving that up means that we can get through Christmas peacefully, then I very well might do that.

I think I'll make the suggestion when I see him.

My phone dings with a text, and I glance down to see that it's from Atlas. Smiling, I open up the text.

Max: On my way to you. Can you grab us drinks to go? I have somewhere I want to take you.

Betty: Of course. What do you want?

Max: Hot cocoa with peppermint.

Betty: You're so cute. See you soon.

I pack up my computer and notebook, and place them in my bag before heading up to the counter, where Tanya is chatting with two ladies I haven't met yet.

"Hello, Betty," Tanya says with a warm smile. "Are you heading out?"

"Actually, Atlas is coming to pick me up and asked if I can grab drinks for us. Two peppermint hot chocolates please."

"Oh, is this the Betty that is dating our Atlas?" one of the ladies asks.

"That would be me," I say with a smile.

"It's nice to meet you. I'm Martha, and this is Mae, my sister. We live across from Cole and Storee, next to the Dankworths."

"It's so nice to meet you. Storee has been such a good friend and has welcomed me into this town with open arms."

"She's really lovely. A great addition to the town," Martha says while Tanya starts making the drinks. "So glad that you changed your mind about the business."

"Oh yeah, well . . . just thought we might need something different here in town," I say, unaware that other people knew about the change of plans.

"Yes, it was difficult looking through the archives to see if there was anything we could do to prevent it from happening," Mae says.

Huh?

Martha nudges her sister with her elbow. "I don't think she knows about that."

"Knows about what?" I ask, looking between the two of them.

"Oh nothing, dear. No need to worry. All is good." Martha smiles nervously. "Well, we best be off. Don't want to be late for a meeting with Bob Krampus." She waves. "Nice meeting you."

"Yeah, nice meeting you," I say, confused. When they take off, I turn to Tanya, who is finishing the drinks, and I say, "What was that about?"

"Didn't hear what you ladies were talking about." She keeps her eyes down as she fidgets with the drink lids. "I'm going to put these on Max's tab. No reason for you to have to pay for a drink he wants." She sets the drinks down in front of me. "Hope you have a good evening."

"Thank you," I say, studying her. "Hey, Tanya?"

She finally looks up, her lips pressed together. "Hmm?"

"Is there something you're not telling me?"

"No, dear. Why would you think that?"

"I don't know. You're acting weird, and then what Martha and Mae said. Just seems like they almost let something slip, and you're trying to avoid talking about it."

"Oh please." She picks up a rag and starts cleaning the counter. "If you hear anything from those two, it's mainly gossip. They don't know what they're saying most of the time."

"Okay, because if there was something I should know, you would tell me, right?"

"Of course." She waves her hand at me and then looks out the window. "Oh, it seems like Max is here."

I glance out the window as well and see his truck pull up. Drinks in hand, I thank Tanya, still feeling uneasy, and carry them outside, where Atlas is getting out of the car and walking up to me.

Wearing a pair of green pants, a red sweater, and an orange shirt underneath, he looks adorable in his reindeer hat, but when he approaches me, he's missing something. The spark in his eye. The smile that stretches from ear to ear.

Something is off.

"Hey," he says as he wraps me in a hug and kisses the top of my head. "How was your day?"

"It was good," I answer as he pulls away. "What about you?"

"Oh, you know, Christmas things at the farm," he answers as I tilt my head to the side, studying him.

"Is everything okay? You seem a little off."

"Do I?" he says, scratching the back of his neck. "Just, uh, just a busy day is all."

I hand him his hot chocolate and ask, "Are you sure? Because if there's something that's bothering you, you know you can talk to me."

"I know." He nods. "Um, should we get going?"

Still skeptical, I allow him to help me into the passenger side of his truck, and when he shuts the door, I set my drink down to buckle up. When he joins me, I look him in the eyes.

"You know, something was a little off in the coffee shop," I say, wanting to be fully transparent.

"What was it?" he asks while blowing on his hot chocolate before he takes a sip.

"Um, well, I met Martha and Mae, and they said something about looking through archives—"

Atlas sputters out his hot chocolate, the liquid dripping down his face.

"Oh God," I say. "Are you okay?"

"Napkin, I need a napkin."

I pop open his glove compartment only for a paper to roll out onto the floor. A stack of napkins sits in the glove compartment, so I grab a few and hand them to Atlas before picking up the paper that rolled out.

Cute crayon drawings are scrolled across the paper, so while he cleans up, I unroll the paper as I say, "Aw, did Florence draw this—" My words are cut short as I take in the stick figures, the precisely drawn stick figures that look a lot like me and a lot like Atlas—not to mention my name is next to the first drawing at the top.

The figures are holding hands, there are hearts in the girl's eyes, and at the very bottom, she's crying with a broken heart next to her. At the top it reads *Battle Plan*.

"Atlas, what is this?" I turn it toward him as he finishes wiping his face. When his eyes read over the paper, they go wide, and I can see panic strike his features.

"Where . . . ? How . . . did you find that?"

"It was in your glove box just now. What is this?"

"Fuck," he says as he turns toward me. "Okay . . . fuck, don't get mad."

"Don't get mad? That's not a way to start an explanation."

"I know, but what I'm about to say is going to sound really fucking bad, okay, but I don't want you—"

"Is this about me?" I look down at the paper again, trying to decipher it.

"Yes," he answers honestly. "It's about you."

"Why does it say *battle plan* at the top?"

He blows out a heavy breath and looks me in the eyes. "Because it's what I put together when, uh . . . when you first started sniffing around the farm, before you knew me."

"I don't understand." I look down at it again. "The pictures almost make it seem like you were trying to get me to fall for you." And then it clicks.

Hits me all at once.

My head snaps up to his, and I feel myself slowly start to inch away. "Oh my God, was this a plan to get me to fall for you?"

He winces, but to his credit, he answers, "Yes."

"Wh-why? And why am I crying at the bottom?"

"Fuck." He scrubs his hand over his face. "Listen, Betty. Fuck, how do I explain this. I—"

Knock, knock.

Startled, I look out my window. Uncle Dwight is standing on the other side, not looking happy at all.

Oh shit.

He opens the door to the truck. "What the hell are you doing?" His eyes glance down at the paper and then back up at me. "What is this?" He snatches it from my grasp and then reads over it. When he's done, his gaze moves right past mine and to Atlas's. "I fucking knew it," he says. "I fucking knew you were trying to fucking lure her in."

"No, that's not . . . Fuck," Atlas says, gripping the steering wheel.

"And why are you in his car? Because he convinced you that I was in the wrong? I told you this was his plan all along, Betty. I fucking told you. He wanted to distract you from what you were doing so he could find a way to save his farm."

Martha's and Mae's comments float through my head, and I turn to Atlas. "Is that what Martha and Mae meant by preventing me from conducting business?"

"Shit," Atlas mutters.

"Oh my God." I unbuckle my seat belt. "Oh my God, Atlas." I hop out of the car. "Has this all been just one giant ruse?"

"Yes," Uncle Dwight says next to me. "I told you that, Betty. Let me guess, the new idea you wanted to talk to me about, it's because he convinced you it would be a good idea?"

"He . . . he did," I say, unable to believe it.

"Wait," Atlas says as he unbuckles and then gets out of the truck. He moves around toward us, but Uncle Dwight holds up his hand.

"Don't you dare come fucking closer."

Atlas holds his hands up, clearly not wanting to start trouble. "Please, just let me explain."

"There's nothing to explain," Uncle Dwight says. "You were using her."

"Wait," I say, crossing my arms. "I want to hear what he has to say."

"Why?" Uncle Dwight asks.

"Because I want him to say it to my face."

Atlas sticks his hands in his pockets, clearly distressed.

"If you have a truth to speak . . . then speak it."

He stares at the ground and takes a few calming breaths before he says, "Yes, I had a master plan to woo you, to get you to fall for me so Martha and Mae had time to look into the town rules, to give me time until my parents were back from vacation and they could handle it. I just wanted time before you started uprooting everything that I've ever known at the farm. The intention was to get you to fall for me and then for me to break it off once we had everything figured out."

Tears well in my eyes as I can't believe what he's saying. "You . . . you were using me?"

"No," he says as he takes a step closer, but Uncle Dwight pulls me back. "Don't come near her."

"Wait," Atlas says, looking distraught. "Yes, that was the plan, but after a few interactions, I told Storee that I couldn't—"

"Wait, Storee was helping you?"

"Fuck." He pulls on his hair.

"Oh my God." Tears fall down my cheek. "I thought . . . oh my God, I thought everyone was being nice to me because they wanted to be my friend, not because they were trying to deceive me." Memories of the "friends" I had in Fort Collins flash in my mind, the aching feeling of being played all over again filling my chest with hurt.

How could I be so stupid?

"Storee is your friend," Atlas says quickly. "She is. Trust me."

I shake my head. "There is no way I can trust you. Everything you've said to me, it's a lie. Everything. And you made me believe you." I wipe at my eyes. "You made me think Uncle Dwight wasn't telling the truth."

"He's not," Atlas says desperately. "I wasn't the one who took the ornament."

"Please stop." I shake my head while Uncle Dwight wraps his arm around me.

"I'm serious. It was Ansel. We have video footage. It wasn't me."

"It was your brother?" Uncle Dwight says. "You're going to blame it on your brother? How does that make it any better? You probably told him to do it."

"No. Fuck." Atlas looks up to the sky. "Please . . . please just listen to me. I'm trying to tell you . . ." He gets choked up, and he takes a deep breath, then his eyes meet up with mine. "Please believe me, Betty. I know I fucked up, but I'm telling you the truth."

"Why does this feel so familiar?" I ask. "You begging me to believe you? Oh, because this keeps happening. You keep asking me to believe you. No relationship should ever have to deal with that."

"Relationship?" Uncle Dwight asks.

"I'm sorry," I say, turning toward him. "I'm . . . I'm sorry. I didn't mean to, but I fell for him, which was clearly his plan all along, and he did a good job at it. And I'm stupid; I know I am. I know I should never have crossed you because now"—I suck in a sharp breath as a sob wants to escape—"I'm just broken."

I move past them, but Atlas grabs my arm. "Please, Betty."

But Atlas is quickly shoved into his truck by Uncle Dwight. "Don't fucking touch her."

Atlas holds his hands up again. "I'm sorry. I just want to explain—"

"You've explained enough," I say and then take off, leaving both of them behind as I find my car and start driving back to my cottage.

I need to get out of here.

I need to get my things, and I need to go.

This entire thing has been a joke.

A fallacy.

And I don't want to be a part of it anymore.

CHAPTER THIRTY
MAX

NARRATOR: WHY DID I KNOW that diagram was going to come back to bite him in the ass?

And why did he think it was okay to keep it?

Men . . . am I right?

That's harsh though. Not really sure if he will be able to fix this, because if I were Betty, the last thing I'd want to see is Max's face. Then again, she was falling for him, so there might be a chance.

We shall see.

_____

"I knew you were going to hurt her," Dwight shouts. "I fucking knew it. The moment I told you to stay away from her, I could see it in your eyes. I could see you wanting to get back at me. Well, you did. Congratulations. You hurt an innocent woman who was just trying to get her feet back on the ground after losing her business. Congratulations, you fuck. You just destroyed her."

"That . . . that wasn't my intention," I say.

"It wasn't? So you weren't intending to make her fall for you only to break her heart in the end to save your stupid, outdated farm?"

I don't know how to fucking deal with this. It's too much, because he's right. He's absolutely right. That was my intention. It's clear as day on the stupid diagram that I drew, but I quickly realized I couldn't make her fall for me, because I was falling faster.

Now it's all fucked up, and I don't know how to handle this.

"That's what I thought." Dwight looks me up and down. "You're pathetic. You know that? You were a pathetic loser back in high school, and you've only carried that through into adulthood." He shakes his head. "I hope you're ashamed."

He starts to walk away, and I say, "I am, Dwight. I'm fucking ashamed." He glances over his shoulder, so I keep going. "I'm ashamed of what I did to her. I'm ashamed I even came up with the plan. I'm ashamed that I didn't try to handle this in a more diplomatic way. I'm ashamed that I haven't spoken to you, talked to you about all this animosity between us but rather let it fester over the years to the point where it is today. I'm ashamed that I let my pride get the best of me. The only thing I'm not ashamed about is falling for Betty. The feelings I have for her, they're genuine." I get choked up as I continue. "She . . . she means so much to me. I've never met anyone like her, and I know I never will again. She's special, and I hate how everything started with her, sparked by animosity, but that quickly faded as I got to know her and spent more time with her. A genuine fondness developed, and that has turned into love."

"Love?" Dwight asks, blinking. "You're telling me you love her?"

"Yes," I say, a tear falling down my cheek, which I quickly wipe away. "I love her, Dwight. I'd do anything for her. Fucking anything. I was actually . . . hell, I was going to take her to the outlook point, and I was going to tell her everything today. That's where we were headed. I was going to tell her how this all started and how it turned into so much more. I was going to tell her that I love her, because I knew you were coming home, I knew I was going to have to have a hard conversation with you, and I wanted her to know how I felt before I had that conversation."

"To manipulate her once again."

I shake my head. "No, to let her know that I love her, so when I had the conversation with you, she at least could hold that close to her heart."

"I don't believe you."

I toss my hands in the air. "I don't know what else to say to convince you. I love her, Dwight. I'm in love with her."

"Hey," a voice booms from the side, pulling both of our attention. Bob Krampus walks toward us, looking none too pleased. "My house, now." He points toward Ornament Park. "That's an order." Then he grabs me by the arm and Dwight by the shirt, and he pushes us in the direction of his house.

Fuck.

And here I thought it couldn't get any worse.

"Sit down," Bob booms when we step inside his living room. "On the couch."

Dwight and I, with our tails tucked between our legs, sit on the couch and watch Bob pace his living room.

"This is not the kind of behavior I like to see in my town, especially right before Christmas." He turns toward us. "Tanya got complaints from patrons about you arguing. Do you think that's the experience I want visitors to have when they come to our town? Two numbskulls arguing outside a coffee shop?"

"No," I say, shaking my head. "I'm sorry."

"I thought that rivalry worked last year when you two were battling out to see who could win the Christmas Kringle competition. It added a lot of hype. But now . . . now you need to look at yourselves and realize you're adult men. We can't have this argument anymore." He takes a seat in his green recliner. "Now what's going on?"

"I fucked up," I admit, wanting to take the blame, because that's what happened. I fucked up. "Dwight was challenging my family farm, bringing in Betty to create a similar business. Instead of acting like an adult and having a conversation with Dwight to clear the air, I was scared and concocted a stupid plan to get Betty to fall for me so I could change her mind into planning a different idea."

"And it worked," Dwight says, crossing his arms.

"It did," I say with shame. "But I fell in love with her along the way, and the bitterness I had quickly turned into so much more. Her idea for the property, for Dwight's property, is so much better than what they initially planned, and I'm not saying that because I'm nervous about my family's business shutting down, but because it truly has merit and she's so smart and she's really thought everything through. And fuck, I don't know what I'm saying. I messed up, Bob. I love her, and now . . . now I know she's not going to ever give me a second chance, especially if Dwight keeps telling her I'm a liar."

"You are a liar," Dwight shouts. "You've lied about so much."

"What has he lied about?" Bob asks in a calmer voice.

"It started back in high school. He lied about not being interested in playing basketball, and then he goes and joins the team, taking my spot. He lied about not liking Jessica, but then I go and find her journals, saying how much she liked him. And then he lied about taking the ornament. He's been lying for fucking ever."

"Hold on," I say, turning toward him. "I didn't lie about basketball."

"You said you didn't like playing and you'd never try out."

"When did I say that?"

"You said that to Duncan."

"No, I didn't," I say. "I was playing basketball before you moved to town, but I skipped my freshman year, when you moved here, because my dad needed help on the farm. He lost some employees because they moved, and basketball season is during the busy Christmas season, but after that, Dad was able to hire, and I could join the team again."

"That is true," Bob nods his head, validating me.

"Really?" Dwight asks, looking stunned. "Duncan said it was because you didn't like basketball."

"Duncan also liked to sniff glue," I point out. "And I never liked Jessica like you did. She was a friend, and we were all pulling for her, but we were never romantically involved. Whatever was in her journals was all from her, man. And I'm sorry if that hurts. I can't imagine finding that out, but I promise you, I had no romantic interactions with her. And the ornament, like I said, that was Ansel, and I still need to confront him about it, but that wasn't me. I'd never do that. The Ornament Park Christmas tree is sacred to my family. Well, at least I thought it was sacred to all of us."

Dwight sits there, staring at his hands. And after a few moments of silence, he says, "It wasn't you?"

"No. I promise you. I know that probably means nothing to you at this point, but I promise you, it wasn't me. We might not have gotten along throughout the years, but I'd never do anything vindictive like that."

He stares out the window and then says, "I want to believe you, but after what you did to Betty—"

"It was stupid," I say. "And I'm going to tell you right now, it took about two interactions with her for my mind to change. I went from wanting to challenge her to wanting her around. I don't know if she told you, but while you were gone, the power went out. And I'm not saying this to win brownie points with you. I'm saying this because I want you to know how much I care for her. I walked through that storm to get to her, from my house to her cottage. Through the snow, through the wind, I walked to see if she was okay. We tried texting and calling, and heard nothing from her. When I got to her cottage, she was nearly frozen, so I carried her back to my place, where I spent the night warming her up and keeping an eye on her because she was not doing well, Dwight. It terrified me. Seeing her like that, it was the first time I realized just how much I liked her, how much I cared for her. From there, I've just kept falling harder and harder."

"You carried her?" he asks.

I nod. "And I even went back for her tarantula once I set her up in front of my fire."

"You saved Buzz?"

"Yeah, hated every second of it, but I'd do anything for her."

"He would," Bob says, chiming in. "I saw him the night he took her out on a date. He was nervous, wanted to make sure she had the perfect night. He is being genuine. There's no doubt in my mind that he has feelings for her."

Dwight lets out a sigh and tugs on the cuffs of his shirt. "Then why . . . why did you have to hurt her?"

"I didn't want to. Trust me, that was the last thing I wanted to do. My intention was to try to talk to you and get you to trust me, to hash out our differences like we are now so that I wouldn't hurt her. I was ready to put aside all the animosity and fighting between us for her."

He slowly nods. "This is . . . this is a lot to take in. Doesn't change the fact that what your brother did was wrong. Duncan told me it was a Maxheimer; I just assumed it was you given our history."

"Either way, should never have happened, and I will get to the bottom of it," I promise. "You deserve an explanation on that."

"I, uh, I appreciate that," Dwight says, throwing me an olive branch that I'll fucking cling to.

"Good," Bob says. "Now, look at each other and apologize." When we don't listen at first, he booms, "Now."

Startled, we both turn toward each other and say, "Sorry," at the same time.

"Thank you," Bob says, pleased with himself. "No more of this fighting, especially in the streets where everyone can hear you. You don't have to be the best of friends, but you can at least understand each other."

"I'd like that," I say.

"Yeah, I mean, we're not friends, but I don't have to be a dick to you," Dwight says.

"Thanks, man."

"I still don't trust you fully."

"I get that," I say. "That will take time. I'll have to earn your trust. And I have no problem doing that."

"Are you saying that just because you like Betty and want to be with her?"

"Honestly, yes," I say. "If she wasn't involved, I probably wouldn't bother trying with you, but I know that she considers you the closest thing she has to a brother, and I'd never want to get in the way of that kind of relationship. So yeah, I want to earn your trust for her."

Dwight slowly nods. "That's a truthful answer I can appreciate. If you said no, I wouldn't have believed you." He rubs his hands over his thighs. "I don't know where to go from here."

"What about Betty?" Bob says. "What are you going to do about her?"

"I need to talk to her," I say in a panic.

Dwight shakes his head. "She's not going to want to talk to you. Not right now at least. I think you need to let her sit in her feelings for a moment."

"I can't," I say. "She's never going to give me a second chance if I let her sit in her feelings, because those feelings will brew, and then she'll just hate me even more."

"She's not going to believe anything you say," Dwight says.

"He's right." Bob sits back in his chair and rubs his beard. "I think you need a bigger plan than just going to talk to her. You can't just tell her you love her. You have to show her you love her."

"As much as it pains me to say it, because I don't like that you love her, he's right," Dwight says.

I shake my head. "No, I should have talked to her from the

beginning. I went with a grand idea, and it came back and bit me in the ass. I'm going to do the thing that I should have done in the first place. Just talk."

Cole: Dude, are you okay? I heard what happened. Tanya called Storee.

Max: No, I'm not okay.

Cole: What can I do?

Max: Nothing. I need to fix this myself.

Cole: What are you going to say?

Max: Just beg her to listen to me.

Cole: And what if she doesn't?

Max: I can't even think about that right now.

Cole: Okay, well, we're here for you if you need us.

Max: Thanks.

I stuff my phone in my back pocket and then drag my hands over my face. I can do this. She has to at least give me a second to explain myself, right?

No, she doesn't. She doesn't have to give me the time of day. I'll be lucky if she even opens the door. But I need to at least try.

I walk up to her porch and give the door a knock. I take a step back only to hear her say, "Go away, Max."

Max.

Fuck, she called me Max.

Not sure she's ever called me that, which can only mean one thing: she wants nothing to do with me. She's put up the boundary, and even though I respect that, I need to try . . . before I walk away.

I knock again. "Betty, please, let me in."

"No," she says, and I can hear the hurt in her voice.

"Please, Betty, I'm not going to leave until I talk to you. I'll stand here all day, all night. Please."

I wait in silence, hoping. I wasn't lying. I'll stand here all goddamn night if I have to, into the next morning. I can't have her leave Kringle without knowing that she wasn't a pawn in a small town's cruel joke. People genuinely adore her. But I hurt that trust, and she needs to know I'll do anything to heal those wounds.

"Betty," I say as I knock quietly. "Please."

After a few seconds, there's movement in the cottage, and then to my utter surprise, the door opens to show Betty on the other side with tearstained cheeks.

Fuck.

My heart sinks, and my initial instinct is to pull her into my arms, to protect her, to shield her from the hurt she's feeling, but unfortunately, I'm the one who brought on the hurt.

"Betty, I—" My voice gets caught in my throat as she shakes her head.

"I can't do this."

She goes to shut the door, but I stop her, my hand to the wood. "Please, Betty, can I just explain?"

"Explain what?" she asks, her voice rising. "How you used my feelings against me? As a weapon?" Her eyes well up with more tears, and it nearly splits me in half, seeing her this upset. "You made me trust you, believe you, only to . . . to use me."

"It wasn't like that," I say.

"It wasn't?" she shouts. "So you didn't set out to try to hurt me?"

"To be fair, you were setting out to hurt me as well," I say. "You were trying to put my family out of business. It wasn't like I was just going to be a dick for no reason. You were attempting to end the farm my family built, that they rely on as a source of income, as a place that provides income for many others. It's *our* livelihood. It's a place where they've grown traditions over the years. I was in a panic, Betty. I was scared, so I did something stupid."

She pauses, her mind thinking about it.

"And listen, I understand where you were coming from. You didn't know me. All you knew was what Dwight told you, which was unflattering at best. There was vengeance on your mind, and I was . . . I was caught off guard. I didn't know how to handle you on so many levels, from your plans to take down the farm to your fucking smile to your gorgeous eyes. I was out of my goddamn mind and just . . . just settled on the most obnoxious idea, which was to try to woo you to get you to stop planning to hurt the farm." I scratch the back of my head as she crosses her arms in front of her. "It was stupid, and if I could, I'd take it all back. If I could do it over again, I'd just talk to you, try to reason with you, and then . . . ask you out on a date."

She shakes her head. "Please don't say things like that."

"Betty, I mean it."

She continues to shake her head. "No. Dwight said you were a manipulator. And he was right."

"He wasn't," I say, feeling desperate. "I'm not that man. I told you that. You believed me—"

"But you were lying!" she shouts. "You were lying the entire time. You weren't interested in me. You were trying to distract and divert me from planning. And you succeeded. You tricked me, made me fall for your every word."

"But that was real," I say. "Betty, I don't know how to explain this to you, but it was real. The intention was to distract you, yes, but the minute I set the plan in motion, I realized that I liked you. That's what I'm trying to say. And the friendship you grew with Storee, that was real. Everything about it. The relationships you've built with the people of this town, those are real too. They love you here. They want you here."

Tears stream down her face.

"And the feelings we grew for each other, to me . . . they were real. The kisses under the mistletoe, there was nothing fake about them. Wanting to see you day in and day out, that was pure desperation to be close to you. The nights we spent together, the days, the conversations, everything about it was real. Please"—I take a step forward—"please, you have to believe me."

She swipes at her eyes, avoiding eye contact with me.

So I take another step forward, testing her boundaries.

Then another step, and when I'm an inch away, I wrap my arms around her, and to my surprise, she leans in.

A wave of relief washes through me right before I feel her hand at my chest and she pushes me away.

"No," she says, shaking her head. "No, you can't just . . . come over here and act like . . . like everything is okay. Like the entire town didn't have this master plan to trick me." Tears stream down her cheeks as her gaze finally meets mine. "Do you know how that makes me feel? Like a fool, Atlas. Like a fucking fool. And I've been there before. Been the object of condescending comments. No one supported me when I failed before, and it looks like Kringle is just as mean."

"It wasn't like that—"

"It wasn't? Because two people I never even met until today were in on it, so you can't tell me it wasn't like that. The friend I thought I had was in on it. The coffee shop owner, probably even Santa Claus, they all knew you were fooling me—"

"They didn't," I say, trying to get my point across. "I need you to understand that—"

"I need you to understand that you need to leave." She points to the door. "Go, Max."

"Betty, please—"

"Go!" she shouts, a sob following. "Just go."

I don't want to make things worse, so I take a step back toward the door. "Betty, I'm . . . I'm sorry."

She shakes her head, not wanting to hear it, so I take that as my sign to leave. *Fuck.*

CHAPTER THIRTY-ONE
MAX

NARRATOR: THE AIR GROWS STILL as Max stands outside Betty's cottage, desperately wanting to go back, desperately wanting to keep trying over and over again to win her back, but he knows talking is not going to do him any good, just like Bob and Dwight said.

So with a heavy heart and a mind bereft of ideas, he goes to the one place where he knows he can find help.

At least he hopes so.

———————

"Can I come in?"

Cole steps aside, letting me into his house. I walk right into the living room, where Storee is holding Florence while Evelyn rocks in her swing.

"How are you?" she asks, sympathy all over her expression. "You can't imagine the number of text messages I've received."

I take a seat on the couch and drag my hand over my eyes. "Oh, I'm sure it's all everyone is talking about."

"I tried texting Betty," Storee says. "But I haven't heard anything from her."

"Yeah, she's really upset. Upset with me, with you, with the whole town. She's embarrassed, and I don't blame her. Fuck, I can't believe I messed this up so much. I was just over there, and she wants nothing to do with me. And do you know what I fear?" I ask. "I fear that she's going to leave town, that she's going to take off, and I'm not going to have a chance at winning her back."

"Then why don't you do something now?" Storee asks while Cole takes a seat as well.

"I tried," I say. "I tried to do something—"

"No, something bigger. You say she's embarrassed and upset with everyone in the town, so then why don't you do something to change that?"

"What do you mean?" I ask.

She rolls her eyes. "God, men are so obtuse." She hands Florence over to Cole and sits on the edge of the couch. "The grand gesture, Atlas. You have to come up with a plan, something that will show just how sorry you are while getting the town involved. That way, she can see that not only are you sorry . . . but everyone still wants her here."

I perk up from the thought. "That's actually . . . that's a good idea."

"I know," Storee says with a smile.

"But what kind of plan?" I ask. "Hell, she didn't even want to look at me. She was fucking crying, Storee. Crying. How am I supposed to convince her to come into town and watch us apologize?"

"You won't be able to, but Dwight might."

I roll my eyes and lean back in my seat, defeat pushing through me. "Look, we have an extremely tentative truce due to Bob's intrusion." Fuck, that was embarrassing. Being led away like a naughty schoolboy to the principal's office. In front of the whole town. "We hashed some things out, and Dwight and I apologized to each other. I told him the truth about Betty, that I love her. He told me to wait for a while and let Betty think. But I'm not sure he'll help me win her back."

Storee shrugs. "Maybe, if you get your brother to apologize to him."

I glance over at her, the idea taking root. Then again, it's Ansel; he doesn't necessarily care for apologizing.

Cole bounces Florence on his knee. "You need to talk to your brother." When his gaze meets mine, I can see just how serious he is. "That relationship has been threadbare for as long as I've known it. This isn't just about having Ansel apologize. This is so much more than that. Think about where all this paranoia stemmed from . . . trying to show your brothers that you could handle the farm. There are some deep-rooted issues there that you need to take care of."

"Let me tell you, the moment you figure out those sibling issues, the better life will be. Take it from someone who struggled with her sister. There were some things we sat on and let stew for a long time, and now that she lives closer and we've been able to build a different bond, a stronger one, life just feels . . . easier. You're going to want that bond with your brothers, especially when you take over the farm one day."

I tug on my hair, thinking about that uncomfortable conversation. "So what you're saying is that I need to fix things with my brother so I can fix things with Dwight so I can fix things with Betty?"

"Yup," Cole says as he tosses Florence in the air and catches her. "Welcome to falling in love with someone."

BETTY

Storee: I'm so sorry, Betty. I'm sorry for my part in you getting hurt. I think you're amazing, and I've honestly enjoyed getting to know you and consider you a dear friend. From the day we first met on the farm, I've wanted to be your friend. And I am deeply sorry that we've hurt you. You didn't deserve that.

I stare at the text, feeling devastated, heartbroken, and embarrassed. Tears continue to fall down my cheeks, sorrow enveloping me.

Why did he have to come here?

Why did he have to beg me to forgive him?

Plead with me?

Because once again, I felt myself believing him. I felt him being genuine. I felt myself leaning into his hold and wanting to bury myself in his chest, where he'd protect me from what was happening, but then that's when I remembered he was the one causing all the chaos.

He was the one causing the hurt.

I swipe at my cheeks and take a deep breath. I need to get out of here. I need to flee.

Bags packed already, I carry my suitcases out to my car and pack them in the trunk. When I turn toward the cottage to go grab Buzz, I feel this sense of loss hit me all at once, because . . . I don't want to leave. I love it here. I love my cottage. I love the property. I love the town and the feel it gives me when I walk around. I felt like I truly found a home here. For the first time since I lost my business, it felt like I had purpose again. Correction: I *loved* my cottage, the town, the property, the sense of purpose. But once again, I'm fleeing with a sense of humiliation on my back.

I can't . . . I can't stay here. Not now.

Even though it leaves me with an empty void in my heart, I know I need to move on.

So I go back into the cottage, making a note to have Uncle Dwight send everything back to my parents' house, and then place Buzz in my car and buckle him up. When I reach the driver's side, I give the cottage one more look and then turn on the ignition.

When nothing happens, I pause for a second and then turn the key, attempting to start the car again.

Nothing.

"Nooo," I say as I try again and again and again.

On the sixth failure, I rest my head on the steering wheel and blow out a frustrated breath.

Why?

Why now?

I take that moment to pull out my phone and dial Uncle Dwight. It takes a few seconds for him to answer and then, "Betty, how are you?"

"Not good," I say on a sob, unable to hold it back. "I'm trying to leave, and I can't because my car won't start, and I just want to be out of here and go back to Fort Collins. I don't want to be here. I don't want to see him again. I don't want to see anybody. I'm just . . . I'm sad and heartbroken and embarrassed, and I wish I never came here at all."

"Shhh," Uncle Dwight says. "First things first. Your car stopped working?"

"Yep," I say, holding back another sob.

"Okay. Well, I can get someone to come and fix it."

"It was already supposed to be fixed. Atlas had someone fix it for me before, or maybe that was all part of the plan. Maybe it was a temporary fix so that when he went to break my heart, he could keep me here so I could live in the sorrow over and over again like a merry-go-round. Do you think that's what the plan was? Well, it's working, and now I have to stay here."

"Listen," he says. "Take a deep breath. I'm so sorry this happened, and I promise I'm going to help. Your parents are on their way, so why don't you just go back to the cottage, relax, and then we can just spend some time here at my place with your parents like we initially wanted to? After the holidays, you can go back with them."

"I really don't think I want to see them. This is all too raw."

"Do you want me to tell them not to come?"

I give it some thought. The last thing I want is for my parents to see me in a failing position again. Not that they would ever judge me or be mad at me, but to have to tell them that I'm heartbroken, that my life once again has fallen off course, and that I have to start all over again—I don't think I can stomach it.

"Yeah, tell them not to come. I can't . . . I can't deal with it right now."

"Okay. I'll tell them that something came up and you're going to be busy during the holiday."

"Thank you."

"I can come pick you up later. We can hang out—"

"I think I just want to be alone right now."

"It's almost Christmas, Betty."

"I know," I answer as I curl up on the couch, the tree Atlas got me lit up in the corner. "And I just think I want to be alone."

"Do you have food? I can bring you some food."

"No, I'm good. Seriously. I have everything I need."

"You sure?"

"I'm sure. Please just . . . just let me be alone."

"Okay," he answers skeptically. "But if that changes, you let me know."

MAX

"To what do we owe the pleasant surprise?" Ansel says, his feet kicked up on his desk while he pulls at a cheese stick.

"I need to talk to you."

"Me?" Ansel points to his chest. "Is this about Mom and Dad walking in on you and Betty? Because I might have told them not to say anything to you about their arrival. Didn't know they were going to walk in on you two with her kneeling—"

"Watch your fucking mouth," I say, coming right up to his desk.

He drops his feet to the ground and scoots back his chair. "Jesus, fuck, what's your deal?"

Calming myself because I know that I can't come in here guns blazing, I say, "I don't appreciate you talking about her like that."

"Just stating facts."

"Facts that don't need to be public," I say.

Ansel looks around his office, not a tourist in sight, since it seems like they don't have any more tours for the day. Seems odd given the time of year, but then again, they could have their secondary crew out there. "There's no one around."

"Just don't fucking talk about her like that. You don't have the right," I growl.

"Okay," he says. "Sheesh." He clears his throat. "Was there a reason you came in here, or was it just to threaten me?"

Deflection at its finest. He fucking started this bullshit. But I have to ignore it because what I need to talk to him about is more important, and I can't have him on the defensive.

So I gather myself and take a seat across from him. "I need to talk to you about something," I say in a calming voice.

He studies me for a moment and then says, "Okay."

"And what I'm about to say, I have video evidence of you doing, so please don't fucking pretend like you have no idea what I'm talking about."

He shifts in his seat uncomfortably. "Okay."

I slide my hands over my thighs, feeling nervous, because Ansel is the kind of guy who will jump down your throat with anger even if he's in the wrong, and it's just not something I want to deal with right now.

"Back when I was in high school, Dwight was going through a lot with Jessica. Remember her? She passed from cancer."

"Yeah," he says skeptically.

"Well, one night during the season, he made a wish on the ornament tree." I can see realization start to form on his face. "It was a wish for Jessica to get better, and when he went to see the tree the next morning, his ornament was gone."

"Fuck," Ansel says as he drags his hand over his face.

"This entire time, Dwight thought it was me who did it, and it's one of the reasons he hates me so much. But from your reaction, I'm going to assume we both know it wasn't me."

"Shit." He places his elbows on the desk and then buries his head in his hands. "That's who it belonged to? Fuck . . ."

"Why?" I ask. "Why did you do it?"

He pushes his palms into his forehead and is silent for a moment before he speaks, and his voice sounds rough . . . jaded. "It was a prank on Felix. He told me he was going to make a wish on the tree for a man in leather pants. He showed me the ornament, and it must have been the same as Dwight's. I grabbed it that night to be a dick, because it was a stupid wish, but the next morning, when I saw that Felix was bragging that his ornament was still on the tree, I felt fucking sick, because I knew I took someone else's. I had no idea whose it was until now." He looks me in the eyes. "It was Dwight's?"

"Yeah," I say. "And he's been blaming it on me all these years."

Ansel nods and then stands from his desk and walks over to a picture on the wall. Confused, I watch him take it off the wall to reveal a safe.

Wait, is he serious?

He opens the safe and then rummages through it for a moment before he pulls out an ornament.

"Wait, you've kept it?"

"Yeah," he says. "I felt so fucking terrible. I felt like I needed to keep it in case I ever found out whose it was."

"Why didn't you just put it back on the tree?"

"Because the damage had been done. It's not like that person was going to go and make another wish or ever go back to the tree, because of the shit experience they had."

"Yeah, I guess you're right."

He stares down at the ornament and then locks up his safe and puts the picture back.

"You should give it back to him," I suggest.

"Yeah, I know."

And to be honest, I'm surprised by the response, because I would have assumed, given my brother's nature, that he would have put up a fight about my suggestion.

"Really?" I ask.

He glances at me. "Really? I can be a nice guy, Atlas. I know right from wrong, and what I did was wrong."

I scratch the back of my head, perplexed. "Um, sorry, I'm just . . . not to be a dick, but I'm having a hard time grasping the idea that you feel bad given how you've been, well, our entire lives."

"What is that supposed to mean?" he asks.

"It means that you've been an asshole to me our entire lives."

His brow creases. "An asshole? Our entire lives? That seems like an awfully big statement, don't you think?"

"Tell me it's not true," I say, feeling vulnerable. "It's always been you and Felix, because you're closer in age. I've been the outsider, and you've treated me like that. You picked on me. You've downplayed my abilities. You've even made it hard for me to date by constantly getting in my business. It hasn't been a walk in the park being your brother, so yeah, I'm a bit surprised."

He takes a seat on the edge of the desk and sets the ornament down. "I didn't know you felt that way. I guess I just thought I was being an older brother."

"Yeah, well . . ."

"And you always had Cole," he says. "I didn't think you cared much because you were always with him. You still are."

"I'm grateful for Cole, don't get me wrong, but don't you think I would have wanted to have the same relationship with my actual brother?"

His eyes meet mine, and I can see the regret in them. "Yeah, I'd think so." He sighs. "Shit, dude, I'm sorry. I should have been better. I should be better."

"I shouldn't have held on to the animosity either." I can see that I've done the exact same thing Dwight has done. *Not talked.* "That's on me too."

He nods. "Maybe we both need to be better."

"I can agree to that," I say.

He lets out a deep sigh. "Christ, didn't think I'd be having this conversation today."

"Yeah, neither did I."

"What brought it up?"

"Betty," I say. "Really fucked up with her, and I'm trying to make it better. It starts with making amends with Dwight, which meant having to see you."

"That's a tangled web." He nods at me. "So you like her?"

"Yeah, I love her, man."

His lips purse, and then he pushes off the desk. "Well then, how can I help?"

"I'm glad you asked."

CHAPTER THIRTY-TWO
MAX

NARRATOR: LOOKS LIKE THERE COULD be some brotherly love finally in Max's life. At least it's a decent start. Now the question is, will he be able to make things better with Betty? It's a large undertaking, given what he put her through, but if I know Max like I think I know him, there is no way he's going to go down without a fight.

And this fight . . . makes me think he's going to go full-on Max.

If you thought dancing in lederhosen was questionable, I think you need to be prepared for what is about to happen.

"Does everyone understand their roles?" I ask as I look around Storee's living room, taking in the people who showed up for me. After talking with Ansel, I knew I had to bring the team together to figure out how to make this better.

And that included everyone in town, because she isn't just hurting because of me; she's embarrassed about the town being a part of my master plan. So . . . I gathered everyone I could to help.

There's Storee and Cole, Taran and Guy—not Gus—Dwight, Bob Krampus and BKJ, Mr. Dankworth, Martha and Mae, and of course Tanya and Sherry. If I'm going to pull this off, I'm going to need all of them.

They all nod as they stare at the plan we've all worked together to create, the ultimate booby-trapped meet-cute. If executed properly, it will give me just enough time to try to talk to her and convince her that I'm still the man she thought I was. At least that's what I'm hoping.

"I can't thank you guys enough. I know I fucked this up royally, but if we're able to pull this off and she gives me a second chance, I'll be indebted to you all."

"Can I get that in writing?" Dwight says, standing off to the side, arms crossed.

"Yes," I say sincerely just as there's a knock at the door.

Knowing exactly who that is, I open it and find Ansel on the other side. I told him to show up a little bit later because I didn't want Dwight to become defensive the moment he stepped foot in the house. I wanted his approval of this plan, so I had Ansel wait.

"Is he here?" he asks.

"He is." I nod for him to come in and point to the dining room, away from everyone else. "Dwight."

He turns to face me, and when he sees Ansel, his brow scrunches.

"Can we have a chat?"

He thinks about it for a second, but then he pushes off the wall and walks toward the dining room as well.

When we're all together, I motion to Ansel. "Go ahead."

Ansel lets out a deep breath, and then reaches into his pocket and pulls out the ornament. Dwight's expression morphs from angry to sad in seconds as he takes the ornament from Ansel and stares down at it.

"I'm really fucking sorry," Ansel says. "I didn't know it was your ornament. And I know what I'm about to say is not an excuse because what I did was shitty, but I was trying to pull a joke on Felix. He said he was putting up an ornament like yours on the tree and wishing for a man in leather pants for Christmas. When I saw the ornament up there, I thought it would be funny to take it down. So I went with some friends, grabbed the ornament, and left. It was stupid and ridiculous, and when I asked Felix about his wish coming true and he said he was excited because his ornament was still on the tree, I was . . . well, I was fucking devastated, because I knew I'd stolen someone else's wish, and it's been a tough pill to swallow. I've held on to the ornament all these years, unsure of what to do with it." He sticks his hands in his pockets. "I'm really sorry, dude. I wish I could take it all back, but unfortunately, I can't. All I can do is apologize and return the ornament."

Dwight runs his finger over the wood ornament, studying it for a good amount of time. When he looks up at Ansel, his eyes are full of tears. "I hate you for taking this."

"I know," Ansel says. "You have the right to hate me."

"But," Dwight continues, "Jessica made this ornament, and it's . . . it's one of few things I have left of her, so . . . thank you for returning it."

"She did?" Ansel asks.

"Yeah, she sold them with her mom over at the vendor booths before BKJ took over. This is . . . this is special. Thank you."

Ansel clears his throat. "You're, uh, you're welcome."

Dwight wipes at his eyes. "Okay. Well, I still hate you."

"Yup, I understand that."

"And if you ever buy another property, I'm charging you extra commission."

"Ehh, is that necessary?" Ansel asks while Dwight gives him a murderous look. "You know what? Yeah, I think you're right. Extra commission it is."

I grip Dwight by the shoulder. "I'm really sorry about Jessica and about all this, man. You deserved better, and I'm sorry you were inserted in a situation you never should have been in."

"Thank you." Dwight nods and then lets out a heavy breath. "Shit, I wasn't expecting this, and now I feel all . . . off." He clears his throat. "We, uh, we better get moving, because you have someone to win back."

"But first, are we good here? Because even though it pains me to ask, I still want your approval. In order for everything to be good with Betty, I need things to be good with us."

He slowly nods. "We're not best friends or even friends at that, but yeah, we're good."

"Okay." I blow out a breath. "Then wish me luck. I'm going to need it."

"Good luck. Don't hurt her again, you motherfucker."

"I won't. Promise." I glance toward Cole. "Hey, is the power cut?"

"Yup. Power is out."

I then look at Dwight. "Okay, you're up. Thanks for doing this."

"Don't forget it."

"I won't."

BETTY

"Noooo," I nearly cry as I attempt to play around with the breaker, hoping the power turns back on. But after the fourth try, I know that I'm out of luck.

Tears fill my eyes as I make my way back into my cottage and flop onto the couch.

Why?

Why is this happening now?

A tear falls down my cheek as I glance over at the battery pack and heater that Atlas left here for me. It might last a little bit, but it's not going to last me all night, I know that for certain. And it's not like I can get in my car and leave.

Nope.

I'm going to have to make a call, despite wanting to be left alone.

I pick up my phone and dial Uncle Dwight's number.

He answers on the second ring. "Hey, heard the power was out over there."

"Wait . . . what? You did?"

"Yeah, was going to show a house, but the power was out, so we had to reschedule. I'm headed your way. Figured you might need someplace to stay."

"I don't think I can stay here, that's for sure. It gets really cold."

"Pack a bag. I'm almost there."

Well, that's easy, given all my things are still packed.

"Okay."

I hang up the phone and then move around the cottage almost like a zombie, waiting for my uncle to rescue me. Again. I really don't want this right now. I just want to be left alone.

When I hear Uncle Dwight pull up, I step outside the cottage with my bag and Buzz, lock up, and then head toward his car, waving at him to stay in it.

I stick my bag in the back seat and buckle up Buzz; then I take a seat on the passenger side, keeping my eyes trained forward.

"You okay?"

"Don't really want to talk about anything."

"Sure, I understand," he says and then pulls out of the driveway. "But you know, I'm here if you want to talk."

"I know," I say, crossing my arms at my chest and staring out the window.

"It might help to talk about it." He drives toward town.

"I know you're trying to help, but honestly, I'm really not in the mood."

"I understand, but . . . you know . . . maybe what he did wasn't so bad."

"What?" I ask, turning toward Uncle Dwight now. Has he lost his mind?

He shrugs. "Just thinking about it. It's one thing, right? But wasn't there . . . more good than bad?"

"What are you talking about? You yourself said he was a liar, a deceiver."

"I know, but what if I was wrong?"

"What if you were wrong? What is happening? Moments ago, you were saying how he's a horrible person and how I should stay away from him."

"Yeah, well, sometimes we make mistakes."

I pause, absolutely floored, because what sort of seventh circle of hell did I enter? Uncle Dwight doesn't say nice things about Atlas. He doesn't give him the benefit of the doubt. He doesn't say that he might have made a mistake.

"What . . . what are you saying?"

"Listen, I know that you're hurt and what he did wasn't right, but do you really think, out of all the things he's done for you, he would be doing them because he's uninterested and just trying to stop you from competing against his business? I mean . . . he went and got your tarantula."

How does he know that?

"I really don't know, okay? I don't know anything. All I know is that I'm hurt and I just want . . . I want this holiday to be over and done with." My throat grows tight as tears build again, attempting to fall down my cheek.

"Betty—"

"Please, don't."

"I want to respect you, I really do, but I also need you to have an open mind."

I stare out the window, the town coming into view. "An open mind about what?" I ask just as someone carting a box of ornaments starts to cross the road. "Watch out," I shout as the box spills over the road, crushing the ornaments.

Uncle Dwight swerves his car across the road, me screaming as he stops right in front of Baubles and Wrappings, knocking over the statue out front.

"Oh my God," I say as I grip his arm, trying to steady my breath.

Someone pops out of the shop and starts shouting, directing his anger at Uncle Dwight. So he steps out of the vehicle and starts shouting back.

The man puffs his chest up to Uncle Dwight, who puffs back, and I can see that this might not end well, so I get out of the car and walk up to them.

"If that is chipped, you're going to have to pay for it."

"Who puts a statue out front like that? Everyone hates that statue. Everyone!"

"That statue is an icon of this town."

"Have you lost your mind?"

"Hey," I say, butting in. "Why don't we just—"

"What's going on out here?" a woman who I think is Mrs. Dankworth says as she comes out of the store holding a pillow.

Why on earth would she need a pillow?

"He ran over the statue."

"The statue shouldn't be there," Uncle Dwight shouts.

"I think if we all just calm down," I say, but it's too late as Mr. Dankworth takes the pillow from his wife and whips it around to hit Uncle Dwight.

At the last second, Uncle Dwight ducks, and the pillow whacks me in the face, sending feathers flying everywhere and pushing me backward as I trip over something behind me.

I twist, I turn, and then I stumble . . . right into the arms of someone behind me.

As I'm being held right above the ground, I glance at my feet, where I spot two paint cans, the culprits for tripping me. When did those get there?

And as I'm about to turn around to thank whoever is holding me up, people start filing out of Baubles and Wrappings. But not just any people: all the people from town. Sherry, Tanya, Bob Krampus, Cole, Storee,

Taran, Guy . . . and then Atlas, who's holding a bouquet of chocolate-covered cherries.

"Give him a chance to explain," a deep voice says into my ear. I turn around and see BKJ right before he brings me back to my feet.

Everyone parts, and Atlas steps forward.

My heart beats rapidly from the mere sight of him. *God, why is he so beautiful?*

"Betty." He clears his throat as I take in everyone watching—everyone who is conveniently here at the same time.

Even his parents are off to the side, along with Martha and Mae.

"The moment I heard about you on the farm, I knew I had to figure out who you were and what you were planning on doing. The instant I saw you, I knew that task wasn't going to be so hard, because you were the prettiest woman I'd ever seen, and I found myself needing to see you every day." He clears his throat and takes another step toward me. "And then I got to know you, I saw myself in you, I saw how well we meshed, how I felt comfortable around you, and I immediately knew, *this is my person.* And I went from seeking revenge to attempting to get you to like me. To make you see who I was past what Dwight was saying. I fell for you . . . hard. And my biggest regret to date is not giving myself a chance to get to know you before I started planning to stop your endeavors."

He takes another step forward, and tears well in my eyes as I glance at Uncle Dwight, who's nodding.

Cole and Storee, gleefully hopeful.

Tanya and Sherry, holding hands.

Bob Krampus . . . popping Tic Tacs into his mouth.

"I know I messed up and that asking for a second chance is bold, but I can't imagine you not being here . . . with me. With us. This entire town loves you."

"We do," Tanya says.

"So much," Sherry adds.

"You're a good friend we can't lose," Storee says, tears in her eyes.

"And someone who makes our boy and everyone else happy," Cole says.

"So please, forgive me . . . forgive us, because we don't want you to go. We want you here, contributing to this town, adding friendship and laughter and smiles. Please stay, Betty, because . . . I love you and I can't fathom you leaving. Not when I just found you."

Tears spill down my cheeks while he takes one more step forward and wipes them away.

He cups my face and then whispers, "Please forgive me. I'm so fucking sorry."

I wet my lips, staring in his beautiful eyes, and all I can think about is that even though I was hurt, I feel the same exact way. I can't fathom leaving this town. I can't fathom not seeing Atlas every day, and a part of the grief I was feeling was not just from being hurt but from putting myself in a situation where I wasn't a part of this town, a part of Atlas's life.

I couldn't stomach it.

And I can't stomach it now.

I lean into his touch and say, "I love you too."

A smile crosses over his face, and he pulls me in tighter. "Please tell me you forgive me. Because I promise, I will not hurt you again. I won't fuck this up."

I nod and whisper, "I forgive you."

He scoops me into his arms and then captures my mouth with his, his body relaxing into mine as his lips lead the way, claiming me as his.

Cheers erupt all around us while I part my mouth ever so slightly for him, melting into his hold and grateful for this town and everyone in it.

When he pulls away, he presses his forehead to mine and whispers, "I love you."

"I love you too," I whisper back as he hands me the bouquet. Chuckling, I say, "Where did you find this?"

"I made it. Took some time."

440 | MEGHAN QUINN

"What else did you do?" I gesture to everyone around us. "Because this seems very convenient."

"Well, I went back to my roots. I had to trap you to talk to me somehow, and I'm just glad I had more hands on deck."

"Can we get hugs too?" Storee asks, waiting patiently. I nod, and she comes running up to me, pulling me in close. "I'm so sorry. Please know, our friendship has always been real."

"I know," I say.

"Good, because I don't think I could stand helping Atlas that much unless I actually liked the person he was hanging with."

I chuckle and pull away just as Uncle Dwight comes up to me and gives me a hug.

"You approved of this?" I ask.

He looks over at Atlas and says, "We had a chat and worked some things out. He's on probation."

Uncle Dwight pulls away, and Atlas scoops me into his arms again, kissing me on the lips. "Fuck, it's going to be a great Christmas now. I have so many things planned, starting with turning the power back on at your cottage."

I gasp, pulling away. "You turned that off?"

"Not the first time," he says in defense. "But today, yeah, as I had to get you out of your cottage somehow."

I shake my head. "I'm not sure if I should be impressed or scared."

"Impressed." He takes my hand and brings me around to the side of the store, out of earshot of everyone else. Growing serious, he says, "I want to make sure you're okay, that you can express your feelings without an audience." He takes his hand in mine, waiting.

"I'm not happy about what happened," I say honestly. "But also, I'm not innocent in this whole thing either. I shouldn't have gone after you so hard. I should have gotten to know you as well before taking Dwight's opinion on the matter. You deserved better."

"I deserve you," he says, squeezing my hand.

"I deserve you as well," I reply. "And I think we can launch from here, forget everything else, and just ... just date."

He nods. "In that case, will you go out with me tomorrow?"

"It's Christmas Eve," I say.

"Yeah, which means you're going to have to double up on days, because I'm going to need to see you on Christmas too. And the day after that, and the one after that ..."

I chuckle. "I'm seeing a pattern."

He tips my chin up and moves in close. "Thank you for loving me and giving me a second chance."

"Thank you for loving me and supporting my second chance."

"Anything for you," he says right before his lips land on mine and I sink into his hold.

EPILOGUE
MAX

NARRATOR: DON'T YOU JUST LOVE *a happily ever after?*

Me too.

And this one was well deserved. In true Max fashion, he couldn't just take the chocolate-covered cherries to her cottage. Nope, he had to shut down the streets of Kringle, clear the sidewalks, have a near accident in front of a store, trip the girl he likes, and then file out with all his comrades to make a show of it.

Just surprised he wasn't wearing any lederhosen for the final scene.

Maybe it's something I need to reconsider. Then again, the feathers and paint can seem a little much.

As for me, I've heard there have been questions as to who I am. Well, let wondering minds rest, because my storytelling days are through. I have bigger, more important jobs to take on now that my father is retiring. And frankly, even though you have some naughty minds, I don't think I can take one more candy cane or chocolate-covered cherry being used inappropriately.

So . . . Merry Christmas, you filthy animals. Bob Krampus Junior, over and out.

———

"Our baby is going to marry your baby one day," I say as I squeeze Betty's hand while sitting on the porch of Cole and Storee's house.

"Yeah, not happening," Cole says while he hands a lemonade to his pregnant wife.

Yup, Storee is pregnant again, with baby number three, and my wife is pregnant with baby number one.

Yeah, you read that right.

Wife.

It took me three months to muster the courage to ask, only for her to accept and tell me the same day that she was pregnant. Talk about a whirlwind of emotions. We kept the wedding small and intimate because Betty was battling some really bad morning sickness but still wanted to get married sooner rather than later. We got married on the farm under the tall pine trees. Florence was the flower girl and stole the show—that was until Betty walked down the aisle in a simple floor-length white dress and a flower crown.

Best day of my life.

We took a small honeymoon up in Estes Park where we got some cherry pie and hung out in Rocky Mountain National Park, sleeping in late and spending our days lounging.

Now that we're back, Cole and Storee shared with us their important news.

"You're right. Our baby will be too good for your baby," I say.

"Hey," Storee says, insulted. "These are unborn children."

"Sorry," I say on a wince. "But your son would be lucky to take my daughter's hand."

"He's right," Betty says with a wink.

"Oh, I know," Storee says. "Because if he's any bit as grumpy as his father, he'll be very lucky."

"I'm not that grumpy," Cole says on a huff.

Not sure who he's kidding. He's incredibly grumpy.

"How are the wedding plans going for Taran and Gus?" I ask.

"Guy," Betty says, correcting me.

"Fuck, why do I keep doing that?"

"Because you have issues," Cole says as he gets down on the porch with his daughters and starts playing with them.

"Good so far," Storee says, "Besides the fact that Guy is set on hiring a polka band for the reception."

"Oh God, really?" Betty asks.

"Yup. The Kenosha Kickers. Says they only charge a hundred and twenty-two fifty an hour, which apparently is cheaper than a DJ."

"But it's polka music," I say, offended as well.

"Taran's point exactly." Storee shakes her head. "I'm not sure it's a battle she's going to be able to win, but we shall see." She sips her lemonade and then asks, "I saw all the cottages were delivered. Are you getting excited? Think you'll be open by Christmas?"

"That's the goal," Betty says with glee. "We've been working hard on getting everything set up. The permits took forever, but now it feels like we're on a roll. We might not have everything ready, but we will be ready enough for at least a soft opening."

After Christmas, Betty presented her idea to Dwight, who was overwhelmed with the plans. His mind was going a mile a minute, and he even agreed it was a much better idea than the initial one. He's been engrossed, planning and executing with Betty ever since. I wouldn't say we're the best of friends, but we've hung out a little while Betty has been around, and we've joked a bit. I think there always will be some tension there, but at least we can get along and appreciate each other.

As for Dwight and Ansel, they're still not friends, and Dwight still hates him, which is understandable. However, Ansel, Felix, and I have been getting together once a month to have lunch. We talk about our businesses and what's going on in our lives, and occasionally reminisce. They've also been prepping me on how to run a business in a more modern way since Mom and Dad tend to be a little more old-school. This Christmas, I'll be taking on the farm myself while Mom and Dad go on another Christmas market vacation, but this time in New York City.

I'm nervous about taking on the farm but excited as well. Over the last twelve months, I've also incorporated many of Betty's excellent ideas for the farm. There are more paved pathways and parking lots, we have secured better rates with more earth-friendly fake tree suppliers, and we're still investigating snack options. It feels like it's *our* farm too now, which is the best of both worlds in my mind.

"That's so exciting, and the house, how is it coming along?" Storee asks.

Betty and I started building our own house on Evergreen Farm. It's been a challenge, but it's been a lot of fun too, putting together a place that we can call our own.

"Should be in it by the time the baby is born. Thank God, because I would not want to have a baby in the cottage."

Yeah, we've been staying in the cottage together . . . for months now.

It's tight, and I keep a lot of my clothes in a shed outside the cottage, but it's better than sharing a house with my parents. Do you know why?

Because I found popcorn garland in their bedroom one day . . . just sitting there on the nightstand, and I will tell you right now, I have not been the same since.

It was at that moment that I realized I could not share a home with them anymore.

"I don't even know where you'd put the baby," Storee says. "Maybe in the aquarium with Buzz."

"If the baby was with Buzz, I wouldn't be changing any diapers," I say.

Betty rolls her eyes. "He gets out of his cage once, and now Atlas is scared out of his life to be near him."

"It's a spider the size of my goddamn fist, so I'm sorry if that is startling."

"Goddamn," Florence says on a laugh, while Cole and Storee both give me an evil look.

I nervously laugh. "At least it's not *boner*."

"Goddamn boner," Florence says while clapping her hands. "Oh, god-damn boner."

Cole points toward my truck. "Leave."

"Yup, I think it's time for us to go." I pull Betty to her feet, offer my friends a wave as Florence continues to repeat herself, and hand in hand, we head to my truck, where I open the door for her.

"You know, you're going to have to watch yourself when our little girl comes around."

I help her into the truck, and she turns toward me, the prettiest smile crossing her lips. "Don't worry. I'll do better."

"I know you will." She cups my cheek. "You're going to be the best father."

I kiss her hand. "Because I have you at my side."

She leans in and kisses me on the lips. When she pulls away, I say, "Maybe when our kids are older, they can enter the Christmas Kringle competition and blow Cole's kids away with their talents."

"Atlas, they are unborn."

"I know, but a dad can only dream."

"You don't need to dream, because that's obviously going to happen."

I chuckle. "God, I love you."

"I love you too."

WANT MORE HOLIDAY CHEER?

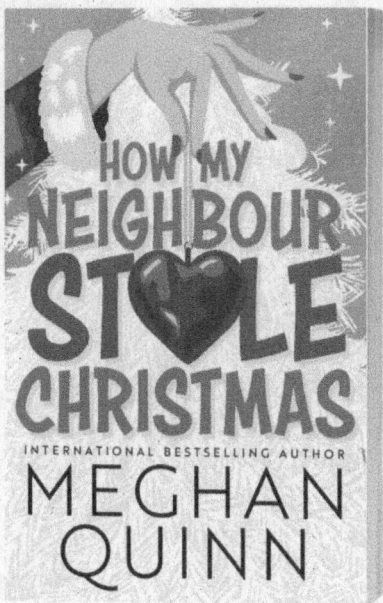

READ ON FOR A SNEAK PEEK AT
MEGHAN QUINN'S BESTSELLING NOVEL

HOW MY NEIGHBOUR
STOLE CHRISTMAS

PROLOGUE

Every Kringle in Kringletown
celebrated Christmas a lot.
But Cole Black on Whistler Lane,
unfortunately, did not.

Cole became a recluse during the
Kringle Christmas season.
No one knew why; no one could quite give a reason.

Martha said it was because he was
alone and very single.
Mae said it was because he was never
named the Town Kringle.

But to me, the true reason is a story far too sad.
For at the age of eighteen, he
lost both Mom and Dad.

Whatever the reason, his loss or
his status of being single,
he spent Christmas in the dark, hating
the cheery people of Kringle.

From his window, he would stare
with a crinkle of a frown,
at the lights and the wreaths spread
all throughout town.

They would sing, they would smile,
they would offer him a wave.
All the while he would scowl from
atop his dim, dreary cave.

For him no decorations, no cookies,
no little boy drumming.
For December 1st was tomorrow, and
he knew what was coming.

The town would awake, the snow
lightly packed in rows.
The baubles would shine; there'd
be tying of the bows.

Because just around the corner, the
bells would soon jingle,
announcing the start of who's
named the Town Kringle.

Cole Black had no interest, not a lick nor a care.
Why would he take part in such an asinine affair?

"Who cares who celebrates Christmas
more?" he would grumpily say,
his motto until a shift of the wind on one blustery day.

From his window he peered at the
commotion over the fence.
The sight of a familiar redhead made
his soulless heart grow tense.

"What is she doing here? There has to be a reason.
She can't possibly be here for the
entire Christmas season."

But her bags stacked high, in the
middle of the driveway,
were a red flag waving, announcing a very long vacay.

But why? It's been years, exactly ten, to be fair,
since she strutted around with her deep red hair.

No, he must find out; he must stop her visit right now.
She can't stay here, not for Christmas;
he must stop it...but how?

CHAPTER ONE
STOREE

"YOU KNOW, YOU NEVER TRULY get over the first pucker of your nips when that mountain air hits you," I say as I stuff my mittened hands into my jacket pockets while I survey the backdrop of freshly powdered mountains.

Taran, my sister, looks at me from over her shoulder and dramatically rolls her eyes. "It's thirty-seven degrees—pretty nice for being at an elevation of over ten thousand feet at the beginning of December."

"Pretty nice?" Good God, this is not pretty nice; this is frigid. "Guess I need to be grateful for global warming then, or else I think my breasts would be two pucks of ice on the ground right now."

Taran stands tall with two duffel bags in hand. "Global warming is never something to joke about." With that, she walks up the snow-cleared sidewalk to Aunt Cindy's pink Victorian house.

In case you didn't catch it from her tone, Taran is the uptight one of the two of us. Being the older sister has led her to adopt a starchy, prickly, slightly severe personality. She's always dealing with a crisis, there's always something to complain about, and nothing ever goes our way in the Taylor family.

Hence the five bags of luggage and trip to Kringletown, Colorado, for the unforeseeable future at the beginning of December.

No, this is not our hometown.

No, this is not the place I'd choose to visit in the wintertime thanks to my body's affinity for the California climate.

And no, I would not jump at the chance to spend Christmas with my cranky, well-mannered, loves-a-good-lecture sister.

I love her, but she sure knows how to take the J-O-Y out of jolly.

Unfortunately for yours truly, Aunt Cindy had a recent fall—the tell-tale occurrence of many an octogenarian.

Once a spry sprite, known throughout her small town as the jolliest of them all, Aunt Cindy was on her way to remove a fresh batch of gingerbread cookies out of her oven when she, as she put it, felt a squeeze in her hip, then a seize in her left butt cheek, which in turn caused her to spin, wobble, and then fall to the ground. And because she's a frail old coot, she had nothing to cushion the blow to the hip, and well... she broke it.

From there, you can imagine what happened. A broken hip to an elderly human is considered a death sentence—according to Aunt Cindy.

So of course, all hell broke loose.

Siren emojis went off in the family group text.

An emergency family meeting was called.

And before I knew it, I was staring at my computer screen, a shot of my father's nostrils clouded in hair as the main image while he attempted to figure out "this Zoom thing."

Mom sobbed in a sarong decorated with birds of paradise from her timeshare balcony in Cancún.

Dad consoled her while he wore a straw hat with a sunblock-painted nose.

Taran rapidly jotted down her issues on a notepad, like the good nurse she is.

And I sat back in my oversized, single-lady recliner, braless and snacking on a canister of chocolate-covered raisins I purchased from Costco that day, watching it all unfold.

"Something has to be done. Someone has to take care of her," Mom squealed about her only living relative.

Did I mention, to me and my sister, she's *Great-Aunt* Cindy? But what a freaking mouthful, so we just say Aunt Cindy.

But she means the world to our mom.

She's the matriarch of a very small family on my mom's side.

And despite the adoration my mom has for this woman who has taken seriously the role of dedicated parent in her life, the Horbachs and the Lindons were just coming into town, and my mother couldn't possibly leave her tropical paradise, because that would mean missing the pinochle tournament that was about to begin—she and Dad have been practicing and they were going to win it this year.

Which meant...I was brought into the picture.

You know, because even though I have a remote job editing Lovemark Channel movies, I have all the time in the world to tend to an elderly woman who broke her hip.

Now, just between you and me, I do have the time because I'm not currently editing anything—currently on a break with editing, putting me more in watch mode right now, leaning into the Lovemark holiday movie schedule—but *they* didn't need to know that.

But it was decided that I, Storee Taylor, was nominated to take care of Aunt Cindy.

And frankly, I have no clue how to take care of an old woman with a bum hip—so probably not a bright move on the family's part.

"Are you just going to stand there or are you going to help with the bags?" Taran asks, snapping me out of my thoughts.

"Just getting used to the thin air," I say and press my hand to my chest. "Oof, hard to breathe. You know, I think I might be experiencing altitude sickness, not sure this is the place for me to be. Perhaps we airlift Aunt Cindy to California."

Taran whips the pillow I couldn't live without into my chest and says, "You're fine," before picking up the bag of snacks I made her stop to get before driving into the mountains and heading back into the house.

She never truly mastered the art of good bedside manner.

Grumbling under my breath—breath that I swear I can see as I huff along the sidewalk—I make my way up the porch of the familiar Victorian house that we used to visit every Christmas before Mom and Dad purchased their Cancún timeshare—Bosom Bungalow. My mom's "bosom" buddy owns part of the timeshare as well, and they think it's a funny name. Ahhh, parents, aren't they fun?

As I get close to the door, I can practically smell the warm gingerbread and freshly harvested pine—a combination of scents that I associate with one person and one person alone—Aunt Cindy.

Hate to admit it, but even though I'd rather be wrapped up in the comfort of my childhood twin-sized Barbie comforter while talking to my ficus, Alexander, about Lovemark's lineup for the season, being here—the scents, the scenery, the snow—it's making me a little—and I mean a little, just the tiniest, minute, so-small-you-can-barely-even-recognize-it bit—warm and fuzzy inside.

And I mean that, because this town and I...we have history.

Sordid history.

Embarrassing history.

The kind of history that has kept me away for ten years.

But my mortifying history doesn't negate the fact that Aunt Cindy's house has always provided a sense of comfort during the holiday season.

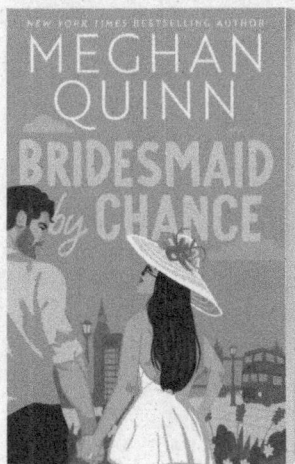